THE MOZART CONSPIRACY

PHIL SWANN

Published by Cygnus Road

The Mozart Conspiracy

For Amanda

The Mozart Conspiracy by Phil Swann

David Webber is a man of prodigious musical talent—and prodigious alcohol consumption—who makes a meager living playing piano in a hotel bar. He's sure he's hit rock bottom. David doesn't realize, however, his boring, depressing life is about to get complicated—and dangerous. When David's college mentor is murdered and his music agent disappears, he becomes the prime suspect. David is hurled into a treacherous world of international assassins, underground crime, and shadowy figures in the US government. Could these events be linked to a few faded scribbles of music his mentor passed on to him years earlier? Two centuries after a chance meeting between Wolfgang Amadeus Mozart and Benjamin Franklin, a washed-up piano player uncovers what might be the most explosive musical discovery ever made. But if David can't put all the pieces together, he could end up like Mozart: a dead musical genius.

Philadelphia, July 4th, 1776

And for the support of this declaration, with a firm reliance on the protection of divine Providence, we mutually pledge to each other our Lives, our Fortunes and our sacred Honor.

—*The Declaration of Independence*

Prologue

Paris, France—June, 1778

If sound could be a color, it would have been bright red. If an emotion, it would have been pure joy. If weather, this surely would have been a hurricane. One unison half note followed by two unison quarter notes exploded allegro double forte from the orchestra, thundering through the salle de Suisse and shaking the collective chest bone of the audience. A flurry of sixteenth notes flew from the string section with the winds and horns following in echo. Those present would later say their very breathing changed as they listened. Others would confess that what they heard was so new and unknown they actually became frightened. While still others would swear that on that summer evening in Paris, God had been revealed in the tension and release of a masterpiece.

The man moved like a ballet dancer as he conducted the orchestra through the lilting melody of the andante and into the third and final movement, yet another frantic allegro. With the precision of a surgeon, the maestro sliced the air with his baton as the violins raced up and down the scale like a flock of butterflies unable to find a place to land. Every second measure seemed to tease the audience with a false ending. Finally, many gave up on anticipating the finish and just stood up and began applauding. When it did come, it came suddenly and with no warning.

...*and three, four!*

Without hesitation or prompting from the king and queen, the entire assembly came to their feet.

With sweat pouring down his face, the conductor smiled to his orchestra and then turned to the audience and bowed. His smile was open-mouthed and broad. The angular, youthful face, only slightly painted and powdered, wore a smile easily and without apology. His wig was blue-white and sat high on his head with a braided ponytail that hung just to the top of his shirt collar. His arms swung without reserve. His eyes moved continuously as if never wanting to miss a moment of the world around him. His slender, almost frail body seemed to dance freely and wildly—even when completely still. To look upon Wolfgang Amadeus Mozart was to look upon pure energy.

King Louis XVI and Marie-Antoinette, though much more sedate, stood and offered their praise. The old man beside them stood but simply gazed at the young composer. The queen, seeing the reaction, whispered in her husband's ear. The king turned with concern. "Doctor, did you not enjoy the program?"

The elderly gentleman wore a scarlet satin *roguelaure*, white silk stockings, and black buckled leather shoes, all topped off with a cocked, matching scarlet felt hat over powdered natural hair pulled back and braided. For a man of seventy-two who suffered from chronic gout, Benjamin Franklin was, by anyone's standard, dapper. "No, Your Majesty, I apologize," he said in perfect French. "Quite the opposite. I am just...awestruck." Franklin began his applause. "That was the most amazing thing I have ever been privileged to hear."

The king smiled. "It is now time to pay our respects. Will you join us, Doctor?"

"I would be honored, Your Majesty," Franklin replied.

Louis, a mere twenty-four years old, stood self-assured in a lavishly adorned gold frock, ruffled at the neck and plumed at the sleeves with silver embroidery on the breast. His wig was white and larger than any man's in the auditorium, and his face was heavily powdered, accenting his blue eyes.

But it was Marie-Antoinette who was the focus of everyone's attention. Her floor-length, cream-colored gown spanned three feet at its base and was embroidered in gold and beaded in rhinestones. The pattern was designed to accentuate the low and revealing neckline, which not so modestly showed the tops of her breasts. The diamond and ruby necklace, which hugged her neck from below her chin to the top of her chest, was so dense with jewels it looked to be a piece of fabric. Her flawless face was heavily powdered and highlighted with a hint of rouge on each cheek. But it was her hair that was the focal point of all who would see the queen. It towered two feet in height. The many braids and folds were too numerous to follow. It was snow-white and accented with a silver comb inlaid with diamonds inserted three-quarters from its zenith.

The trio, flanked by numerous valets and maids, were ushered from the salle to a salon located in the eastern wing of the palace. The musicians were happily chattering among themselves when the royal couple and Franklin entered. At once, they fell silent and to one knee. The king and queen proceeded to the middle of the room. "We thank you for the gift of music you bestowed upon us tonight. The king's blessing is upon you, and may God give you peace and health on this most blessed day. Adieu."

The musicians remained kneeling as the royal couple turned to depart. Franklin, standing off to the side, continued smiling at the musicians, shaking his clasped hands in front of him in a gesture of triumphant congratulations.

A small man stood wringing his hands three feet from the king. With his head down, he stepped forward. "Your Majesty, I am Jean Le Gros, director of the Concert Spirituel. Thank you for honoring us with your presence on this opening of the concert series."

Louis stopped and turned. "Monsieur Le Gros, we thank you for the gift of music you bestowed upon us tonight. The king's blessing is upon you, and may God give you peace and health on this most blessed day. Adieu."

Le Gros smiled awkwardly and stammered as the king and

queen once again began to move away. "Tha-tha-thank you, most gracious Majesty. As always you are too kind. But if I may, Your Majesty and Your Highness, before you depart, be allowed to present to you the composer of the work you heard tonight." Le Gros turned and motioned quickly for Mozart to approach. Mozart walked slowly from the corner of the room where he'd been standing. Le Gros, irritated with Mozart's casualness, gritted his teeth and as covertly as possible motioned for him to kneel. Mozart reluctantly complied. "I might add, most modestly of course, it was I who commissioned the piece you heard tonight. I felt the king and queen would enjoy something new for this opening."

The king sighed heavily, approached the young composer, and said once again, but this time with waning enthusiasm, "Monsieur Mozart, we thank you for the gift of music you bestowed upon us tonight. The king's blessing is upon you, and may God give you peace and health on this most blessed day. Adieu."

As the king and queen began to leave, Mozart, still kneeling, spoke. "What exactly pleased you?"

An audible gasp echoed through the salon. The king looked back at the composer and raised one heavily stenciled eyebrow. "You spoke, monsieur?"

"Yes," Mozart said, looking up. "What exactly pleased Your Majesty about my work?"

A mortified Le Gros jumped in. "Your Majesty, please excuse the impudence of Monsieur Mozart, he does not wish to—"

"Yes I do, Le Gros!" Mozart interrupted. "I want to know what the king enjoyed. He said the same thing to me as he did to you and the rest of the orchestra. I am left wondering if he slept through—"

"Your Excellency," Le Gros begged, "I ask for your forgiveness for—"

The King shot up his hand for silence. He stepped close to Mozart's bowed head and glared down at him. Never taking his eyes from Mozart's skull, the king removed a pewter snuff tin from his vest, retrieved a pinch with his thumb and index finger, delicately placed it beneath his nostrils, and inhaled. The room was silent, anticipating the wrath of the notoriously quick-tempered king. The king closed his eyes, enjoying the rush of the stimulant. When he opened them, it was with a broad smile, which blossomed into a yellow toothy grin that erupted into a shrill, almost effeminate laugh. At first no one was sure if the king's amusement was genuine, so only an uneasy smattering of laughter pecked through the room. But as it became clear that it was genuine, all roared, all except for Mozart, who remained motionless before Louis. "Monsieur Mozart, I shall excuse your rudeness because you are not from France," Louis stuttered over his laughter. "But please be aware that for displaying such disrespect to the king, I, with a mere word, could have you shot!" Louis continued, "When the King of France praises you, you are to accept that praise with joy and humility, not with an interrogation." Louis looked back at his queen, who was daintily holding her hand in front of her mouth. "Oh, you Austrians! You are such a headstrong people." Marie-Antoinette threw her hand forward toward Louis in a gesture of coquettish denial.

Mozart, still kneeling with his head down, replied calmly, "Yes, Your Majesty. Please accept my sincere apology. It was not my intent to show disrespect. I thank you for your kind words and your kind forgiveness of my..." Mozart swallowed hard as if he was about to choke, "stupidity."

Louis continued his belly laugh, only half hearing Mozart. "Very well, adieu." The king and queen turned and once again began their departure, laughing and whispering to each other as if sharing a private joke. Mozart, keeping his head down, stood, turned around, and walked back to the corner of the salon.

Throughout the bizarre exchange between Mozart and the king, Franklin's eyes never wavered from the brash young composer. In his two years in France he had never witnessed such open face-to-face hostility toward the king and queen.

"Your Majesty and Your Highness?" Franklin said. "With your permission, I would very much love to stay for a while and tour some of this beautiful palace. That is, of course, if it meets with your approval."

"The Louvre is yours, Doctor. And I'm sure Monsieur Le Gros

would be honored to show you around. Is that not correct, Le Gros?"

"Indeed, Your Majesty," Le Gros responded.

"Good. I look forward to seeing you again soon, Doctor. I know we still have great matters of importance to discuss between our two lands. But for now, enjoy the rest of your evening. And for the last time, I trust, we wish you all adieu." And with that, King Louis XVI and Marie-Antoinette, with maids steadying her hair, left the salon.

Le Gros leaped before Franklin. "Doctor, 'tis my privilege to show you the Louvre."

"Monsieur Le Gros, you are too kind. But I was wondering if I might wander around on my own? I just love experiencing the grandeur of such a magical place like this in solitude. 'Tis one of my many little peccadilloes."

"As you wish, monsieur. I shall be available if you need me."

"Actually, Monsieur Le Gros," Franklin begged, "there is one thing you can do for me. I would very much like to speak to Monsieur Mozart."

"Mozart, monsieur?" The request noticeably petrified Le Gros.

"Yes," Franklin answered with a smile.

"As you wish, monsieur." Le Gros walked over to the corner of the salon where Mozart was gathering his music. Franklin watched as Le Gros shook his finger in the composer's face, obviously chastising him for the incident with the king and warning him to behave himself with this next encounter.

Mozart nodded dutifully, approached Franklin, and kneeled.

Franklin looked down, let out a chuckle, and then spoke in German, "Herr Mozart, please rise. I am no one's royalty."

Mozart looked up, surprised. "Monsieur, you speak my language."

"I do. A very beautiful language it is too. Now please stand up. My hearing is not what it used to be and conversing with the top of a man's head is...well...just odd."

Mozart stood. The two were eye level, though Mozart seemed taller due to his lanky build. Franklin continued in German, "Your composition was extraordinary. May I inquire as to its name?"

Mozart's eyes widened, and he grinned as he spoke. "I call it *'Sinfonia 'a 10 instrumenti'*. Did you really enjoy it, monsieur?"

Franklin laughed, "Yes, I surely did. Why do you seem so surprised?"

Mozart licked his lips nervously. "You see, monsieur, this was the first time it has ever been performed. I just created it last week."

"Ah, I see. So that's why you were inquiring to the king what he especially enjoyed about the piece?"

"No, monsieur," Mozart replied. "I *was* being intentionally rude to the king. I should not have been, and I apologize to you as well."

Franklin grinned. "No need, I'm not French," Franklin said, changing effortlessly back to speaking French. "But if I were, I would accept your apology." Back to German, "There now, your... what was the word...ah, yes, stupidity is internationally forgiven."

Mozart, feeling as if he was being mocked by yet another of the pompous French aristocracy, could not hold his tongue. This time he spoke in French. "Monsieur, you said my composition was...what was your word...ah, yes, extraordinary. May I ask what you enjoyed so much about it...specifically?"

Franklin never blinked. "Specifically?"

"Yes," Mozart replied, "specifically."

"Well, specifically, first I would have to say that the expansion of the principal movements and the complete deletion of the minuet was a very interesting choice. I realize that this is France and the minuet is often overlooked, however, you are Austrian, and being Austrian, I thought sure a minuet would be offered—it was not. That was very crafty of you, young man. Secondly, I liked the way you took into account your audience's preference for the...how shall I say it...the *'Premier coup d'archet'* with that magnificent introductory D-major unison in the strings. And, if I might add, the heavy participation of the winds in the first movement lends it a highly contrasted, almost concerto-like character. Now, as for the second movement...lovely as it was...I think I would prefer a shorter andante. But alas, you may choose to take that as the personal taste of a silly old man. The final movement, ah, now that was a glorious surprise. The way you fooled us by preceding the expected unison forte with a *piano* introduction by the violins, that, my young friend, was simple genius."

Franklin smiled.

Mozart's mouth hung open.

"Herr Mozart, are you quite all right?" Franklin asked, tilting his head.

Mozart stuttered, "Uh, well—uh, yes. Did you really think the andante was too long?"

"Maybe just a shade, but please do not change it on my account."

"No, I shall consider it. I felt that also," a bewildered Mozart said. "Monsieur, may I ask your name? Are you a composer yourself?"

Franklin let out a robust laugh. "Oh, if only Tom Jefferson could hear you ask me that. He fancies himself a violinist and the best musician in the Continental Congress. He just loves to tell me how my musical ear is akin to that of a gnat—they are quite deaf, you see." Franklin laughed again. "No, young man, I am not a composer. My name is Benjamin Franklin. I am from the American Colonies, and I just recognize brilliance when I hear it."

Mozart raised his chin and assumed a more respectful posture. He began to speak, but this time in broken English, "Mister Franklin, my English not as good as your German, for that I apologize. I also very sorry for rudeness. Please forgive, sir. Thank you for complimenting my music. It is great honor I have for you to hear it. I know some little about your America. You desire freedom and independence. These are words good. I would love to hear more about your America. Also, you not deaf as gnat."

Franklin broke with laughter. After a moment, Mozart joined him.

Franklin removed his eyeglasses to wipe the tears from his eyes. "Oh thank you, young man, and I would love to hear more of your music sometime."

"I would love to play more of my music for you. I can now, if you wish?"

"Now?" Franklin replied.

"Yes. Monsieur Le Gros keeps private salon. He has an original Bartolomeo Cristofori fortepiano. If we could beg Le Gros to let us in, I could play you my music, and you could tell me about America."

"Doctor Franklin, is everything satisfactory?" Franklin hadn't noticed the anxious man as he approached.

"Thank you, monsieur Le Gros, yes, everything is splendid." Franklin then began to do what he knew he did best. "Monsieur Le Gros, I have made an outrageous faux pas."

Le Gros became even more rigid. "What, monsieur, is that?"

"I believe that I have neglected expressing to you my appreciation for such a magical evening. It is obvious that beyond the fine orchestra and this talented young composer, the real genius behind tonight's festivities is yourself. Was it not you, monsieur, who so expertly choreographed the entire performance this evening?"

"Well, monsieur, I might have played a small role." Le Gros replied, growing by inches as Franklin spoke.

"A small role indeed, monsieur, you are the whole cast. But you are far too modest to ever acknowledge any of these things yourself."

"Yes, I guess I am," Le Gros said with a faraway look.

"Can you ever forgive me for my thoughtlessness?"

Le Gros stood with his chest out and head high. "Monsieur Franklin, I am honored. If your evening was enjoyable, then my work has been a success."

"It has been memorable," Franklin announced.

Le Gros beamed.

"But alas," Franklin continued with a falling tone, "there is only one other thing that would have made this evening completely unforgettable."

Le Gros's smile diminished slightly. "What would that be, monsieur? If it is in my power, I will make it so."

Franklin sighed. "No, monsieur, I believe this request would be even beyond your incredible abilities."

"Monsieur, I humbly demand you allow me the chance to provide the impossible."

Franklin looked at Mozart, and with his left eye, the one Le Gros couldn't see but Mozart could, winked. "If you insist. I have always had the desire to see and hear an original Bartolomeo Cristofori fortepiano. I have heard about them, but that is all. I had some hope that I might see one tonight, but it was not to be. Perhaps you may know someone in Paris who has one?"

A smile slowly reappeared across Le Gros's face. "Monsieur, I have in my possession just such an instrument."

"No, monsieur, you jest," Franklin exclaimed.

"No, Monsieur, I do not," Le Gros exclaimed back.

"Monsieur, you are indeed a truly remarkable man."

Le Gros gloated, "And I can even do better than that. It just so happens that Monsieur Mozart is a virtuoso on the fortepiano."

"Is he really? Do you think he'd play for me?" Franklin scammed.

"He shall if I so instruct him to. Monsieur Mozart," Le Gros said, turning to Mozart, "you will take our honored guest to my private salon. My valet will lead you. Upon arriving, you will play the fortepiano for monsieur Franklin until he instructs you to stop. Is that understood?"

Mozart, who was totally aware of Franklin's ruse, couldn't resist his own bit of theater. "Monsieur Le Gros, I was commissioned to compose a piece for the opening and conduct it. I did, now my job is finished. I am not being paid to—"

Le Gros lowered his head like a bull. "You are lucky to be paid at all after your exhibition before the king and queen. You will do as I say, or you will never have a commission in Paris again. That, monsieur, is a promise."

Mozart played the part to the hilt. "It seems I have little choice."

"Indeed, monsieur," Le Gros replied.

Mozart turned to Franklin and winked with his right eye, the one Le Gros couldn't see. "Monsieur Franklin, it would appear that I am at your service."

Franklin bit his upper lip to keep from smiling.

"Garçon!" Le Gros barked to the young valet waiting in the

wings. "Please escort Doctor Franklin and Monsieur Mozart to my private salon."

The valet leaped forward, bowed, and then gestured for Franklin and Mozart to follow.

Mozart whispered, "Doctor Franklin, you are a conniving gentleman."

Franklin, looking straight ahead, whispered back, "And you, Herr Mozart, have a touch of larceny in you as well."

The young musician and the old philosopher exited through the large double doors on the east side of the hall and entered the lush tuilerie gardens of the Louvre. A light rain had given way to a balmy Paris evening, and the moon reflected off a fountain in the center of the garden. The smell of rose and honeysuckle permeated the air.

"Oh, what a lovely night, would you not agree, Herr Mozart?"

"Yes, it surely is. But please, Doctor Franklin, call me Wolfgang."

"Wolfgang, what a delightful name! I am Ben."

"I am honored, Ben. So tell me—Ben—about your America."

"'Tis a tall order, Wolfgang. Let me see." Ben put his hand on Wolfgang's shoulder as they strolled through the palatial garden. "First off, it is not my America, 'tis all the colonists' America. I should begin at the beginning, always a fine place to start. Some years ago a few of us got together in Philadelphia—that is my home. Oh, what a bevy we are too. There's young Tom Jefferson, I have already told you a little about him. A fellow named John Adams, nice chap but can be somewhat of a horse's rear end at times—oh, but John's bride Abigail—let me tell you about Abigail. Taking nothing away from the queen of France of course, Abigail possesses two of the most heavenly—"

"Ben," Mozart exclaimed. "You are a Frenchman."

"My young friend," Ben replied, "when it comes to food or a man's loins, we are all Frenchmen."

Mozart howled.

Part I

Chapter 1

Los Angeles, California

They were connected, man and music. With eyes closed and with a gentle sway, the pianist's hands glided over the keyboard without a moment of indecision. *A tri-tone passing chord. Damn, that's nice. I'll do it again in the second verse.* And he did, seamlessly modulating from one key to another, wrapping the familiar refrain in chords voiced so warmly as to melt stone. It was "Moon River" that filled the lobby-bar of the Los Angeles Airport Holiday Inn. Some listened, most didn't, but the man at the piano couldn't have cared less. He kept his eyes closed and played. He was at peace—totally at peace.

"Hey, piano boy, you deaf?"

Without so much as a *ritardando*, the pianist turned his head and opened one eye.

"I asked you," the man yelled from across the room, "to play me and my little lady here a song."

Reclosing the one eye, the musician stopped, took a deep breath, and then reopened both. "What would you and…your little lady like to hear?"

"How about something good?" The man let out a laugh that could be heard throughout the hotel's lobby.

The pianist only slightly moved his lips before he closed his eyes and returned where he left off in the song.

"What the fuck did you just say?" the man yelled, leaping to his feet.

The piano player stopped abruptly and looked at the man with a cold smile. "Oh, did I say that out loud?"

Two highball glasses and a bowl of mixed nuts crashed to the ground as the irate man lunged from his table. "You wanna get it on, you little homo?" he said, ripping off his sport jacket. "Come on, right now. It's you and me, piano boy."

The beer-bellied businessman was now standing directly over the piano player. Without changing expression or even missing a beat, the musician ran an arpeggio up the keyboard, concluding with a right-handed uppercut into the businessman's groin. The man fell to his knees, coughing and gasping for air. As his left hand began playing an old-time gospel-style stride, his right hand yanked in rhythm on the businessman's tie, bouncing the man's face onto the upper register of the keyboard. Blood spit over the keys as the man's nose slammed into them.

From the first angry word, the bartender, a formidable young black man, sped from behind the bar. By the time he reached the action, the businessman was a limp and bloody rag. The bartender grabbed the piano player by the back of his tuxedo jacket and flung him off the bench. He picked up the businessman and sat him in a nearby chair. "Just keep your head back, sir. Janet," he yelled to the waitress cowering in the corner, "get some ice for Mr. Harshbarger here."

A short, balding man in a conservative gray suit frantically excused himself through the spectators. "Sir, are you okay? John, who did this?"

"David Webber."

"The piano player?" The manager shouted. "Where the hell is he?"

The bartender pointed toward the bar.

Sitting casually on a barstool with his legs crossed, smoking a cigarette and sipping a glass of whiskey, was a dark-haired, moderately handsome thirty-something-year-old man in a blood-stained tuxedo.

"Call security," the manager said. "Then call the police."

Chapter 2

"Sign right here, sir."

David Webber, tie undone and tuxedo jacket draped over his arm, signed the document the elderly officer pushed toward him.

The officer opened a manila envelope and poured the contents onto the counter. "Now, sir, I'd like for you to verify this is the personal property you had on your person when you were brought in and that it's all accounted for. You can sign right here."

David remained expressionless as the officer pushed another form in front of him. He took his wallet, a half pack of Marlboro Lights, a tarnished silver Zippo lighter, sixty-four cents in change, and an almost new roll of breath mints.

"Yeah, it's all here," he said, dropping the items into his bloodied tuxedo jacket pocket and signing the form.

"Okay, sir, that's it. Here's your receipt," the officer said, handing David the pink carbon. "Ms. Peterson said you should wait for her out front."

"Thanks," David mumbled, putting on his jacket.

"You're welcome, and you have a nice evening, sir," the old officer crooned with a tone David knew was perfected for the sole purpose of pissing off people like himself even more than they already were.

David put on his jacket, turned up the lapel, and walked out the front door of the LAPD Pacific Division. The rain had become drizzle, and a record low for Southern California in mid-June was forecast. He pulled a cigarette from his pocket, lit it, and looked at his watch. It was a little before one thirty in the morning. He looked down Centinela Boulevard. He saw two police officers on the sidewalk, a homeless woman, and a taxicab, but no J.P. He looked the other direction down Culver Boulevard—two taxicabs, a green sedan, and a sheriff's cruiser, but again, no J.P. "Where the hell are you?" he moaned aloud.

A second later, a '75 red Mercedes 450SL slowly rolled from the LAPD car garage and stopped at the side entrance where the word BOOKING hung over the door. A young LAPD officer stepped from the passenger side of the car laughing. David watched the officer exchange a few words with the driver before shutting the door and heading inside. The car rolled onto Culver Boulevard, made a U-turn, and pulled over to the curb, stopping in front of David.

Jean Ann Peterson rolled down the passenger side window and pushed her nose sideways with her index finger. "I'm bustin' outta here. Ya with me?"

"Very funny," David said, getting in the car. "What were you doing with the cop? Getting a date?"

"I can't believe you, luv," the attractive, red-haired woman said with a British accent. "I knew you'd never win a personality of the year award, but assault with a deadly weapon? Good lord, David, what were you thinking?"

"Assault with a deadly weapon? What weapon?" David replied as J.P. pulled onto Culver Boulevard.

"The piano."

"A piano classifies as a deadly weapon?"

"It does when you use it as a springboard for someone's face. Luckily for you, neither your victim nor the hotel wants to press charges."

"Lucky me. Why?"

"Well it seems the man's wife, you remember her, the one you affectionately referred to as—let's see, how did you put it? 'Your cow in lipstick.'"

"Actually, it was your heifer in high heels—still can't believe he heard me," David said, flicking his cigarette out the open window.

"Whatever. At any rate, it turns out she was not his wife after all. The very charming officer Josh, that was the dreamboat's name, and yes, I was trying to get a date, told me the real Lady Harshbarger is back in Missouri doing the Donna Reed gig with their three children. Once it was pointed out to Mr. Harshbarger if he pressed charges, he'd have to testify to why he was there, whom he was with, and what started the altercation, he became very forgiving. As for the hotel, they'd just as soon avoid bad press and forget the whole thing."

"Those weasels," David laughed. "They could give a shit about bad press. What they're afraid of is me bringing up in open court the little matter of illegals working in their kitchen for fifty cents an hour."

J.P. shook her head. "David, luv, you're one of a kind."

"So I'm off the hook?"

"Not entirely. The police are still charging you with reckless endangerment and disturbing the peace. By the way, you owe me seven hundred and fifty dollars."

David looked at her.

"Bail amount, luv."

David rubbed his face and sighed. He retrieved another cigarette and lit it.

"You have another one of those?"

"Thought you quit."

"It was more of a good idea." David handed her a cigarette. "Besides, it goes well with the whole look tonight."

"And what look would that be?"

She pushed in the cigarette lighter, letting the cigarette dangle from her lips. "You know, the incredibly sexy and mysterious older woman—that would be me, of course—who rushes out in the middle of the night to a seedy police station to bailout her helpless, troubled, not-too-intelligent yet irresistible young lover—that would be you. I think the black scarf is a nice touch, don't you?" She pulled a black silk scarf from around her neck, took both hands momentarily off the wheel, and wrapped it around her head.

Smoke came out of David's nose and mouth as he laughed. "J.P., you're my agent. In the ten years we've known each other, we've slept together twice. Once when you were drunk, the other when I was. That hardly qualifies us as lovers."

J.P. pulled the scarf off, lit the cigarette, and blew smoke. "It's my fantasy, luv. And one would think that out of sheer gratitude one would be happy to indulge one's fantasy for springing one's bum out of the clink."

"What *one* thinks is that one's read one too many Jackie Collins's books."

"Hush," J.P. said, slapping David on the knee.

She turned the car onto the northbound 405. The rain began falling steadily, turning the freeway into a river of taillights. J.P. rolled both her and David's windows up just enough to keep the rain out but let their smoke escape. She turned on the windshield wipers and the radio to a light jazz station. "So, you want to tell me about it?"

David stared out the passenger side window. "What's left to tell? I told you pretty much everything that happened on the phone. The guy was an asshole. I was minding my business just playing the gig. This guy yells from his table if I take requests. I ask what he wants to hear. He yells at the top of his lungs, something good. Then he starts busting a gut like that's the most original joke ever. That's when I made the cow comment. Next thing I know, he's coming after me. I was just defending myself."

"That's not what I'm talking about," J.P. said.

"Then I don't know what you're talking about," David replied, blowing smoke out the window.

She spoke firmly but still softly. "Don't bullshit me, Webber. You know exactly what I'm talking about."

"No, I really don't."

J.P. turned off the radio, reached across the console, and took David's hand. "David, it's me. Don't treat me like one of your little actress–slash–cocktail waitress Twinkies. I know you better than anybody, and I'm probably the only friend you have left."

"Great. I'm a musician, and my only friend is my agent. Priceless."

"Luv, you can be a real dick sometimes," J.P. said, removing her hand. She turned the radio back on, and the two sat in silence as the Mercedes crept up the Santa Monica Mountains.

As is often the case in a place where oceans, deserts, mountains, and valleys lay within a few miles of each other, weather can change quickly. As the car came over the apex, the sky cleared, and the lights of the San Fernando Valley sparkled below like a million diamonds on black velvet.

David reached over and turned down the radio. "Sorry, Jeep."

J.P. responded with a sigh. Jeep, the name David always used to signal the end of the jokes and sarcastic banter the two had become so good at over the years.

"You're right, J.P. Hell, you probably *are* my only friend."

J.P. looked at David. He looked tired and sad. She took his hand again. "What's wrong, David? You've always been the angry young man type. But as dark and brooding as you've always been, you still retained a sense of humor about things—demented sense of humor, I admit, but…"

David smiled.

J.P. returned a sad smile of her own. "But, David, the past month or so, it's like there's no joy in life at all for you anymore."

David stared out the window for a long moment. When he spoke, it came almost as a mumble. "It wasn't supposed to turn out like this."

"Like what?"

"Like this. Who I am. It wasn't supposed to turn out this way."

"How was it supposed to turn out?"

J.P. could see that David looked like someone who needed to empty his soul. Confess every fear and demon he had locked inside.

But she wasn't surprised when he answered, "Different, just different."

J.P. didn't push. She knew better. She smiled and nodded.

"Oh, hell. I'll be all right, J.P., just my time of the month."

And the moment was gone.

"Tell you what," David said, sitting up in his seat. "Why don't you jump off the next exit, and I'll get us a bottle. We'll go to my place and watch something old and black and white and get drunk."

"Not me. It's Thursday, and I still have a job."

"Come on. So what if a bar manager or worthless musician doesn't reach you by ten, the world won't end."

"Sorry, luv. Meeting at nine a.m. with an entertainment buyer from South Pacific Cruises. And, I need the booking. Hey, you need me to get that booking. I'm running out of places on dry land that will put up with you."

"All right. But would you at least pull over and let me get a bottle and pack of smokes for myself?"

J.P. exited at Burbank Boulevard and pulled into a liquor store located at the corner of a small strip mall.

"Sure you don't want anything?" David asked, getting out of the car.

"No, I'm fine."

"Then can you float me a twenty?"

J.P. shook her head. She opened her purse and handed David the money. "You now owe me seven hundred and seventy dollars."

J.P. WATCHED as David trotted into the liquor store. She loved him. She knew it. She wondered if he knew it—probably not. She remembered that night they slept together the first time. He was wrong, she wasn't drunk. She pretended to be, of course. That somehow made it easier the next day. It allowed them the license to laugh about it. She wondered how they might have turned out had she not used the ruse. Would they have become more than just friends? And what was so special about David Webber anyway?

Over the years she'd known a lot of talented men. Many better looking and all with considerably better personalities than David Webber. But from the moment he walked into her office that day —*good lord, was it really ten years ago*—there was a connection. He was glib, sarcastic, and sometimes downright rude. But underneath, there was a soul that exploded with sensitivity and passion. It sometimes showed itself in moments of weakness, other times in moments of intoxication. But always when he played. Good lord, could he play. She had lost count of the many times she had had to say to an irate club manager, *"I know he's a pain in the ass and totally lacking in any social skills, but listen to him play."* In her seventeen years in the business, David Webber was quite simply the best she'd ever heard.

DAVID TOOK his time scanning the various spirits, his main concern being which gave him the most alcohol bang-for-his-buck. He decided on a bottle of Black Velvet and two packs of generic brand cigarettes. Beside the counter was a lone copy of the early edition of the *Los Angeles Times*. As David reached over to pick up the paper, another customer behind him reached for the same one.

David turned around.

"It's yours," the giant man in a dark tailored suit said with a raspy voice.

"No, go ahead and take it," David said, handing the paper to the man. "Nothing in there I really care about anyway."

"Thanks." The man threw some change on the counter, nodded to David, and left.

David was getting back into J.P.'s Benz, when he glanced across the parking lot and saw the man in the suit getting into the passenger side of a green sedan.

"It's about time."

David didn't reply.

J.P. looked in the direction David was staring. "Somebody you know?"

Still no reply.

"David," J.P. said.

"What…sorry…no it's nothing, just…"

"Just what?"

"What did you say that guy—what was his name —Harshberger…?"

"Harshbarger."

"Yeah, right Harshbarger. What did you say he did back in Missouri?"

"I didn't. But Officer Dreamboat told me he owned some sort of machine parts company, or something like that. Why?"

David dropped his head. "Oh God."

"What in the world is wrong now?"

"Just get me the hell home," David mumbled. "And take the surface streets."

J.P. headed east on Burbank Boulevard through Van Nuys. David remained hunched in his seat, periodically rising up for a quick look out the rear window.

"You mind telling me what is going on?"

"That green car, a Taurus, I think…the one at the liquor store that guy got in. I saw it in front of the police station."

J.P. let out a held breath and laughed. "Oh lord, David, you must be kidding? You know how many green Tauruses there are in Los Angeles?"

David didn't smile. "Yeah, a lot. But not all of them are following us."

J.P.'s smile vanished. She turned to look out the back.

"Don't do that," David ordered. "Just keep driving. When we get to my apartment, drive past it and pull over down the street. Don't park in front."

"David, what's going on?"

"A machine parts company, that's what."

"I don't understand."

"I'm from the Midwest too, J.P."

"What…does—"

"I know how guys like Harshbarger operate. When I was a growing up, there was a kid down the corner from where I lived. His old man owned a trucking company, among a few more lucrative and less legal enterprises. One year this kid doesn't make the junior high basketball team. So his old man calls up the coach and tells him that he must have made a mistake. The coach said he hadn't. The guy said, think about it again. The coach didn't. The coach was rushed to the hospital that night with a broken arm, a broken nose, and severe internal bleeding. He was out the rest of the year. His kid, by the way, was on the basketball team the next day. No, Harshbarger's not going to press charges. He's just going to send his bent-noses to get justice."

"Are you sure? We need to call the police." J.P. reached for her cell phone.

"No," David replied. "That would just make it worse."

"What are we going to do?"

"I don't know. My apartment's coming up. Just pull over down the street."

J.P. pulled over a block past David's apartment building. She turned off the headlights, and both scrunched down in their seats. A late model pick-up truck, a city bus, and the green sedan whizzed by, the green sedan not so much as flashing its brake lights.

"Then again, I guess I could be wrong."

"Damn it, Webber, you scared the shit out of me."

"I really thought that car was following us. It was at the police station—"

"David, get some bloody help. Now we can add paranoia to your list of neuroses."

David rubbed his eyes and fell back in his seat. J.P. turned on the headlights and backed up to David's apartment building. "Go get some sleep, we'll talk tomorrow."

David opened the door but stopped before he got out. "I'm sorry, J.P., for everything. I don't know what I'd do without you."

J.P.'s lips turned up slightly. "I don't either, luv."

David leaned over and kissed her on the cheek.

Spanish in style with chipped paint and palm trees, the four-story apartment complex looked no different than hundreds of others in the Valley. David opened the security gate and walked to the elevators located across the modest courtyard. He heard meowing from the other side of his door the instant he inserted the key into the lock.

"What's happening, Ravel? Have a good night?" David said as the cat rubbed against his leg. "Mine? Buddy, you wouldn't believe me if I told you."

He whipped off his tux jacket, tossed it across a dining room chair, and picked up the TV remote sitting on the back of a tan couch. He pulled his whiskey and cigarettes from the bag, grabbed a glass with ice from the kitchen, and came back into his tiny living room. He set the bottle on the coffee table, using a *celebrity m*agazine as a coaster, lit a cigarette, and fell onto the couch with an audible *ugh!* The feline jumped onto David's lap as he cracked the seal and poured himself three fingers worth. He took a gulp and began stroking Ravel's head, curiously watching as his left hand slid off the cat's back. He paused and tentatively made a fist. He threw back another gulp and then reopened his hand again. "No," David whispered, staring at his hand and repeating the motion. "It just wasn't supposed to turn out this way, Ravee."

THE MAN in the passenger seat dialed a number on the cell phone. "It's me." He listened. "No sir, not yet." He listened again. "Yeah, we're out front, we have a full view." Silence once more. "Got it." The man placed the phone inside his suit jacket. "I'm to stay here. You go back to the hotel."

The driver nodded and started the car as the man in the tailored suit got out of the green sedan.

Chapter 3

The man in the royal blue satin robe who stood on the balcony looking over the Upper East Side of Central Park was the picture of elegance. His six-feet-one-inch frame was lean and strong. His features were sharp and defined. His hair gleamed dark and wavy, teeth sparkled white, and his skin shone a smooth golden brown. The man was beautiful, and he carried himself with an air of knowing it.

He pushed the Off button on the phone and slowly sipped the amber liqueur from the crystal snifter he held between his perfectly manicured fingers.

"Anything?" asked a voice from the living room.

"No."

"Maybe we're barkin' up the wrong tree. Ever think of that?" the man in the black leather jacket said in rough Brooklynese.

"No," was the cold reply.

"Well, maybe you oughta."

Anthony Depriest walked from the balcony into the plush pastel-colored living room without comment.

"Yo, maestro. You hearing me?"

"Keep your voice down, you idiot," Depriest ordered in a sharp half-whisper. "My wife is sleeping."

"Hey." The barrel-chested Italian lunged to the edge of the couch. "You gonna have more problems than me waking up the missus if you call me an idiot again. I don't give a fuck if you are family."

Depriest's face contorted. "Please, don't remind me. God, I can't believe you and I are from the same gene pool."

"Yeah, well we are, Mister Hoity-toity, and don't forget it. Under those pretty little jammies, you just a dumb Flatbush wop like me."

"I don't think so, James," Depriest replied.

"You are too, and you oughta be proud of it. And the name's Jimmy. You know I don't go by no fairy name like James. Pop made you what you are, don't forget it."

"I made me what I am, my talent and genius," Depriest said. "I would have become what I am with or without my uncle."

"Yeah right," Jimmy laughed. "Well, all's I got to say, Mister Genius, is the family's got a lot riding on this, and Pop's not gonna like it if it gets fucked up because of you."

Depriest took another drink and leered at his cousin through his glass. Jimmy was right—he better not fuck this up.

Jimmy went on. "Now, you look. I gotta report to Pop in the morning about how things are going, and it would be in your best interest if I got something good to say."

"Tell him everything is proceeding as planned."

"What plan? All we seem to be doing is chasing some old man around. Now two of my best are in Cali-fuckin'-fornia. I say just give Leo and Sal fifteen minutes with the old fart, and he'll be forever working for us."

The crystal rattled as Depriest slammed his glass onto the silver tray beside the etched brandy decanter. "Me, James. Working for me. And you'd be wise to remember for whom you're working. Must I remind you of our little arrangement? As far as not giving a fuck *who* is family or not, how do you think your old man would react if he learned of your little shenanigans with the Goudio woman, hmmm? Not well, I imagine. Besides, I'm paying you twice what your illustrious father is, aren't I?"

Jimmy cowered into the sofa saying nothing.

"Leo and Sal do not touch the old man, is that clear? I've told you a thousand times, the old man is the key. All we need to do is let him lead us to it." Depriest softened his tone. "I know him, Jimmy. He's as methodical as they come. He doesn't take a crap unless it's for two good reasons."

"Yeah, but California?"

"Yes. California makes the most sense out of everything he's done thus far."

"Because of that piano player?" Jimmy asked.

"Yes. Because of that piano player."

"So, if this piano player guy is so important, why don't we just get him and put the screws to him ourselves?"

"Because I wouldn't know what to ask him, but I'm quite sure the good professor does. Besides, he'd rather die a slow and painful death than assist me in any way."

"Why? You know this guy?"

"Oh, yes, I know him. And he knows me." Depriest strolled to the open sliding glass door, looked out across the Manhattan skyline, and smiled. "He knows me, all right. I'm the man who destroyed David Webber's life."

Chapter 4

The shrill ringing was like an ice pick puncturing David's eardrum. Slowly, and painfully, he raised his head from the couch and attempted a sitting position. After several unsuccessful tries, he surrendered by rolling off the couch and onto the floor. One knee to one knee, one foot to one foot, David stood. Once erect, he saw the problem. His shirt was sopping wet and twisted around his torso in such a way it was restricting the movement of his arms. He had one shoe still on, and his cummerbund had crept its way up around his chest—he had passed out in his clothes. "Jesus Christ," he moaned, rubbing the crust away from the corners of his mouth. He looked around the room and noticed the ringing had stopped. He saw the television was still on and blaring out testimonials from people singing the praises of a new and revolutionary spot remover. An eight hundred number was pasted at the bottom of the screen. No sooner had David decided the ringing had come from the television than it began again. From the living room, he could see the clock hanging in the kitchen. Three fifty-eight a.m. "Who in the hell?" He picked up the phone from the coffee table. "Yeah?" he answered with a rasp.

The voice on the other end was weak and cracked. Between

David's alcohol delirium and the caller's inaudible tone, it was impossible to make out what the caller was saying. He was about to hang up when the voice suddenly became familiar.

"Davey, Davey."

David's chest tightened—his breath got short.

"Davey, it's me."

A wave passed through his body.

"Davey, are you there?"

David swallowed hard. "Yes, I'm here."

"Hello, Davey," the elderly voice said.

David couldn't reply

"Davey, are you there?"

"Hello, Professor," David said, trying to keep the shake out his voice.

"Hello, Davey."

David took a breath and tried to sound casual. "Henry, I can't believe—"

"Yes, I know, it's been too long since we've spoken."

"Too long?" David said with a nervous laugh. "Try a lifetime or two."

"Yes, it has." There was a long pause before the man spoke again. "I'm sorry, Davey, I shouldn't have called, but—"

"No," David interrupted, "please, Henry, don't hang up."

"I'm not hanging up, Davey. But I realize this intrusion—"

"No, Professor, please—" David closed his eyes. "I want to talk to you—so badly I want to…need to talk to you."

"Davey, I know we have a lot to—"

David jumped on the man's words. "There's so much I need to say. I just…" His thoughts were all over the place; he couldn't focus. Was he dreaming? He wasn't sure. "I don't know where to begin, and…I'm still not quite awake. You must have forgotten about the time change. It's the middle of the night here."

"I did not forget. I'm in Los Angeles. My apologies for the hour. I need—"

"Los Angeles?" David said, "Professor, why are—"

"Davey, please," Henry interrupted. "We will reunion at another time. At this moment though, you must listen to me very carefully, please."

"Sure, but Henry, why—"

"Damn it, Davey, please."

David was stunned. The Professor Henry Shoewalter he remembered never used profanity. "Okay, Henry, I'm listening."

David heard a strained sigh on the other end of the line. "I'm sorry too, Davey," the old man said, lowering his voice. "I know you and I have much to talk about. I realize that after the long silence between us, me calling you now from out of the blue must seem strange. But Davey, right now I must ask we save what needs to be said between us for another time."

"I don't understand, Professor, but whatever you say."

"Thank you, Davey." The old man sighed again. "I have a question for you. Do you remember the gift I gave you at the conservatory?"

"The gift?"

"Yes, the gift. The one I gave you from the master."

The combination of David's half-drunk-half-hung-over state, the hour, and the surprise of hearing from the most important person in his life still had him reeling. "The master? The gift, the gift, oh you mean the—"

"Yes. Do you still have it?"

"Of course, Henry. It's just about the only thing from my past I've held onto." David's hand shook as he tried lighting a cigarette.

"Good. Davey, listen to me. I need you to bring it to me. I promise I'll give it back, but it's very important that I borrow it for a while. There are also some questions I need to ask you."

"What?"

"Not over the telephone. I'll ask you when I see you. Where can we meet?"

David sat down on the couch. "Anywhere you want, Henry. If you have a car, you could come over here."

"No, I have no car, you must come to me."

"Okay, that's fine, I'll come to you—oh shit—I mean shoot. I forgot, I don't have my car, it's still at the hotel, and—"

"You mean the Airport Holiday Inn?" Shoewalter interrupted.

"Yeah, the Airport Holiday Inn. Henry, how did you know——"

"I'm calling you from there right now."

"You mean, out of all the hotels in Los Angeles, you just happen to be at the Airport Holiday Inn?"

"Yes, of course," Henry answered. "I found out through the union that was where you worked. Odd though, when I asked for you tonight, they said you were no longer under their employment."

David shut his eyes in disbelief. "About what time was that, Professor?"

"I believe it was around midnight."

David dropped his head. "Well, Professor, let's just say sometimes things have a way of changing quickly out here."

"Quickly, indeed."

David shook his head and allowed himself a silent chuckle. "In a way, Professor, I'm glad we didn't meet up last night."

"Why, David?" the professor asked. "Do you still hate me so?"

A lump filled David's throat. "No, sir. Oh God, no, sir. I never... I mean...I was young, I said a lot of things I didn't...I just had a...I——"

The old man spoke calmly. "I know, Davey, I know. You don't have to say any more. I deserve so much blame."

"No you don't, sir," David replied. "Sir, the reason I'm glad you didn't see me last night is...well, you see, Professor..." David could hardly get the words out. "I'm just a saloon piano player now."

"Davey," the old man replied. "You are not now, nor ever will be, just a saloon piano player. You may make your living playing a saloon, but you are and always will be so much more. Where you must, or choose, to exhibit your gift is up to you. But what you are, really are, is beyond your power. Because that, Davey, was created by God."

He had forgotten the power the man possessed when he spoke. "Thank you, Professor," David replied in a near whisper.

"Now, back to how I can procure that item from you."

"The guy that lives next door works at the airport. He'll give me a lift down."

"Great, then it's—"

"Oh, there is another small problem of me getting my hands on it, but—"

"You don't have it?" Shoewalter responded. "You've given it to someone else? Who did you give it to?"

"No, no, it's not like that," David replied. "I didn't give it to anybody. It's almost four in the morning. It's in a safety deposit box at my bank. In fact, except for a passport, it's the only thing of value in there."

David heard the old man swallow hard. "Of course, my apologies once again, Davey. These are just stressful times."

"What's going on, Henry?" David asked.

"I'll explain everything when I see you, but it's all very exciting, Davey. Shall we meet in the morning after the bank opens?"

"Sure."

"The lobby of the Airport Holiday Inn, then?"

David laughed. "You know, that might not be the best idea. How about you meet me out front at eleven o'clock? I'll get my car, then we'll go grab some brunch or something and…talk. I'd really like to just talk."

"That sounds splendid, Davey. But ten would be better. I have a bit of business to handle at eleven. In fact, it would be perfect if you could join me. Then afterward, we could spend the day together if you like?"

"I would like that very much," David replied.

"Wonderful. I'll be waiting in the lobby for you to pull up. I think I'll still recognize you."

David could hear the old man smile. "Henry?" David said quickly. "It's going to be great seeing you again. I think about you all the time and…I—"

"Davey," the old man interrupted, "it's going to be wonderful seeing you too. I think about you often, as well. Goodbye, Davey."

"Goodbye, Henry."

David turned off the phone and just stared. His stomach jumped, and he felt an excitement in his chest so strong he thought his heart was going to pound straight through his skin. *My Henry.*

Over the years, there wasn't a day that had gone by he didn't think of him. There wasn't a day he didn't consider picking up a telephone, calling him, and finally just saying the words, "I'm sorry." But as the years passed and his life went to hell, that call became ever more impossible. "Stupid," he mumbled out loud.

David got up from the couch, went into the kitchen, and started a pot of coffee. A half hour later, he stepped from the shower feeling almost human again. Ravel, who had been curled up on the corner of the bed, rose from his slumber with a "what the hell are we doin' up at this hour" look and followed David back to the kitchen.

"Hey buddy, you want an early breakfast?"

Ravel jumped onto the counter and meowed.

"I think I could stand some food too."

David pulled a carton of eggs, a dish of butter, a half-block of Swiss cheese, and some sandwich meat out of the refrigerator. He picked up a dirty skillet, ran some soap and water over it, and dried it off. As he struck a match to light the gas burner, he gave voice to what had started bugging him in the shower. "First of all, how did he find me?" he said as Ravel raised his nose to the smell of frying butter. "Secondly, why call me in the middle of the night? After twelve years, what's a few more hours?" Ravel watched as David cracked four eggs into the skillet. "And third, fourth, and fifth, what's suddenly so important about that old piece of music? I'd forgotten I had it. And why didn't—" David stopped himself. "Oh, shut up, Webber. For cryin' out loud, he's an old man."

David battled back Ravel as he cut thin slices of cheese and placed them into the frying eggs. He opened the package of lunch-meat, took out a piece and began tearing it into strips. Out of self-defense, he gave a strip to Ravel. As David tossed the remaining pieces of meat in the pan, he was suddenly eleven years old again. Memories of South Bend and a man named Mr. Ramsey flooded his mind. As a professor at Notre Dame University, Ramsey only took on a few private students and absolutely no children. But David's foster parents, with the assistance of the social worker, were able to convince Ramsey that he should listen to David play. After he did, he took him on immediately. David remembered how everyone told him how lucky he was to have a teacher like Mr. Ramsey. David, however, only remembered Ramsey as a half-in-the-bag hack. The music he was required to play was never that challenging, and most of the time old Ramsey would fall asleep halfway through the lesson. But Ramsey wasn't a complete idiot. He recognized a gift and knew he wasn't the instructor to nurture it. The one thing Ramsey did right was calling his old friend in New York, professor of piano at Juilliard, Doctor Henry Shoewalter. As if it were yesterday, David recalled the day he was practicing scales from the dreaded Hannon book when Ramsey wobbled into the room. With him was a man, who at the time seemed like the oldest man David had ever seen. David smiled thinking of that too. Twenty-five years ago Henry probably wasn't much over fifty-five years old, maybe younger.

"David this is Professor Shoewalter from New York."

"Pleased to meet you, sir," a young David said.

"Very pleased to make your acquaintance too, young man. I shall call you Davey—David seems so out of place for a boy your size."

"Yes sir, but I am almost five foot two inches tall," protested David.

"I see. But I will call you Davey until David feels comfortable for me. Okay?"

"Okay, sir," replied David.

"Good. Now, I've come a long way. Thurman here tells me you're something of a prodigy. You will play for me now, please."

"A pro-to-jee?"

"Yes. You show me now."

Ramsey cut in, *"David, play the Chopin in C minor for Professor Shoewalter."*

David pulled two plates out of the cupboard. He slid the concoction onto one plate, took his fork, and cut it three-quarters from the top. He slid the smaller piece onto the other plate and set it on the floor for Ravel.

"As long as I live I will never be as scared as I was at that moment," David said out loud as he ate. "I didn't even know who this guy was, and I was still petrified. All I knew was old Ramsey wanted him to hear me play and made it clear they'd gone to a great deal of trouble to make it happen. I can't believe I choked." David laughed remembering Ramsey's face when he duffed the second variation. But the laugh turned to a smile when he remembered what Henry said, *"Very fine, that section always gives me fits too."* David shook his head, "How cool was that?"

"From that point on, life would never be the same. Henry took me back to New York, enrolled me in the Westchester County School for Boys, and gave me private lessons every Tuesday and Thursday for two hours. I grew to love that old fart, Ravel. He was there for all the important stuff, the competitions, the concerts, even —" David stopped. He still couldn't say her name.

Ravel was sitting on the table washing. David ran his hand over the feline's black–and-gray striped head, got up, and took their dishes into the kitchen. He looked at the clock, and it was still only a little after five in the morning. He couldn't remember the last time he'd seen five in the morning. Going to bed was out of the question, and for some reason, he suddenly felt like straightening up his long-neglected apartment. He picked up dirty clothes from the floor and threw away junk mail that had accumulated on his favorite dumping ground, the piano. That's when he had the thought. *How about practicing the piano? Whoa.* He hadn't sat at the piano and just played for his own enjoyment in years, but that's what he felt like doing.

Like a man approaching an old lover after a long separation, David moved to the piano and tossed the old newspapers, magazines, and unread books off the bench. He lifted the seat and saw a copy of George Gershwin's "Rhapsody in Blue." "Whew, I haven't touched this bear in years."

He lost all track of time. With Ravel sitting atop of the piano, David chicken-pecked his way through the "Rhapsody." After that came Schumann, Haydn, and Brahms. He amazed himself, and possibly even Ravel, as he tore through the Bach inventions as if he'd been playing them every day for the past twenty years. But it was in the middle of Debussy's "Claire de Lune," he would later recall, that he happened to look over at the television. The morning news was on, and a reporter was on the scene for breaking news.

The location was the Airport Holiday Inn. David jumped from the piano and went to the couch for the remote.

...there's been a brutal murder at this airport hotel. Eyewitness News has information that the victim is an elderly man.

David went cold as he grabbed the telephone.

Sources have told Eyewitness News that it appears the victim was beaten, then shot to death in his room on the twenty-seventh floor. We were told that two shots...

"I need the number for the Airport Holiday Inn."

...fired at point blank range into the back of the man's head.

"Airport Holiday Inn, how may I direct your call?"

It's also said that nothing is left of the man's head—hang on, we're getting new information. An unidentified source at the hotel has informed us that the man's name was Henry Theodore Shoewalter. We're being told identification has been confirmed.

"Hello, Airport Holiday Inn, how may I—"

David dropped the phone and fell onto the couch.

John, this is a brutal murder down here. Many guests of the hotel, noticeably shaken, are telling me that they are moving to other accommodations. The management of the hotel says...

David sat in silence as the reporter went on with her story. He sat in silence as the local news went off and the national morning show with the funny weatherman came on. No words, no expression, and no tears, David Webber, with his cat in his lap, simply sat in silence as the sun rose to meet a perfect Southern California morning.

Chapter 5

Horns blared and tires screeched as the yellow Volkswagen convertible whipped across two lanes of Interstate 66 rush-hour traffic. Obscene gestures from irate morning commuters were met with an *I'm sorry* wave as the small car careened into the center lane, crossing the Theodore Roosevelt Bridge and onto Constitution Boulevard. Without slowing down, much less stopping, the automobile made a right-turn-on-red onto Fourteenth Street and brought cars to another screeching halt by turning left into oncoming traffic and entering a driveway marked Museum Employees Only, where the driver was forced to lock up the breaks to keep from crashing through a wooden security gate. With a swipe of a card through an electronic box, the gate lifted and the car lunged forward, speeding down the driveway into the underground garage, ending its assault by turning into an assigned parking space. A young woman with chestnut hair pulled into a ponytail bounded from the vehicle. Wearing white sneakers, khaki pants, denim shirt, and carrying a backpack, Dr. Dani Parsons looked more like a college freshman late for class than curator of American Musical Antiquities for the Smithsonian Institution.

Using the fire escape stairwell, Dani scaled the steps two at a time and bolted through the steel door marked Security Check-In. A gray-haired black man in his late sixties wearing the traditional security guard wardrobe of navy pants and light blue shirt was there to meet her.

"Dr. Parsons, right on time I see," the guard said with a Mississippi drawl.

"Very funny, Charlie," Dani replied, rummaging through her bag for her I.D. card. "I can't believe I'm late today of all days. Beckman is going to have my head."

Charlie laughed. "Dr. P, if I've told you once, I've told you a hundred times, all you need to do is get yourself a man and start popping out some babies. That'll get you up in the morning, all right."

"Is that an offer, Charlie?" Dani said, finding her I.D. and handing it to the security man.

The old man pursed his lips. "Oh, now, Dr. P, you watch what you say. I just might have to call up mother and tell her to find herself another buck." He scanned the I.D. card, and a green LED light appeared. "Here you are, Dr. P," he said, handing Dani back her I.D. "You have a good day, now."

Dani raced into the elevator, pushed the button for the fifth floor, and nibbled a fingernail as the elevator ascended. Before the doors had completely opened, she was running down the plaster and stone hallway until reaching the end of the corridor, where she stopped to compose herself. Feeling as if she had the pretense of calm firmly in hand, she entered a large oak door bearing the words DIVISION OF MUSICAL HISTORY, NATIONAL MUSEUM OF NATURAL HISTORY.

"They're waiting for you inside, kiddo," said the woman at the desk.

"Thanks, Millie," Dani replied.

Dani opened the inner office door, and twelve sets of accusing eyes looked through her. She stiffly entered the conference room and sat on the lone empty chair located at the corner of a long rectangular conference table.

At the head of the table sat a man in his early fifties. The man was reclined in a high-back leather chair, staring blankly at the ceiling and tapping a fountain pen on the table. Except for the *click click click* of the man's pen, there was silence. Finally, the man spoke. "Dr. Parsons, thank you for joining us. And dressed so well too. I hope this meeting is not putting you out too much."

Dani wanted to evaporate. "No, sir, not at all. I'm very sorry for being late, Dr. Beckman, and everyone else. The Roosevelt was a mess."

"I took the Roosevelt, thought it was fine," offered the dweeby, bald man who sat across from Dani.

Dani stared at him.

The dweeb dropped his head.

"Is that so? Thank you, Herbert," Beckman said. "How about you, Dr. Rogers? You use the Roosevelt if I'm not mistaken, how did you find it?"

"Fine, sir," mumbled the bearded young man seated next to Dani.

"Isn't that something? Anybody else here find the Roosevelt particularly a mess this morning? No? Me either. Well, Dr. Parsons, it seems that the Roosevelt was just a mess on your behalf this morning. I wonder why?"

Beckman smiled directly at Dani, but the smile did not disguise anything. Dani knew Beckman didn't like her. When she had interviewed for her position, Dr. Dennis Beckman, the director of the Division of Musical History, was the only nay vote on the hiring committee. She didn't know the reason. Was it because she was from Oklahoma and he was an old money Virginia Southerner? Was it because she went to OU, not an Ivy League? Was it because he had a buddy he wanted to give the job to? Or was it simply the old tried and true reason that she was a woman? Dani suspected the latter. She had met many men like Beckman since getting her PhD, traditional male chauvinists in every sense of the word. He was okay around females as long as he had the upper hand. But take that away, put him with a woman who was not only his mental equal but attractive as well, and he couldn't handle it. He was just another short, middle-aged man with a receding hairline. Whatever the reason, he was out-voted, she was hired, and he'd been a thorn in her side ever since.

"Dr. Parsons, do you have nothing to say?" Beckman asked.

"I'm sorry," Dani replied, staring into the man's eyes.

Beckman nodded and then opened the file in front of him. "Let's get started."

For the next forty-five minutes the meeting consisted of Beckman reviewing budget overruns as well as projections for the following quarter. Each person at the table headed a specific department. All were middle-aged men except for Paul Rogers, who was roughly Dani's age and her only real friend at work.

Dr. Paul Rogers was curator of wind instruments. He and Dani first worked together two years earlier while collaborating on an exhibition called Music from the Swing Era. The exhibit was Paul's idea and was a huge success. Dani was successful in securing several personal instruments of famous bandleaders as well as original handwritten charts to many swing standards. It was her first exhibit, and she and Paul had been close ever since.

"Now, I'd like to move on to another matter," Beckman said. "Is everyone familiar with Mrs. Gertrude Sugarberry?"

Everyone looked at each other in hopes they weren't the only one who didn't know the name.

"Well, you all should because Mrs. Sugarberry pays your salaries—well, at least a large chunk of it. Mrs. Sugarberry is a major—underline major—contributor to the Smithsonian Major Acquisition Fund. That fund, gentlemen…and lady, enables this department to operate. As well as being filthy rich, Mrs. Sugarberry is a rather eccentric old woman—actually she's crazy as a loon, but be that as it may, she still represents a major part of the health of this department. So when she makes a request, the boys and girls on Capitol Hill do their damnedest to see it's fulfilled. She's made a request. It seems Mrs. Sugarberry possesses a collection of old sheet music she would like to donate to the museum. Now, that's all well and good, except she wants them viewed. That means an exhibit. Unfortunately, her collection is not large enough for an exhibit. So the powers that be have decided to include her collection with others, thereby creating an American Sheet Music Exhibit."

"But, Dr. Beckman, we don't have a large cataloged collection of American sheet music," the dweeb named Herbert offered.

"We don't yet," Beckman said.

Everyone understood.

"Parsons," Beckman barked. "You and Rogers are heading this up."

The rest sighed in relief.

"Dr. Beckman," Rogers said, "I'm honored by your trust in me to co-head this project, but I'm not the best candidate. I'm in wind instruments—as of course you know—I'm not sure what use I would be in acquiring sheet music."

"Forget it, Rogers, you're doing it," Beckman interrupted.

Dani started to speak, but Beckman cut her off. "Don't you even start. You're doing this. Everyone else has assignments that must be completed before the next quarter. You two are the only ones who don't have anything pressing."

Dani was fuming. "What about the Women in Song project I'm planning?"

"It can wait," Beckman said.

"But—"

"It can wait," Beckman said, emphasizing each word.

Dani threw her pencil down onto the table.

Beckman ignored her.

"After getting the collection together, you will coordinate with the Archives Center, which is where the pieces will be housed. I want the exhibit to exploit the enormous value the collection has in understanding this country's musical past. It should entail the mainstream, tributaries, and streamlets of American music. It should also highlight American social and cultural history, and history of graphic arts. Is that understood?"

Paul patted Dani's leg under the table, urging her to calm down.

"This could take the rest of the year," Dani said.

Beckman grinned. "Yes, it could. Maybe longer."

Dani thought at that moment how lucky Beckman was she

wasn't a man. For if she were, she would fly across the table and thoroughly kick his butt.

"I think that's it. We're adjourned. Have a good day."

Beckman was the first out the door. Everyone rose from their chairs and gathered their papers. Dani rammed her file folders in her bag.

"Sorry, Dani," Paul said.

"That man is a world class jerk."

"I know."

"Does he practice being a butthead, or does it just come naturally? Did you see that look on his face when he said the Women in Song project could wait? Joy. It was joy."

"I know," Paul replied.

Millie was standing behind her desk as Dani and Paul left the conference room. "Here you go, kiddo," she said, handing Dani a slip of paper.

"What's this?"

"Mrs. Gertrude Sugarberry's phone number. Dr. Beckman told me to make sure you got it. She's expecting your call."

Dani looked at Paul like a puppy begging for a treat.

"Oh, no," Paul said, shaking his hands in front of him.

"Please, oh please, oh pleeeeeeease."

"Nah huh. Beckman told Millie to give you the number, right, Mil?"

Millie nodded. "I'm afraid so, honey."

"Ugh," Dani groaned, taking the slip of paper. "It's not fair."

Chapter 6

Ravel leaped from David's lap the moment the pounding started. David didn't move. He didn't notice. The pounding continued. Then came the demand.

"Los Angeles Police Department, open the door. We have a warrant."

David still didn't budge. He sat on the couch, all senses shut down. He stared at the television but didn't see it. His eyes were bloodshot, and he was still in his robe.

Over the next sixty seconds, David was totally oblivious to the mayhem. The door crashed open. Splinters of wood from the door's frame flew into the entranceway of the apartment. Four officers entered in a crouch with their side arms drawn. Two officers held their position at the door with shotguns leveled.

"Get on the floor, get on the floor!"

The coffee table was kicked out of the way. David was grabbed by his hair and dragged belly first to the ground. His arms were twisted around his back, and his wrists were cuffed, pinching his skin as the sharp metal locked into place. David was pulled to his knees, and then to his feet and frisked.

A man in a tweed sport coat, white shirt, and dark pants walked in as David was sat on the couch. The square-jawed man with salt and pepper hair carried himself with the air of a soldier. His voice was low and sharp. "He say anything?"

"Nothing, Lieutenant. He may be on something," the young officer standing over David answered.

"Mr. Webber, I'm Lieutenant Pete Ryan of the LAPD."

David looked up but said nothing.

"Mr. Webber, can you understand what I'm saying? Are you on something?"

David blinked twice as if waking up from a deep sleep. He looked around his apartment at the strangers. Men and women were going through his drawers, cabinets, clothes hamper, and closets. Everything was being invaded.

"I want everyone to be careful," the detective said, looking over David's shoulder. "Don't touch anything unless you're wearing latex. The boys in the white coats will be here shortly to get trace, and they better not come-up with anything off you screwballs."

"What's going on?" David mumbled.

"Mr. Webber, are you on something?" Ryan asked again.

David opened his eyes wide and stammered. "On something? What? You mean drugs? No. I'm...who are you? What are you doing here?"

"I'm Lieutenant Pete Ryan of the LAPD. We're investigating a murder. I need to tell you that you have the right to remain—"

David hung his head. "Henry."

"Yes, Henry. So, you do know Henry Shoewalter?"

David began whispering. Ryan couldn't make out what he was saying. "Okay, hang on, Mr. Webber, we'll talk about Henry." Ryan motioned to the officer standing behind the couch. "Get everyone out of here. Sanchez and Gilbert are getting statements from the neighbors. Get them here pronto."

The officer nodded and began moving people out into the hallway. A minute later, two plain-clothed detectives entered the apartment. Ryan motioned for the detectives to come close. Both detectives pulled out note pads.

"Mr. Webber? David?" Ryan asked, his voice becoming calm, almost serene. "What do you know about Henry?"

"He's dead," David answered as if he were in a trance.

"How do you know, David?"

"Television."

Ryan looked at the two detectives. "Were there any names released?"

Sanchez and Gilbert looked at each another. Sanchez responded. "Afraid so, Lieutenant."

Ryan shook his head in disgust.

"No, David, not television," Ryan corrected.

David looked up and nodded his head yes.

Ryan let out a breath. "Okay, David, I'm going to ask you something, and I want you to think before you answer. What have you been doing since last night?"

"Nothing."

"You must have done something, David. Think hard. Did you go to the Airport Holiday Inn?"

"Yes," David answered.

All three police officers looked at each other.

"And you saw Henry, is that right?"

"No, I went to work."

Ryan took another deep breath. "Okay. That's right, David, you went to work. You got in a fight and got arrested. Is that correct?"

"Yeah."

"Then what?"

"J.P. picked me up."

"That would be Ms. Peterson, correct?"

"Yeah."

"Then what?"

At that moment David's brain clicked in.

"Oh my God," David whispered. "You think I—you think I killed Henry."

"Come on, David, stay with me. We're doin' good here, don't stop."

"You can't be serious?"

Ryan went on. "What did you do after Ms. Peterson picked you up?"

"You idiots," David said.

"What did you do after Ms. Peterson picked you up from jail?" Ryan repeated even stronger, ignoring David's sudden belligerence.

David tried to adjust himself on the couch, but became aware of the pain caused by the handcuffs. The detective standing over him put his hand on his shoulder. He shut his eyes and answered, "She drove me home."

"You came straight home?"

"Yes...no."

"Which is it?"

His voice quivered when he spoke. "We stopped at a liquor store. I bought a bottle and some cigarettes, then she drove me straight home."

"This bottle here?" Ryan said, holding up the three-quarters empty bottle of whiskey.

"Yes."

"My, you did some drinkin' last night," laughed the short but muscular Latino detective named Sanchez.

"You know, David," Ryan said, "back in my drinkin' days, I used to drink so much that I'd forget entire days. I'd walk around, even go to work, but I was so plastered I couldn't tell you a thing about it. Remember, guys?"

"Sure do, Lieutenant."

"That ever happen to you, David?"

"No," David replied. "I came home, I drank, I fell asleep. I might have passed out, but I did not kill Henry." The words were strangled but were now carried by rage. "Oh God, poor Henry. Why would someone kill that sweet old man?"

David swung his shoulders, fighting the handcuffs and causing the uniformed officer standing above to restrain him.

"Okay, David. Let's take a break." Ryan stood and took off his jacket. "Gilbert, see if the criminologists are here. Take this place apart, and don't forget his car."

"DMV says it's a black '94 Honda Accord." Sanchez read from his notebook. "Parking is down below. I'll get a team."

"That's it," David suddenly yelled. "You won't find it. It's still at the hotel. I couldn't have gone anywhere after J.P. dropped me off last night 'cause I don't have a car." David fell back into the couch.

Ryan looked at Gilbert. "Check it out." Ryan rubbed the bridge of his nose. "Sanchez, call Ms. Peterson, confirm she brought him back here last night. I'm sure Mr. Webber won't mind if you use his telephone, will you Mr. Webber?"

"No," David answered, breathing heavily.

"I'll use the one in the bedroom," Sanchez said. "You wouldn't know her number off the top of your head, would you?"

David took a deep breath and gave him J.P.'s home and office numbers.

Sanchez left the room, but fifteen seconds later he was back. "Hey, you've got another phone in this place, don't you?"

David looked down at the cordless on the floor. Sanchez picked it up. "That's what I thought—man, your phone's turned on."

Sanchez turned off the phone, set it back in its cradle, and went back into the bedroom.

The criminologists overtook David's apartment. Everything from dirty clothes to bath towels to garbage was inspected and labeled.

Ryan sat down in a chair across from David and crossed his legs. "This should only take a few minutes. Why don't we just continue talking a little."

"I didn't do anything," David said.

"Relax. I mean just talk. That's all. So you're a piano player, huh?"

David went limp. "Yeah, I'm a piano player."

"Wow, a guy can really make a living doin' that?"

"Just barely."

"My folks gave me piano lessons. I lost interest, you know how it is?"

"Yeah," David replied. "Can you unhandcuff me? This really hurts."

Ryan brushed off the request. "So how did you know Shoewalter, uh–Henry, anyway?"

"He was my piano teacher as a kid, and became my professor in college."

"No kidding, what college?"

"Juilliard."

"That's in New York, right?"

"Right," David said, getting more agitated.

"So, Shoewalter was from New York?"

"Yes. But you knew that already from his I.D."

"Yeah, I guess you're right, we did," Ryan said with a slight laugh.

"What have you done with Henry? Have you called anyone back east?"

"We're taking care of it. So what do you think he was doing out here?"

David sighed again, "I don't know."

"He must have told you. I mean, David, we know he talked to you. We have the phone records from the hotel."

"If you have the phone records, then you know what time we talked. How could I have talked to him here and been there at the same time to do what you guys think I did?"

"Great question," Ryan said with a chuckle. "You're a bright guy. Well, to be honest, that was a concern. But it's lookin' like Shoewalter wasn't killed until after five-thirty a.m. We know that because he ordered room service—strudel and coffee. We figure it happened right after that. To be honest, David, you could've talked to him, gotten into an argument, and had plenty of time to get down there and get back. Sorry to be so blunt, but that's the truth."

"Right," David said, feeling like someone was hitting him in the stomach every time Henry's name was spoken.

"So, what did you two talk about?"

"I was supposed to see him today."

"Really, why?"

David didn't get a chance to respond. Sanchez came from the

bedroom wearing a frown. David couldn't hear what he was saying to Ryan.

Ryan got up from the chair and paced in front of the couch. "We're unable to locate Ms. Peterson, David."

David rolled his eyes. "Did you call her at home?"

"First place I tried," Sanchez responded. "Her maid answered. Said she hasn't seen her all morning. Says she must've left for work before she arrived."

Ryan broke in, "Then he called her office. Her secretary, Sherry, isn't that her name, Sanchez?"

David interrupted, "No, it's Cherry."

"Okay, Cherry said she hasn't seen her all morning."

David thought for a second. "Wait a minute, what time is it?"

"Quarter 'til ten," Ryan answered.

"I know where she is. She told me she had a morning breakfast meeting with a buyer. Some guy from a cruise ship company, what was the name…?"

"South Pacific Cruises." This time Sanchez interrupted. "We know. Cherry said the guy's been calling all morning. Ms. Peterson never showed."

David's face went numb.

Detective Gilbert walked in.

"Lieutenant?" Gilbert smiled as he came toward Ryan and Sanchez, who were standing at the television in front of David. "It's down there, '94 Honda Accord, plates check out. And Lieutenant, the engine's still warm."

David looked at the detective.

Lieutenant Ryan looked at David. "Mr. Webber, you have a problem." He nodded to Sanchez and Gilbert.

The detectives grabbed David by each arm and lifted him off the couch. Sanchez spoke methodically, "Mr. Webber, let's get some clothes. David Webber, you are under arrest for murder. You have the right to remain silent. Anything you say…"

David went deaf. He heard nothing but the sound of his own heart beating in his ears. As he was led out of his apartment, he looked back to see Ravel being placed in a cage by a man in an orange jumpsuit with the words "Animal Control" embroidered on the back.

David Webber was led into the elevator. As the doors shut, his wail echoed through the apartment complex. "What's going on?"

Chapter 7

The black limousine sputtered through midtown Manhattan, crossing Seventh Avenue on Broadway at Forty-fourth Street. Anthony Depriest, adorned in a perfectly pressed black tuxedo, sat with legs crossed, fingers locked, and eyes closed, oblivious to the carnival that was New York City on a Friday night.

This was his favorite time, the moment before. The moment where he could sit in anticipation of the accolades that were sure to be bestowed upon him by evening's end. This is where he could be still and take in all of himself and his life—the what was, the what is, and the what soon shall be.

The what was: it never ceased to amaze him how far he'd come. The limo and the clothes were light years away from little Tony Roberto Depriestiano of Flatbush and Avenue J. Son of a pathetic fish merchant and the smelliest, smallest kid in the neighborhood. The one all the boys liked to call tuna-fishy-sissy-ass and queer bait —the one who was too scared to fight, too slow to run, and just too talented for his own goddamn good. From the moment Father Francis of Sacred Heart parochial school realized nine-year-old Tony had an ear for music, his life became a never-ending roulette of beatings by playground bullies and sexual liaisons with Father Francis after music lessons.

By age eleven he had consciously surrendered his childhood. He recalled, in awe really, how he so willingly and beautifully accepted it. Buying time, and not for one instant considering himself the abused and manipulated. But instead, knowing he was the ultimate abuser and manipulator. For he knew, even then with the mind of a child, his time was coming. A time when Father Francis and all the kids on Flatbush and Avenue J would look upon him with respect, admiration, guilt, and, yes, even fear. So he took it. And used it. The bullies were his motivation, the good Father's penis his manipulation.

He was thirteen when his father died. He didn't cry. He rejoiced. He hated him for his poverty and good-for-nothing decency. Had his old man been more like his brother, life most certainly would have been easier for him, and the mother he never knew would still be alive. She had died when he was a toddler. They told him it was cancer, but he knew the truth. She died from being poor.

So off he went to live with Uncle Nick, and he knew it was time to make his move. No one in the neighborhood had much fear of the police, least of all a respected priest that shepherded many of New York's finest. But everyone feared Nicholas Depriestiano, the crime lord of Flatbush.

It was so easy, Depriest recalled. A few simple insinuations, some strategically placed tantrums, a well-rehearsed seduction, and *poof!* Father Francis was his obedient servant, ready and more than willing to do his bidding. And his bidding was to be out of Flatbush, across the East River to Manhattan and the High School of the Performing Arts, the place where the city's best of the best attended. Though tuition was free, acceptance each year went only to a select few based on audition and academic excellence. The audition wasn't a problem—academic excellence was. A problem easily solved, however, by a motivated priest who was the headmaster of Tony's school. Tony's permanent record was adjusted accordingly, and after a flawless audition, he was accepted into the school without debate.

Depriest smiled as he remembered. From there it was an easy

jump to Juilliard. As the legal ward of Nicholas Depriestiano, doors seemed to fly open. The old man was an idiot, no doubt about that, little more than a street thug with a nice suit, but he had been useful in those early days, especially to someone as sharp as himself. He adopted the formal variation of Tony his second year at Juilliard, as well as dropping the "iano" at the end of his surname. Tony Roberto Depriestiano was dead for all time. Anthony Depriest was on the way up.

Which brought him to the what is: Resident Conductor of the New York Philharmonic, one of the foremost symphony orchestras in the world, and frequent guest, and host, of royalty and politicos. Honored philanthropist, noted musical scholar, and voted one of the ten sexiest men in America, it was indeed a long way from Flatbush and Avenue J.

The what shall soon be: children would be reading the name Anthony Depriest in history books. Courses on his life would be offered in universities. And, of course, he would be wealthier than he ever dared to imagine. "It will happen. I will make history. It is my destiny," Depriest said out loud.

"Sir?" came the voice over the intercom. "Brooklyn on line one."

"Thank you, Leon." Depriest waited before picking up, a technique he adopted after reading a biography of General Douglas MacArthur. Whenever an irate President Truman would call the renegade general, MacArthur would always wait ten seconds before picking up the phone, even though he knew it was the president of the United States on the line. More importantly to the general, however, was the fact he knew the president of the United States knew he knew it was the president of the United States on the line.

Depriest cleared his throat and smiled—another technique of the general's. "Yes? Uncle, how are you? Good to hear your—"

The voice on the other end interrupted. Depriest grit his teeth. *That voice, God, that wretched atonal voice.*

"Sir, I would love to see you, but I am currently on my way to the Center. I have a concert tonight. We're performing Beethoven's Ninth—"

"Yes, Uncle, certainly I'm on top of the situation in Los Angeles," Depriest said, continuing to force a smile as he squeezed the handset of the phone.

Suddenly the blood raced from Depriest's head. What was he hearing?

"No...sir...I didn't know. How did you find—"

Depriest's face fell, the smile gone. A rush of heat overtook his body. This wasn't happening. Why didn't he know about this? Why wasn't he informed?

He had to regain his composure. He couldn't let the old man think he wasn't in control. *Think Anthony, calm down and think. You're smarter than these people. You can handle this. Take back control. Take a breath and take control.*

"Sir, this is surprising news, but only in the sense that you heard about it first. I will chastise my L.A. contacts for not notifying me promptly. It is surprising but not unexpected. It changes the strategy somewhat, but perhaps for the better. Only minutes ago, I was reevaluating the situation, and—"

Once again, Depriest was cut off. "Tomorrow afternoon? Well, certainly, sir, but I fear I might be late. You see, I'm having lunch with the mayor and his wife at...yes, I understand the importance of me being there. Absolutely, sir, I understand. I'll be there. Thank you, sir. Not to worry, everything's under—" The phone went dead.

Depriest slammed the phone in its cradle and tapped his fingers on the console. *Air, I need air!* He rolled down the tinted window and breathed in the New York night. It was loud and electric, but the circus outside the confines of the limousine seemed to calm him. *Action, Anthony, action.*

Depriest pressed a button on the console. "Leon, call the mayor's office. Tell him that the maestro must regrettably cancel lunch tomorrow. Tell him a family emergency has arisen. Afterward, call my wife and tell her I have some bad—" He caught himself, reevaluating his strategy. "No, strike that. Call and tell her we're eating with Uncle Nick and the family tomorrow." Depriest leaned his head back. "Also tell her I'll be late tonight—publicity pictures or something—you know how to handle it." Depriest rolled his head from one side to another. "I'm very tense, Leon, please call Mrs.

Rochelle and inform her I'll have a seventy-two Rothschild chilling in my dressing room after the concert."

"Understood, sir. Anything else?"

"Yes," Depriest spit. "See if you can locate my stupid cousin. Tell him to get ahold of Sal and Leo. Then tell him I expect to speak to him alone tomorrow before I see his father. No excuses. Tell him I said his worthless life might depend on it."

Chapter 8

A weeping-willow stood in the middle of a vast open meadow. David sat under the tree alone. It was morning, the ground was damp with dew—there was complete silence.

David saw himself turn his head and look to the right. There, holding hands and smiling warmly, were Fred and Joanna Webber, his mother and father. "Mommy, Daddy."

Behind them was Aunt Elva, her big bottom swinging behind her like a lead bucket. A few steps behind her was a crowd of people David recognized as the foster families he had been sent to live with after his parents were killed and Aunt Elva was no longer able to care for him. There were the Witherspoons, the family in South Bend where he eventually ended up. "Hey, Mr. Witherspoon."

Then, to his left, a shape walked out of the sun. "Oh my, Kathryn. You're so beautiful." A breeze that seemed to blow only on her caused her yellow cotton dress to ripple as she walked. "Oh, Kathryn."

Behind her was Henry. He laughed while bobbing his head and flailing his arms in utter joy. David began to laugh. He doubled over, laughing harder and harder until the muscles in his stomach began to cramp. He looked around. Everyone was laughing.

He felt a hand on his shoulder. It was J.P. "Jeep, what are you...why are you crying?" She turned and walked away. Then David saw the tree from a distance. Everyone was leaving, except David. "Don't leave! Where is everyone going?" No one said anything. David was stricken with a rush of terror. "Come back! Please, don't leave me!" He tried to follow, but his legs were numb. He began sobbing.

Then there was silence—not even the sound of his own breathing. David was alone under the tree. The tree was barren now. The meadow had become a harsh, cracked desert. The sky was dark gray. Silence.

David looked around. He was alone, totally alone. "No!"

David, dripping in sweat, lunged forward in the cot.

"Shut the fuck up, you idiot," yelled a voice from down the concrete corridor.

"You wanna give me a heart attack?" a voice yelled from the cot above.

"Hey, brother, what gives with that dude?" came another faceless voice from another direction.

"I don't know, man, he's like freakin' out, man. Hey, guard, get me the fuck oughta here. Man, this dude's crazy. Put me in another cell. I don't be needin' to be locked up with no mental, man. Get me the fuck oughta here."

DAVID WAS PRACTICALLY COMATOSE when he appeared before the judge at his bail hearing. Legal assistance from the public defender's office was offered to David and rejected. He was held without bail. It was a little after four p.m. when he was led from his cell to a twelve by twelve interrogation room located on the third floor of the Van Nuys division. For over two hours, the tag team of Gilbert and Sanchez questioned their suspect. The walls were solid white cinder block, the light was garish florescent, and the room was stiflingly hot.

Gilbert: "So once again, Mr. Webber, you claim Ms. Peterson dropped you off at your apartment at a little past midnight."

David responded with silence.

Sanchez: "You drank until you passed out. You were awoken by a phone call from Shoewalter around four. Correct?"

Once again, silence.

Like tennis players exchanging volleys, Gilbert and Sanchez recounted the previous night's events, interjecting their own speculations as to what they believed had occurred.

Gilbert: "So, you talked to him, got into an argument, went over the hill to his hotel, and killed him. Isn't that correct, Mr. Webber?"

Silence.

Again Gilbert: "Where's the gun, Mr. Webber?"

Silence.

By six twenty-two p.m., David, Gilbert, and Sanchez looked like boxers after fifteen rounds. Sanchez' methodical cool disappeared. He came within inches of David's face, the two men's noses almost touching. "So, man, how'd it feel to blow that old man's brains across the room, huh? Come on, tell me. I've always wanted to know what that feels like. Bet it was awesome, man. Made you feel real big, yeah? Yeah, I know your type, you little piece of crap. Bet you'd like to blow my brains out right now too, wouldn't you? You want me to get you a gun? Hey, yeah, little man, why don't I get you a gun, and you show me just how you'd do it? You want me to do that, little man? Hey, let me ask you somethin', little man. That Peterson chick, you offed her too, didn't you? Yeah, I know you did. But tell me something, little man, you got some before you splattered her brains? You hit that fine stuff before you made guacamole out of her skull?"

And with that, for the first time since his arrest, David spoke. "You son of a bitch!" David lunged for Sanchez' throat, but Sanchez was not taken by surprise. He routinely stepped back. The small wooden table in front of David screeched as it slipped across the white tile floor. David lost his balance and fell to his knees, hitting his chin on the edge of the table and biting his tongue.

The door opened, and Ryan casually walked in. "Help him up."

Blood was trickling from the corner of David's mouth. Ryan took a handkerchief from his pocket and gave it to David as Gilbert assisted him back into the chair. "Here, put this on your mouth. Sanchez, call the nurse, tell her we're bringing someone down who had an accident. Afterward, help Mr. Webber retrieve his personals from the desk. He's free to go."

"What?" Gilbert yelled.

"You heard me. Mr. Webber's free to go. We're cutting him loose."

Sanchez fell into the chair across from David. "Lieutenant, you can't be serious?"

"Yep, I am, now call the nurse, pronto."

Sanchez slammed his fist on the table, got up, and stormed from the room. Gilbert stood still and stared coldly at David.

"You got a problem, Gilbert?" Ryan sniped.

"No, sir," Gilbert replied, reluctantly walking out the door.

"Okay, Webber, they'll take care of you downstairs, then you're free to go."

David held the handkerchief inside his bleeding mouth. He painfully got up from the chair and moved toward the door with a slight limp. He stopped in the doorway, put his hand on the frame, and looked back at Ryan.

"Why?"

"You tell me?"

David paused before he answered. "You must've realized I didn't do it—that I couldn't do anything like what you guys thought I did."

Ryan smiled. "Oh, come on, Mr. Webber, you can do better than that."

"I don't know what you're talking about."

"Uh-huh," Ryan muttered.

David looked at Ryan confused.

"All right, listen, Webber. I don't know who you know, but whoever it is, you owe them big."

David ran his hand through his hair and looked helplessly at the lieutenant. He noticed that Ryan seemed much older than the man who was in his apartment that morning.

"I don't know what you're talking about."

"Yeah, right. D.A. calls less than ten hours after arresting a man for murder and tells me to cut him loose because we don't have enough evidence. Funny, isn't it? The judge that arraigned you this morning thought we did. Who the hell do you know?"

David closed his eyes and turned to leave.

"Let me tell you something, Mr. Webber. I don't care what the D.A. thinks. I think I do have enough evidence, at least enough to hold you 'til I get the rest of what I need. You see, I think you did it. I think you killed Shoewalter and maybe the Peterson woman too. Why, I'm not sure. But I'm gonna find out. I just wanted to let you know that. Don't think you're off the hook, 'cause I'm gonna getcha." Ryan made a clicking sound and winked at David.

David threw Ryan's handkerchief toward the table. It missed and fell on the floor. "I don't need the nurse. I just want to go home."

As David left the interrogation room, Sanchez and Gilbert were leaning against the wall in the hallway. Both eyed David accusingly as he walked past, but neither spoke. Lieutenant Ryan appeared in the doorway behind David, and both officers looked at their superior, questioning if they should follow. Ryan shook his head in the negative.

Once again inside a twenty-four hour period, David found himself standing in front of a police officer signing forms and identifying his belongings.

"Mr. Webber?"

"Yeah?" David answered, turning around.

"Hi, my name's Bowen."

"Yeah?"

"I think we have a mutual friend. Ms. Peterson."

David's body chilled. "What do you know about J.P.? Where is she?"

"Not here. Come on, I'll drive you home."

"Who are you? Where the hell is J.P.?"

"Please lower your voice, Mr. Webber," the young man said with a frightened look in his eyes. "Yelling is not going to do either of us any good. Who I am is not important right now. And I know Ms. Peterson—Jean Ann, because—" He looked from side to side. "I spent the night with her last night."

Chapter 9

"My name is Joshua Bowen."

The evening sun reflected off the sidewalk and blinded David as he and Bowen exited the tinted glass doors of the Van Nuys Division. It was oppressively hot, and the infamous L.A. smog was lying low in the Valley.

"Jean Ann and I met last night. We really dug each other."

At first glance, the faded Levi's, T-shirt, and manner of speech gave the illusion that Bowen was nothing more than some California surfer dude. The thick blond hair and sunburned nose only added to the perception. But as David studied the young man, there were contradictions. His hands were callused and scarred. His nose was uneven, obviously from many fractures, and his eyes were wise—far too wise, David thought.

"I've just never met anyone like her before and…"

Bowen talked nervously and continuously, and David had to rush to keep up as they crossed Van Nuys Boulevard. Try as he did to listen to Bowen, David kept getting interrupted by his own private conversation. *I've seen him before. Where?* David's mind suddenly focused. *The garage area of the police station last night—a young man laughing as he got out of J.P.'s car—Josh.*

"…we just connected, you know? Like we'd known each other for—"

"You're a cop."

Joshua Bowen stopped speaking and looked straight ahead. The two entered a parking lot adjacent to an outdoor burrito stand. Bowen raised his arm, pointed at an endless row of cars, and pressed a button on his key chain. Two high pitched chirps belched from a charcoal gray Ford Focus.

"Answer me, damn it. You're a cop, aren't you?"

Bowen opened his door, got in, and turned the ignition. David opened the passenger side door but remained outside the car, staring at Bowen. Bowen looked straight ahead as he spoke. "Yes. Please get in the car."

David didn't move.

Bowen lowered his forehead onto the steering wheel and closed his eyes. "Look, Mr. Webber, I am a cop, all of three months out of the academy. Man, I'm putting my career on the line here. I shouldn't even be seen talking to you. If you'll just get in the car, I can explain everything—or at least what I know."

David stood motionless for a moment longer. His eyes never left Bowen as he got into the vehicle. Both men were silent until Bowen turned onto the entrance ramp of the 101 freeway.

"Where's J.P.?" David demanded.

"I don't know."

David's glare never wavered from the driver.

"Really, I don't know," he repeated. Bowen's left knee bounced nonstop. He turned the radio on and then off again, adjusted the air conditioner several times, and sprayed the windshield with washer fluid twice.

"I don't think that window's gonna get any cleaner," David said.

"Sorry." Bowen let go a long exhale.

"You said you spent the night with her."

"Yeah, I did," Bowen replied, looking like a boy confessing to his priest.

"Where?"

"Her place."

"You're lying. J.P. had an early appointment today. She was going home and going to bed."

"What can I say? She changed her mind," Bowen nearly squeaked. "Look, when she dropped you off, she didn't know I was going to call her and beg her to let me come over. If it means anything to you, it took a hell of a lot of convincing on my part before she said yes. I'm glad she did, though. It was the most incredible night of my life. I've never felt so much..."

David looked out the window as Bowen recounted his passionate rendezvous with J.P. It felt weird, and he didn't know why. He and J.P. had always been very open about their flings and one-night-stands. But this was different somehow.

"...she's funny too. I've never laughed so much in bed in my life—"

David slammed his hand on the dashboard. "Shut up. I don't need to know the details, okay? I just want to know where she is. Now either you know something or you don't. If you don't, then fine, I'll thank you for the ride home, and you can be on your way. But if she's hurt, and I find out that you had anything to do with it, I swear, cop or no cop, I'll rip your heart out your mouth."

Bowen's reaction took David by surprise. He smiled.

"What the hell's so funny?"

"Jean Ann said you had a temper. She talked about you a lot last night. She really described you perfectly. Except for what a talented musician you are, I wouldn't know about that. But everything else, wow, she really nailed you. Tell you the truth, it was getting kind of annoying. I was beginning to think she was in love with you or something. But she explained your relationship."

David scowled at Bowen. "Yeah, and what would that be?"

"You know, friends...best friends...really special friends. Right?"

David rubbed his hands over his face. *I don't even know where to start.* "Okay, I need some answers," David said, leaning his head back on the headrest. "Let's backup. You met J.P. last night at the police station."

"Right, the Pacific Division."

"How?"

"What do you mean, how?" Bowen asked with a slight chuckle.

Bowen's casualness irritated David. Venom filled his words. "How does a cop get a damned date with someone who's at the jail to bail out a friend?"

"Oh that," Bowen said, seemingly a little embarrassed, "Well, from what I hear, it's not really that uncommon, if you know what I mean. Anyway, I wasn't really on duty. I mean, I was in uniform, but I was coming off my watch and getting ready to go home. Mr. Webber, I never intended for what happened to happen. It was just...fate, I guess."

David was growing more impatient. "Go on."

"Well, like I said, I was leaving, and there was this woman—Jean Ann—standing in front of booking looking kind of lost. I asked if she needed help. She said a friend of hers was brought in, and she was there to bail him out. She was really cute, you know?"

David didn't reply.

"Anyway, I showed her where she needed to go. What more do you want me to say? We talked—we connected—we just clicked. Hasn't that ever happened to you, Mr. Webber?"

David looked at the young police officer. *Oh, jeez, J.P. He's so young.*

"Anyway, she got you cut loose, and by the time you were released, we'd decided to get together this weekend. We said good-bye, and that was it. But I just couldn't wait until the weekend. You know how it is. I couldn't stop thinking about her. So I called her last night after I got home. I knew it was nuts, and I told her so. But you know what she said? She said, that's okay, I like nuts, luv. You know how she talks. Oh man, she's just great."

David closed his eyes. "Yeah, she is that."

Bowen pulled over to the curb in front of David's apartment and turned off the engine. "She was fine when I left. About an hour later, I get a call from a buddy down at Pacific. He wanted to double check to see if I'd hooked up with the woman I was talking to. That really pissed me off too. I mean, it was none of his business, and I told him so. But he said the reason he was asking was because the woman's friend had an All Points out on him. That was you, Mr. Webber. He just wanted me to be careful."

David took a deep breath and put his face in his hands.

Bowen continued, "I had to call Jean Ann and tell her. But there was no answer. So I jumped in my car and drove back to her place. I must've knocked a hundred times on her door, but nothing. I figured she must've heard, so I raced over here to your place. I got here as you were being put into the squad."

Bowen looked at David for the first time since stopping the car. "A buddy works the desk at Van Nuys. That's how I learned that Jean Ann was missing and you'd become the number one suspect."

David talked into his hands, "But you knew I couldn't have had anything to do with J.P. being missing 'cause you were with her?"

"Right. I didn't leave until close to seven, and she was fine. They didn't come for you until after seven. You couldn't have done anything to Jean Ann. It was impossible. Plus, Mr. Webber, the way Jean Ann talked about you guys, I knew you wouldn't do anything to her."

David raised his head from his hands and looked at the young police officer. The boy was sincere.

"Well," David said, "at least that explains how I got out of jail. An LAPD officer is a pretty damn good alibi."

Bowen looked away.

"What's wrong?"

"Mr. Webber, that's not why you're out of jail, and I'm not your alibi. You're only one of two people who know I was with Jean Ann last night."

"What the hell are you talking about?"

"Mr. Webber, the department can't know about me and Jean Ann."

"The hell they can't," David replied. "You can tell them—"

"I can tell them nothing," Bowen shouted back.

"Why?"

"Because I'm a cop. And my old man is Arthur Bowen."

"Who the hell is Arthur Bowen, and why should I give a shit?"

"Jesus, man, don't you read the papers or watch the news? Dad —Arthur Bowen—is the deputy district attorney of Los Angeles county. That's the other person who knows."

David laughed. "I don't give a shit if he's the president of the United States, you're gonna tell the police you were with J.P. last night, and she was fine this morning when you left her place."

"No, I'm not," Bowen said, his voice almost squeaking again.

"Then I will."

Bowen looked David directly in the eye. "And if you do, you'll be back in jail so fast you won't know what hit you."

David took in Bowen's cold stare. The understanding came like a punch in the face.

"Holy shit," David whispered. "Your old man got me out."

Bowen looked away.

"Why get me out? Why not just keep your mouth shut?"

An expression of sheer pain covered Bowen's face. "Because that would have been wrong, Mr. Webber, and I'm a decent guy and so is Dad. Mr. Webber, there is no hard evidence against you, as far as I can tell. Everything they got on you is circumstantial. You know what that means?"

"I've watched a cop show once or twice in my life, Bowen— yeah, I know what it means," David answered.

"The circumstances look like you killed the guy at the hotel and are responsible for Jean Ann's disappearance. Now, I don't know much about the murder. Hell, for all I know you could have done it, but I doubt it, not the way Jean Ann talked about you. And I know you didn't do anything to Jean Ann, but Mr. Webber, why should I destroy my life and my dad's career if I don't have to? I told Dad about it, and he got you out. But only because he reviewed the evidence and decided there wasn't enough to keep you locked up. I promise you if there were, you'd still be in there right now. Dad's an honest man. He would sacrifice me, and himself, in a second if it were the right thing to do."

"Well, isn't that noble," David replied. "I still don't get it. You could've just as easily let your dad pull a few strings, get me out, and never tell me. Your conscience would be clear, and no one would be the wiser. Why risk telling me?"

Bowen tightened his jaw and looked at David like a man about to explode. "Because I want you to help me find Jean Ann."

"You've gotta be kidding?"

"No, I'm not. I don't know how, and I don't know why, but we— I mean we the police—are right about one thing. You're the connection. The murder of the old man at the hotel and Jean Ann's disappearance, you're the common thread, the common circumstance." The young man paused. "Don't you want to help?"

David lifted his finger in front of the boy's face. "Bowen, I'm going to move heaven and earth to find J.P. But the idea of you getting me out of jail to help you find her is just a little too—"

"Too what," Bowen said, sounding even younger.

"Movie of the week. Look, Bowen, you're a cop. Doesn't this go against everything you guys are taught? And isn't it illegal for me to—"

"I think I love her!" Bowen broke, dropping his head in defeat.

Oh J.P., you really did a number on this one.

"I can't lose her, Mr. Webber. She's got to be alive."

David's body jerked. A part of him wanted to hit Bowen for even suggesting otherwise. Another part wanted to break down and bawl his eyes out at the possibility.

"You know how many active missing person cases LAPD has? Over twelve hundred. That's twelve hundred people a department of five thousand is supposed to find, while at the same time trying to protect and serve a city of eight million. Mr. Webber, I don't want Jean Ann to be just another file in a drawer. I'm going find her, Mr. Webber, with or without your help."

David drew a breath and fell back into his seat. A young Asian boy rode by on the sidewalk, popping wheelies and blowing bubbles with his gum. On the grassy area at the corner of his apartment building, a young African-American girl was standing under a maple tree, plastic bag at the ready, coaxing her poodle to take care of business. Mr. and Mrs. Schwartz, the friendly elderly couple that lived above David, were coming out for their nightly constitutional. Life was going on all around him. *How can this be? Don't they understand? Henry's dead. Murdered. And J.P.'s missing. Don't they get it?*

"Please, Mr. Webber, I know I can—"

"I'll help," David said.

"What?"

"I'll help. We are going to find her, we've got to."

Bowen closed his eyes and sighed in relief.

"So what now?" David said leaning forward, trying to focus his mind.

"Well, first you must understand something—we do this my way. I can get my hands on everything the department has up to now. But I can't be connected to this case. It would kill my career and my father's. Understood?"

David flinched inside. *I could still give a shit about what happens to you or your old man's career.* "Okay."

"All right. First, we have to find out what connection the old man and—"

"Henry."

"What?"

"Henry, his name is Henry Shoewalter. Not just the old man at the hotel. And he was my friend."

"I'm sorry. Okay, we find the connection between Henry, Jean Ann, and you. There's got to be one. I know I haven't been a police officer very long, but the one thing I have learned is not to believe in coincidences."

"I have no idea. I can't believe I could—"

"Believe it, Mr. Webber," said Bowen, stopping him. "I know I'm right. Why did Henry call you so late last night?"

David explained he hadn't talked to Henry in several years and recounted what he could remember of the telephone conversation.

Bowen looked off into the distance. "So you say he was adamant about getting that music he gave you?"

"Very."

"What's the song?"

"It's not a song—it's a sketch."

"I thought you said it was music?"

"A sketch is music." David rubbed his tired eyes. The last thing he felt like doing right now was giving this kid a music lesson. "Before a composer writes a full score for an opera or symphony or something, he'll write it first on the piano. That piano arrangement is called a sketch. What I have is an old piece of staff paper with sixteen bars of music. It's a sketch—or at least part of one."

"And that was the gift?"

"Yeah, quite an expensive one too."

"Okay, I give."

"The eight bars were written over two hundred years ago. It's a partial sketch by Mozart."

"Mozart, like in the composer?"

"Yeah, like in the composer."

"Cool. Any idea why he'd want it back?"

"None. Look, Bowen, don't you think I've gone over this a thousand times in my head? I don't know why he wanted it back or why it was so important for him to call me in the middle of the night to get it."

"Is it worth a lot of money?" Bowen continued grilling.

"I guess—hell, I don't know." David's frustration was mounting. "I had it appraised seven, eight years ago. A guy down at Christie's said it would probably go for about five thousand on the low side, twenty on the high."

Bowen shook his head. "That's a lot of dough but not enough to die over."

David didn't respond.

"Okay look, we need to look at—"

"Don't have it," David interrupted as if by rote. "My bank—safety deposit box."

Bowen nodded. "Okay. Tomorrow's Saturday, banks close early, so we need to get it first thing in the morning. Until then, I want you to write down everything you can remember about the conversation with Henry. What he said, how he said it—everything. Then I want you to totally recount on paper the events of the past twenty-four hours. Leave nothing out. Anything you saw, heard, smelled, said, or even thought."

David yawned. His head was pounding. A dull pain pushed from behind his brow just above his eyelids. "You mean like how my car got back here last night if I didn't drive it?" he said almost to himself. "Okay, I'll try. Let's get out of this car. We can work in my place."

"No, I can't," Bowen replied.

"Why, afraid to be seen with me?"

Bowen smiled. "Now that you mention it, yeah. Wouldn't be too cool for me to be seen coming in and out of your apartment. But the fact is I have to be at work in an hour. You're going to have to start without me. Looks like you could use some sleep anyway. Get it. It'll help the memory."

David nodded in agreement as Bowen started the car.

"This is something we're going to have to deal with. I can only work on this with you when I'm off duty, and even then we've got to be very discreet, because like I said, it wouldn't be cool for me to be seen with you. Actually, it would be disastrous and hurt the case. They'd start looking at us instead of the people who are really responsible."

"What if I come up with anything or J.P. calls me or something? How do I get in touch with you? Call the station and ask—"

"No," Bowen shot back. "Under no circumstances are you to contact me through the department." He took out a pen and wrote something on a slip of paper. "Here. This is my cell number. I'll always have it on. You'll be able to reach me anytime. Leave a message if I don't pick up. And if I'm ever in a situation where I can't talk, I'll just say, sorry you have a wrong number. I'll call you back when I can. Okay?"

"Yeah, I got it," David said, opening the door and stepping out.

"You get some rest, Mr. Webber. I'll come by in the morning when I get off, and we'll go to your bank."

"One last thing," David said, standing on the curb holding the top of the car door.

"What?"

"How did you know where I lived?"

"Please, man," Bowen replied. "I'm a cop. I got it from your arrest report."

David nodded.

"Get some rest, Mr. Webber. We'll find her."

David shut the car door and watched Bowen drive off.

Chapter 10

Saturday morning found the Potomac its usual alive and vital late-spring self. Sailboats, fishing boats, and yachts of every shape, color, and kind painted the mariner's paradise like an artist's palette. Dani sat at a traffic light on Rosslyn and Washington Boulevard frantically hoisting her sail, the ragtop of her VW. The beautiful morning that had greeted Dani for her daily seven a.m. run was gone by eight. It was now a little after nine, and the mercury had dropped a full fifteen degrees; ominous clouds lay to the west. To everyone else in the nation's capital, this was a loss of good fortune, to Dani, a chance to put on the forest green angora sweater and navy cords she'd gotten on sale last weekend.

The signal changed just as Dani hooked the last latch into place. With the precision of a cluster bomb, she whipped the car into the right lane and assaulted the Key Bridge exit. As she crossed the bridge, she was reminded of March 25th, the last time she'd been to Georgetown. She remembered it so specifically because it was her birthday and her last date with Jerry. *Ah yes,* Jerry Slater, handsome, smart, a congressional aide, and a law student on the way up the ladder of success, and unfortunately…gay as Tinkerbelle. It figured, she bemused, that the first man she'd ever met who enjoyed all the same things she enjoyed—music, art, theater, shopping—*God, did he have impeccable taste in clothes*—also turned out to have impeccable taste in men. For as long she'd live, she would never forget sitting in that bistro on M Street, listening in amazement as Jerry shared his revelation. The revelation being the captain of the sculling team at Georgetown—he did have taste. She could still hear him apologizing for leading her on and thanking her for making him see the truth about himself. "No thanks necessary, Jer," was all she could think to say at the time. "Glad to help."

Exiting the Key Bridge, Dani turned right onto M Street and landed in the middle of trendy boutiques, cafes, and antique shops. The stop-and-go traffic gave Dani a chance to spruce up her makeup in the rearview mirror and double check the address of Mrs. Gertrude Sugarberry. A reluctant, and brief, call on Friday evening had garnered an invitation from Madam Sugarberry for pie and tea. Dani decided the sooner she got it over with the better, so she accepted without hesitation. Besides, she reconciled, her Saturdays usually consisted of little more than balancing her checkbook, tidying up her Arlington condo, and returning emails from her dad back in Oklahoma. Ever since she'd gotten him his first computer for Christmas, email and the Internet had become the old fellow's life, three emails a day since January.

She turned north onto Wisconsin and cruised past the cobblestone sidewalks and ancient oak and hickory trees that canopied both sides of the street. She realized this small burg represented everything she both loved and hated about Washington, DC.

What she loved, not surprisingly, was the history. Every brick of the small but elegant Federal and Victorian style homes were layered with it. Washington, Jefferson, and Adams seemed to pour from their very mortar. The spirit of Roosevelt and Kennedy resonated from the monuments of the obelisks and weeping angels that studded the many terraces. The stately mansions of tobacco merchants, the ones who built the town, seemed to still emit the sweet smell of the much sought after commodity long after the days when their ships docked at the foot of Wisconsin and cows ambled down M Street. Yes, Dani mused, in Georgetown history is in the present tense.

But as much as she embraced the town for its past, she despised it for what it now was, the exclusive hamlet of the rich and power-ful. Senators, cabinet members, and other politicos infected its history like locusts, all suffering from the same blight inside the beltway blindness. "Don't go there, Dani," she begged out loud, grit-ting her teeth and pushing the accelerator harder. *No sooner did these people get elected to public service in their home states than they began matching swatches for their new homes here in Shangri La. Safely out of touch with their constituents and the concerns of Joe Six-Pack.* "Folks like Daddy," Dani said, hitting the steering wheel. *It's not fair. Why should a man who never missed a single day of work, or was never late on April 15th, suffer like this?* Tears welled. She removed a tissue from the glove box and dabbed the corners of her eyes. "Oh frigg," Dani huffed, looking in the rearview mirror and seeing her newly applied mascara running down her cheek.

"I wonder if these people ever get cancer?" she said, fixing her face. "I wonder if they've ever been told by an insurance company they can't have any more treatment, or medicine?" She threw the blackened tissue on the floor. "No, because they probably own the friggin' insurance company."

She looked at the speedometer. She was doing fifty in a thirty-five. She lifted her foot off the accelerator and coasted the car to a stop at the top of the hill. She rested her head back and took a deep breath. It was always with her; pain, anger, and helplessness. She'd gotten better at controlling it, but it was with always with her. And that, probably more than anything, was what irritated her most about this assignment. The fact Capitol Hill was at the beck and call of some old lady simply because she had the right address.

The loud honk from behind brought Dani back. She waved the driver around and then looked at the street sign. She was in an area known as Georgetown Heights. The slip of paper where she'd written Sugarberry's address had suffered her wrath and was now a crumpled ball. "Okay, Dan, calm down," she said to herself, unwadding the paper and checking the address again. "Just interview the old biddy, get what you need, and be done with it."

Dani saw she had to make a left or right, as continuing straight would lead her into the private driveway of an old civil war cemetery. She read the numbers in both directions and elected to turn right. As luck would have it, it was the first house. House, however, was a ridiculous understatement.

Dani pulled over to the curb, got out of her car, and gawked at the sight before her. Unlike the other small but stately homes in Georgetown, the red brick Tudor mansion before her was massive. Marigolds and pansies lined a cobblestone walkway that wound from the street through a perfectly manicured front lawn. Three giant sycamores, two on one side of the walk, one on another, shaded most of the yard. On the right corner of the house, an elderly oak rose high in the air, resting one of its mammoth limbs on the tip of a bleached wood steeple protruding from the second tier of the manse. Dani smelled the burning wood before she saw the smoke billowing from a chimney on the right rear of the house. Four bay windows, one that looked to be on a third floor, three of which looked to be on a second, were the focal point of the house. All were adorned with redwood flower boxes.

Dani pulled her backpack from the backseat and started up the walk toward the granite staircase that led to what she hoped was the front door. "I wonder how many bathrooms this dump has?"

She ascended the stairs onto a covered veranda where six large wicker rocking chairs sat in row. The huge double doors that greeted her were dark wood and embellished with solid brass knockers on each side. She knocked twice. At that moment, she wouldn't have been surprised if Lurch opened the door with a deep, *"you rang?"*

He didn't.

Instead, an elderly African-American woman appeared. "Yes?"

"Hello, my name is Dr. Dani Parsons. I'm from the Smithsonian, and I have an appointment with Mrs. Sugarberry."

The next words spoken were the last words Dani ever expected to hear. "Yes, I'm Mrs. Sugarberry," the old black woman said with a smile and refined southern drawl.

"Gertrude Sugarberry?" Dani asked, unable to hide her surprise.

"Yes, dear, one and the same," the woman replied with a slight laugh.

"Oh...well...hi."

Sugarberry laughed harder. "Well, hi to you too, dear. It's getting a tad chilly out there, won't you come in before we both catch our death?"

"Uh...yes—thank you, I'd love to."

Dani's immediate impression was that there was a youthfulness about the woman that contradicted her seventy-plus, possibly even eighty-plus years. She walked slowly but not cautiously. Her skin was smooth, only her hands and neck showing the wrinkles of age. Her hair was black except for a shock of gray above her left temple, and the southern accent didn't disguise the fact that she was very well educated.

Dani followed the woman from the gracious foyer, down two steps, and into a large living room area. Dani was overwhelmed. If the outside was breathtaking, the inside was full-blown asthma. Elegant didn't begin to describe the décor. It was as if she were looking at a magazine. The whole room had a quiet, peaceful ambiance. Exquisite antique furnishings, eighteenth century, Dani surmised, sat on polished hardwood floors and a richly colored braided wool rug. Tiffany lamps softly illuminated everything, the largest being the one on a simple mahogany table beside a cream-colored divan in the center.

"Your home is magnificent."

"Oh, thank you, dear. I must confess I love it too. Won't you please have a seat? Can I get you a cup of tea?"

"Yes, thank you, that'd be lovely," Dani replied, putting down her backpack and sitting on the over-stuffed divan.

"I'll be just a minute, you make yourself at home."

In the far left corner, a fireplace was crackling as expected. The house was warm but not hot. Dani got up and walked over to the fire and put out her hands. The heat flushed Dani's face, and it felt good; it felt wholesome. She closed her eyes and drew a long breath.

The burning wood blended with the aroma of the jasmine potpourri that filled the house. She could easily understand how one could forget about the outside world here.

The fireplace itself was unlike any Dani had ever seen. The hearth was high—very high, at least two-feet tall, and it extended far into the room. The heavy oak mantle that stretched over the firebox was bare, no framed photographs, no special keepsakes, and no porcelain figurines, the things one would expect to see in such a house. Instead, a large oil painting, the only such piece of artwork in the room, hung above the mantle. Dani studied the art. The painting depicted numerous families, obviously slaves, huddled together by a riverbank. It looked as if it was supposed to be dawn, but she couldn't tell for sure. The sun, if that's what it was, seemed to be neither rising nor setting, it was just sort of there, casting no shadows or light. On the bluff above the bank, men, both black and white, sat on horses with shotguns and pistols at their side. Their expressions were determined. The look on the faces of the slave families was—

"Beautiful, isn't it?"

Dani turned to see Mrs. Sugarberry reentering the room with a silver tea service.

"Can I help you?" Dani said, moving toward the elderly woman.

"No, no, I'm fine. I'll just set it right here."

Nonetheless, Dani assisted in placing the tray on the coffee table in front of the sofa. "Yes, it is beautiful, but I'm embarrassed to say I'm confused by the depiction."

"Really, why?"

"They look—I mean the slaves—they look so…hopeful, almost happy."

The stately woman let herself fall onto the couch. After a brief adjustment, she sat straight with her back arched and looked at Dani. Her brown eyes sparkled. "I'm going to become very fond of you, dear."

"Excuse me?"

"You are very observant and have a very empathetic soul, dear. There are not five people in this town who could walk into this house and make that observation about that painting. Yes," Mrs. Sugarberry nodded as she poured the tea, "I'm going to become very fond of you. Cream or sugar?"

"No, thank you."

"Now then, you're from the Smithsonian. I gather from your reaction at the door that Dr. Beckman didn't inform you I was colored?"

Dani sat down. "No, ma'am, he didn't. I'm sorry for—"

"Oh, stop it, I'm not offended, dear. An old colored woman is the last person I'd expect to live in these parts too. Don't tell anyone, but I'm what you might call a minority." Sugarberry put her napkin up to her mouth and let out a low and husky laugh.

Dani joined in. "Yes, I guess you are."

"Oh, lordy me, I'm awful."

Dani took a sip of tea.

"Now, where were we, oh yes, Dennis Beckman. Now there's an interesting person. You know, I don't think he cares for people of color very much. Mmm mmm, not one bit. He's never been exactly warm to me, if you know what I mean. I believe he puts up with me because he feels he must. Rather funny, don't you think?"

"Yes ma'am, I guess it's—"

Sugarberry moaned and set down her teacup and saucer. "Oh, would you listen to me? I'm sorry, dear, where are my manners? Your Dr. Beckman is a colleague and probably a friend. I do apologize."

Dani responded quickly, "No, Mrs. Sugarberry, please don't apologize. Dr. Beckman is neither my friend nor what you'd call a colleague. He's my boss. And quite honestly, I don't think he cares much for me either. And though I feel absolutely no desire to defend the little—" Dani stopped herself. "Well anyway, I do feel the fact that you're a woman is more of an issue with him than your race. He's not what you'd call a modern man."

"Ah, I see." Sugarberry smiled. "One of those."

Dani returned the smile. "Yes, ma'am, one of those."

"Then let me apologize."

"For what?" Dani asked, setting down her tea.

"I'm sure I must be a punishment of sorts. I can't believe Dennis Beckman would send someone to me he actually liked. I'm sure he thinks I'm cuckoo." She chuckled again. "So, I am sorry. I hope you'll find me worthwhile in the end."

Dani wasn't sure if she was being conned or not. But she was quite aware she was having her blue cords charmed right off of her. If Sugarberry's intent was to make her feel guilty about all the mean things she'd said and thought since getting this assignment, she'd succeeded. If it was to merely win her over with grace and hospitality, she'd succeeded at that too.

"Ma'am, if he is punishing me, then the laugh's on him, because I am delighted to be here."

"You are a dear." Sugarberry reached out and patted Dani's hand. "I guess that leads us to the task at hand, my collection. Would you like to see it?"

"Yes, but first I'd like to start by asking you a few questions."

"Okay, I'm all answers. You go right ahead."

"Great. I'd like to learn a little about you. Like where you're from, how you came to live in Georgetown, things like that."

"Me? Oh, I didn't expect that. Is that really important?"

"Is that a problem? I assure you I have no desire to intrude into your personal life. It's just I've found the more I know about the contributor of artifacts, the better I can recreate its history for display."

The husky laugh resonated again. "No, dear, I'm not worried about you exposing any dirty laundry. In fact, at my age, it would be quite a hoot if you could dig up some juicy dirt. No, I'm just surprised anyone would care about me. I'm just not that interesting."

There go my pants again, Dani thought.

"Okay, well let's see now. I was born and raised in New Orleans —you don't need the year, do you? I'd like to keep some secrets."

Dani chuckled as she took out a pen and note pad from her backpack. "No, that won't be necessary."

The old woman nodded and continued. "Well, being from New Orleans, of course I developed a great love for two things: food—

oh, my girl, you just wait until I cook for you, mmm, mmm—and the other, of course, was music. Yes, music was always a part of my family. You see, Daddy was a preacher, fire and brimstone, don't you know? Oh, child, he could get a place going like nobody's business. The devil didn't stand a chance when Daddy got to testifyin'," she said, waving her arm in the air, momentarily taking on a cliché dialect. "A good man, a real good man. And he could sing too, all the old Negro spirituals. We'd sit up at night, my five sisters and me —can you imagine, five sisters—yes, we'd sit up and listen to Daddy sing and sing and sing."

Dani saw water filling the old woman's eyes.

"Oh, now look at me." She dabbed her eyes with her napkin. "I'm such a sentimental old coot."

"It sounds wonderful. My daddy used to sing to my younger brother and me when we were young too—we were Methodists though. Our songs weren't nearly as good."

Both laughed.

Dani added, "It's one of my favorite memories from childhood."

"Music's a powerful thing. Is your daddy and mamma still alive?"

Dani smiled. "Dad is, Mom died when I was eleven. He raised us on his own. Both my brother and I are still very close to him."

"That's wonderful. Family is the most important thing there is."

Dani noticed a sad and distant look on her face, the first time she'd seen that expression.

"Anyway," she continued, snapping back to her previous self, "that was where my love of music began. When I got older, I would sneak down to the Quarters—Daddy didn't know about that. Preservation Hall was the place. I was little more than a child, but I was big for my age, so I got in with little trouble. I'd listen to The Dukes of Dixieland, with this kid on trumpet named Armstrong. You may have heard of him," she said mockingly. "Yes, dear, that's where the love affair started. And not just one love affair, either." She laughed loudly only to suddenly become very quiet. "I met my Edgar down there. Oh, that was so many years ago."

"Edgar was your husband?" Dani asked.

"Yes, we were married a month after we met. Daddy threw a fit, but he eventually got over it, and he and Edgar became quite close."

"How long were you married?"

"Forty-five years. I still talk to him. Perhaps your Dr. Beckman is right and I am cuckoo."

Dani felt a warmth go through her and a chill down her arm. "No you're not. You're very lucky."

"I take it you're not—"

"Married? No, I haven't as yet found my Edgar."

"You will, you will," she said, patting Dani on the hand again.

"So how did you end up here in Georgetown?"

"Edgar. Can you believe it? The man didn't have two nickels to rub together when we met, but he had an imagination. Edgar was nothing but a cotton picker down in Baton Rouge. Every night all the men would go out after a day in the field. Well, Edgar was younger and smaller than all the other men, so he had to work harder at fitting in—this may be the one time that blasted male ego actually paid off. Anyway, all the other men smoked. Edgar tried but would get sick every time he'd taste the tobacco. It was very embarrassing for him. So Edgar had this idea. He started taking little pieces of cotton with him from the field and wrapping it at the end of his hand-rolled cigarettes. He said it took the sting away and kept his tongue from tasting the tobacco."

"Wait a minute," Dani interrupted. "Are you telling me Edgar invented the filtered cigarette?"

"Can you believe it? No one was more shocked than I was when he came home one night and told me he'd met some fellow from the Phillip Morris Company down at the saloon, and they wanted to buy his invention. We moved up here two weeks later—not into this house, that came later—but to Maryland. This was where, what did they call it—the research and development center was located. They gave Edgar a lot of money for his invention and a job as well."

"It must have been quite a change, moving from the South up here."

"Dear, you can say that again. I'm a regular pig in a pastry shop," she said, covering her mouth and laughing.

Dani didn't laugh with her this time. Instead she smiled a smile of admiration. Some quick arithmetic in her head told Dani that Sugarberry's husband must have died somewhere around the late sixties, early seventies. That would have put her living here in Georgetown alone right in the middle of the civil rights movement. She was sure she wasn't getting the entire story and that there had to have been very trying, if not downright scary, days. Her off-handed casualness about being a minority living in this largely white community, Dani suspected, was a complete façade.

"Well, ma'am, may I say this is one pastry shop that is considerably sweeter for your being here."

Sugarberry blushed. "Oh, dear, aren't you charming."

Praise indeed was all Dani could think. "So, about the collection?"

"Yes, the collection." Sugarberry's face lit up.

"How did you get started collecting old and rare sheet music?"

"Well, come with me to the music room while I explain."

Sugarberry lifted herself from the divan. Dani followed her from the living room back across the foyer into a small study. The room was sparsely furnished with an antique rolltop secretary, two chairs, and a bookcase. The room looked as if it wasn't used, and Dani guessed it was probably her late husband's study.

"It all started when I was growing up in New Orleans. There was a piano player in the Quarters—he played ragtime—for the life of me I can't remember his name. Anyway, I used to love to hear him play. I think he was sweet on me and was trying to impress me, so he gave me an autographed copy of the Maple Leaf Rag. Now in all honesty, I don't know for sure if it's the actual handwriting of Scott Joplin. It could well be the piano player signed it himself and just told me it was Joplin's, but the music is quite old and in very good condition. But that was the start. I began picking up music all over the place after that, second-hand music stores, garage sales, church bazaars, just about anywhere I ran across something that looked special to me."

Dani loved seeing the passion and enthusiasm of a child bubble from the old woman. Dani could swear she was watching her grow fifty years younger and two feet taller. The two exited the study through another door at the rear and descended a small stairwell that curved forty-five degrees to the right and emptied into a light, bright room at the back of the house.

The morning sun twisted through the old oaks of the lush back-yard and sprinkled light through a large picture window, gently brushing the soft lavender walls of the lanai music room. Books filled the shelves of a built-in bookcase directly in front of Dani as she entered the room. She could make out a few titles of the larger ones: *Oxford Dictionary of Music*, *Portrait of a Genius*, *Baker's Biographical Dictionary of Musicians*, and *Reader's Digest's World's Best Loved Love Songs*. The long wall opposite the window was filled with photographs of some of the world's greatest jazz musicians. Dani's eye was immediately caught by her favorites, Basie, Ellington, Parker, and of course, Armstrong. In the corner atop a small ivory pedestal was an enormous ebony bust of...Chopin? *She does have eclectic taste.* But directly across from it, filling most of the room, was a satin-black seven-foot Steinway.

"Oh, Mrs. Sugarberry, this is beautiful," Dani said, making a beeline for the instrument and looking under the open lid.

"Thank you, dear. Once again, you must forgive me, but I love it too."

"It's pre-war, isn't it?" Dani's voice reverberated off the soundboard.

"Yes, 1914," Sugarberry said with pride.

"It's in magnificent condition."

"Please, dear, won't you play it?" Sugarberry asked, suddenly excited.

Dani lifted her head out of the instrument and smiled. "I'm sorry. I don't play piano. Cello's my instrument. I learned just enough to get me through the required courses in college. I stopped altogether in graduate school. One of my many regrets."

Sugarberry's face went sad. Dani noticed and tried to recover. "But please, won't you play me something? I'd love to hear this instrument."

"Oh, I don't play, either. I tried learning years ago but just couldn't seem to get the knack of it. Still, I do love this old piano," she said, stroking the top of the piano with her hand. Dani saw she had gone somewhere else, perhaps to a time and place kept alive by the instrument.

"Well, dear," Sugarberry snapped back, "let me show you my pride and joy. Why don't you have a seat here beside the piano, and I'll get the music."

Sugarberry went to a cedar chest under the picture window and began lifting out large photo albums. She set them on the table.

Dani opened the first album and began thumbing through the page—she'd study them more closely later back in her office. Each page contained a piece of sheet music, many dating back to before the turn of the century. There were marches by Sousa, a first edition of "St. Louis Blues" by W.C. Handy, as well as many very rare original works by the New England Impressionists, Horatio Parker, Arthur Foote, and even Charles Griffes. Legendary publishing companies such as Jerome H. Remick & Company and Whitney Warner were proudly displayed on many of the pieces.

As much as she resented Beckman for pulling her off the Women of Song project, she had to admit this was going to be a wonderful addition to the museum. All the pieces were in their own individual, non-acidic plastic sleeve and appeared to be in mint condition.

"Mrs. Sugarberry, these are magnificent," Dani said, not looking up.

"Do you think they're suitable for the museum?" Sugarberry asked cautiously.

Dani closed the album and looked kindly at the woman. Sugarberry was sitting wide-eyed on the piano bench, knees tightly locked and hands together on her lap. She had the look of a six-year-old waiting for a sign from a parent that she had done good.

"Yes, ma'am," Dani declared with authority. "The Smithsonian Institution and the National Archives of the United States of America will be honored to exhibit your fine collection. And on behalf of the Division of Musical History and this nation, I thank you for this very generous and historical contribution."

As the tears started falling down the proud lady's face, Dani decided that everything—the four years for the BA, the two years that followed for the masters, and the two years after that for her PhD—had all been worth it.

"Would you look at me." Sugarberry said, retrieving a tissue from the table.

"May I join you?" Dani said, reaching for a tissue as well. The two women dabbed their eyes and then looked at each other. Both broke into laughter.

"Why don't I go get us another warm pot of tea and some strawberry pie? I pulled it from the oven before you arrived, should be perfect now."

"Sounds wonderful."

After Sugarberry left the room, Dani went to the piano and sat down. She plucked a few keys in the middle of the keyboard and tried to remember some of the songs she'd learned back in college. It seemed so long ago now.

She hadn't noticed the music stand in the far-left corner of the room. She rose from the piano and walked over for a closer view. The stand was mahogany and stood about four feet high with the top in the shape of a lyre. Displayed was a single page of music, a very old page of music. Dani got very close but didn't dare touch it. There was one melody line, no accompaniment, handwritten with no title and no claim of authorship. It was twelve bars in length, but the twelfth bar ended with a tied B-flat quarter note, obviously an incomplete phrase leading to a second page. Dani, still not wanting to touch the music, looked around the back of the stand. The carving of the lyre was such that she could see through to the back of the music—it was blank. *Frigg, no second page.*

"I see you've found the Cook," Sugarberry said, entering the room with the same tea service, but this time sporting two pieces of pie.

"The what?" Dani replied, startled.

"Well, I think it's a Cook. Maybe you can tell me for sure?"

"I'm not familiar with that composer."

"He wasn't really a composer. That's why no one's sure if it's his or not."

"Ma'am?" Dani asked.

"Doctor James Cook was a medical doctor and a member of the free black community in these parts during the days of slavery. He was also a violin teacher. I picked that up several years ago at an auction. The person selling it confessed he wasn't sure if it was authentic or not, but that didn't matter to me. I just loved the way it looked and felt. I also think it's a beautiful melody. I guess I just like things old."

"The music is interrupted. Do you have a second page?"

"Oh, aren't you clever to see that. No, that's all I have."

Dani thought for a second. "Can't someone do an analysis of the handwriting to authenticate it? There must be other examples of his writing."

"Oh, there are plenty. No musical works though, just letters and things like that. I've had it analyzed, and it's definitely his writing. You see the thing is, no one knows if he actually composed the piece or just copied it."

"That's fascinating."

"Oh, isn't it though? I just love a mystery," the woman said, making a face as she took a bite of strawberry pie. "Mmm, mmm. Oh, dear, you must try this pie. If I say so, I have outdone myself with this one."

Dani returned to the table where Sugarberry was sitting and dug into the pie. She was right—it was *mmm, mmm*.

As the two ate, Sugarberry asked about Dani's life, and the two talked for almost an hour until the tea was gone. Dani looked at her watch. "I really must be going now. Thank you for a wonderful morning."

"No, dear, thank you. You have been a delight. Now, I presume you'll be taking my sheet music with you?"

"No, ma'am. For security sake, the institution will send a courier from Brink's by on Monday to retrieve the items."

"I see. That's very serious."

"No, ma'am, it's just standard procedure. They are very well trained in transporting important artifacts for the museum." Dani caught the look on Sugarberry's face. "Don't worry, ma'am, I'll be here to make sure everything goes okay."

Sugarberry's face relaxed into a contented smile.

"However," Dani said hesitantly. "No, never mind."

"What, dear?"

"No, I can't, it's not a part of this project, so I have no authority to ask."

"What? Please, dear, do ask me," Sugarberry begged.

"Well…it's just…that piece on the music stand."

"The Cook?"

"Yes, the Cook. I was wondering if I could borrow it for a few days? I'd like to do some digging myself in my spare time."

"Well," Sugarberry hemmed, "I guess there'd be no harm, you—"

"No, I'm sorry, Mrs. Sugarberry, I should have never asked."

"No, you take it. If you can learn something about it, that would be delightful."

"Are you sure? I promise I'll take very good care of it."

"Of course, dear. You take it and return it whenever you're through." Sugarberry took the old music from the music stand. "I even think I have something we can put it in."

"Thank you, Mrs. Sugarberry. I'll take very good care of this and return it in a few days."

"Whenever, dear."

GERTRUDE SUGARBERRY STOOD at the door, smiling and waving goodbye as Dani bounced down the cobblestone walkway and into her car. Sugarberry closed the door and walked back into the study where she and Dani had walked through to get to the music room. She rolled up the top of the desk and pulled the old black telephone close to her. She slowly dialed—not punched—a number and waited for an answer. It came on the second ring. "She's gone, dear." Sugarberry listened. "Yes, she took it with her, and I believe she may be just who we need." Sugarberry smiled. "I love you too, dear."

Chapter 11

Joshua Bowen turned onto Ventura Boulevard as David sat beside him writing on a yellow note pad. Bowen's knock had awakened David at seven-thirty a.m.—he'd slept for ten hours straight. After Bowen had dropped him off, David spent the first two hours tracking down the whereabouts of Ravel. After getting the runaround from the LAPD, David decided to call the Department of Animal Control directly. As it turned out, Ravel was being kept at a shelter two miles away. After retrieving the cat that, except for being thoroughly petrified, was none the worse for wear, David swung by the grocery store for cigarettes, a pre-roasted chicken, and some cat food. It was after nine by the time he got back to his apartment and began writing down the events of the past twenty-four hours as instructed by Bowen. A half-hour into the assignment, both he and the cat surrendered to exhaustion.

"Coming up with anything?"

"I don't know, maybe," David replied without looking up from the page.

"Well, what?"

"Hang on, I'm almost done." David scratched furiously over the page. "Yeah, that must be it. I knew it. I even told Jeep."

"What, tell me?"

"Okay," David said, taking a deep breath. "It has to go back to Harshbarger. Everything started going to hell after that."

"Wait, who's Harshbarger?"

"He's the guy I got in a fight with at the hotel."

Bowen looked confused.

"The guy I got arrested for beating up, and how you met J.P."

"Oh, okay, I'm with you."

"Okay, I get arrested, but Harshbarger doesn't want to press charges because he's got a wife. So he gets a couple of his henchmen to tail me."

Bowen reacted, "Wait, you were tailed? When?"

"After J.P. picked me up from the police station. J.P. thought it was my imagination, but I knew it wasn't."

"So you were tailed by Harshbarger. Why?"

"Retaliation. Only I'm with J.P., so they can't carry out the vendetta."

"Mr. Webber, this doesn't make any sense. What do they care if Jean Ann's with you or not?"

"She's a witness. She'd know it was Harshbarger's men."

"So? So would you. Unless they were planning on killing you, which I find hard to believe. You could report Harshbarger's harassment as easily as Jean Ann. Which leads me to the obvious question. Why didn't they just do whatever it is you think they wanted to do to you after Jean Ann dropped you off? And what does this have to do with what happened to Jean Ann?"

"Well, he must've kidnapped her," David answered.

"For retaliation?"

"Yeah."

"And Henry? Harshbarger just happened to know an old friend of yours you haven't seen in over ten years was staying at that hotel, so he decided to have him murdered to get back at you too? And he set all of this up to frame you because of a stupid barroom fight? Oh, and I forgot about your car. He would have also had to—"

"Okay, I got it already," David said. "So you got any better ideas?"

"No, but I know——"

"You wanted me to write down what I thought happened, that's what——"

"No, I told you to write down everything you could remember about the events leading up to Jean Ann's disappearance. There's a difference."

"What's the difference?"

"Stop trying to make sense of the picture and just paint me the picture."

David came back with nothing. He knew Bowen was right. He was grasping at straws. Searching for anything that might make the insanity make sense.

"It's over there," David muttered.

Bowen pulled into the parking lot of the Bank of America.

David opened the door. "I'll be back in a minute."

"Mr. Webber," Bowen said. "I'm sorry, I know it's tough, but I just don't think Harshbarger's the key."

David responded with a nod and shut the door.

Fifteen minutes later, David emerged from the bank carrying a leather pouch.

"That's it?" Bowen asked.

"This is it."

"Okay. Let's grab some breakfast. My treat."

BOWEN CUT into his pastry as David opened the leather pouch.

"I haven't looked at this in years," David said, gently removing the clear laminate that housed the fragile work. A lump caught in his throat. It was a moment ago—no twelve years ago. He, Kathryn, and Henry were at Sardi's toasting the success of an A plus on his music history final. David would graduate with honors. Henry walked over, kissed him on the cheek, told him he was proud of him, and that he loved him. Then, he handed him the music and said it was the only thing of value he had and wanted him to have it.

"Wow, how old did you say it was?" Bowen asked.

"1790-91 is everyone's best guess. It's definitely toward the end of Mozart's life when he lived in Vienna."

"Really, how do you know?"

"The watermark embossed on this sheet is consistent with the stock Mozart used on other pieces he's known to have written at the time."

"Cool, when did he die?"

"December 5, 1791."

"It's held up pretty good."

"Yeah. So now what?"

"We go over it. Does it have anything written on it other than music?"

"Yeah," David answered.

"Really, let me see?"

David smiled slightly and handed him the music in the plastic sleeve.

Bowen put down his coffee and carefully took it. David watched as Bowen scanned the page.

"Hey, it's all written in—"

"German," David said with a smile. "You'll make detective in no time."

Bowen handed the music back to David. "So, what does it say?"

"Not much. It's part of some unfinished symphony, or opera, or something. Basically, it's just notes to himself about things he wanted to do with the instruments. There's a lot of scribbles too, seems ol' Wolfgang was a doodler."

"Is this a one-of-a-kind—I mean are there other half-written, what did you call it, sketches out there?"

"There are parts of the guy spread all over the place. Wolfy was incredibly prolific. He composed more important works than any other composer in history. Sixteen operas, forty-one symphonies, twenty-seven piano and five violin concertos, twenty-five string quartets, nineteen masses, and about five hundred other works in every style. And the son of a bitch died at thirty-six."

"Over five hundred. You're exaggerating, right?"

"Nope. He accumulated a catalog of over six hundred and

twenty works. But one of the by-products of being a genius is also being a bit absent-minded. He would start something, forget where he put it, and just write it down again somewhere else."

"He could remember all that music and just write it down again?"

"Yeah. But he didn't always finish everything he started. There's a lot of unfinished shit floating around, as well as first drafts of works he revised later. This is all pretty common knowledge."

"Common knowledge to you. I don't know anything about the guy. Well, I did see part of that movie once. What was it called?"

"*Amadeus*. Good movie—bad history."

"What do you mean?"

"It wasn't accurate. It portrayed Mozart as some uncouth sex-crazed, drunken lunatic. In truth, he was quite religious, drank very lightly, and was deeply in love with his wife, Constanze." A distant smile filled David's eyes, "That was another reason Henry gave me the music. He thought it was right I should own it because Constanze's maiden name was the same as mine, Weber—but with one *b*. Yeah, Mozart was definitely different, maybe even a bit mad. And he did rub people the wrong way, but hey, the guy was a genius. Everyone knew it, even then."

"Wasn't he killed or something?"

David shook his head and raised his coffee cup. "More theatrical license. Lots of rumors like that started popping up after his death. Everyone from Leopold the Second to a supposed lover of Constanze was bandied about. Some even blamed the Freemasons."

Bowen's eyes widened. "The Freemasons, why?"

"Mozart was a Mason—pretty avid one too. One of his last operas was *The Magic Flute*. It's known as a Masonic opera because it's filled with the secret symbols and numerology crap of the brotherhood. Some speculated the Freemasons got pissed at Mozart for divulging sacred lodge secrets and killed him—total horseshit."

Bowen nodded.

David continued, "But the most famous was that Salieri had poisoned him. He was a composer in the Viennese imperial court. Salieri went totally bonkers in his last year of life—today we'd probably call it Alzheimer's—and he supposedly confessed to killing Mozart. The rumor even reached Beethoven and a lot of famous composers of that time. Even Constanze jumped on that one for a while. But ultimately, too many people around Salieri came forward and said Salieri had never said it, and it was just that, a rumor. No, there's no evidence his death was deliberate. In fact, most historians agree he died of pneumonia brought on by all the infections going around Vienna at the time. The little guy never was very healthy. Not too sexy, huh?"

Bowen shook his head and smiled at David.

"What?" David asked.

"Nothing."

"You have a bad habit of that, you know it, Bowen?"

"Sorry, man. It's just, like, you really know your shit. You sound so like…I don't know, an expert or something."

David responded by taking a bite of his scrambled eggs.

"Sorry, man, I didn't mean anything by—"

"Ol' Wolfy was kind of my thing," David said, chewing.

"What do you mean?"

"He was my specialty—I had an affinity for the guy. I wrote a ton of research papers on him and worked on a couple of special projects."

"You must have been good."

David ignored the compliment. "And for some weird reason, I played him better than I did any other composer."

"Why do you think?"

"Beats me. I guess that was another reason Henry gave me this music."

"I'd like to hear you play sometime."

David responded quickly, "I can't play that stuff anymore."

His tone was enough for Bowen to let it drop. "Can we talk about Henry?"

David adjusted in his chair. "All right."

"You said you hadn't talked to him in a long time. Why?"

"That's personal," David answered.

"Did you guys like have a falling out or—"

David laid down his fork. "I said, it doesn't have anything to do with this."

Bowen nodded and moved on. "Was he still teaching?"

"I heard he retired about five years ago," David answered.

"What was he doing with his time?"

"Don't know, probably writing."

"Songs?"

David chuckled. "Guys like Professor Henry Shoewalter don't write songs. Symphonies maybe, not songs. More likely he was writing books. The guy was a real scholar."

"Books about what?"

"Music history, criticisms, composers, that sort of thing."

Bowen sat back in his chair and put his hand on his chin.

"What are you thinking, Bowen?"

"What if he was writing a book on Mozart?"

"Okay, so?"

"That would explain why he needed this music. Maybe there's something important about this sketch we're not seeing?" Bowen began talking faster, "Hey, what if he found out there was something in this music no one else knew—you know, like some startling revelation about Mozart?"

David wiped his mouth with his napkin and tossed it on the table. "Okay Bowen, my turn—it doesn't make any sense. First of all, Henry had this for a long time before he gave it to me, so he would have already known everything there is to know about it. Second, even if there was some 'startling revelation' as you call it hidden here in an eighth rest or something, what could be so urgent to warrant him flying clear across the country and calling me in the middle of the night to get it? Why not just call me from New York and have me send it to him? Thirdly, what in the hell could be important enough to get himself killed over? And lastly, what does any of this have to do with J.P. being missing and me being set up to look like I did it?"

Bowen's excitement didn't recede. "I don't know, but I think we're onto something here. Look, Mr. Webber, the fact is Henry did fly clear across the country and call you in the middle of the night to get this page of music. And he *was* murdered, and Jean Ann *is* missing, and you *have been* set up. Pretty darn convincingly too."

David caught the emphasis on the last statement.

Bowen continued, "I went by homicide this morning. Everyone's talking about you. They're all pretty pissed you were released and are damn sure you did it. Mr. Webber, they're really gunnin' for you. We gotta come up with something quick, or you'll be back in jail, and this time I don't think there's anything even my father will be able to do to get you out."

"That can't happen. I've gotta find J.P.," David yelled, inviting stares from the other customers.

"Lower your voice. Remember, I don't want to be seen with you."

David sat back.

"And that's another thing. We can't meet face to face anymore unless it's absolutely necessary. We'll have to communicate by phone from here on out. I think they've got you under surveillance."

"What?"

"This morning, I'm sure I saw an unmarked car sitting in front of your building. They're probably out there right now watching us. But by the time they figure out who I am, we should be done with this. I'll just explain that because of my relationship with Jean Ann, I was carrying on my own investigation off the clock. They'll reprimand me, but that's all—maybe not even that if we're successful. So we have to be successful."

David turned his head, scanning Ventura Boulevard.

"Don't do that," Bowen scolded.

David rested his elbows on the table and put his face in his hands. His muffled voice was desperate. "What are we gonna do, Bowen?"

"Find Jean Ann, that's what."

David looked up. "How? All we have is a theory on why Henry contacted me after all these years. You may be right, maybe this music is important, but that still doesn't get us any closer to finding J.P. or who killed Henry."

Bowen leaned in. "I know, man. But we have to start somewhere. We can't give up hope. We have to believe that Jean Ann is out there somewhere waiting for us to find her. At least that's what I have to do. How about you?"

David nodded. No matter how naïve the kid's feeling for J.P. might have been, he was happy he wasn't in this alone. *How do you do it, J.P.?* he thought. *Even now, you've found a way to take care of me.*

"So look," Bowen started again, "when I went by homicide, I did find out some details about the murder."

David swallowed. "I'm not sure I wanna hear this."

"I went down to property. That's where they keep all the evidence and personal effects from the cases. I went through Henry's stuff. I found something."

"What?"

"This." Bowen reached in his back pocket and withdrew a faded brown leather address book and handed it to David.

David struggled for breath.

"You all right, man?"

David coughed to clear his throat. "Yeah, it's Henry's address book. I gave it to him for his birthday years ago."

"Get out of here, really?"

David couldn't respond.

"I've looked through it. I want you to do the same. See if anything jumps out at...hey," Bowen interrupted himself, "DHW, the initials burned inside the flap here, that's you, isn't it?"

David nodded, fighting his emotion, "Yeah, David Henry Webber."

"Henry. That's your middle name, wow, what a coincidence."

"Not really," David uttered softly as his memory took over.

"Are you sure about this, Davey? A name is an important thing. It'll be with you for the rest of your life."

"Yes, sir, I am. I've thought about it a lot. I want you to know, sir, that I first thought about changing my last name to Shoewalter but then decided that would be disrespectful to my real parents. So, I thought since I didn't have a middle name, I could use yours. I think David Henry Webber sounds better than David Shoewalter Webber, don't you?"

"I think it sounds wonderful."

"Man, if they find out I took that, I won't only be fired, I'll be arrested."

David folded back the back flap of the book and pulled on a tiny piece of leather that hung from the inside stitching. The back lining of the wallet opened, revealing a secret pouch sewn into the fabric.

"Cool," Bowen said.

A folded white slip of paper fell onto the table.

Bowen grabbed the paper and unfolded it.

"What is it?" David asked.

"It's a phone number and an extension, but no name, just a number."

"That's a lot of help."

Bowen handed David the slip of paper. "Look at the heading on the stationary."

David took the slip of paper. *The Airport Holiday Inn, Los Angeles.*

"Didn't you tell me he arrived about midnight?"

"Yeah," David said, knowing where Bowen was heading.

"He'd only been at the hotel for a few hours. He must have just written that number down before he was—" Bowen stopped himself. "Sorry, man."

A chill went down David's back.

"I want you to call that number and see who answers," Bowen ordered.

"Why me? Why not you?"

"Because whoever answers may mean nothing to me but something to you." Bowen handed David his cell phone. "No time like the present."

David took the phone and dialed the number off the slip of paper. On the third ring the line was answered.

"Smithsonian Institution, how may I direct your call?"

David was taken off-guard, "The Smithsonian Institution?" he repeated for Bowen's behalf. "Uh…I'm not sure. I have an extension, five—two—zero?"

"That's the office of Doctor Dani Parsons—one moment and I'll connect you."

Chapter 12

The fifth floor of the museum was deserted on weekends and the primary reason why Dani always enjoyed dropping by. It still made her smile when she stepped off the elevator into the vacant hallway. Sure, there was nothing she could do here that she couldn't do from her computer at home, but here just felt better, more scholarly. Especially on weekends when the business of running the nation's historical Mecca wasn't in full gear. When it was just a place of history. It even smelled different.

Dani unlocked the door and turned on the light to her small, cluttered office located down the hall from the conference room. She tossed her backpack on the chair in front of her desk and hit the space bar on her computer keyboard, causing the dancing gophers of her screen saver to abruptly bow and then disappear. As the computer booted up, Dani opened Mrs. Sugarberry's green satchel and retrieved the old manuscript. She laid the sheet of music on her desk and sat down, one leg tucked under her. "What are you and where did you come from?"

Not taking her eyes off the piece of music, Dani typed in her password. Seconds later she heard the expected words, "*You've got mail.*" She looked at the screen and saw she had seven new emails.

One from a college roommate she had recently started corresponding with again and two from an Internet company that offered discount prices on designer fashions. "Only two, don't you guys love me anymore?" And sure enough, four emails from her dad.

Dani saved the messages as "new," deciding she would respond later from home. She closed her mailbox and typed in a new address. Seconds later, the web page to the Smithsonian Institution came on screen. She typed in another password and waited. One short beep followed by two long beeps. The computer asked for another set of commands, which Dani entered. The screen went black before the words National Archives Research Library rolled across the screen.

Dani positioned her mouse in the search field, typed the word cook, and then hit Return. She waited as the computer searched the massive database. "Nothing matching your request" appeared on the screen. She reentered Doctor James Cook and Georgetown. Nothing. She tried one more time, Doctor James Cook and Georgetown and free black. Again nothing.

"Wishful thinking, Dan," she muttered aloud.

Dani looked long at the music again. "Oh, just for laughs."

"Gertrude Sugarberry."

"Nothing matching your request."

"You're batting a thousand, Dan."

Dani logged off and thought for another minute. She picked up the music and started humming the melody. "It's beautiful," she said with a sigh. She looked at her watch and then picked up her telephone and dialed.

"Paul, you there? Paul, it's Dan, pick up the phone." Dani smiled and then spoke again in a singsong way, "Paul, it's safe. I've already met with Sugarberry."

The phone clicked, and Dani heard the machine on the other end feed back, "Hello? Hello?"

"What a wiener."

"What do you mean?"

"You were screening me because you thought I was going to try and get you to go see Sugarberry."

"I was not."

"You were too, you little turd."

Paul laughed.

"Well, just so you know, it was your loss. I did meet with her, and she's delightful, and her collection is amazing. Maybe this won't be so bad after all."

"Really? That's great, Dan. I can't wait to see it."

"Glad to hear you say that, Paul."

"Uh oh."

"Actually this doesn't have anything to do with the collection, I don't think."

"What do you mean you don't think?"

"Well, to tell you the truth, I don't know what I have."

Dani told Paul about the old piece of music and how it was attributed to a Dr. James Cook. She summarized her impressions of the piece and relayed Sugarberry's tale of how there was thought to be more works by Dr. Cook.

"Fascinating."

"Isn't it? Paul, this may be a wild goose chase, but I think there might be something special here. What if there are other pieces by this guy? We may have stumbled onto one of America's foremost composers no one's ever heard of. And Paul, he's African-American —pre-civil war. Can you imagine the ramifications?"

"Yeah, I can imagine. I can also imagine what Beckman's going to say when he finds out. He'll shut it down, Dan. He'll either shut it down or give it to someone else."

"Beckman doesn't have to know. As far as I'm concerned, this is just part of the American Sheet Music Exhibit he put us on."

Paul said nothing for a moment. "Okay, I'll go along with that for now, but if stuff starts turning up, we have to tell Beckman, agreed?"

"Agreed," Dani responded, rolling her eyes and crossing her fingers in the air. "So what are you doing right now?"

"Laundry," Paul answered dryly.

"Laundry? Paul you gotta get a life. I'm coming over."

"Okay."

"I'm going to stop by my place first and get my cello. I want to hear how this thing sounds."

"You eaten?" Paul asked.

"No."

"I'll order a pizza."

"Perfect, see you in an hour."

Dani hung up and went to a copy machine buried under a stack of textbooks. After making three copies of the piece, she went to the safe in the opposite corner and dialed in the combination. She opened the safe, withdrew a metal briefcase, placed the copies in the safe, and put the original in the briefcase. She shut the safe's door and spun the tumbler. She walked over to the bookcase behind her desk, scanned the titles, grabbed three large tomes, and placed them in her backpack. She grunted as she threw the heavy sack over her shoulder. She grabbed the briefcase, turned out the light, and closed the door.

Thirty seconds later her phone rang.

Chapter 13

"I'm sorry, sir, there's no answer. Would you like Dr. Parsons's voice mail?"

"No, thank you, I'll call back. Thank you." David turned off the phone.

"What time is it?" Bowen asked.

"Almost ten thirty, why?"

"The Smithsonian...interesting."

David said nothing, handing the phone back to Bowen.

"What do you think?" Bowen asked.

David raised his eyebrows and nodded. "I think you might be right. Henry must have been researching something on Mozart and needed the sketch."

Bowen replied, "Now we just have to figure out what it was and why it was so important." Bowen thought for a moment. "Did he ever work for them?"

"The Smithsonian? Not that I'm aware of, but it's been years since I've talked to Henry. He very well could've. He probably knew people there. He played off and on with the National Symphony for years."

The waitress came by the table and asked if they would like

anything else. Bowen declined and handed the waitress a twenty. Neither spoke, both lost in thought, until she returned with the change.

"What was the person's name again?" Bowen asked, taking a pen from his shirt pocket.

"Dr. Danny Parsons."

"Okay, it's ten thirty, that makes it one thirty on the east. Must be out for the weekend."

"Or out to lunch," David interjected.

Bowen didn't hear. "We'll call again Monday morning." Bowen wrote the name on the back of the receipt and then thought for moment. "In the meantime, can you…like…I don't know what's the word…analyze this music?"

"What do you mean, analyze?"

"We need to find out what Henry was working on."

David shrugged. "That would help."

"Well, maybe you can find out what *that* was by going over this thing, you know, really study it."

"Bowen, that's not exactly my expertise. Yes, I know a lot about Mozart, and I used to play the shit out of his Concerto in B-flat, but what you're asking is completely out of my wheelhouse. There are highly skilled people who do that sort of thing, and I'm not one of them. Plus, what the hell am I even supposed to be looking for?"

"Anything odd, out of place, I don't know, I'm not a musician. Look for something that Henry might have seen as—"

"Why?" David interrupted. "Why would anyone do this, Bowen?"

Bowen choose his words carefully. "Well, the framing you is easy to answer. It's to throw the police off the trail. Taking Jean Ann, if that's what has happened, I still don't get, unless—" Bowen stopped.

"What?"

"Unless it's to motivate you."

"Motivate me? To do what?"

"Whatever it was that Henry was doing."

David fell back in his chair. "Bowen, it's crazy. If this really is all about Mozart and this sketch, then why kill Henry? Why not just follow him and let him get it from me? Why kill him first? It's stupid. Then they kidnap J.P. and frame me so I'd continue Henry's work? Bowen—"

"I know," Bowen said calmly. "It's weird. But we don't have all the pieces yet. David, I know we're on the right track here."

David looked at Bowen. The kid truly believed what he was saying. "And you're still sure they're connected. Henry's murder and J.P.'s disappearance?"

"I am," Bowen said without hesitation. "I think you are too."

David looked down and rubbed his temples. "Yeah, I guess I am."

"Then we have to follow this lead, no matter how off-the-wall it might be."

David didn't reply.

"So look at this music, okay?"

David nodded.

Bowen stood. "Let's get out of here."

David pushed his chair back, but Bowen stopped him. "I don't think I should take you home. No reason to give my brothers in blue more than they already have. Can you get a cab?"

"Yeah, sure," David said, resting back in his seat. "Call me, okay?"

"I'll call you later."

David watched as Bowen exited the front door of the restaurant and looked up and down the street before jumping in his Ford. David picked up the music. *What did you want, Henry?* David laid the music back on the table. He'd never felt so helpless and out of control. No, he remembered, he had—twice, as a matter of fact. The first time was when his parents were killed. He'd always wondered how he'd rebounded so fast from that. He wrote it off to the power of youth. When a person hasn't had enough time to make dreams and set goals, the ability to roll with life's detours must come easier.

But the second time, that was a different story altogether. He had made dreams—he had set goals. And he lost the two, no three, loves of his life, almost at once—Kathryn, Henry, and his career.

The knotting in his stomach started the way it always did.

I'm sorry, David.

The words still cut, the wound still bled.

Henry was just helping me. More words, more blood.

I'm sorry, Davey, I didn't know what to do.

Turn it off, David pleaded to himself.

You knew. You knew, and you didn't tell me. How could you?

Stop it, Webber. For cryin' out loud, he's dead.

Go to hell, old man!

The words still cut. The wound still bled.

You're very lucky, Mr. Webber. If you hadn't been drunk, you would have probably been killed. Your hand went through the windshield—we were able to save the hand, but you'll have some nerve damage.

It always played out in his mind the same way, slowly. David began flexing his left hand.

"Who's your friend?"

David jumped when he heard the familiar baritone voice from behind. Lieutenant Pete Ryan, clad in tan Dockers and a green Polo shirt, set his coffee mug on the table and slid into Bowen's former chair. "Mind if I join you?"

David stiffened and didn't reply.

"Small world, huh? I was just grabbing some breakfast, and lo and behold, look who I see across the room. How are you doing?"

"Fine," David answered.

"How's your mouth? Did you need stitches?"

"No, it's fine."

"Good."

For a moment David considered just getting up and walking away. That's what everything inside him wanted to do. But the words came out of his mouth before he knew he was saying them. "Are you here to arrest me again?"

Ryan laughed with no sound. "No, I'm not going to arrest you." He took a drink. "Though, I guess I can understand why you'd ask. You've had a pretty traumatic last couple of days, haven't you?"

Again, David didn't reply.

"No, actually I wanted to tell you that I think we might have screwed up after all. I'm now pretty sure that you're not responsible for Mr. Shoewalter's death. I saw you over here and thought I'd save myself a phone call. I want to apologize. I'm sorry, sometimes these things happen."

More than anything David wanted to believe what he was hearing, but he couldn't. *Mr. Webber, they're really gunnin' for you.*

"What about J.P.?" David asked, not looking at Ryan.

"Or her too. That's another thing I wanted to tell you. We found Ms. Peterson's car."

"You found J.P.?" David shouted.

"No, we found her car, red '75 Mercedes SL, no Ms. Peterson."

"Where?"

"Mr. Webber, the car was found in an alley three blocks from your apartment." David went numb. "And there's something else. The car was clean except for the registration, a pair of sunglasses, a scarf, and a key card. The kind hotels are using nowadays for room keys. The card was for the Airport Holiday Inn. Care to guess which room it was to?"

"Henry's?" David said almost under his breath.

"Henry's. Care to guess whose prints were all over the car—except of course for Ms. Peterson's?"

"Mine."

"Yours." Ryan confirmed.

David's chest tightened, and he could barely form the words. "How did Henry's key...why...but you don't think I have anything to do with it?"

"No, that's not accurate. I said I don't think you're responsible. See, we've found no trace evidence that puts you in Shoewalter's room—that's hair, powder residue, prints at the murder scene, stuff like that. Also, nothing turned up in your apartment that puts you with Shoewalter. You not being a professional killer would make that practically impossible if you'd been there. But we do have the connection between that room key and the Peterson woman, so it's pretty obvious you have something to do with this case whether you know it or not."

Was Ryan being straight with him? Was Ryan now thinking the

same as Bowen, or was all this a ploy? Maybe he should tell him about Bowen? But if he did and Ryan was bullshitting him? Bowen would deny everything out of self-preservation, and he'd be back in jail. Bowen's dad would make sure of it.

"Any ideas how Shoewalter's room key got in Ms. Peterson's car?"

David shook his head.

"And the two of you didn't go back to the hotel after she picked you up from the police station Thursday night?"

"No."

"Okay then, any ideas how your car got back to your apartment?"

"No."

"Why did Henry call you in the first place, Mr. Webber? You never told us."

"I don't know."

Ryan looked long at David. He didn't speak, but David knew exactly what the detective was saying, *"You're not telling me everything,"* and now, for the first time, he wasn't. He couldn't, not yet, not until he found out what Henry was working on.

"Mr. Webber, David, listen to my words," Ryan said, squinting his steel-blue eyes. "I'm telling you I don't think you're a murderer. Do you understand? I do think, however, you're a mouthy, arrogant, quick-tempered basket case who is about to get into something way over his head. I've seen this more times than I can count. Every husband whose wife has been killed, every father who loses a child, it's always the same, and I tell them all exactly what I'm going to tell you now: this isn't television, and you're not Magnum PI. If you know something that might help me, you've got to tell me. Because, beyond the stupidity of thinking you're smarter than an entire force of trained professionals, it's also, in your case, potentially very dangerous. Remember, David, whoever has done this has intention-ally involved you. And if you start playing Dick Tracy, you could wind up as dead as Shoewalter. Am I clear?"

David stared at the police lieutenant. God, he looked sincere. But that was his job, wasn't it? He remembered how he was when he arrested him; he was sincere then too. No, he had to wait. He had to find out what Henry was doing.

"I don't know anything, Lieutenant Ryan. I wish I did."

Ryan held David's eyes without saying anything until David became uncomfortable and had to look away.

"Okay, have it your way." Ryan stood abruptly, picking up the coffee mug. "Here's my card. Call me when you decide to help. By the way, that piece of music doesn't have anything to do with this, does it?"

David had forgotten it was in view and replied as matter-of-factly as he could. "No, just something of mine I'm working on."

Ryan's jaw remained clenched as he continued his accusatory stare. He turned with no goodbye and walked from the restaurant—with the coffee mug.

David watched Ryan exit the same door as Bowen and disappear around the corner of the building to the back parking lot. David waited until he saw a black sedan with Ryan behind the wheel pull onto the street and head down Ventura Boulevard.

David exhaled, sure that he had been holding his breath ever since Ryan had walked up to his table. *My god, Bowen, you're right. J.P. and Henry are connected.* What if Ryan was telling the truth? What if he wasn't a suspect? What if Bowen was wrong? *Stop it,* Ben thought. *Don't try to make sense out of the picture. Just paint it.*

David picked up the music again and stared at the ink marks made so long ago. Dots and stems—that's all it really was, dots and stems. Nothing more than a language some learned to express their emotions. Some better at it than others, for sure, but...really nothing more than dots and stems. Certainly nothing worth dying for, or killing for. "She's dead," David whispered to himself, his eyes filling with tears, his mind darting from one thought to another. "She has to be." *It's like all those news stories. When someone disappears, there's never a happy ending.* David scanned the page again. *What could be so important? Henry and J.P. are connected. That makes me the common denominator.* Heat rose in David's body. He began tapping his spoon on his empty coffee cup in a slow rhythm as confusion and helplessness turned to anger and then rage. Ryan's words echoed, *"You could wind up as dead as Shoewalter."* David's face turned to stone. "So the fuck what?"

David gently put the old music back into the leather pouch. He got up from the table, oblivious to the looks around him, and headed for the hostess stand.

"Hi, can I use your phone? I need a cab, and I've lost my cell."

The hostess gave David the phone and the number to the taxi service. He ordered a cab, hung up, and immediately dialed another number.

David listened and then said, "Yes. I need to book a flight from Los Angeles to Washington, DC."

GILBERT WAS BEHIND THE WHEEL, and Sanchez was looking through binoculars as Ryan pulled into the parking lot of the convenience store. Gilbert rolled down the window.

"What's he doing?" Ryan said, bringing the car to a stop.

"He's probably calling a cab."

"All right, you guys, stay on him," Ryan said, shifting the car into gear. "I'm heading back." Ryan held up the coffee mug from David's table with a handkerchief. "I'm gonna find out who Mr. Webber's friend is."

As Ryan turned the black sedan back onto Ventura Boulevard, neither he nor the two other detectives noticed the charcoal-gray Ford Focus that pulled out of the gas station a block away as Ryan drove past.

Chapter 14

Dearest,

I didn't want to wake you. I could tell you had a long night. I trust your performance was...adequate. I received your message and am so looking forward to seeing Uncle Nick and family for lunch—oh joy! You can pick me up at the spa. Have Leon call Charise and let me know you're on your way.

Ciao, K

ANTHONY SAT at a table on the balcony in his satin robe and read the note over his glass of fresh squeezed. Showered, shaved, and oozing with the renowned Depriest polish, he bore little resemblance to the belching, red-eyed, and thoroughly disheveled man who staggered through the front door earlier that morning. Having neither the desire, nor the ability, to climb the spiral staircase and get into bed with his wife, he opted instead to pass out on the couch in his downstairs study. Had he, however, he would have found the bed empty. His wife wouldn't arrive home for another hour.

Anthony wadded up the note and lobbed it over the ledge. He picked up the cordless and dialed. "Leon, phone my wife's spa. I'll pick her up in forty-five minutes."

THE DOOR-SLASH-SECURITY-MAN of the very exclusive Park Avenue Health and Beauty Spa was whistling a familiar refrain as smiling Upper Eastsiders strolled by. It was an ideal, sunshiny Saturday afternoon in the Big Apple.

Kathryn Depriest emerged from the tinted glass doors exactly forty-three minutes after she was given the message from her husband. From the immaculate pedicure to the perfectly applied makeup on a flawlessly featured face, the tall, slender blonde had gotten what she came for, the look that epitomized health, wealth, and beauty.

As the only child of Joseph Junior and Annabelle Whitebridge of Boston, Massachusetts, and granddaughter of oil baron Joseph Whitebridge Senior, Kathryn had grown to wear her station in life with ease. She had always known the truth of who she was and what was expected of her. It was a truth she had once rebelled against, but one she rediscovered after marrying Anthony and began the catapult into the thick of the New York elite. She'd also reacquainted herself with the weapons of such breeding, one of which being the coquettish smile she now offered to the Irish-American Goliath holding the door.

"Thank you, Michael."

"You're welcome, ma'am. Did you have a nice workout?"

"Lovely, Michael."

"Did you sleep well last night?" the man said with a sly grin.

Kathryn scanned the avenue in both directions for the black limo before reaching for the back of the young man's head and running her bright red fingernails down the back of his thick neck. "Hard as a rock, Michael."

The young Irishman's breath got short. "You look incredible," he said, discreetly touching the neckline of her blouse.

"You like it?" Kathryn replied, adding a twirl.

Like many of the women at the club, Kathryn kept a partial wardrobe on the premises for all occasions, formal, casual, and somewhere in between. Lunch with the Depriestiano clan, however, always posed a particular problem. She surrendered to yellow pastel slacks and a cream-colored satin blouse.

Long ago she'd ceased hiding her true feelings about her husband's family. She found them crude and revolting. When she married Anthony, just out of college, she wasn't fully aware of, nor cared to know, his background. For no reason at all, she'd just presumed he was from wealthy upstate stock. In the years that followed, Anthony spoke little about his childhood except to say it was "challenging." The awareness of her husband's true lineage, and the reputation of Uncle Nick and the Depriestianos' of Flatbush, came slowly. In the beginning, she'd found it somewhat charming—married to the mob, what a hoot. Not that Anthony was a mobster—a ludicrous thought to say the least. True, she'd come to know her dear husband to be a liar, a cheat, and a spoiled brat, but a mobster? Anthony Depriest wouldn't know which end of the barrel to point. But he was the nephew of Nicholas Depriestiano and that made divorce tricky, if not downright suicide. Not physical of course, but certainly financial. Mummy and Daddy had all but disowned her, and she'd come to the conclusion early on that she'd rather live a charade with Anthony than go running back to them for anything. Besides, the arrangement did have its advantages.

She dropped her hand and released the valet's gaze when she saw the limo round Seventy-first. She arrived at the curb the same moment as the car. The door-slash-security man dutifully opened the car door, she stepped in, and the door was shut without the two uttering a word or giving a passing glance. Anthony was deep in a copy of the *New York Times*.

"Afternoon, dear," Kathryn said, adjusting the collar of her blouse.

"Afternoon, dear," came the reply from behind the newspaper.

Kathryn retrieved the Arts and Leisure section from the seat, and the two read in silence as Leon navigated east to the FDR and then south to East River Drive and the Brooklyn Bridge. Anthony pretended to read, waiting for his moment. As the car moved onto the Prospect Park Express Parkway, Anthony folded the paper and dropped the bomb.

"Dear, do you remember Professor Shoewalter?"

Kathryn lowered the paper with a look of disgust. "Of course, I do. I told you just a few months ago I had spoken to Henry."

"Oh, that's right, where is my mind going? What was it he wanted again?"

"Research. He asked me to do some research for him."

"Just like the old days, huh?" Anthony said, with a wide grin.

Kathryn looked out the window. "He said I was the best research assistant he ever had. That was nice of him to say, those were good times. I was sure I'd never hear from him again after—" Kathryn stopped herself.

"What type of research?" Anthony asked.

"Just some historical data on Mozart, nothing too complex."

"So you did it, then, the research?"

"Yes, of course I did, I told you that also. About three months ago I gave him everything he asked for. Really, Anthony, if you're not going to listen to me when I speak, I might as well stop talking to you."

"Have you talked to him since?"

"No, that was it. Why the sudden interest in Henry Shoewalter?"

Anthony's eyes became sad. He took Kathryn's hand. "Dear, I-I don't know how to say this."

"Say what?"

"Well…it's just that—oh my, this is difficult."

"Anthony, what are you talking about?"

"Dear, last night, a few of the musicians were talking. Most of them knew the professor—hell, I guess most of them studied under the old man. Well, dear, this will come as a terrible shock, but Professor Shoewalter is dead."

Kathryn's mouth fell open, and she had to catch her breath.

"I'm so sorry, dear. It gets worse. It seems the old man was murdered."

"Murdered? Why? How?" Kathryn's eyes filled.

"I don't know, except that it happened in Los Angeles. It's quite a news story out there, television, newspapers, everybody is talking about it."

Kathryn let her newspaper fall. "Oh, my God. That poor, sweet man." Kathryn was working hard at collecting herself. "Have they arrested anyone?"

"Yes. But he's been released."

"Who?" Kathryn asked.

Anthony paused to set up for the knockout punch. "David Webber."

Kathryn's face went flush. It was as if she'd been thrown into a dark tunnel, unable to distinguish up from down. David Webber. A name she hadn't heard in nearly a dozen years. Unless she counted the endless times she'd let it speak to her within the intimacy of a memory. A memory she kept on reserve. A memory she went to when life got too dirty and complicated. A memory that was decent and simple. A name from another life, a life perhaps that should've been. But a life that lived only in that mythical place called what if.

"Are you okay, dear?" Anthony said, putting his arm around his wife.

Kathryn placed her head on Anthony's shoulder and wept.

IT WAS while he was getting a suitcase from a closet in the bedroom that he found it. When he had told Henry that "the gift"—the Mozart piece—was the only thing from his past that had survived, he'd forgotten about the box. For a moment he thought about just carrying it out to the dumpster and tossing it. Why open it? Why go there? But before he knew it, he had the cardboard box sitting on the bed. Ravel jumped up and curiously watched as David began cutting away the duct tape that had been hastily applied so many years ago.

"You wanna see how screwed up I was back then, Rav?" David asked as the cat chased the falling tape. "I'm not sure I do."

It was just after he'd been released from the hospital—or more accurately, not released. From day one, he had refused visitors. He wanted to see no one, Henry and Kathryn topping the list of those who were persona non grata. And though months of rehab were scheduled for his hand, he had no intentions of sticking around. So, after two and a half weeks of partial recovery, he got out of bed, put on his clothes, and hobbled out, telling no one, signing nothing. He took the train into the city, stopped by the bank and emptied his account, went straight to his apartment on the Upper West Side, and tossed what he thought was important into a suitcase—the box was an afterthought, a brief moment of sentimentality, the only such moment. After that, nothing was ceremonious. He simply shut the door to his apartment, not even caring to lock it, made an offer the doorman couldn't refuse on an old Impala sitting in the parking garage, and hit the road. No fanfare, no drama, no poignant good-bye, he just left. And now, almost twelve years later, for the first time, he was looking back.

What did I think was so important back then to save? With the last piece of tape falling to the floor, David took a deep breath and pulled back the flaps. To his relief, the first thing he saw made him smile. It was a baseball glove, old, cracked, and about four sizes too small. It had been a gift from his foster father, Mr. Witherspoon. David could still see the joy on Mr. Witherspoon's face when he gave him the glove on his ninth birthday. David pushed the tiny mitt over his fingers and smacked it with his fist. It still had the smell of Vaseline. *You should have kept in touch, you self-involved bastard.*

Though he'd only lived with the Witherspoons for a little over three years before he went to live with Henry, of all the people he stayed with after his parents were killed, the Witherspoons were special. After he left, his only contact with them was through Christmas and birthday cards—from the Witherspoons to him, never the other way around. The cards continued up until about seven years ago. It was from one of those Christmas cards, this time from Gladys alone, that David learned George had died. It took him four months to call. By the time he did, he learned from Gladys's sister that, as is often the case with couples who've been together most of their lives, Gladys had gone to be with George two months earlier. *I should have stayed in touch.*

He set the glove beside him and continued lifting memories from the box. There were award, scores of them, first-place trophies and plaques from piano competitions from all over. There were long-forgotten compositions he'd composed, and arrangements he'd written for the Westchester High School band. He found an envelope, his letter of acceptance to Juilliard, and his diploma. *Funny how something that was once so important could end up in the bottom of a cardboard box.*

There were items whose significance he couldn't fathom; a menu from some restaurant, a *Time* magazine, a bag of subway tokens, and a cheap ink pen. "I must've been sleepwalking when I filled this thing."

Then he saw them, the picture frames. He froze. *You should stop now, Webber,* he told himself. He lifted out the first picture. It was of him and his parents. He couldn't have been more than six or seven. It showed the typical American family, striking the typical pose. He stared at the photo for several minutes before setting it down and picking up the next frame. He knew it was coming. He'd remembered it was in there the moment he opened the box. He held the frame low and gazed at the photograph. He felt nothing. He continued staring, raising the frame closer. Still nothing. It was a photo taken on graduation day. He, Kathryn, Henry, and Anthony Depriest were standing in front of Lincoln Center. He didn't know then. He wouldn't know for two weeks. He looked at Kathryn's eyes. He looked at Depriest's eyes. Neither gave anything away. But Henry's eyes looked…tense. No…sad. Henry's eyes looked sad. David settled back on the bed and held the picture above his head. Ravel bounded onto his chest. The cat purred as David stroked its head. *What am I feeling?*

After a moment, David raised up, causing Ravel to leap to the floor. He tossed the picture back into the box. "Okay, buddy, we gotta get ready for a trip. You better like peanuts 'cause you're coming too. I don't have anybody to leave you with." It brought David to a sudden stop. He heard the echo of what J.P. had said to him in the car. *"I may be the only friend you have left…"*

"Indeed, Jeep," David whispered.

He was putting the other items back into the box when several pieces of notebook paper fell out of the *Time* magazine. David noticed the scribbles on the paper and immediately remembered why he had saved that magazine all those years ago. In his hand-writing, he read: *Missing Mozart Mass.*

"Well, I'll be damned. Talk about your coincidences."

He opened the magazine, and there it was—an article about a professor from UCLA, a Dr. Raymond Sullivan. In the article, Sullivan speculated about a mass Mozart may have composed after the death of his mother, Anna-Maria, a mass that had never been found. He remembered he was preparing to write a rebuttal thesis challenging Sullivan's assumptions and proving Mozart didn't write a mass for his mother. The thesis would have been the height of arrogance—an undergrad challenging the work of a tenured profes-sor. It was just the type of thing David was becoming known for. It would have been brilliant. "Or at least stir up some shit!" he said with a grin.

David inserted the notebook paper back into the magazine and put the magazine in a briefcase alongside the Mozart piece. *How appropriate,* he thought.

Chapter 15

Paul Rogers hunched over the keyboard of a walnut baby grand and blocked sparse chords around the melody Dani bowed on the cello. As both came to a simultaneous stop, Dani grinned sheepishly. "That could be right."

"Hmm, I don't know," Paul mumbled, stroking his reddish-brown goatee. "Let's try it again. This time I'll change the four-chord in the second measure to an E-flat minor instead of an E-flat major, then I'll go to a G-minor instead of back to the E-flat in the fourth measure. I'll count it off—and one and two and three and…"

The duet began again, Dani following the notes written on the ancient manuscript, Paul embellishing with his improvised accompaniment. At the end of the last bar, it was Paul who smiled. "Now that's nice."

"Yeah, it is. But is it right?" Dani replied.

Paul yawned and stretched his arms into the air. "There's just no way to tell, Dan. We've been at this for over an hour, whatta ya say we call it?"

Dani laid down her bow, picked up a bottle of Budweiser, and fell back. She drained the last swallow from the bottle. The warm beer caused her to make a sour face. "Why couldn't she have a second page? There might be some variations on the theme, which would give us a clue to where it should go."

"True. But without knowing what period this is from, the accompaniment could still go ten different ways. If it's earlier classical period, as the melody in the first three bars tends to suggest, then it's going to be more emotionally restrained, more homophonic with that melody staying predominant and the chordal accompaniment remaining pretty tame. However, there is that A-flat in the fourth measure, which is totally unexpected and very emotional, especially if it's accompanied by an E-flat suspended chord like I played. But that type of writing is very expressive. We could be talking late Romantic Age or the Impressionists."

"It can't be, not the Impressionists. That would put it well after Dr. Cook."

"Well, maybe Cook didn't write it after all."

"No, Sugarberry told me that it's been authenticated as his handwriting. He definitely put these notes on this page."

"Then that takes us back to Classical or Romantic. It's not Baroque."

Dani smiled. "What you're trying to say is you don't have a clue, do you?"

Paul feigned shock. "Whatever gave you that idea?"

Dani chuckled. "Neither do I."

Paul picked up the music. "But I'll say this, if that Dr. Cook guy did write this, then he's one of the most overlooked composers of the nineteenth century, because this is brilliant."

"I couldn't agree more. So now what do we do?"

Paul handed Dani the music, grabbed the empty pizza box off the coffee table, and headed for the kitchen. "First thing Monday morning let's get this over to the lab and see if we can identify and date the paper stock. That'll at least tell us the when and where. Then we'll go to the studio and have Marcus download the melody. Let's let the computer spit out some accompaniments. My guess is it's not going to come up with anything better than we did."

Dani half-yelled toward the kitchen, "Okay, that's Monday, today's Saturday, what do I do in the meantime?"

Paul reentered the living room. "And you tell me I should get a life? It's the weekend, Dan."

Dani puffed out her lip in pretend sadness.

Paul rolled his eyes and sighed. "Okay, in the meantime, why don't we find out what we can about Dr. James Cook?"

"I've already been on the Net. Archives aren't showing anything."

Paul thought for a moment and then snapped his fingers. "Got it. Cook is from Georgetown, right? I have a friend at the University library. I'll get a hold of him tonight and set us up a meeting on Monday."

Dani beamed. "Perfect. I have to be at Sugarberry's on Monday anyway for the pickup of the sheet music. That'll give you a chance to meet her too."

Paul shot Dani a look.

"Relax, Paul, I told you, she's delightful."

"Okay," Paul chuckled. "You know, Wilbur's also a member of the Georgetown Historical Society. I'll bet he knows something about Dr. Cook."

"He's a librarian and his name is Wilbur?"

Paul shook his head.

"I'm just kidding. That sounds great, Paul."

"I'll call him tonight."

"Perfect," Dani said, jumping from the couch with the music and gathering her things. "Okay, I'm oughta here."

"Really, I thought we'd catch a movie or something."

"Nah, I wouldn't be able to stop thinking about this. Besides, I've got to swing by the office on the way home. I want to get this in the safe. I made copies, so we'll use them if we need to see the music. Then I need to get home and take Hemingway out. He's been locked up all day."

"Perhaps if you didn't spend so much time with that mangy mutt, you'd have time to get yourself a life, or a man, like me for instance."

Dani smiled and gave Paul a quick kiss on the cheek. "We'd drive each other nuts, and you know it. Plus, Hemingway isn't a musician."

To her relief, Paul let the subject drop. He'd tried on other occasions to go down that road, but she just wasn't interested. Paul was sweet, but not for her.

Paul gave Dani a hand with her backpack, cello, and the steel briefcase containing the music. "I'll see you tomorrow, then."

She stopped and looked questioningly at him. "You will?"

Paul rolled his eyes in exasperation.

The light came on. "Oh frigg, the concert! I forgot all about it." Dani moaned, setting down her cello.

"How could you forget a concert we've been rehearsing two weeks for?"

"I know, I know…it's just with this Sugarberry thing and the… oh you know me. Paul, can't you get someone else to——"

"No, and don't you dare even think about backing out."

"Please."

"Dan, I can't find another cellist by tomorrow. You're a member of the Smithsonian Chamber Orchestra, and we've got a gig. You're playing. Besides, it'll be good brownies for you with Beckman."

"Yeah, if it was for anything other than *his* birthday." Dani sighed in surrender. "Okay, I'll be there."

"It won't be so bad. You'll be outside, and there'll be lots of happy tourists."

"Yeah, and Beckman," Dani droned, picking up her cello again.

"We start at noon. Don't be late."

"All right, all right, I won't. I'll see you tomorrow."

Chapter 16

The brownstone manse on Church Avenue was beyond respectable
—it was honorable. Though large, it was not ostentatious. Sitting in
the middle of a tree-lined block, the Depriestiano home was flanked
on both sides by similar looking structures housing a circuit court
judge on one side and a private Hebrew school on the other. The
pace and noise synonymous with New York City was nowhere to be
found in this quiet, dignified neighborhood of Flatbush.

Leon pulled the limo into the driveway and hustled to open the
door for his passengers. Anthony stepped from the car, turned, and
offered his hand to Kathryn. Kathryn ignored her husband's
newfound chivalry and got out unassisted. Kathryn dabbed her eyes
and tousled her bangs as they walked around the side of the house
to the backyard. Her legs were like lead, and she felt very tired. This
was the last place she wanted to be.

The backyard of the Depriestiano house was like an Italian
greeting card. Red lanterns hung on wire crisscrossing above a red
brick patio protruding off a screened-in porch. A piñata for the kids
hung from a branch of a maple tree in the middle of the lush yard,
and sunflowers shot up five feet high in the flower garden along the
back fence. It seemed to Kathryn every son, daughter, cousin,

nephew, and niece in the Depriestiano family had gathered, all eager to see their famous kin. Anthony plastered a smile on his face as if he were posing for the camera. Kathryn regained her composure, swallowed hard, and mustered an expression to hide how totally miserable she felt.

"Little Tony," an elderly female voice with the heavy Italian accent cried, pushing her way through the throng. "Look, everyone, it's little Tony and his beautiful wife."

"Auntie Mar," Anthony replied with an even broader smile.

"Little Tony, you have not been eating. You are as skinny as a grapevine."

"But just as sweet, Auntie Mar, just as sweet."

"Oh, listen to you. Well, we'll just have to ask your bride about that, won't we, little Tony?" the small Italian woman said, pinching Anthony's cheek. "So, dear, is he or isn't he?"

Kathryn allowed a faint smile to the only member of the clan she could actually tolerate. "Yes, Auntie Mar, he is. But like the wine from that vine, I'm hoping he'll improve with age."

Anthony responded to his wife's mild jab with a peripheral glance.

The woman laughed and followed it with a kiss on Kathryn's cheek. "Little Tony, I have made something very special for you."

"You didn't, Auntie Mar."

"I did. Your uncle told me you were coming, so I made my cabbage balls just for you. What do you think of that?"

"I think I should call my tailor immediately and tell him to start adding an inch or two onto the waist of all my trousers, that's what I think about that."

The woman laughed and pinched on Anthony's cheek again.

"Auntie Mar, is that handsome son of yours around?"

"Jimmy?" the woman answered, waving her hand in the air with disgust. "Yes, he's in the alley playing stickball with the kids. Can you imagine, playing stickball at his age? When will he ever grow up, I ask you? Blessed Saints, he's turned out just like his papa."

"Well that's not such a bad thing," Anthony said, kissing the woman on the forehead. "Kathryn, I'm sure Auntie Mar needs some help in the kitchen."

Kathryn looked at her husband with contempt. Every time they came here it was 1950 again—get in the kitchen, woman, take care of the kids.

"Is Uncle Nick around?"

"He's in his study with some friends. Do you want me to get him?"

"No, I'll see him in a *momento*. I'll go say hello to my cousin. Maybe I'll even take a turn of stickball."

The woman turned for the house. "Now don't get all sweaty. Food will be ready in a half hour."

KATHRYN FOLLOWED her into the house, and Anthony headed for the back of the yard. The gate was open, and Anthony walked into the alley.

A half-smoked cigarette dangled from Jimmy's lips as he stood at the makeshift home plate—a garbage lid—holding a stick in his hand. The young boy hurled the small ball, bouncing it off the concrete. Jimmy shifted his weight and twisted his thick body toward the approaching orb. He missed the ball by a foot.

"Fuck! Son of a bitch, fuck!"

All six boys in the street laughed.

"Shut the fuck up and throw the ball again, damn it."

"You're out. Give someone else a turn," the nine-year old at first base yelled.

"Yeah, you've already had ten tries. Give someone else a bat," hollered the eleven-year-old in right field.

"Hey, I said throw the fuckin' ball before I wrap this stick round your tiny little heads." Jimmy took his stance. The boy threw the ball, and once again the stick failed to make contact. "Fuck! Son of a bitch, fuck!"

The boys broke out with laughter again, with the kid on first falling down and holding his stomach. Anthony's chuckle cut through the others. Jimmy saw his cousin and snarled, "You think you can do any better, pretty boy?"

Anthony smiled. "Probably not, pitching was always my forte."

Jimmy drew hard on his smoke. "Well come on, maestro. I'd just love to take your ass downtown."

Anthony walked over to the kid with the ball. "May I?" The boy handed Anthony the ball. "Ready, cousin?"

Jimmy threw down his cigarette butt and spit on the garbage lid. "Bring it on, mutherfucker."

Anthony reached back in a deep wind-up and brought his arm over his head. The ball flew from his hand like a bullet. Jimmy had no time to react. The ball found its target just above Jimmy's left eye. First the stick fell, then the knees buckled, and then the tough Italian lay prone on the street. Every boy ran to check on the injured man. Anthony casually walked.

"He'll be okay, boys, don't worry. You are okay, aren't you, cousin?"

Jimmy responded with a grunt.

"Yeah, he'll be fine. Okay, boys, I'll take care of Babe Ruth here while you guys get in and get cleaned up for lunch."

The boys looked at each other.

"Go on now, Jimmy's fine. We'll be along in a second."

The boys obeyed Anthony's order and ran off through the gate and into the backyard. Anthony grabbed Jimmy by the back of his T-shirt and lifted him into a sitting position.

"Come on, you're not hurt."

"You mutherfucker," Jimmy mumbled, recovering his senses.

"Right back at you, cousin."

"I'm gonna fuckin' break your skull."

"Tsk, tsk, let's not lose our head," Anthony said, slapping the man on the face. "Let's not forget who you're talking to, or should I remind you about—"

"Shut the fuck up about that. I'm sick of you bringin' that up. What the fuck's eating you, anyway?"

"You know exactly what's wrong, Jimmy. Now, what I want to

know is why I didn't know anything about it until your father called me last night?"

"You mean the old man gettin' whacked? How the fuck should I know? I didn't know anything about it either 'til pop told me."

"What about Leo and Sal?"

"I can't find 'em."

"What do you mean you can't find them?"

"I mean, I've tried calling and I can't find 'em."

Anthony kneeled down and looked his cousin in the eye. "Jimmy, you wouldn't be fucking with me, would you?"

"What the fuck you talkin' about?"

"You wouldn't have had Sal and Leo whack the old man to make me look bad in front of your father, would you? Because if you did—"

"You're a fuckin' lunatic. I told you I haven't talked to Leo and Sal, and I didn't know about the old man 'til Pop told me last night. What, you think I'm stupid or something?"

"Yes, I do." Anthony stared at Jimmy's face for a moment. "But not that stupid, or smart, whichever the case may be." Anthony helped his cousin up. "So, where is Leo and Sal?"

"I don't know, this ain't like 'em. They're two of my best. Hell, I've known 'em both since fourth grade."

"Someone else is in the picture," Anthony said, tossing the ball in the air.

"Someone else? You mean somebody else is lookin' for this thing too?"

Anthony didn't reply.

"Hey, maybe it's that piano guy the old man wanted to see."

"Not likely, but we can't rule it out. You keep trying to locate Leo and Sal. Call everybody out there you know who might be of assistance. If we haven't heard from them by tonight, we can probably expect we won't."

Jimmy looked at Anthony. "You thinkin' they got whacked too?"

Anthony didn't respond to the question. "You should put some ice on that."

"Little Tony! Jimmy!" Auntie Maria yelled from over the gate.

"Boys, your father and uncle would like to see you both in his study."

"Thank you, Auntie Maria, tell him we'll be right there."

The woman nodded and scurried back to the house.

"Any idea what your father's going to want to do?"

"No, all I know is the nigger and the Jew are both here."

Anthony dropped the ball. "Here? Why?"

"Relax. Knowin' Pop, it's just because he likes all the players on the same page. You know how he is."

Anthony tightened his jaw in frustration.

"Come on, Pop gets pissed when he's kept waiting."

SMALL, light, and bright, Nicholas Depriestiano's private study was very much like the house itself, the total antithesis of what you'd expect from the head one of New York's most powerful crime families. Depriestiano prided himself on that fact. While others of his ilk chose the profile and reputation of a Bensonhurst address, Old Nick rejoiced in the simplicity and wholesomeness of his stately Church Avenue residence.

The old man seated behind the desk seemed himself to be a contradiction to his profession as well. Slight in build, with wavy, snow-white hair that made his dark complexion appear even darker, he wore gray slacks with a light pink pullover. One could easily visualize the man walking up the seventeenth fairway at Pebble Beach.

Jimmy entered first, announcing their arrival with two brief raps on the door. Despite the smiles on the faces in the room, the tension was obvious.

Nicholas remained seated. "Here are my boys," Old Nick whined with a bagpipe-ish voice. "Come in, boys, it's time you met our new friend face to face."

An African-American man wearing a crisp white shirt, red bow tie, and frameless round eyeglasses rose from a rocking chair sitting in front of Nicholas's desk. Jimmy extended his hand.

"Boys, this is Thurman Winfield. Thurman, this is my son Jimmy and my nephew—"

"The maestro needs no introduction, Mr. Depriestiano," the man cut in, releasing Jimmy's hand and quickly offering it, and a sparkling smile, to Anthony. "I have enjoyed the maestro's work on many occasions. It's a pleasure to finally meet you, Mr. Depriest."

Anthony shook the hand and returned the smile. "You are kind, Mr. Winfield. And likewise it's a pleasure to finally meet you, but please call me Anthony."

"Thank you. Call me Thurman?"

"Hey, Bernie, look, it's my boys," Nick said to the somewhat disheveled man relaxing on a floral sofa by the wall.

Jimmy nodded casually but Anthony hurried across the room.

"Hello, Mr. Freeman, good to see you again," Anthony said, offering both his hands to the seated little man, who appeared to be only slightly younger than the elder Depriestiano.

"Hello, Tony. You look good," Bernard Freeman replied with a thick New York Jewish accent.

"As do you. How's Lady Justice treating you?"

"Oh, you know, win a few, lose a few. I guess it all works out in the end. What can I say, I should have listened to my mother and been a barber."

"Well, let me speak for all of us when I say that I'm glad you didn't. I'd hate to think where our family would be had we not had your wisdom and counsel over the years."

Bernie threw both hands forward.

Old Nick broke in. "Whatta you say we all have a seat."

Winfield sat back in the rocking chair. Anthony took a seat in the matching one beside him. Jimmy joined the lawyer on the sofa.

Nicholas rested his folded hands in front of him on the desk as he spoke. "The reason I called this little meeting was to gather all the principals in one room and discuss the progress of our little enterprise. I've always found it wise to keep everyone on the same page."

Anthony subtly glanced over his shoulder and saw Jimmy looking at him with a conceited smile.

"Thurman and I have been discussing the situation on the coast. I have informed him, Tony, that this unfortunate event was not unexpected by you, and in no way should hamper our mutually desired result. I'd now like for you to take over with where things are at present."

Anthony remained relaxed, gently rocking back and forth in his chair. "I'd be happy to, Uncle. Well, as my uncle said, the recent event in California came as little surprise. It was only a matter of time before something like this was going to happen. When you're dealing with any treasure as desirable as this one, it can become quite dangerous."

Winfield listened expressionless. Anthony continued. "Therefore, since it was anticipated, there is no reason to consider this a setback in any form or fashion. It should only be regarded as what it is—an unfortunate bit of bad luck for someone who was in way over his head."

"May I interrupt for a moment?" Winfield asked.

Everyone looked at Nicholas, who nodded to Winfield.

"I'm a little confused, Mr. Depriest."

"Anthony," Depriest corrected with a smile.

"I'm sorry. Anthony."

"How so?"

"When Mr. Freeman approached me and my representatives at Electric Chair Records with this venture, he made it clear in no uncertain terms one of the most important elements was this professor. I'm sorry, what was the elderly man's name?"

"Shoewalter," Bernie Freeman offered.

"Yes, Shoewalter. He reiterated over and over how Professor Shoewalter was the key to the success of this venture and how fortunate we all were that you, and you alone, had access to him and what he knew. Now, I learn he has been killed, and you say I should not be concerned. Do you see my confusion?"

Anthony didn't blink. "Absolutely, Thurman. I can well imagine your shock when my uncle informed you that Shoewalter had been murdered. But you must take—"

"Excuse me, Anthony," Winfield interrupted, "But your uncle didn't inform me, I informed him."

Anthony looked at Nicholas, who was staring right at him. At that point, Anthony knew his uncle had set him up—a little payback. Old Nick, above everything, hated to look stupid. And Anthony now understood that in his uncle's opinion, Anthony had committed the cardinal sin—allowing him to look stupid, to a black man at that.

"I see. Thurman, may I ask how you learned of the incident?"

"Anthony, surely you must know as a record executive many of my dealings are in Los Angeles. I was notified by one of my close associates."

"I see. Thurman, it's not my intent to butt in on how you run your business, but is it wise to let out the delicate particulars of what we're doing?"

Winfield spoke directly. "I said he was a *close* associate, Anthony."

"Ah, of course, my apologies." Anthony bowed his head. *What would MacArthur do?* Anthony stood and faced the room. "Thurman, I sincerely hope what I'm about to say does not make you uncomfortable, but I must make this statement. I would like to most humbly apologize to you, my uncle, Mr. Freeman, and my dear cousin for the egregious breakdown in communication in regards to the California incident. The blame should rest solidly upon my shoulders. There is no excuse for such sloppy—and make no mistake, it was sloppy—intelligence. If it's of any consequence, I can assure you all I have taken the necessary steps to ensure such a blunder shall not be repeated in the future. I hope this unfortunate mistake has not lessened your faith in my abilities to execute the rest of this worthwhile, and what I'm sure will be profitable, endeavor."

Winfield adjusted his glasses. Old Nick nodded approvingly.

"Your apology is most gracious and impressive, Anthony," Winfield said.

"Thank you, Thurman."

"Now," Winfield said, first scanning the room and then looking right at Old Nick, "can we cut through all this polite bullshit and get to the matter at hand?"

Anthony's smile abruptly vanished. Bernie and Jimmy adjusted themselves on the couch. Old Nick shifted his eyes on Winfield. Anthony stayed still, waiting to see how the old man would react— Nicholas Depriestiano was not accustomed to being spoken to in such a manner.

Old Nick settled back in his chair and smiled. "Have a seat, Tony. Okay, Winfield, the floor is yours."

Anthony sat down.

Winfield leaned back in his chair, folded his hands, and looked at the ceiling as he began to speak. "Gentlemen, I don't give a rat's ass about some old man in California getting in over his head. What I do care about is Electric Chair Records. Pardon the cliché, but it is my baby. I built this company from a home studio in my bedroom in Harlem to one of the most successful rap labels in the country. You know how I did that? Foresight. Foresight and organization. You know what I'm not seeing here? Foresight and organization. Now, I have been approached with joint venture deals from every major record label in the country. I've said no to every one of them. See, I like being in control. I like knowing what's going on at all times with my baby. When Mr. Freeman came to me with this joint venture deal, four months ago I might add, I was intrigued. You know why? Because you, Mr. Depriestiano, have a reputation for knowing what's going on within your organization—a reputation I now question."

All eyes looked at Old Nick for a response. He gave none.

"Bottom line, gentlemen, is this: it's stipulated in the offering memorandum, that we all agreed to, that if at any time there is dissatisfaction by either party, then either party could pull out of the deal before the full partnership goes into effect. Now, besides the incompetence of how this operation has been run heretofore, let me remind you that it's also stated in the agreement that you have three months to match your initial five hundred thousand investment or lose it all. Your three months ran out two days ago, gentlemen, and I'm," Winfield paused for effect, "dissatisfied. As I see it, you need this deal considerably more than Electric Chair Records does. I'm here to be persuaded why I should continue this relationship."

The room was silent while Old Nick stared blankly at the man. Finally he looked at Anthony. "Tony, do you wish to respond to Mr. Winfield?"

"Yes." Anthony folded his hands, leaned back in his chair, and looked at the ceiling. "Thurman...fuck you!"

"Excuse me?"

Bernie raised forward on the couch, "Now, gentlemen, there's no need—"

"Shut up, Bernie," Nicholas commanded sharply.

"You heard me. Fuck you. If you want out, no one here's stopping you. You must really think we're stupid. Do you actually believe we'd give you a half million dollars in good faith money and not know everything that's going on within your little record company? Well, allow me to enlighten you. Let's start with your big gun artist, BJ Jam, alias Lester Tyron Waters, alias Maxwell Washington, Jr. That is the little felon's real name, isn't it? Oh yeah, we know about his little stint in Attica for child molestation—registration of sex offenders is a bitch, isn't it? I wonder what would happen to his record sales if that got out? And while we're talking about record sales, let's talk about your other artists—and I use that term in the broadest possible sense. All of their sales have been down for the past eight quarters. That's gotta hurt. I mean, how does one keep a cash flow with those types of numbers—perhaps some extracurricular activities in the old accounting department? Perhaps an inventive little sell-through arrangement?"

Winfield maintained his cool, but Anthony knew he was getting to him.

"Oh, yes, I know about sell-through. I believe it's pretty common practice in the independent record world. Tell me if this isn't how it works? You, as the record company, don't get paid from your distributor until the CDs you ship to them, that they in turn distribute to retailers, online or otherwise, go off the shelf as it were, and remain off the shelf for ninety days, correct? It's a way the distributor has of protecting itself from returns of unsold merchandise."

Winfield didn't respond.

"Hmm, that's a terrible arrangement, isn't it? Unless of course you happen to, one: own, the distribution company in question, silently, of course, and two: have a habit of making buyout deals with foreign distributors—no royalties, no nothing, just cash in hand. Then that wouldn't be so bad, would it? Certainly would offset the cost of doing business. I just wonder, though, how the Feds would look at that little arrangement? I mean, you are paying taxes on all that ill-gotten gain, aren't you, Thurman? Of course they'd probably be the least of your worries. Imagine if your Gangsta Rap buddies were to find out you were withholding their royalties in a nice little offshore account. I don't even want to think about that, do you? By the way, how is Belize this time of year?"

"All right, Depriest, I got it. So you've done your homework. Your point?"

"Point is, Winfield, your baby is sucking air. The hell you don't need this joint venture. The only reason you haven't done one with a major is because you can't. The first thing they'd do is audit your books. You poor fool. You've been skimming off the top for years. The IRS would have a field day with you."

The two men stared at one another.

Finally, Winfield dropped his head. "So what do you want from me?"

"To shut up and enjoy the gift, because that's what we're giving you. And, if you do exactly as we instruct, you just might stay out of prison and alive."

Winfield withdrew a handkerchief and dabbed his lips. "What do I have to do? And I don't mean that garbage in the agreement I signed. I see that thing's pretty much worthless. I want to know what I've really gotten into."

Anthony looked at his uncle. The sun was breaking through the window behind the old don, wrapping him in ethereal radiance. He nodded affirmatively, giving his okay for Anthony to continue.

Anthony rose from his chair with a smile, walked behind Winfield, and put his hands on his shoulders. He whispered into the man's ear, but still loud enough for all to hear. "Nothing, just relax and let us make you legit. Once we're in possession of the piece, you'll shut down Electric Chair Records."

Winfield stiffened and closed his eyes.

"After we make the recording, you'll reopen the label under the new name, Renaissance Records. A new and exciting record label specializing in classical music. Your first release will be a never before heard Mozart piece."

Winfield's voice broke. "I'll be a laughing stock."

"*Au contraire*, you'll be heralded as a genius—a true Renaissance man. I can see the headline in *Billboard* now: Thurman Winfield, from Rap to Rapture. And here's the best part, everything's PD, public domain, no pesky publishing royalties to pay out. You keep all the money, legally this time."

Winfield took a deep breath and looked at the old man in front of him. Old Nick was like a mother lion watching her young make its first kill.

"And what's in this for you?" Winfield asked the old man.

He looked at Anthony, who picked up the cue. "We handle the distribution and all print publishing. You'll be paid accordingly."

"I guess it doesn't matter if I should say I don't like this arrangement. You've got me, don't you?"

Finally, lord Depriestiano spoke, "The moment you took the half-million."

Winfield got up and walked toward the door. He turned. "You'll be in touch?"

"We will. Good day, Winfield," Old Nick said.

Anthony added. "It's a pleasure finally meeting you, Thurman."

Winfield glared at Anthony, opened the door, and left.

Old Nick smiled. "You were very good."

Anthony turned to his uncle. "Thank you, sir."

"Don't you think he told him too much?" Jimmy scowled.

"I think he told him just enough," Nicholas countered.

"And I do once again apologize for California," Anthony added.

Nicholas waved his hand. "It's forgotten. So, now that all that unpleasantness is out of the way, what's next, Tony?"

Anthony sat in Winfield's former chair. "David Webber."

"The piano player they arrested for Shoewalter's murder?"

"Yes, he's also an old acquaintance of mine, sir."

"Really? Can he help us?" Nicholas asked, cutting to the heart of the matter.

"I believe so, sir. You see, as well as being a piano player, he's somewhat of a Mozart authority. I believe that's why Shoewalter was out there."

"Tony, do you think this Webber really killed Shoewalter?"

"I don't know, and I don't really care. It would make it easier if he did."

"Yes, I see what you mean. You're, of course, following Webber?"

"We were, but my intention now is not to."

Nicholas's eyes got wide. "Why not? Don't you think—"

"I said *we* weren't going to follow him any longer. I didn't, however, say anything about my wife. You see, sir, they used to be very close."

THURMAN WINFIELD GOT in the passenger side of the black Escalade parked in front of Depriestiano's house. The man behind the wheel started the car.

"Everything go okay?"

Winfield buckled his seatbelt. "They were patronizing, condescending, and downright threatening."

"So it went well?"

Winfield smiled, "Perfect."

Chapter 17

David dialed the phone number written on the slip of paper that Bowen had given him. The outgoing message was simple.

"This is Joshua Bowen, please leave a message."

"Bowen, it's Webber. I'm going to DC to meet this Dr. Parsons face to face. I'll call you tonight. Call me if you hear anything, Bowen. Okay? Bye."

David hung up. He took another look around the room, picked up his briefcase, a small leather duffel bag, and Ravel.

"HE'S LEAVING, and he's got a suitcase."

"What do you think we should do?"

Sanchez lowered the binoculars. "Follow him. Call the lieutenant."

David looked down Coldwater. Three minutes later a taxi pulled up.

As the cab pulled away from the curb, Sanchez started the car and followed. "Tell him I think he's headed to Burbank Airport."

"Lieutenant, Sanchez thinks he's heading to Burbank Airport."

Gilbert listened as Sanchez kept a three-car separation from the taxi.

"Okay, Lieutenant, you got it. See you there." Gilbert shut off the phone. "He wants us to call for black-and-whites and to stay on him, but no contact—he'll meet us at the airport. Then he said something really weird."

"What?"

"He said we should get ready to get our names in the paper."

"HEY, WAKE UP," the woman said, tossing her cigarette out the window.

The man beside her sprung forward rubbing his eyes. "What?"

"He's moving, and he's got a tail," the woman said.

"No surprise there. Let's join the convoy?"

"Ten-four, good buddy."

The car pulled away, following Gilbert and Sanchez.

RYAN FINISHED his call and looked again at the printout—so much for a quiet weekend. He stuffed the paper in his pocket and picked up the phone again.

"It's me. I might be late tonight. Best you don't hold dinner. I know…" Ryan closed his eyes as he listened. How much more could one marriage take? Last weekend it was supposed to be a family weekend at Magic Mountain. Before that, his son's little league baseball game, before that…he couldn't remember, but he knew it was something. "We'll talk when I get home. I'm sorry, but I really have to go. I love—" the line went dead.

Ryan came out the rear exit of the Van Nuys Division. He'd parked on a residential street behind the police station on purpose. Traffic on Van Nuys Boulevard was a nightmare on Saturday afternoons, and the only exit out of the police garage dumped you right in the middle of it.

As he approached his car, he saw a homeless man sprawled

against the front tire. The man was obviously wasted. "Come on, pal. You can't be lying around back here." The wretch mumbled something as Ryan assisted him to his feet. "Don't you know leaning against cars in L.A. is a capital offense?"

The homeless man stumbled away. Ryan unlocked the car door and got in. As he buckled his seatbelt, he glanced in the rearview mirror and saw that the man was already gone. He put the key in the ignition and turned. He heard no sound; the engine didn't turn over, but he did smell sulfur. At that moment, he thought of his wife and a little league game he wished he hadn't missed.

The explosion was deafening. Chunks of stucco were ripped off the Spanish-style house across the street from the vehicle. The windows on the east side of the police station shattered like peanut brittle from the violent crush of air. Black smoke billowed, and shards of metal and glass rained down.

As screams began echoing through the neighborhood, the homeless man reappeared from behind a cinder block wall. He looked upon the destruction, nodded approvingly, and casually walked away.

Chapter 18

Anthony moved the golden Grammy statuette to one side. He felt behind the shelf, and with little effort, found the button on the back of the bookcase. A moment later the etched mirror on the opposite wall slid to the right, disappearing into the wall and revealing a gray steel door to a safe. Anthony crossed the room and sipped a whiskey as he entered a series of numbers on the keypad. The red LED light on the left of the pad went out, and the green one on the right came on. He turned the latch and opened the safe.

A thick, brown, accordion-like folder was all that was in the safe. Anthony removed it and took it to the piano in the middle of the study. His eyes were emotionless as he pulled out a photocopied letter beginning *Dear Kathryn*. The letter was signed, *Sincerely, Henry*. There was another photocopied letter. This one began *Dear Henry* and was signed, *Kathryn*. Next, he pulled out a stack of legal size papers resembling a report, yet another photocopy. On the top of the first page it read:

RESEARCH NOTES on Mozart 1778
   By: Kathryn Depriest For: Dr. Henry Shoewalter

. . .

ANTHONY LAID the bundle on top of the envelopes and went back to the folder. "Ahhhhh," he moaned softly with a grin. He slid a photocopied sheet from the packet and placed it on the music holder of the piano. He looked lovingly at the composition and waved his right hand in a triangle. He closed his eyes, lowered his hand onto the keyboard, and without reading the music, played the piece perfectly from memory.

Kathryn opened the door to Anthony's study and saw her husband in his satin robe sitting at the piano.

"I'm turning in," she said with no inflection.

Anthony opened his eyes and saw his wife in her nightgown. He apathetically glanced at his watch and spoke to her through the open lid. "Little early for you, isn't it?"

"I'm exhausted. I'll see you in the morning—or are you going out tonight?"

Anthony smiled. "Good night, dear."

KATHRYN SHUT the door to the study and climbed the stairs to the master bedroom. But she wasn't turning in—not yet. There was something she needed to see again.

The bedroom's walk-in closet was a room to itself. With over three hundred outfits and two hundred pairs of shoes, it had to be. She found what she was looking for in the corner tucked behind two dozen or so hatboxes.

On her knees, she pulled the boxes away, revealing a stack of photo albums. One by one she flicked through the pages. In the middle of the third album, she stopped. The eight by ten was cracked in the middle and had suffered some discoloration. A tear ran down her cheek as she ran her fingers over the picture of the three young faces and one older one. The picture was of her, David, Anthony, and Henry on graduation day.

DANI TURNED on the computer with her toothbrush still in her mouth and entered her password. Hemingway, a challenged-looking dishwater-brown mixed terrier, was all-fours-in-the-air on the couch. Dani was spitting into the sink in the bathroom when it occurred to her what she *didn't* hear.

She went back to the computer sitting on a table in the corner of her small living room and sat down.

Hemingway stumbled off the couch, trotted over, and leaped onto her lap.

"Oh lord, boy, do you have to do that?"

Hemingway responded with a lick to her face.

"I should have mail, Hem. I know I saved them as new." Dani clicked on the mailbox icon. Indeed, there was nothing. "Well, frigg. What happened?"

She thought for a moment and then moved her cursor to the icon "old mail." She clicked, and there it was—the one from her college roommate, the two from the Internet clothing company, and the four from her father, all of the emails from earlier in the day she hadn't read or responded to. "How the heck did that happen? Stupid computer."

With Hemingway on her lap, Dani settled back in her chair and opened the first email from her father.

THREE HOURS INTO THE FLIGHT, David surrendered to the ache in the back of his neck. He'd gone over every inch of the sketch, searching his memory banks for knowledge learned and forgotten. There was a time when doing this, composition study, getting into the composer's head, was as easy for him as playing a C scale. But that seemed like a lifetime ago.

He laid down his pen and viewed the notes he'd written in the red spiral notebook he'd purchased in the airport before boarding the plane. The significance of the red notebook didn't occur to him until the plane was in the air. The purchase of a red spiral notebook was a ritual he always employed at Juilliard before beginning a new research project. David rolled his head in both directions and then began to read.

Notes on Mozart sketch:

Autograph in upper right corner appears authentic. <u>*In DC confirm water-mark dating is correct.*</u> *Check major works in 1791, omitting dances, minuets, songs, etc... Look at "Concerto for Horn in D," "Sehnsucht nach dem Frühling," "Adagio and Rondo for Glass Harmonica," "Adagio in C for Glass Harmonica," "Cantata," "Die ihr des unermeßlichen Weltalls," "Con-trapuntal Study," "La clemenza di Tito," "Die Zauberflöte"—The Magic Flute—"Concerto in A for Clarinet," "Freimaurerkantate", Requiem in D minor.* <u>*In DC confirm list—see if you forgot anything.*</u> *Reconfirm sketch* <u>*does not match these works.*</u>

Analysis

Key: Bb major

Time signature: 3/4—but too complex to be a Minuet.

Expression markings

Up lt-corner notation—adg.—must mean adagio

Up rt -corner instrument notation interrupted

Middle rt—doodles, pictures, errant ink drippings

Lower rt-corner marking—More doodles, letters CKF—unknown

Lower lt-corner—errant ink drippings, more doodles

Treble clef: Melody Very legato—predominately whole and half notes. Surprise in measure 4. Uncharacteristic suspension.

Bass clef: interesting contrast to treble clef—staccato—probably pizzicato cello and/or contrabass.

Summarize:

Sketch appears to be for symphony or concerto. Lack of any libretto notations makes it doubtful that it's for an opera—<u>however could be a Mass.</u> The missing mass for his mother? Could it be? NO, DATE DOESN'T WORK! Mozart's mother died at least a dozen years earlier. <u>*Must reconfirm watermark date and reread Time mag. article.*</u>

David closed the notebook and put it and the music back into his briefcase. *Brother, have I been out of this world for a while,* he thought. He raised the tray table and turned out the overhead light.

It was dark now. The plane wasn't even half full, and the ride was smooth. He looked in the small crate sitting on the empty seat beside him and saw Ravel sleeping peacefully. He looked out the window and saw nothing but blackness. He guessed he was somewhere over the Midwest by now. As he looked into the void, it occurred to him he hadn't ventured out of California since his self-imposed exile landed him there. When he decided to escape to the West, that meant everything, and everyone, in the East would no longer exist. His plan was to disappear, and he felt he could safely dub the plan "mission accomplished." *But have I forgotten to stop running?* The question had been eating at him all day. Ever since looking at the picture of Kathryn. *Am I over it?* It felt strange even to consider. He wondered if he'd gotten so used to feeling lousy it had become habit? What if he'd gotten over Kathryn years ago but had plain forgotten how to be happy? He remembered the night J.P. picked him up at the jail. When she mentioned how different, sadder he was, what were her exact words? *"It's like there's no joy in life for you at all anymore, David."* He was too embarrassed to tell her that it was a stupid celebrity magazine article that brought it on. Anthony Depriest: one of the ten sexiest men in America. Complete with full color photo of Depriest and Kathryn. Under the picture was the caption, THE MAESTRO AT HOME—A MATCH MADE IN HEAVEN. *God was I an asshole to J.P. that night*, he remembered. "I'm sorry, Jeep," David whispered as he reclined his seat and closed his eyes.

THE ROOM WAS DIM. The only light being that of a nearby neon sign trickling through the bottom of the drawn curtains. It was furnished with a single end table, a couch, a chair, and a bed. In the bed, a woman tossed restlessly, mumbling indistinguishable phrases.

A man sat by the woman and ran his hand over her forehead. "Shhh, relax."

The woman moaned, blinking furiously in an attempt to open her eyes. Her breath became hard and labored, and her mumbles grew louder.

"Shhh, help is coming."

The man opened the drawer of the end table and removed a small vial and syringe. He placed the needle into the bottle and withdrew the clear liquid. He tapped the syringe and then opened the woman's arm flat onto the bed. He rested his knee on top of her forearm.

"Here we are, just what you need. Sleep, we're going on a little trip."

The needle was inserted into the vein and the plunger compressed, dispensing the fluid into the woman's bloodstream. He wiped the blood from the needle and placed the syringe and the vial back in the drawer.

It was quick. Her breath became slow and regular, and her body became still. Within thirty seconds of the injection, J.P. was once again unconscious.

Part II

Chapter 19

Thomas Liam Fowler hated working on Sundays, and after thirty-two years with the Bureau, he seldom had to. But during communion at the Hillcrest Methodist church, he got a text. The message was direct. *Needed immediately at office.* So, during the singing of "They Will Know We Are Christians by Our Love," he kissed his wife goodbye, asked his grandson to drive his grandmother home, and quietly slipped from the second pew and out the side door of the church. Twenty minutes later, Fowler was at Pennsylvania Avenue and Tenth Street, the J. Edgar Hoover building.

Fowler got off the elevator on the sixth floor and walked directly to the office of Assistant Director Robert Greenfield. He gave three short raps on the door and entered without invitation. Robert Greenfield looked up from behind his desk. The two men sitting across from him stood as Fowler walked in.

"Tom," Greenfield said, "sorry to pull you away from your family. Let me introduce you. Agent Thomas Fowler, this is Scott Douglas from State."

"Agent Fowler, pleasure," Douglas said, extending his hand.

"And this is Conrad Woo from Central Intelligence." Fowler

shot Greenfield a look as he extended his hand to the young Chinese-American.

"Good morning, Agent Fowler, pleasure."

"Likewise," he said, shaking the man's hand. "Berkeley?"

"Yes, how did you know?"

"Your class ring," Fowler said, pointing at the man's finger. "My youngest daughter is graduating from there this year—architecture."

"Congratulations, very good program—one of the best in the nation."

"Yeah, that's what they say. Thank God for scholarships."

"Indeed," Woo replied with a smile.

"Bob, what's Central Intelligence doing here?" Fowler said without segue.

Greenfield leaned back in his chair and chuckled. "Gentlemen, you've just been introduced to the famous Fowler tact. He's legendary around here for it. He should be sitting in this chair except for the fact he's as lousy at politics as he is brilliant at criminology."

"I don't want your job, Bob," Fowler came back. "You work Sundays."

Greenfield smiled. "Okay, have a seat, Tom, we'll get right to it."

The three men sat down. Greenfield leaned forward in his chair.

"We've got ops colliding, Tom. That's why CIA is here. Now that you know that, it should be obvious why State is interested."

"They want to coordinate," Fowler said, with an edge of contempt.

"No," Douglas interrupted, "not coordinate, just observe. State has no interest in interfering with your operation or the one at Central Intelligence, but for national security reasons, the Secretary thinks it would be prudent if we stayed up to speed."

Fowler said nothing but looked doubtfully at the formal man from the State department. He then looked at Woo. He wasn't sure, but he thought he detected a look of doubt on his face as well.

"Okay, Bob," Fowler said, looking at Greenfield. "What's the conflict?"

"The floor's yours, Mr. Woo," Greenfield said.

Conrad Woo nodded to the assistant director and adjusted himself in his chair to face Fowler. "A little formality first, Agent Fowler. This is of course all classified. It can't leave this room. I've been given the okay from my director to bring you into the loop."

"Son, I've been doing this since before you were born. I'm cleared."

"Of course, my apologies." Woo reached into his attaché case, removed an eight by ten photograph, and handed it to Fowler. "Four years ago this photograph was taken in Jerusalem. The man on the left is a rabbi named Ezar Bloc. Years ago, Bloc had done the impossible. He succeeded in befriending Arafat. It was Bloc's relationship with Arafat that brought Arafat and Rabin to the table for the '95 accords. He was assassinated outside a restaurant in Tel Aviv two hours after this photo was taken."

"And the other man?" Fowler asked, studying the photo.

"The man who killed him. His name is Viktor Petrovic, a.k.a. *Das Kind*. Translation: The Child."

"Why do I get the feeling he's neither *kind* nor *childlike*?"

"For lack of a better term, he's a mercenary, and the worst kind, one with an ideology. He's an assassin for hire to anyone who shares his beliefs."

"Islamic extremist?" Fowler asked.

"Believe it or not, no—white Euro-Christian superiority and a united Eastern Europe. Besides the murder of Bloc, he's suspected in at least five bombings throughout Europe, two bank robberies, and the recent kidnapping of the Israeli Ambassador's eight year-old daughter in London. He's a good Nazi, and very good at what he does."

"Okay," Fowler said, tossing the photo on Greenfield's desk. "What's this got to do with the Bureau?"

"Petrovic is on American soil," the man from State answered.

"How do you know?"

"Because you found him," Woo said, looking directly at Fowler.

Fowler glanced at Greenfield.

Woo continued, "Petrovic changes his appearance like we change our socks. It's uncanny, he can become anybody, including someone very young, thus the name *Das Kind*. After that picture with Bloc was taken, it was two days before we realized it was him. We were quicker identifying him in this picture."

Woo reached into his attaché case and pulled out another photograph.

This one Fowler recognized. "You've got to be kidding?"

The photo was of two men getting into a charcoal-gray Ford Focus in Van Nuys, California. Adhered to the bottom boarder of the photo was an FBI sticker. It read: *David Henry Webber &*_____*?*

Chapter 20

"Now you see why I'm here," Woo said, leaning back in his chair.

Fowler rubbed his forehead. "How did you get an FBI surveillance photograph?"

Douglas answered, "Given the circumstances, Agent Fowler, I hardly think that's relevant."

"You would think that, wouldn't you?" Fowler responded. He looked at the assistant director. He had known Bob Greenfield thirty years and knew this wasn't sitting well with him, either.

"You guys at Langley are shameless," Fowler said, shaking his head.

Woo responded with an emotionless stare.

Fowler continued, "Bob, why am I here? I'm sure these guys know more about the cases we're working on than we do."

Greenfield remained typically relaxed. He was a man who wasn't easily rattled, and if he were, few would ever know it. "Let's just fill them in, Bob."

"Is that an order?"

"From the very top," Greenfield answered.

Fowler sighed. "You want to save me some time and tell me what you already know, or are you going to make me start from the beginning?"

Douglas answered, "Why don't you start from the beginning, agent?"

The knot in Fowler's gut twisted tighter, but Greenfield's look told him to calm down. He reminded himself that Greenfield probably despised the arrogance of the man from the State Department as much as he did. Fowler took a deep breath and exhaled in surrender. "Okay. How much do you guys know about the mafia?"

"I saw *The Godfather*," Woo answered.

"Well, Nicholas Depriestiano makes Don Corleone look like Pope Francis."

"Old Nick, right?" Woo interjected.

"Yeah that's what he's called," Fowler responded, aware this was Woo's way of letting all in the room know he knew more than he should have known.

Fowler continued, "For the past thirty-five years, the Depriestiano family of Brooklyn has been connected to just about every illegal enterprise you can come up with: gambling, prostitution, black-market, drugs, money laundering, loan-sharking, not to mention good old-fashioned murder. Old Nick himself has shaken down half the businesses in Flatbush at one time or the other. No one's ever been able to nail him. Hell, he's never even been indicted. We're trying to change that."

"How long have you had him under surveillance?" Douglas asked.

"About a year. We got a break about six months ago."

"What kind of break?"

Fowler looked at Greenfield again. Greenfield nodded. Fowler sighed. "Anthony Depriest."

"The conductor?" Douglas said as animated as he ever got.

"Yeah. Anthony Depriest was born Antonio Depriestiano."

Woo broke in, "You mean he's Old Nick's son?"

"Nephew, but he was raised by Old Nick after his father died. So we played a hunch and put Depriest under twenty-four-hour surveillance. We figured since he'd done such a good job all these years hiding the fact he's Old Nick's nephew, he might be hiding other family secrets as well."

"And it paid off," Woo stated.

Fowler looked again at Greenfield. Greenfield nodded once more. Fowler rolled his eyes. "Depriest currently has a business deal with the family."

"The missing Mozart," Woo stated matter-of-factly.

This brought Fowler out of his seat. "Jesus Christ! What don't you know?"

"Tom," Greenfield ordered.

Fowler sat down and put his hand over his mouth. His eyes were on fire.

"What we don't know," Woo answered, "is the whereabouts of Viktor Petrovic, and that's all we care to know. He's on US soil. That's why we need the bureau's help."

"Is Petrovic in cahoots with Depriest?" Greenfield asked.

"Not likely. Petrovic works alone," Woo answered.

"So what does he want?"

Woo said, "The same thing Depriestiano wants, the Mozart. The only difference being what they do with the money. Petrovic has visions of a new Fourth Reich and anointing himself Fuehrer. With the money he'd make from the sale of the piece, he could do it."

"You're not serious?" Fowler blurted.

Douglas answered, "Painfully so. At last count, no less than fifteen countries, all seething anti-West sentiment, are making overtures to their new leader, Viktor Petrovic."

"How much is this damn thing worth, anyway?" Greenfield asked.

"Enough," Woo answered.

Douglas shifted gears. "Why is this picture in the Depriestiano file, Agent Fowler? How does David Henry Webber play into this?"

"We're not sure is the answer to the second question. The answer to the first is simple. Two of Depriestiano's wise guys were sent to L.A. last week. They were tailing a retired music professor from Juilliard named Henry Shoewalter. Since the old guy was a music professor, we assumed he was connected to Depriest, so we followed them. Early Friday morning Shoewalter turns up dead, and this David Webber fellow is arrested. Webber's a new player, it was the first we'd ever heard of him. The picture you have was taken as he was being released from custody, which is why it's in *our* file," Fowler said to Woo. "We've been working overtime trying to find out who the other guy is. We assumed he was one of Old Nick's men. Thanks for clearing up the mystery."

"Does LAPD know about the surveillance?" Woo asked.

"No."

"Is that protocol?"

Fowler chuckled. "Are you kidding me? *You're* talking about protocol?"

"Tom," Greenfield snapped.

Fowler raised his hand. "We know Depriestiano has moles inside the LAPD."

Woo nodded. "I assume you still have Depriestiano's men covered?"

"Depriestiano's wise guys are MIA."

"What happened to them?" Douglas asked.

"We don't know, otherwise they wouldn't be MIA."

All were silent until Woo uttered mechanically, "Petrovic."

"When was Petrovic last seen?" Douglas asked.

"Yesterday," Fowler said. "Two agents were assigned to cover Webber. He had breakfast with him. LAPD is also tailing Webber. I'm sure they're as confounded as we are—or *were*—about who the other guy is."

Douglas stood with authority. "Can we get him?"

Fowler looked up with disgust. "Yeah, we'll get him. It'll give us away to Depriestiano and a year's worth of work goes down the tubes, but we'll get him."

"Maybe not, Tom," Greenfield said. "If Petrovic is freelance, then Old Nick probably isn't even aware of him."

Douglas stood. "Gentlemen, I said I was here to just observe. I meant it. You're the professionals, so I'll stay out of your way."

"Agent Fowler," Woo added, "this shouldn't hamper your

Depriestiano op. We just need to get Petrovic—alive if possible. Given the crowd he runs with, the potential intel is invaluable."

Fowler nodded.

"Tom, do we know Petrovic's current whereabouts?" Greenfield asked.

"No. But he'll contact Webber again. Then he's ours."

"Be careful, Agent Fowler," Woo said as he stood. "Petrovic is a very dangerous man. Make sure you've got a small army when you take him."

"Thanks for the advice," Fowler responded. "We'll handle it."

Douglas headed for the door. "Assistant Director, I assume you will instigate an open line of communication with Mr. Woo?"

"Of course," Greenfield answered.

Douglas turned for the door with Woo behind.

"So," Fowler said, "you guys seem to know everything else. Do you know where this mysterious Mozart music is?"

Woo and Douglas looked at each other, but it was Douglas who answered, "No. We have no idea where it is. Do you?"

Fowler cracked a half smile. "No. No idea at all."

DOUGLAS AND WOO exited the elevator into the FBI's subterranean parking garage. Douglas looked straight ahead as he spoke. "You were good up there."

"Thanks," Woo replied.

"Any chance they could actually get Petrovic?"

"None. Fowler's a dinosaur. He won't get within fifty feet of him. God help him if he does. But he'll lead us to him."

Douglas nodded. "Status in Pyongyang?"

"The general's scheduled to be in Hong Kong in seven days."

Douglas stopped. "Not much time. Are we ready?"

Woo nodded. "Everything's in place. Just one missing ingredient."

"Indeed, just one missing ingredient," Douglas said, opening his car door.

"So why didn't we tell them what the Mozart piece really is?"

Douglas got in the car, looked up at Woo, and smiled. "Because then we'd have to tell them how we know that bit of information, wouldn't we?"

"So? We explain it to them."

"Mr. Woo," Douglas said, starting the black sedan, "after twenty-two years in government and four Presidents, you learn a few fundamental truths."

"And those would be?"

"Keep it simple."

Woo didn't reply.

Douglas continued, "Find Petrovic, that's all they need to know."

"And David Webber? He's not part of this. We could have at least told them he didn't kill Professor Henry Shoewalter."

"That's where you're wrong, Mr. Woo. Webber is a big part of this. He's also a walking testament to another truth."

Woo raised an eyebrow.

Douglas smiled and shifted the car into drive. "Chaos brings results."

Chapter 21

The calliope played at a deafening volume, getting louder as the merry-go-round spun faster. David sat on a snow-white steed, tremulously holding onto the pole, pushing his left ear against his left shoulder in an attempt to muffle the agonizing cacophony. Then, in a moment of painful desperation, he raised both hands to his ears, completely letting go of the pole. The carousel continued to speed up. David felt the inside of his thighs begin to burn from the strain of hanging onto the giant horse. Finally, David was hurled into the air, spinning and twisting with no discernible design as he flew through black empty space.

He landed hard on concrete, but felt no pain. He looked up and saw off in the distance Joshua Bowen running toward him. He tried calling out but couldn't make the air go over his larynx. Then he felt it, dampness soaking through his pants and onto his skin. He looked down and saw that his legs were gone, sunken into the cement. The concrete was now quicksand, and his torso was all that was now visible. He could barely move his arms. They were so heavy from the weight of the morass. He looked for Bowen again. He was still running toward him but not getting any closer. He tried calling out, but still no sound. He was sinking, sinking, sinking.

"Housekeeping," the female voice bellowed, accompanied by three knocks.

David sprung up, unsure of his surroundings. He struggled out of bed and stumbled to the door. Looking through the peephole, he saw a small black woman, all in white, standing patiently behind her cart. He felt a sudden pang of fear before he spoke. "Can you come back later? I'm just getting up," he said, for some reason surprised and relieved by the sound of his own croupy voice.

"Sorry to disturb you, sir," came the reply through the door.

David rubbed his eyes and looked at the clock on the nightstand. It was 10:22 a.m., 7:22 a.m. by his internal West Coast clock. Left-over pizza, an empty cigarette box, and an emptied bottle of Jim Beam flanked the clock. The last time he remembered looking, it read four thirty a.m.

Ravel was wound on the bed, nose snuggled between the mattress and the headboard. He hadn't budged since being let out of his cage following David's clandestine operation of sneaking him past the front desk and up to the room. Many were impressed with the fancy downtown Washington, DC, hotel. Ravel wasn't one of them. Neither was David. To him, it was too small and insanely overpriced. But given its location, roughly six blocks from the Smithsonian, the free transportation to and from Reagan National, and the fact he hadn't had a vacation since…forever, David decided, *what the hell, I got a Visa.*

It was an hour, a shower, and a cup of coffee later before David felt cognizant and the pounding in his head had subsided. Even Ravel had grown more comfortable with the surroundings, finally venturing off the bed to the bowl of food David had placed under the wash basin, along with a makeshift litterbox David had constructed from the pizza box—the litter came courtesy of the drug store on the corner. The cat was crunching away as David, now in jeans and a white button-down, picked up the telephone and dialed.

This is Joshua Bowen, please leave a message.

"Bowen, it's Webber again. Don't you ever pickup? I left you a couple of messages last night, so you should have my number here at the hotel—again, I'm in room 1470, okay? I'm heading over to the Smithsonian now. Call me. If I'm not here, leave me a message and let me know when I can get a hold of you. I've been doing like you asked and going over the sketch. I found some interesting things, I...so—" David stumbled for something else to say. He really wanted to talk to Bowen. Not because he actually had any new information on the Mozart, he didn't, He just needed to talk. He needed to hear again he wasn't alone. "Well, okay, call me, all right?"

David hung up the telephone and ran his hand through his damp hair. He slipped on a pair of brown loafers, grabbed his brief-case, the room keycard off the desk, and headed for the door. Ravel stopped eating and looked up at him as he unlocked the deadbolt. "Shit, what am I going to do about you?"

David picked up the purring cat, stroked its head, and returned him back to the pillow on the bed. He picked up the phone again.

"Hi, this is David Webber in room 1470. I'll be working all day in my room and won't require maid service. In fact, I won't for my entire stay. Can you please inform housekeeping to just leave fresh towels outside my door? Thank you."

"There you go, buddy," David said, picking up his briefcase again. "You have the place all to yourself. I'll even turn on the TV for you. Don't order room service. We can't afford this hole as it is."

SIX ROOMS down from David's sat an abandoned maid's cart. As David stepped into the elevator, a maid emerged from a room. She lifted a stack of towels off the second shelf of the cart and retrieved a small, black rectangular object. Looking both ways down the hall-way, she raised her wrist to her mouth. "He's coming down, car number three, blue jeans, white shirt."

"I'm on him, hold for clear," came the reply.

"Holding," the woman said, her eyes continuing to scan the hallway.

The voice came back, "Okay, he's out of the hotel. Do your stuff, Sheila."

The woman pushed her cart back in front of room 1470, with-drew a keycard, and inserted it into the door.

HE NEVER NOTICED it when he was growing up, but now it was like breathing paste. David stood in front of the hotel already wiping sweat from his brow. Twelve years in L.A. had spoiled him, weakened his resistance to the humidity of the East coast. He unfolded a map he'd gotten from the concierge and turned it three different times before coordinating his position. Then, with a wipe to his forehead, he entered the herd of sightseers trampling down Tenth Street.

A taxi would be faster, and sightseeing was the last thing on his mind, but there was one historic place he wanted to see, and if he walked, it was on his way—plus he needed to move. He had begun to think he'd gone in the wrong direction, but just after crossing F Street, he saw it, Ford's Theatre.

David's interest in Abraham Lincoln had started as a child. The first time he heard the story of the Great Emancipator, his humor, his honor, his bravery, he was hooked. As an adult, his fascination with the sixteenth president never waned. He was one of the few human beings David Webber actually admired. He remembered J.P. saying to him how ironic that was. *"It's hard to believe, luv, that such a hopeless and cynical bastard like you would be drawn to the epitome of hopefulness and virtue."*

As he stood in front of the infamous theatre, a quiet shiver raced through his body. He was amazed at how bland it seemed, how unimportant. Disgust ran through his body when he noticed the Hard Rock Café that had been built beside the theater, practically connected to each other. David looked through the old box office window. As he gazed at a photograph of Lincoln memorialized inside the theater's door, the faces of Henry and J.P. burned in his mind. He turned and began walking again.

Twenty minutes later David leaned against a tree beside a concession stand, smoking a cigarette and gulping a can of Coke. Just across Madison Drive, roughly two hundred feet away, David stared at the pinkish-white marble building, The Smithsonian Institution, National Museum of American History. He took one last puff of his smoke, tossed the soda can in the bin beside him, and headed for the entrance. It was time to get some answers.

A BEARDED MAN with a black ponytail sat cross-legged on the grass several yards away from where David was standing. He wore tan hiking shorts, a tie-dyed T-shirt, and a Yankees' baseball cap. Around his neck hung a camera. He lifted the camera and aimed the telescopic lens in David's direction. Then he panned west toward the Washington Monument. The image through the viewfinder, however, was not of the famous statue but of two men, casually dressed, aiming cameras of their own.

He watched as the men lowered their cameras and jogged toward the museum. He panned to the museum's entrance just as David walked through the glass doors. He lowered his camera, picked up a black bag, and followed.

Chapter 22

The elderly woman sitting at the information desk loved her job. David tapped his fingers on the counter while the woman spoke enthusiastically, and in detail, to a young couple from Ames, Iowa, on everything the National Museum of American History had to offer. When the couple finally stepped away from the counter, David approached.

"How may I help you, sir?"

"I'm looking for a Dr. Danny Parsons," David demanded more than asked.

"Dr. Parsons," her smile fading. "Does he work for the institution?"

"Yes, I'm looking for his office."

"Uh...oh my...I'm sorry, sir," the woman mumbled, frantically scanning down a clipboard, noticeably unnerved at David's very untourist-like manner, "that's a little out of my area. I'm not familiar with all the curators here at the museum—we have so many—and all the offices on the fourth and fifth floors are closed. Uh, what department is he in?"

"Music."

"Music," the woman muttered. "Well, uh...I'm sorry. All I can suggest is that you go to the third floor Archives Center and inquire at the desk up there if they know him. They have more direct contact with the music division."

David nodded. "Third floor, got it."

"Yes, east wing, third floor, the elevators are right around the corner, sir."

As David turned in the direction the woman was pointing, a shrill howl bellowed from his knee area.

"What the fu...!" David stifled his vulgarity when he looked down and saw a small boy lifting himself off the marble floor. Oblivious to the near collision, the boy continued his pursuit of another slightly older boy racing around David's back.

"Jeremiah, Zechariah, boys watch where you're goin'," commanded the old African-American man in the white Panama hat and bright yellow T-shirt boasting the words WORLD'S GREATEST GRANDPA across the chest.

"I'm sorry, sir," the man said with a flustered smile and thick Mississippi-drawl, grabbing the smaller of the two youngsters by the arm. "They's young and fast, and I'm just too cotton-pickin' old and slow."

"No problem," David replied, remaining intent on the elevators.

"Sir, excuse me for eavesdropping, but I couldn't help overhearing. You looking for Dr. P?"

David stopped and looked back at the old man. "Uh...yeah... Dr. Parsons. You know Dr. Parsons?"

"Oh yes, me and the doc are old friends—but Dr. P's not in today."

"Do you work with Dr. Parsons?"

"Sure do. I'm security here. This is my day off, but I got my grandchildren today, so—"

"So Parsons won't be in 'til tomorrow then, right?"

"Right—tomorrow but—"

"Do you know what time?"

The old man laughed. "Well, now with Dr. P, that could be just about any time. You see, Dr. P has some trouble with time—always kinda runnin' a step behind the ol' tomato cart."

Tomorrow damn it, more waiting. "Okay thanks, I'll come back tomorrow."

"'But if you'd liked to see Dr. P today, you know you can."

David stopped. "I can? How?"

"That's what I've been trying to tell you, son. The doc's in a little musical group that plays around here sometimes—heck of a fiddle player, Dr. P is."

"Where, what time?"

"Well, right now, in the garden over at the castle."

"The castle?"

"The old Smithsonian building across the Mall. They're having a birthday party for one of the uppity-ups here at the institution, but it's outside and all are welcome. I'm taking the young'uns there now. Come on, walk with us."

"The name's Charlie, Charlie Cheevers," Charlie said, extending his hand as the two men stepped onto the thick green grass of the Mall and the two small boys raced ahead.

"David Webber," David said, taking the man's hand.

"Now, I'm not gonna get in any trouble with Dr. P, am I?"

"What do you mean?"

"You're not some bill collector or somebody the doc ain't gonna wanna see."

David's anxiety was growing with every step. He just wanted to take off running to meet Parsons face to face and start getting some answers about Henry. Instead, he was forced to slow his gait to that of the older man's.

"No, nothing like that. I just need to ask a musical question. You're not going to get in any trouble."

"Where you from, David? It is all right I call you David, isn't it?"

"Yeah, sure, I'm from L.A."

"Ooo-wee, Los Angeles. I was out there once, back in my Army days. Spent two—no, three nights there before getting shipped out. Mighty big ol' place, always something going on. And you can call me Charlie."

"Yeah, there sure is, Charlie, there sure is."

"So, are you a doctor yourself, David?"

"A doctor?"

"Yeah, you know, like Dr. P."

David had to chuckle at the mere thought. "No, I'm just a piano player."

"A piano player, you say? Well, that's mighty fine, mighty fine."

David looked at the grinning old man. His teeth were almost the color of his shirt, but there was sincerity in his eyes and warmth to his voice. David felt this man actually thought being a piano player was truly mighty fine.

For several minutes the two walked in silence, Charlie having to periodically corral the two young boys from running too far off. David's brain sizzled. How would he introduce himself to Parsons and how would he break the news about Henry?

"Well, there it is."

David was mildly startled by Charlie's pronouncement. He had paid no attention to where he was walking. He looked ahead and saw the impressive structure towering above the sycamores. It was aptly named The Castle. The red sandstone palace looked like something out of a fairy tale.

"Wow," David whispered, unconsciously counting the steeples that jutted from the edifice.

"You can say that again. I've worked here for purtin' near forty years, and I still get all stirred up inside when I see it. Built in eighteen fifty-five, it's the original Smithsonian Institution building. The fella that designed it also did St. Patrick's Cathedral in New York City, ain't that something?"

"Yeah, it is. So, where's this party?"

"It's just 'round the corner, you follow me."

Charlie wrangled the two raucous boys by their hands, and David followed as the old man led them across Jefferson Drive and between two small buildings to the right of the castle. A cool breeze accompanied the momentary relief from the sun, and David began hearing music faintly blowing through the blooming Magnolia trees that canopied the crushed gravel and sand pathway—*Strauss*, he thought to himself, *small orchestra*.

David winced as they turned the corner and emerged from the

shade into the afternoon sunlight bathing the lush floral landscape in front of the castle.

"Here we are, Haupt Garden."

A red brick pathway lined with cherry-blossom trees wound through the deep blue-green grass of the garden. As David and the trio strolled further into the garden, he began having to excuse himself around an increasing number of people holding paper cups and plates, and either standing around or sitting comfortably on wrought-iron benches. The crowd grew denser the closer they came to the castle's entrance. David saw who he suspected was the guest of honor smiling and shaking hands with well-wishers.

"Looks like the party's in full stride," Charlie said, keeping a tight grip on his boys.

The clustered mass made it difficult to move and impossible to see where the music was coming from. David climbed on one of the benches, turned, and surveyed the grounds.

People milled around everywhere, and though David heard the music, he was unable to see where the orchestra was located. He focused on the center of the park-like yard where a large rectangular flowerbed bursting with a colorful array of pansies, Chrysanthemums, and daisies spanned the length of the castle. He panned up the flowerbed. "Charlie, the orchestra's over there," he said, looking like a ship's lookout pointing over the partygoers' heads.

David followed Charlie and the boys down the brick pathway toward the other end of the garden, happily finding the crowd thinning out the farther they moved away from the building's entrance. Nevertheless, David still briefly lost sight of Charlie and the boys when he was held up by a group of people congregating in the middle of the pathway. David pushed through and was relieved to see the back of Charlie's white Panama hat bobbing up and down.

Some people were sitting with their eyes closed, some were standing and bouncing their heads like Charlie, and some were even dancing. The small orchestra of fifteen musicians sat on a slightly raised platform facing back into the garden. They were indeed playing a Strauss waltz. David walked up beside the old man. Charlie smiled and pointed to the stage.

"That's Dr. P right there."

"Where?" David asked, searching every face in the orchestra.

"There, playing that big ol' fiddle."

David looked where Charlie was pointing and saw two men and one woman sitting in the first row, each with their backs arched bowing a cello.

"Which one is Dr. Parsons?"

Charlie smiled. "That's easy, Doctor P. is the pretty one."

Chapter 23

A smattering of applause rippled through the garden when Paul Rogers let his arms fall to his side. He turned and dropped his head in a humble bow. Dennis Beckman sauntered onto the platform and up to the microphone.

"Thank you, Dr. Rogers and orchestra, that was lovely," he said with a too-big smile. "Let's give them another hand, shall we? The Smithsonian Chamber Orchestra, ladies and gentlemen." Beckman stepped to the side and delicately clapped his hands as Paul bowed his head again and then extended his arm acknowledging the orchestra.

"Thank you, Dr. Rogers, and thank all of you. This has been such a special day. I'm overwhelmed, so I'll just leave you with a most humble thank you." The audience applauded. Paul turned to the orchestra and nodded. One by one the musicians began to rise and pack up their instruments.

Dani was shaking hands with her fellow cellists when Paul approached. "Congratulations, Maestro," Dani said.

"He hated it."

"What are you talking about?"

"He hated it. I shouldn't have played Strauss. He hates Strauss."

"Paul, you're being ridiculous. Didn't you hear him, he said—"

"Yeah, I heard him, 'thank you Dr. Rogers, that was *lovely.*' Dr. Rogers, not Paul. Lovely, not wonderful—he hated it."

"Paul, will you relax, he liked it—he loved it."

"Doctor P.," a voice came from the crowd. "Doctor P."

Dani scanned the front of the stage. She grinned when she saw the Panama hat riding over the wave of heads below. "Charlie, you made it."

"Of course I did, Doctor P., wouldn't have missed it for nothing."

"Hang on, I'll come down there." Dani patted Paul on the arm and then walked to the corner of the stage and down the stairs.

She wore a tailored black sheath dress with a pearl barrette holding back her chestnut hair, allowing only a single highlighted curly wisp to dangle down each side of her face.

Charlie was standing with his grandsons in front of him, one hand on each of the youngsters' shoulders.

"Hi, good lookin'," Dani said, kissing Charlie on the cheek as the two boys giggled. "Good heavens." She put both hands over her heart. "Jeremiah and Zechariah, look at you boys. Charlie, are you sure I can't date these young men? They're about the handsomest gentlemen I've ever seen."

"Oh, I don't know. They'd just break your heart, these two would."

"No we wouldn't, Pappa."

"Uh-huh, Pappa."

Dani laughed and rubbed both boys on the head. "Like grandfather, like grandsons, right, Charlie?"

Charlie let out a husky laugh.

"So, did you enjoy the concert?"

"Oh my yes, y'all were really playing now."

"Hear that, Paul?" Dani said as Paul was coming down the stairs.

"Hear what?" Paul replied, walking up.

"Dr. Rogers, you're really something. Boy, oh boy, I just don't see how you keep all them people playing together like you do."

"Thank you, Charlie."

David nudged the back of Charlie's hand.

"I'm sorry, where are my manners? Doctor P., Doctor Rogers, I'd like you to meet a new friend of mine. This is David Webber from Los Angeles."

David stepped around and extended his hand, first to Paul and then to Dani.

"Pleasure to meet you, Mr. Webber," Paul said.

"Hi there, David Webber, welcome to Washington. Did you enjoy the concert?" Dani asked with a perky smile.

He didn't know who, or what, he was expecting, but *she* wasn't it. "I did. It was very good," David answered.

"See, Paul, another satisfied customer. Now stop worrying."

"What're you worried about, Dr. Rogers?"

"He's afraid Beckman didn't like the concert because we played Strauss and Beckman hates Strauss."

"Well, I thought it was wonderful, didn't you, David?"

"Yes," David mumbled again.

"And he would know too, he's a piano player."

"Really," Dani responded. "Professionally?"

"Uh, yeah," David stammered as he wrestled with how to bring up the subject of Henry. "Just bars, clubs, places like that."

"Oh, I see," Dani responded. "Charlie, you're full of surprises. How do you know a piano player from L.A.?"

Charlie laughed, putting his hand on David's shoulder. "Well, I met him over at the museum. He was looking for you."

Dani looked at David, then Paul, then Charlie, and then back to David.

"Me? You were looking for me, Mr. Webber?"

"Uh, yes, Dr. Parsons, I was."

"Why?"

David swallowed hard and decided it was time to get on with it. "Dr. Parsons, may I speak to you in private for a moment?"

"Private?" Dani said, glancing again at Paul.

"Yes, may we speak in private?"

"Why?"

"Uh…I'd really rather tell you in private, Dr. Parsons."

"What's this about, Mr. Webber?" Paul asked.

"Dr. Parsons, if you don't mind—"

Dani's smile suddenly fell. Her knees went numb, and a rush of heat surged through her body. Her weight fell onto Paul as Charlie moved quickly to grab her by the arm. "Is this about my father—is he okay—has something happened to my dad?" Dani cried out as her eyes began to tear-up.

"Your father? Uh—no this doesn't have anything to do with your father—"

"Mr. Webber, what's this all about?" Paul demanded.

"David?" Charlie said, his trademark smile totally absent.

"I'm sorry. I didn't mean to scare her. I just need to ask her a couple of questions about…a mutual friend. Dr. Parsons, I'm sorry, but this will only take a few minutes, and it's very important."

"David, perhaps this could wait 'til later?" Charlie said.

"No, it can't," David snapped.

"Well, maybe it just has to, Mr. Webber," Paul said back.

"No, Paul, Charlie, it's okay," Dani broke in, regaining her composure. "I'm sorry, Mr. Webber, my father's 's been ill, and I thought that you were—"

"I understand," David said. "I'm sorry I scared you."

"No, it was my fault for jumping to conclusions." Dani took a deep breath and exhaled with a smile. "Whew, I really need to get a grip. Me, falling into the arms of two men, can you believe it?"

Charlie laughed out loud. Paul was less amused.

"So, you say we have a mutual friend?"

"Yes, I believe we do."

"Can I ask who the friend is?"

Dani caught the frustration on David's face.

"Got it—in private. Okay, Mr. Webber, tell you what. I was just leaving. If you'd like to walk with me to my car, we can talk on the way."

"That'll be fine."

"Great, you can carry my cello."

Paul's arm was still around Dani's waist. "Dan, are you sure you're okay? I'll be glad to walk with you to your car."

Dani smiled and pulled away. "I'm fine, Paul. I'll see you tomorrow."

"Yeah." Paul surrendered, letting his arm fall.

"Will I see you in the morning, Charlie?"

"No, ma'am. I got the late shift next week, but I'll see you after five."

"Okay, then. Hey, where'd your boys go to? I wanted to say goodbye." Dani asked, looking around.

Charlie looked down. "Oh lordy, where'd those rascals run off to?"

Paul pointed to the stage. "There they are, by the tympani."

Charlie took off for the stage. "Jeremiah, Zechariah, you boys get away from there. That's not a toy for you two hoodlums. I'll be seeing you, David. Nice to have met you."

David allowed a smile. "You too, Charlie, and thank you."

"Call me when you get home, okay, Dan?" Paul said, looking at David.

"I will," Dani replied with a kiss on his cheek. "And, Paul, you did great. I'm sure Beckman is very pleased."

Paul let go of a smile. "Good afternoon, Mr. Webber, enjoy your stay."

"Thank you," David replied without expression.

"Well, shall we, Mr. Webber?"

"Yes, thank you, Dr. Parsons."

"Oh please, eighty-six the doctor stuff, call me Dani."

"All right, I'm David."

DANI HAD TRADED her black pumps for white Nikes. David struggled to keep up with her runner's pace as the two exited the garden on the east side of the castle behind the Arts and Industry building.

"Okay, David, what can I do for you? Who's this friend of ours?"

"Could we slow down? This cello isn't exactly light, and I'm in no shape for a sprint."

Dani stopped. "I'm sorry, old habit. I'm usually late for something or another, so racing around this place feels very natural to me."

"Yeah, so I hear."

Dani shot David a questioning look, and David responded quickly, "Charlie."

Dani nodded. "Got it."

"Dani, uh…" David stumbled, not knowing how to start as they began walking again—this time much slower. "I'm a friend of Henry Shoewalter."

David held his breath.

"Yes?" Dani came back.

David's heart began beating faster—it was time to go for broke. "Dani, I'm afraid I have some very bad news. Henry is dead."

Dani stopped. "That's terrible. I'm very sorry."

"Yeah, it is terrible. Dani…I need to know what you and—"

Dani interrupted, "But I don't know any Henry Shoewalter."

David was silent for a moment, and then he looked hard into Dani's eyes. "You don't understand. I'm a friend of Henry's. You can trust me."

Dani looked back just as hard. "I don't know what you're talking about."

A volcano began churning in the pit of David's stomach. This couldn't be a dead end. He wouldn't accept it, not after what he'd been through.

"I know Henry was in contact with you," David said with more edge.

"In contact with me?"

"Yes, I know Henry was in contact with you."

"David, I'm sorry for your loss, but I don't know—"

"He had your number when he died," David shouted, his jaw clenched, his eyes turning to fire. "What were you two working on? You've gotta tell me."

Dani's mouth dropped. She widened the space between her and David and began looking around to see if there were people nearby.

David felt all control slipping away. *Why is she lying?* He closed his eyes and took a deep breath. His mind began flashing on snapshots of Henry and J.P., the police, and the interrogation. He spoke softly, "I'm sorry, I shouldn't have shouted, I just…uh, Henry was, uh… and you and he were…an address book with your number." He was shocked when he heard his own voice shouting again. He wasn't doing it, the voice wasn't connected to his body, but it was his voice. "I've got to know! I've got to know!"

Dani flinched. "Look, I don't know who you are, but this is getting weird. I told you, I don't know your friend, and I certainly don't know why he had my phone number. I swear I've never spoken to a Henry Shoewalter before in——"

"Stop lying!" David shouted, dropping the case and falling to the ground.

He rubbed his hands over his face. *Why was this happening?* He looked up at the young woman. He could see from her expression he'd scared her.

When Dani spoke, it was almost comically calm. "So, listen, David, I'm sorry I can't be of more help, but…it was nice meeting you…." She moved closer, and once she got within inches of her instrument case, she snatched it and began backing up again. "There's no need for you to walk me to my car, I'll take it from here. So, good luck…I hope you…have a nice…goodbye, Mr.… David."

David said nothing as Dani hustled away. Twenty yards into her escape, he saw her glance back at him. Then to David's surprise, she stopped, turned, and came back.

"Listen, are you okay? Can I do anything? Call anybody?"

David shook his head.

"But, are you okay?" she asked again.

David nodded. "Yes."

"Do you need a lift somewhere, or anything like that?"

"No," David answered. "I'm sorry I uh——"

"Freaked out?"

She wasn't trying to be funny, but her honesty forced him to smile. "Yeah, I guess that's what I did, didn't I?"

"Yeah, I think that's what they call it."

David looked at the pretty young woman. Her face was open and honest. She wasn't lying. She wasn't hiding anything. He had a sense that for this person deception was completely unknown. Unfortunately, that also meant she truly didn't know Henry, and he had come to Washington, DC, for nothing.

"Have you eaten lunch?" Dani asked.

"Lunch?" David thought for a second. "No, I haven't eaten for a while."

"Well, that's your problem. I tell you what. I was going to grab a salad at this little place at the museum. Would you like to join me?"

David was about to decline when—

"If you'd like, we can talk more about your friend I'm supposed to know."

"Really?"

"Yeah. I mean he had my phone number, so maybe we can figure out why."

David let out a breath. "That'd be great."

"Let me drop this elephant off at my car first. I promise to keep it to a jog."

David started to stand.

"By the way, how did your friend die?"

"He was murdered," David said bluntly as he lifted himself off the grass.

Dani's face went flush. "Oh my. Murdered? By who?"

"The police don't know, but they think me. Lead the way."

Dani swallowed hard as the two started walking across the Mall.

"HER NAME IS Dr. Dani Parsons. She's a curator at the Museum of American History," said the voice over the radio.

Fowler listened as he sat in his car on Jefferson Drive and Fourteenth. "Any sign of a Depriestiano, Agent Sanders?"

"Negative, sir."

"How about our other friend?"

"Negative. No sign of Petrovic."

"Well, from what I understand, he could be sitting on your lap and you still wouldn't notice him. Are you getting pictures of the perimeter?"

"Affirmative, everybody within two hundred yards of Webber."

"Good. Okay, here's the drill. Sanders, I want you to stay on Webber and the girl. I want Stevens back at the office to download the pictures. Mr. Woo is waiting—he'll assist in analyzing the photos. Got it?"

"Yes, sir. Stevens is on his way now—out."

Fowler's cell phone rang.

"Fowler."

"Tom, it's Bob."

"Long time no talk. What can I do for you, Assistant Director?"

"Any sign of Petrovic?"

"No, not yet. But we got Webber covered like a blanket. We'll find him."

"Find him fast, Tom."

Fowler could hear the tension in the man's voice.

"What's happened, Bob?"

"An LAPD lieutenant who was investigating the Shoewalter murder. He was killed yesterday evening—car bomb. The Los Angeles DA is on his way to DC right now. He's asked for the bureau's help."

"Lord," Fowler breathed.

"Yeah. They want Webber."

"Bob, I don't think Webber has anything to do with a car bombing, or the Shoewalter murder for that matter."

"Tom, pictures don't lie. He is connected to Petrovic somehow."

"Yeah, if he knows it's Petrovic."

"What do you mean?"

"I have a suspicion David Webber is the proverbial unlucky man in the wrong place at the right time."

"How about Depriestiano? Have you connected Webber to the family?"

"Only that he and Anthony Depriest were in college together."

"So, when do we decide to bring him in?"

"When we're sure. Right now he's all we got to get Petrovic."

"Okay, but it means we come clean with the DA. It's the only way to keep the DC police from picking up Webber themselves."

Fowler sighed. "All right, we tell the DA. Just make sure it's hands off Webber. One other thing, Bob. How well do you know Douglas and Woo?"

"Woo not at all. Douglas has been around for years. Typical bureaucrat, a real beltway operator. Why?"

"Because I have a feeling they weren't exactly forthcoming with us."

"What makes you say that?"

"Call it a hunch, Bob. Just a good old-fashioned hunch."

THE MAN with the ponytail and ball cap lay prostrate on the grass. As David and Dani neared, he placed his camera to his side and rolled over. David and Dani passed, giving no attention to the lounging tourist.

Chapter 24

Los Angeles police detective Stuart Gilbert stood at the outermost end of the Santa Monica pier tossing bread crumbs from a plastic bag into the cold gray water below. A stubborn marine layer hung over the ocean, explaining the unseasonably brisk spring morning and the reason why the otherwise bustling pier was almost deserted. Except for the honking armada of gulls swarming above his head, the policeman was alone.

He didn't turn around when he heard the clacking of the wooden planks behind him. He was expecting the arrival. Gilbert glanced at the man and smiled. The portly man's nose was completely covered with tape and bandage.

"Look at the bright side," Gilbert said, staring out at the crashing waves.

The man looked at him bewildered.

"The ocean these days is nothing but sewage. At least you can't smell it."

"I thought this was supposed to be paradise? I'm freezing my ass off."

"No, paradise is Hawaii. This is California, land of fruits and nuts."

"Huh, you got that right. I hate this fucking place. You Gilbert?"

"Yeah."

"All right, whatta ya got for me?"

"Well, that depends. Whatta ya got for me?"

The man withdrew a bundle wrapped in deli paper and set it on the wooden railing. "You need to count it?"

"Nope. Old Nick's never screwed me before," Gilbert said, stuffing the package in the pocket of his hooded sweatshirt. "Doubt he's going start now."

Gilbert scanned the pier. "Would you mind?"

The man rolled his eyes and raised his arms. Gilbert went down the man's body with his hands, giving special attention to his abdomen and chest area.

"Satisfied?" the man said, lowering his arms.

"Thanks." Gilbert turned back toward the ocean. "Everyone is loony over Ryan's murder. The chief is personally overseeing the case. DA's involved too."

"Where's Webber?"

"DC—at least I think he is. Before Ryan was blown to smithereens, he gave explicit orders not to touch him, no matter what. So we didn't. He boarded the plane and was off before we knew anything about Ryan getting toasted."

"That was stupid."

"Yeah, not one of our finer moments. We're coordinating with the FBI."

"That's it?"

"That's it."

"Any idea why he's in DC?"

"Haven't the faintest."

The man nodded. "Okay, I'll pass it on. I'm sure Old Nick will still want you to keep your ears open. This could turn out to be very profitable for you."

"Hey, I didn't get myself assigned to this case for nothing. Tell Old Nick I'm here for him. Does it hurt?" Gilbert asked, looking at the man's nose.

"Only my pride. I could've beaten the shit out of that faggot, but—"

"Yeah, I know. Old Nick does have a way, doesn't he?"

"Yeah, he does," the man said, rubbing his thumb and middle finger together. "I'm going home. I got a real business to run."

"Where's that?"

"Joplin. You ever need ball bearings, look me up. Name's Harshbarger."

ANTHONY delicately spread butter over a small slice of sourdough and listened to his cousin's report. The cafe, as usual for a Sunday afternoon, was busy, so Jimmy was forced to lean across the table to keep from being heard by surrounding diners.

"That's it. Harshbarger says Webber's in DC."

"Are they going to arrest him when they find him?"

"They can't connect him to the cop's death, so—"

"So they just want to make sure they know where he is."

"Yeah, that's what it sounds like."

"That's all you have?"

"That's everything."

"Okay, Jimmy, good work. Now get lost."

"Hey, the least you could do is buy me a freakin' lunch. I'm starvin'."

"Another time, James. Did you drive your car here, or did you take a cab?"

"It's Jimmy, and I drove myself. Why?"

"Good. I want you to go to your car and wait. Kathryn will be here shortly. When she leaves, follow her, and I mean follow her, cousin, wherever she goes. Don't lose her, and don't let her see you. Do you understand?"

"Yeah, sure, but where do you think she'll go?"

"Just do it, Jimmy. You got it?"

"Yeah, I got it."

"Good. Also, see who your father knows at the FBI."

Jimmy nodded.

"There she is, now beat it."

Beautiful and fashionable people are not in short supply on the Upper West Side of Manhattan. But when Kathryn walked through the upscale Central Park cafe, heads turned. She moved like a runway model, eyes fixed, walking with purpose. Her blonde hair was pulled up, showing off her evenly tanned shoulders, and her aqua-green sundress danced around the tops of her smooth long legs.

Jimmy stood just as Kathryn arrived at the table.

"Not leaving on my account are you, Jimmy?"

Anthony spoke before Jimmy could respond, "Jimmy was leaving anyway."

"Sure you can't stay for lunch? I see you didn't eat."

Jimmy started to answer, but again was interrupted.

"I tried, dear. Seems my cousin is in demand these days. Jimmy, do try to make some time to dine with Kathryn and me. It's been such a long time since the three of us have had a chance to catch up."

"Yeah, I'll do that. Well, I gotta get going. Good to see you, Kathryn...you sure look righteous."

Kathryn smiled. "Thank you, Jimmy, that's very sweet."

"Yeah...well...see you guys."

"So long, cousin," Anthony replied.

Kathryn continued to smile until Jimmy left the table. Her face fell as she sat down and picked up the menu.

"How's the swordfish today?" Kathryn asked from behind the menu.

"I didn't ask, but I'm sure it's splendid as usual."

"I think I'll just have a Caesar," Kathryn said, putting down the menu."

Anthony dabbed the edges of his mouth with his napkin. "You didn't sleep well last night. You got up more than once."

"Sorry if I woke you."

"Don't be. I didn't sleep well, either."

Kathryn didn't respond. She looked out the picture window

overlooking the park. A young couple holding hands walked past with a dog. The sweet, innocent image filled her with sadness.

"Dear, could the reason for your sleepless night and your lack of appetite have anything to do with Henry Shoewalter and David Webber?"

Kathryn adjusted herself in her chair. The very mention of the names ripped at her. "Don't be ridiculous," she lied, realizing she would have made a terrible actress. "Sure, it's disturbing. Henry was a very sweet man, and David was—"

"Someone you were once in love with. Someone who you were going to marry if you hadn't—"

"Someone who I used to know," Kathryn interrupted with as much casualness as she could muster. "But that was many years ago. Good lord, I haven't thought about David Webber in…really, Anthony, don't be so melodramatic, it doesn't become you."

Anthony reached across the table and took Kathryn's hand. The physical contact with her husband took her by surprise.

"It's okay," said Anthony softly. "I understand. For heaven's sakes, if I were you, I'd be upset too. It's only natural. You needn't hide it from me."

Tears began to well in her eyes. She tried to stop them, but it was no use. She dropped her head as the first tear rolled down her cheek. "I'm sorry, Anthony."

"It's okay, I understand. Go ahead, let it out."

Anthony reached in his pocket, retrieved a handkerchief, and handed it to her. The waiter stepped up to the table, and Anthony ordered for both. Afterward, Anthony said nothing, patiently waiting for his wife to gather herself.

"Why are you being so understanding about this? It's not like you," Kathryn asked, dabbing her eyes.

Anthony leaned forward and wiped a tear from her cheek. When he spoke, his voice carried a gentleness Kathryn had seldom, if ever, heard. "I know, Kathryn, I know." Anthony slowly sat back in his chair, letting his shoulders fall and his strong square chin melt into his chest. "Oh, Kathryn, I am so sorry." Anthony looked up, revealing two moist eyes. "I guess it wouldn't matter if I said I know I've been a terrible husband? My, doesn't that sound trite?"

Kathryn watched as the cockiest and most pretentious man she'd ever known struggled for words.

"What happened to us? It wasn't always like this—*we* weren't always like this. Do you remember…the beginning…back when we were in school?"

Kathryn whispered, "I try very hard not to remember that time."

Anthony nodded. "I understand."

Kathryn avoided her husband's gaze and took a drink of water.

"But, I'm talking about the very beginning when we first… connected. Can you remember that time, Kathryn? It was good. It was so—"

"You didn't see his face," she whispered.

"I know. But there was a time before that when…"

Anthony continued speaking, but Kathryn didn't hear a word. She went away, reliving a rainy afternoon twelve years past as if it were yesterday.

"An abortion. You killed our baby!" David yelled.

Henry and Kathryn jerked as David entered Henry's study. He was carrying a piece of paper. Kathryn was shaking. Henry's eyes filled with tears.

"Why? Why?" David screamed, throwing the thin sheet of paper at Kathryn.

"Davey, please, calm—"

"You killed our baby." David grabbed Kathryn by the arm. "How could you?"

Henry jumped from his chair and hurried around the desk to restrain the out-of-control young man.

"You bitch. You killed our…"

"It wasn't your baby," Kathryn screamed, falling to her knees. "It wasn't your baby. It wasn't your baby," she repeated, her voice trailing off in pain.

David's face went flush. He let go of Kathryn's arm and fell against the doorframe.

Henry kneeled next to Kathryn.

"Anthony," David whispered to no one.

194

Kathryn cowered on the floor and nodded her head.

David took in a long breath and looked up at the ceiling. "How long?"

Kathryn didn't answer.

David found his hand on the bookshelf. He heaved a row of books to the floor. "How long?"

"A couple of months," Kathryn mumbled.

David looked at Henry, his eyes wide and insane. "You knew. Jesus Christ, you knew and you didn't..." David stopped mid-sentence and looked back at Kathryn and then back to Henry. He looked around the floor and found the paper he had hurled. It was the hospital's report and discharge. It was paid and signed by Henry Shoewalter.

"You son of a bitch," David whispered.

"Henry was just helping me," Kathryn wailed.

Henry hung his head. "I'm sorry, Davey. I love you both so—"

"It's my fucking life!" David howled like a wounded animal.

"I know, oh, I'm so sorry, Davey—"

"Sorry?" David shouted, hitting the wall with his fist. "Go to hell, old man...all of you can just go to hell. I don't fucking need any of you."

"He was devastated," Kathryn whispered, as if she were in a trance. "It nearly killed him, literally. Henry and I searched for three days. We never heard about the accident. We just found him in the hospital. He'd refused to tell anybody his name. That was the last time I saw him. Everyone he'd ever loved had left him, and I was just one more. He even thought Henry had abandoned him, which may have hurt him even—" her voice trailed off. "I never should have told Henry. I never should have gotten him involved. I just needed help, and money. I was so stupid back then."

Both were silent for a moment, Kathryn locked in a memory, Anthony setting up for his next move.

"Kathryn, I have a confession."

Kathryn looked up.

"It's the reason I didn't sleep well last night myself. It was because of Henry Shoewalter and David Webber. They've been on my mind as well."

"Why? You weren't that close to Henry and never cared much for David."

"That's not true. I had nothing against Webber. I was just…well, jealous, I guess. He had a part of you I could never touch…still can't."

"Anthony—"

"No, let me finish. We're into this, so we might as well stop avoiding it. And it's time I came clean, anyway—confessed to my sins, as it were. Kathryn, it's no secret to either of us that our marriage is less than blissful. We both know it and have just come to accept it. But I can't just accept anymore. I want my wife, my beautiful wife. When I mentioned David Webber's name yesterday and saw the look on your face—"

"Anthony—"

"Please, Kathryn. I did something."

"What?"

Anthony paused for effect. "You know Uncle Nick has contacts everywhere, including with the Los Angeles police department. I asked him to see if he could get me information about the murder, specifically about David's involvement."

"Why?"

"Because I'm pathetic and desperate. Kathryn, that time twelve years ago still haunts me too. You see, I used to believe that your getting pregnant was my good fortune. You and David split up. I won. I got the girl. I now see how wrong I was. Had you not gotten pregnant, I believe things would have turned out differently. Maybe I'm being foolish, or maybe just wishful thinking, but I honestly think I would have won you anyway. I believe you would have left David on your own accord instead of what happened. I believe you would have fallen as much in love with me as I was with you—as much as I am still in love with you, Kathryn. But I never got that chance, which is why I've gone through our marriage feeling like a consolation prize."

Kathryn was stunned. She didn't know how to respond, especially since much of what he was saying was true. For even though it had taken over two and a half years from that horrible afternoon at Henry's before she'd accepted Anthony's persistent proposal of marriage, she remembered thinking even then Anthony was a consolation prize. And, at times, perhaps her punishment.

"I had my uncle look into Henry's murder because I thought if I could show you what they had on David—what kind of man he turned out to be—then you'd realize you had made the right choice. I'm not proud of it, but that's what I did, and I'm sorry." Anthony hung his head.

Kathryn didn't know if she wanted to hear this or not. But she had to ask.

"What did you find out, Anthony?"

"No, Kathryn, I can't—"

"Anthony, what did you find out? I have to know. Did David kill Henry?"

Anthony closed his eyes and spoke through a deep sigh. "The police have no other suspects. The police believe that Henry contacted David because of something the old man was working on. It must have had something to do with the Mozart project Henry contacted you about a few months ago. If you recall, David was a whiz when it came to Wolfgang. It only makes sense that Henry would go to him for help. Anyway, the police think for some reason a fight ensued, and David lost control."

"No, that's not possible. Henry was like a father to David, he'd never—"

"I'm sorry, dear. But the truth is you haven't seen David in a very long time. You don't know what he's like now. Uncle Nick learned that David has become a pretty hard drinker. He was even arrested earlier the night Henry was killed for a barroom brawl. He was probably still drunk when he saw Henry. Anyway, the police suspect a crime of passion."

"I can't believe it. David loved Henry..." Kathryn's breath stopped and she brought her trembling hands to her mouth. "It had to do with me. Oh God."

"No, it was so many years ago. David couldn't still be holding that anger."

"Yes, Anthony, he could. Henry must have told him I assisted in the Mozart research and that sent David back twelve years. Oh God."

Anthony grabbed his wife's shaking hands. "Sweetheart, you don't know any of this. We don't know if Henry told David about his project. And we also don't know with certainty that David is responsible for Henry's death."

"But you said the police weren't looking for anybody else," Kathryn said, barely able to get out the words.

"That doesn't mean David is responsible. Henry's murder might not be connected to David at all. Maybe it has to do with his Mozart project."

"What…why, why would you say that?" Kathryn stammered, eager to accept any other explanation.

"Well, I don't know. I'm just throwing out other possibilities. But we don't know what Henry was working on."

"No, we don't." Kathryn's posture abruptly changed. "Anthony, I do remember something."

"What?"

Kathryn squinted, trying to make the memory focus. "Henry said something when we first talked. When he asked me to do the research. He said something like…he was working on something that was going to be very big news."

"He did? He said, 'very big news?'"

"Yes, he did. I'm sure of it. He said this project could be the biggest music story of the century. Those were his words. But I just thought it was Henry's usual hyperbole. But what if it wasn't? What if it was something very important? Important enough to get killed over?"

Anthony's eyes widened. Inside, however, he felt calm confidence. *This is way too easy.* "You mean, maybe it wasn't David," he said, his voice bursting with hope. "Maybe his murder had something to do with his Mozart research?"

"Right," Kathryn responded. "And…and what if the police don't know anything about Henry's work? I must find out what he was working on. They need to look at other suspects other than David. Is David in jail now?"

"No. They didn't have enough to hold him. Now they can't find him. They think he's fled to Washington, DC."

"Why Washington?"

"Nobody knows, but you know what? It might have something to do with whatever Henry was working on." Anthony let his words sink in for a second. "Or, maybe he's just running."

Kathryn stared out the window.

"I'm sorry, Kathryn, please forgive me. I wish I'd never opened this wound up for you." *Yes, just way too damn easy.*

Chapter 25

The self-serve food court/gift shop located in the basement of the Museum of American History was bustling with tourists. Dani and David sat outside in the patio area located on the west end of the building. As David inhaled a heaping Chinese chicken salad and second basket of bread, Dani, still stunned at David's pronouncement he was a murder suspect, picked at a Caesar and rambled on with trivial facts about the museum.

"...so until nineteen-eighty, this museum was known as the National Museum of History and Technology. There are sixteen Smithsonian buildings in total, nine located right here on the Mall. Feeling better?"

"Uh-huh," David said, without looking up.

Would this guy be the date from hell or what? Dani thought to herself.

Dissecting men had become one of Dani's favorite pastimes—and she knew she was good at it too. Excluding the doomed relationship with gay Jerry, which she could easily rationalize as being blinded by his delicious ability to spot a sale, she usually had most males figured out pretty quickly—they were so transparent. It wasn't that she had a low opinion of men, quite the opposite. She suspected she liked men better than women. There was something

comforting about their overtness. But the guy across the table was…
she couldn't even think of the word. Everything was a contradiction.
He wasn't bad looking, but carried himself as if he could care less if
anyone thought so or not. Obviously very bright, but certainly not
the cleverest conversationalist she'd ever met. And though at times
he exhibited moments of crudeness, bordering on being rude, she
had a sense he was a decent person—at least she hoped so.

David leaned back from the table and took out a cigarette.

"There's no smoking here. Also, I'm allergic."

David removed the unlit cigarette from his lips.

"Thanks, sorry." *Why am I even sitting with this drone?* Dani said to
herself, wrestling with ways to make a graceful exit.

"Can we talk about Henry now?" David asked.

"Yeah, I guess." Dani replied, adding total lack of finesse to the
list.

"Where'd you go to school?"

"Oklahoma, why?"

David's face showed his disappointment. "Henry was a professor
at Juilliard. I thought you and he might—"

"David, I told you I've never heard the name Henry Shoewalter
before. I think I would remember if he'd been one of my
professors."

David conceded with a nod.

"Hey, Paul went to Juilliard, though."

David looked at her confused.

"You just met him, the conductor of the orchestra. Maybe it was
his number—"

"No, it was yours," David cut in. "I called it and got your voice
mail."

"Well, I bet Paul knows him…I mean, knew him." *Frig!* She
wanted to crawl in a hole, but David didn't react.

"I doubt it. I hear Henry's been retired for a while."

"You hear? I thought you and he were…"

"It's a long story and not important."

"Oh, I see," Dani said, not seeing at all.

Both were silent for a moment. But David's next question told

Dani her own face must have been shouting volumes. "So why don't you ask me?"

"Ask you what?" Dani lied, knowing exactly what he meant.

"What it is you want to know. Did I kill Henry?"

Dani opened her mouth, but no words came out.

"No, I didn't," David said. "Or don't you believe me, either?"

"Uh, yeah…of course I do. I mean, why shouldn't I?"

David didn't answer.

"Do you think I'd be sitting here if I thought you were a—"

"A murderer?"

"Yes, a murderer," Dani said, swallowing hard. "Pardon me for saying so, David," she realized she should shut up as the words were coming out of her mouth, "but you seem a little…paranoid."

"Dani, I'm very fucking para—"

"Please don't use that word," Dani winced, still with a smile.

David reacted with a surprised half-laugh. "No smoking, no swearing—what, you some kind of Jesus freak or something?"

Dani's smile completely disappeared, and again there was silence.

As before, David spoke without segue. "You married?"

"No, you?"

"What do you think?"

You're right, you weirdo. What a stupid question, Dani thought, but instead said, "I presume not." *Okay, two can play this game.* "So how was Henry killed?"

"He was shot in the head."

"Oh, gee." Her brief attempt at callousness was short lived.

"Yeah, my sentiments exactly—oh gee," David replied.

Enough was enough, and Dani had had more than enough. She dabbed her mouth with a paper napkin and stood from the table.

"Where're you going?"

"I'm sorry, I need to take off."

"But we haven't figured out why Henry…"

"I know, but I really don't think I can be of any help."

"I pissed you off, didn't I?"

"No, of course not," Dani said, lowering her head.

"Yeah, I did."

"David," Dani said, forcing a smile, "I don't know you well enough for you to piss me off. And quite frankly, you don't know me well enough to be rude."

"Rude? What the hell are you talking—"

"David," Dani interrupted, "I understand you've suffered a terrible loss, but I get the feeling that doesn't have a lot to do with your shitty personality."

"Wow, a vulgarity."

Dani smiled and shook her head as she cleaned off her side of the table.

"You got a problem with my personality?"

Dani sighed and looked David in the eye. "Not that it matters, since you and I will probably never see each other again, but since you asked, yes, I have a huge problem with your personality. But it's probably my problem, so you shouldn't concern yourself."

"Okay, what's *your* problem?"

Dani put her tongue in her cheek, thought for a moment, and then decided what the hell, he deserves it. "I believe you're one of those types of people who think of themselves as an honest, get-to-the-point, no BS type of person. I don't like those types of people. You know why? Because in reality, I find those types of people to be rude, obnoxious, self-centered assholes. Like I said, it's my problem. Good luck, and again, I'm sorry about your friend." Dani turned, tossed her plastic salad bowl and cup in the trash can, and started through the food court toward the elevators.

David stared at Dani's empty chair and then got up and followed. "Dani...Dr. Parsons...hey wait up. I'm sorry."

Dani didn't turn around and didn't stop her stride.

David continued his pursuit, dodging tourists. "Hey, I'm sorry...please—"

"What? There's nothing to be sorry about," she said not stopping. "We just have personalities that don't click—no biggie."

"But I need your help."

"I can't help you."

"Why, because I'm a jerk? Come on, Dani. Dani, would you please stop?"

Dani did stop, but not until she'd reached the elevators. "What?"

David leaned over and put his hands on his knees to catch his breath. "I've got to stop smoking."

Dani crossed her arms and waited.

"Look, I know I'm a...it's just habit...you don't deserve it."

Dani said nothing.

"I'm sorry...really...I...usually do have better manners."

"David," Dani said, getting into the elevator with David close behind. "I was just trying to help you. The way you looked out there in the mall, you looked like you needed it. That's why I came back. How could you be such a jerk to someone trying to help you? That's not very nice."

"Yeah, I know, I'm...bad at nice. I'm sorry." The elevator doors closed. "Look, Dani, you don't know me and have absolutely no reason to help me...or believe me...or anything. But please, just a few more minutes. And...thank you for coming back."

Dani didn't reply. The doors opened onto the first floor, and Dani got out and walked around the corner to an alcove just inside the museum's entrance to another pair of elevators marked MUSEUM STAFF ONLY.

"I'm taking the employees' elevator down to the parking garage. There's a security check, so you're probably not allowed down there."

David closed his eyes and exhaled. "Dani, one of the most important people in my life was killed three nights ago. If that's not bad enough, my best friend is missing too. The police think it's all connected and I'm responsible. My life, for what it's worth, is coming apart, and I don't know what to do. You're right, I do need help, and you're the only lead I have."

"David, are you wanted by the police?"

"No, I'm not. They suspect me, but that's all, I swear."

Dani looked in David's eyes. Two thoughts ran through her mind at once. *This is too weird*, and, *why am I such a sucker for needy men?* "David, I don't know what I can do."

"Me either. But Henry had your number. And it looks like he got it the night he was killed, maybe hours before. It was important to him, Dani. Why?"

Dani studied David for a moment and then let out her own surrendering breath. "Okay, David, just a few more minutes. What do you suggest?"

He wasted no time. "Somehow, there's a connection between you and Henry, even if you don't know what it is."

"I'm a music historian. People don't die because of me."

David ran a hand through his hair and tried to decide where to fish next. "I think Henry was working on a book, or something to do with Mozart."

"Okay."

"That means nothing to you?"

Dani shook her head, feeling only sympathy again for David. "I'm sorry."

He didn't have the faintest idea where to go next.

"Why do you think he was working on something to do with Mozart?" Dani asked.

"Because I talked to him the night he was killed. He was frantic about borrowing something he had given me a long time ago. A sketch by Mozart."

"Wow. Original?" The elevator arrived, but Dani ignored it.

"Yeah."

"That must be worth a fortune. What's it from?"

"I don't know. It's only a partial sketch and doesn't fit any known work. But the autograph and watermark have been authenticated."

"Really, what year?"

"Ninety, ninety-one, or thereabouts. It's from the Vienna paper stock."

"That must be one of the last sketches Mozart ever did. Of course, you checked it against the D minor Requiem?"

"First place, not even close."

"Do you think Henry had learned what it was from?"

"I don't know. But I thought that's why he had your number."

"That doesn't make sense, David. If he wanted assistance from the Institution, there are other curators here who know more about Mozart than me. Especially when it comes to analyzing a sketch. Paul, for one."

David said nothing.

"Did you bring the sketch to DC?"

"Yeah, it's in here," David said, nodding to his briefcase.

"You're carrying it around? An authentic sketch by Mozart, and you're carrying it around Washington, DC?"

"Yeah, I thought you might want to see it," David replied. He opened his briefcase and withdrew the plastic laminate. He gently took the parchment from the cover and handed it to Dani.

She didn't see it immediately. She was too busy studying the paper stock and the scribbles. But when she finally looked at the notes on the staff, it only took seconds. There it was—right down to the accidental A flat in measure four.

"Oh my God," Dani whispered.

"What's wrong?"

Dani looked up in shock. "You need to come with me. Now."

Chapter 26

Fowler had moved his car to the Madison Avenue side of the Mall and was sitting on the north side of the street a hundred yards east of the museum when the call came in.

"Agent Fowler, it's Sanders, we got him. Petrovic."

"Are you sure?"

"He's wearing tan shorts, a tie-dyed shirt, and a Yankee's cap. He's in a gift shop on the main floor."

"I'm on my way," Fowler said, jumping from his car.

"IT'S THE SAME MELODY. Where did you get this?" David asked, staring at the parchment given to Dani by Sugarberry.

"From a woman named Gertrude Sugarberry. She claims it's a Cook."

"A what?"

"Not a what, a who. Dr. James Cook was a medical doctor and free slave in the mid-eighteen hundreds. He also played the violin. She thinks he wrote it."

"Well, he didn't," David replied. "Mozart did."

"If your sketch is authentic, it—"

"It is," David cut in. "It's been authenticated more than once."

"I believe you, David, but—"

"How did a—"

"Right," Dani interrupted, finishing David's thought. "How was a free-slave from the eighteen hundreds able to transcribe a Mozart work no one's ever heard before? I don't know."

"Have you had this—"

"No," Dani interrupted again, "I haven't done anything yet except play it with Paul. I've only had it since yesterday."

"Yesterday?" David responded.

"Yeah, quite a coincidence, huh?"

A chill went down David's back. "Someone told me recently there are no such things as coincidences."

Dani took the Sugarberry music from David and laid it on her desk beside David's Mozart sketch. The two musicians went to work.

David spoke first. "The melodies are the same, but the transcriptions are different."

Dani added, "Sugarberry's is a single melody line and yours is a complete sketch, and four bars longer."

"Mine has Mozart's autograph, yours has no claim of authorship."

Dani said, "Yours is written on traditional eighteenth century scoring paper, brownish-white, longer horizontally than vertically. Sugarberry's is lighter in color and longer vertically than horizontally. And look at this, at bar twelve, Sugarberry's ends with the tied B-flat quarter note, yours continues to a dotted-C half note followed by a quarter rest. I was right. Sugarberry's *does* end in the middle of a phrase." Then Dani noticed bar four, the A-flat quarter note. "Well, I'll be."

"What?" David responded.

"When Paul and I played this last night, we speculated this might be an E-flat suspended chord."

"Well done," David said. "I see both pieces are in the same key and time signature."

Dani nodded. "Yes, but where mine only has the abbreviation

adg, yours has the complete word *adagio* handwritten in the upper left corner. Yours also has expression marks. *Pianissimo* in the first five bars, with a *crescendo* notation to *mezzo piano* in bar eight, then a *diminuendo decrescendo* to bar twelve, returning to *pianissimo* for the remaining four bars. Sugarberry's has no such markings. What are these?"

"Just doodles," David answered. "It appears Mozart never meant for this to go to a copyist."

"Are you sure that's all they are? They look familiar."

"What's that?" David asked, pointing to the lower left edge of Sugarberry's music.

"Just ink drippings, I think."

"No, here, on the corner."

"Hang on." Dani opened a drawer and pulled out a magnifying glass. "Where?"

"Here, where my finger is."

Dani lowered the glass to the manuscript. "It looks like…letters or something."

"Let me see."

Dani handed David the glass.

"Yeah, they are. It's a C and a K and a F."

"Here, let me see?"

David handed Dani back the eyeglass.

"You're right, C-K-F."

"Okay, now look here at mine—right here," David instructed.

Dani focused the glass to the lower right edge of David's sheet. "C—K—F." Dani looked up. "What's C-K-F mean? I've never heard of it before."

"Neither have I."

"The title?"

"Strange place to put it if it is," David responded.

Neither spoke for several seconds.

"Well, at least I know why Henry had your number," David finally said.

Dani's head snapped toward David. "Really? I don't."

David answered Dani's statement with a stare.

"David, didn't you tell me Henry was killed only a few nights ago?"

"Yeah, Thursday night...actually I guess it was Friday morning."

"I didn't get the Sugarberry assignment until Friday morning. Before then, I didn't even know Gertrude Sugarberry existed, much less this music. Besides, she didn't even show this to me. I stumbled onto it by accident."

David offered no rebuttal. Instead, he walked around her desk and sat down in her chair and crossed his arms.

Dani looked at David, his face was relaxed, and his eyes were calm. The calmest they'd looked since she'd met him. "Are you okay?" Dani asked.

"I'm fine," David answered, almost serenely.

"David, did you hear what I said? I didn't get this music until yesterday, and the assignment the day before yesterday."

"I heard you."

"And that makes sense to you?"

"No, it makes no sense at all."

"So why are you suddenly so——"

"Because now I know there's something going on—that there's a tangible reason behind all of the insanity. Until now, I wasn't sure if Henry's death and J.P.'s disappearance weren't just random acts. I mean, I thought they were connected—everyone said they were—but I still wasn't sure. But now, I know. Henry was working on something, something that started all of this."

"And this piece of music is the key?" Dani asked.

"Yes, it is," David answered.

"But I——"

"I know, Dani, it's..." David searched for the words, "Don't try and make sense out of the picture. Just paint the picture."

"What?"

"What were you planning to do with this?"

Dani sighed and sat on the corner of her desk. "I'm meeting Paul in the morning." Dani chuckled, interrupting herself. "Boy, is this going to freak him out. We're dropping it off at the lab to have the paper analyzed and dated. We also have a ProTools studio where we were going to run some possible accompaniment—guess that won't be necessary now."

"No," David broke in, "I think you should still do it."

Dani thought for a second and then nodded. "Yeah, you're right. If nothing else, the computer can do a sparse orchestral arrangement based on the notes Mozart made himself."

David nodded.

"Then Paul and I planned to go over to Georgetown and meet an historian to see if he knows anything about this Cook guy. Who knows, now that we know it's a Mozart, maybe we can figure out how Cook got it."

"What about the woman who owns it, Sugar…"

"Sugarberry. Yeah, I need to go by there too. I still have to pick up her collection of sheet music. Maybe I should call her now…" Dani said, reaching for the phone. "No. I'll wait 'til we talk to the historian in Georgetown."

"Can I come?" David blurted, ignoring any subtlety.

Dani looked at David and thought for a moment. Then she smiled. "On two conditions. One, you let our lab analyze your sketch. It's not that I don't believe you, it's just if we're going to be working together on this, I want us both to be using the same information. Besides, we have the latest technology when it comes to carbon dating and watermark ID'ing. We also have the latest Kochel catalog in ProTools, so we can download your sketch and see if it matches any known Mozart work—you are familiar with Kochel, aren't you?"

"Viennese botanist, mineralogist, and educator who was the first to catalog Mozart's work in eighteen sixty-two," David said.

Dani raised an eyebrow. "Okay, I'm impressed."

David continued, "But it might be helpful to look at earlier Kochel catalogs to check it against work that was omitted over the six revised editions."

Dani smiled. "Smart, but not too smart—seven."

"What?"

"Seven editions. A couple of years ago, Breitkof & Hartel revised another one. It's called The New Kochel."

"Oh," David said with an apathetic shrug, "whatta you know? Guess I've been out of the serious music world for a while." He pretended not to care, but there was a time when he would have known that fact like his own name.

"At any rate, it's no problem. Our computer has all seven revisions as well as the original Kochel catalog downloaded."

David nodded. "What's the second condition?"

Dani picked up David's parchment. "That you let me keep this in the safe here in my office. You shouldn't be walking around the streets of DC with it."

"You got it."

"Okay, then. Where are you staying?" she asked, picking up both pieces of music and walking to her safe.

David stood. "A hotel on Tenth."

"I'll drop you off. Paul and I will pick you up in the morning, okay?"

"Okay."

Dani heard a sadness in David's reply. "What's wrong?"

David shook his head as he picked up his briefcase. "No, nothing…it's just, I wish there was more I could do tonight. I sure doubt I'm going to sleep much."

Dani grinned as she opened the door to the safe. "You sound like me."

"Do you have dinner plans?"

Dani closed the door to the safe and looked back mildly surprised. "Wow, you don't waste any time, do you?" she said, spinning the tumbler.

"What?" David blanched, realizing the way his innocent question sounded. "No, I don't mean like—"

"Are you asking me out on a date?" Dani asked, fully knowing that he wasn't, but enjoying David's awkwardness too much to let him off the hook.

"No…uh…I…wasn't…"

"Must be an L.A. thing."

"No, of course not…I mean, I assume you and Paul are——"

"Me and Paul?" Dani laughed and decided David had had enough. "Paul and I are just colleagues and friends. I'm sorry, I know what you meant."

"I'm asking if you want to eat with me tonight. I owe you at least a decent dinner…you know, after the way I acted."

Dani picked up her bag and walked toward the door. She turned and looked back at David with an accusatory expression. "You know, I'm still not sure I trust you or not, or even like you for that matter. I haven't forgotten what a jerk you were downstairs in the restaurant, or how you freaked out in the Mall."

David said nothing in his defense.

"Do you like to shop?"

"What?" David responded, taken completely off guard.

"Shop. Do you like to shop?"

"No, I hate it."

"Figures," Dani said, rolling her eyes. "Well, look, I was going to do some shopping tonight. There's a new outdoor promenade on the east side of town. If you'd like, you can join me, and maybe I'll let you buy me dinner after——"

"What time?" David's face gave no reaction, but inside was a different story. He was both happy and relieved. Happy as any man would be to spend an evening with a beautiful woman, and relieved he wouldn't have to face the night alone with his thoughts.

Dani chuckled. "I should probably have my head examined for this. Let's see, it's a little after three now, how about seven?"

"Sounds good, that'll give me time to make some calls and feed my cat."

"Your cat? You brought your cat to DC with you?"

"Yeah," David answered.

Dani shook her head. "You're a strange man, David Webber."

Chapter 27

Fowler spoke as he jogged toward the museum's entrance, "Sanders, where—"

"He's in a gift shop just as you enter the museum," Sanders interrupted.

"What's he doing?" Fowler asked, adjusting the volume on his headset.

"Just meandering. He must have had the same problem I had when Webber and the woman took the employee elevator to the museum's offices. There was no way to follow them without being spotted, so I stationed myself in the foyer beside guest services. We both have a view of the elevator, and he's watching it like a...wait... the elevator's coming down...it's not stopping, it must be going to the garage. He's moving, sir, he's leaving the gift shop and heading for the doors. He'll be walking past you any second."

Just as Fowler completed a one-eighty, Petrovic came out the museum's glass doors and trotted down the steps, passing within feet of the FBI man. Fowler waited until he got a ways down the sidewalk before he followed. If Petrovic was in a hurry, he didn't show it. He casually walked east on Madison, keeping stride with the rest of the tourists. Fowler felt sure he'd turn left onto Twelfth and head toward the east exit of the museum's underground garage to wait for Webber and Parsons. He did, but instead of stopping, he continued down Twelfth.

"Sanders, where are you?"

"I'm in the car now, sir. I'm rounding Fourteenth onto Constitution."

"I'm at the corner of Constitution and Twelfth. Get over here and give me the car. I'm too damn old for a foot pursuit. I want a man at Pennsylvania and Twelfth, Tenth and Fourteenth. If he crosses Penn, have everyone rotate to the next block. Converge at Fourteenth. We do not lose him."

The young agent pulled up to the curb and jumped out of the car. Fowler got in on the passenger side, slid over into the driver's seat, and rolled down the window as the door was shutting. "He's at Constitution. See him, son?" Fowler said pointing.

"Yes sir," Sanders said, watching Petrovic cross the street.

Fowler talked as he picked up his cell. "I don't know what this guy's doing, but he's not following Webber and the girl. Get moving."

With a nod, Sanders was off. Fowler watched as the young agent crossed Constitution in the middle of the street and closed the distance on Petrovic.

"Bob, it's Tom. You've heard?"

"Yes, Tom, where is he?"

"He's on Twelfth. A perimeter is being established. He's in a cage."

Fowler heard Greenfield sigh in relief. "Good, how about Webber?"

"We had to drop him when we found Petrovic. He's probably heading back to his hotel. In fact, that might be where Petrovic's heading."

"Do you think they're rendezvousing?"

"No, I don't. I'm positive Webber isn't with Petrovic."

"Why?"

"Because Petrovic worked too hard at staying out of sight while staying on Webber's heels. No, Webber doesn't have a clue who this guy is."

"Then David Webber's in danger."

"Petrovic wants something. I believe he thinks Webber will lead him to it."

"The music," Greenfield stated.

"That'd be my guess."

Fowler heard Sanders's voice on his radio. "Hang on, Bob. Go ahead, Sanders."

"Sir, we may have a problem. He's entered the subway. Twelfth Street station."

"Shit, of course."

Fowler went back to the phone. "We got a problem, Bob. He's taking the Metro. I blew it. I should have anticipated this."

"Resign later, Tom. Right now, don't lose Petrovic."

Fowler whipped the car down Twelfth Street. "Talk to me, Sanders."

"I'm on him," Sanders replied. "He's walking through the station."

"Is he waiting on a train?"

"It doesn't look like...I can't tell. Wait...I've lost him."

"Where'd he go?"

"No...it's okay...I think I got him again...hang on."

Fowler screeched to a stop across the street from the station's entrance and jumped out of the car. He crossed the street and ran down the steps into the Metro station. He walked slowly through the tunnel, looking in all directions for Petrovic or Sanders. "Sanders? Sanders, do you copy?" There was no reply. He walked deeper into the subway station, dodging people along the way. Finally, he reached the middle of the terminal just as a train was pulling in. The noise forced him to raise his hand to his ear to hear. As a stampede of commuters exited the train and another horde battled to get on, Fowler searched every face he could—no Sanders, no Petrovic. The doors closed, and the train pulled out. Fowler heard a commotion off to his left. People were huddled together, many yelling for police. Fowler withdrew his badge and raised it in the air as he broke through the cluster. "Federal agent." In the middle of the crowd a woman was huddled on a bench. The woman's eyes were locked wide open, and she was white as a ghost. "Ma'am, I'm a Federal agent, what's the matter?"

She moved her mouth, but no words came out. She pointed in the direction of the woman's restroom. Fowler withdrew his sidearm.

"Federal agent!" Fowler yelled, kicking open the door and entering with his gun leveled. Three steps in and he was brought to an abrupt stop. "Oh, God." he mumbled, putting his hand over his mouth. Thirty-two years with the bureau and he'd never seen anything so savage. Blood was streaked across the floor from the stall to where Agent Sanders was lying in a pool of blood. His terrified eyes were frozen open. His throat had been cut so deeply that Fowler could see the back of the boy's spine. The young FBI agent had practically been decapitated.

Chapter 28

The statuesque woman walked through the lobby of the Marriott Hotel. Her flaming red hair was heavily sprayed, and her makeup was painted on thick under tortoiseshell eyeglasses. She wore sensible shoes that matched her oversized black leather purse but did little to diminish her height. She was attired in a blue pantsuit with a green ascot tied around her thick neck. She was not an attractive woman.

"Mrs. Black?" the concierge called out.

The woman turned but came no closer to the girl.

"Mrs. Black, I know it's none of my business, and forgive me if I'm being forward, but I just wanted to tell you something."

"What's that, dear?" the woman replied in a soft voice.

"It's about your sister. I was here when you checked in last night, and I just wanted to tell you last year my sister was in a car accident too. She was in a coma for three months. But she's fine now, practically back to her old self. I wanted to tell you to not give up hope. What hospital are you taking her to?"

"Hospital?"

"Yes, hospital. That's why you brought her to Washington, isn't it?"

"Oh, yes, of course it is. I'm sorry, it's the jetlag—Bethesda, I'm taking her to Bethesda Hospital."

"Great. That's where my sister was. She's going to be fine, Mrs. Black."

"Thank you, dear. That's so reassuring."

The woman smiled and turned for the elevators. Just as the doors opened and she stepped in, a high-pitched chirping came from her handbag. She withdrew a phone and looked at the caller ID. It was the call she was expecting.

"Bowen, I can't believe I got you," David exclaimed.

"Mr. Webber, I'm sorry, the department has had me working doubles."

"Have you gotten my messages?"

"Yeah, thanks. How's DC? Have you met Parsons?"

"Yes, and you're not going to believe it. She has the same Mozart piece that I do—not exactly the same, but it's the same."

"Where'd she get it?

"From a woman in Georgetown named Sugarberry. It's weird, Bowen. She found it by accident, and only a couple of days ago. We still can't figure out how or why Henry had her number."

"Man, that is weird."

"I'm on to something here, Bowen, I know it." David paused and changed his tone. "Any word about J.P.?"

Bowen sighed. "Nothing, and it's making me crazy. I've called in every favor I have on the force to try and get someone to give the case special attention. Everyone just tells me the same thing, 'we're doing all we can.' I hope you come up with something."

"How about me? Are they still gunnin' for me?"

"Now more than ever. It's totally freaked them out you left town. But Dad says you're not under arrest, so there's nothing they can do. When are you coming back?"

"I don't know. I'm going to go to Georgetown tomorrow with Dani —uh, Dr. Parsons—to meet a man at the university who might know something about the guy who supposedly wrote the piece Sugarberry owns. Then we're going to meet Sugarberry. I'll keep you informed."

"Okay, and I'll do the same at this end."

"Do that, Bowen. If you hear anything about J.P., call me."

"Of course, Mr. Webber. I'll call you if anything develops. Good luck."

"Thanks. I'll talk to you tomorrow."

Joshua Bowen clicked off his phone and stepped off the elevator. Three minutes later, he was in his room looking in the mirror at his ridiculously painted face. With a cold stare, he pulled the red wig from his head. He turned on the hot water in the shower and took off the ascot and blue pantsuit. Ten minutes later, the lean, hard, naked body of Viktor Petrovic stepped out.

Petrovic, still naked, walked into the main room carrying the leather bag. He reached under the nightstand, retrieved an empty trash can, took out the plastic lining, and neatly spread it on top of the bedspread. One by one, he began lifting out the contents of the bag and placing them on the plastic—a Nikon camera, baseball cap, black beard, a wig, and a bloody shirt.

"I was told a few minutes ago not to worry, that you were going to be all right. What do you think?"

J.P. lay in the bed on her back. Her wild eyes darted around the room in frantic confusion. She tried to speak but was unable.

"I think it depends on the resourcefulness of your Mr. Webber, that's what I think."

Petrovic removed a wadded up, bloody shirt from the bag and unfolded it. With two fingers, he lifted out a bloody serrated nine-inch blade. He swung it like a pendulum in front of J.P. "Yes, let's hope he's very resourceful."

"MOZART, yes, I saw it with my own eyes," Dani said, the phone tucked between her ear and shoulder as she folded laundry on her dining room table.

Paul was silent for a moment.

"Paul, you there?"

"Yeah, sorry, Dan. Webber's friend who was killed, what did you say his name was?"

"Henry Shoewalter. You might have heard of him. David said he used to be a professor at Juilliard."

Paul was silent again.

"Paul?"

"Yeah, I'm here…hang on a sec."

Dani heard Paul put down the phone. A minute later he was back.

"Holy Moses. Yeah, I remember now."

"Remember what?" Dani heard Paul turning pages in a book.

"Mozart, you say? Well, it stands to reason."

"Why? Paul, what—"

"I haven't thought about these guys since school."

"Paul, what are you talking about?"

"Dan, I'm sitting here with my yearbook from Juilliard. Professor Henry Shoewalter wasn't teaching when I was there, but he was on every advisory board imaginable. He was a big shot to beat all big shots."

"Well, there you go."

"There's something else—jeez, it's just such a common name, I didn't even connect it," Paul said almost to himself.

"Who?"

"David Webber. I've also heard of David Webber."

Dani stopped and took the phone in her hand.

"You have? How?"

"David Webber's legendary. Well, that might be an exaggeration, but not much of one, especially to a Juilliard student."

Dani sat down on her sofa. "Why?"

"When I was in school, I remember hearing stories of the young phenom David Webber. A few years before I got there, he was a hotshot student who got off challenging his professors' interpretations of famous works. As it turns out, Webber's critiques were so brilliant, many were adopted as curriculum. He was like a child prodigy or something, heralded as a genuine musical genius. When I was there, it was said he was the last great virtuoso pianist

Juilliard graduated. He's in my yearbook's list of who's who alumni."

"There's got to be a mistake. It can't be the same person. The David Webber I met today is a crude lounge piano player from L.A."

"Well, I don't know about crude, but the David Webber who went to Juilliard was no lounge piano player. I'm reading a list of accomplishments right here under his name. International Tchaikovsky Competition winner, gold medalist at the Arthur Rubinstein Competition, first place at the San Antonio Piano Competition, the list goes on and on."

"Lord, he's another Van Cliburn."

Paul laughed, "Yeah, that's another competition he won...twice."

Dani was both stunned and bewildered. This couldn't be the same guy. "Does it say what happened to him? A person with credits like that doesn't just fade into obscurity."

"No, I..." Paul stopped himself. "Wait...you know...for some reason..."

"What?" Dani begged.

"Well, I don't know, but—and I base this on nothing—but I seem to remember there was talk of him being dead—killed in a car accident or something."

"A car accident?"

"Yeah, I'm sure of it. When I was at Juilliard, the rumor was David Webber had been killed in a car accident." Paul chuckled. "Well whaddaya know about that, the great David Webber lives."

"Yeah," Dani mumbled as Hemingway jumped on her lap. "He sure does."

DAVID REACHED for a cigarette but stopped it halfway to his lips. With a sigh, he put it back in the pack and settled back just in time for Ravel to amble onto his chest. David closed his eyes and stroked the purring cat's head. "I met someone today, Ravee."

Chapter 29

Dani picked David up at his hotel at twenty past seven. When David got into the car, he saw a different Dr. Dani Parsons from the one he'd met earlier in the day. Her hair was down, she was in cowboy boots, a pair of faded Levi's, and an untucked red plaid flannel shirt over a gray T-shirt. David realized he was overdressed in slacks, white Polo, and a tweed sport coat and was a little miffed he hadn't been warned this was a casual outing. But for once in his life, he vowed to hold his tongue.

"How's your cat?" Dani said as David maneuvered his six-foot frame into the small vehicle.

"Still a little unnerved by the flight," David replied.

"You usually travel with her?"

"It's a him, and I don't usually travel."

Dani shook her head. "Is it just me, or is talking to you like trying to talk to a fortune-cookie?"

"What do you mean?" David responded, worried he'd inadvertently said something wrong.

"Meaning, you make all of these *delightfully* cryptic statements, but don't follow them up with any explanation."

Realizing that Dani wasn't really mad, David laughed.

"What's so funny?"

"Sorry. It's just that of all the up-front girls I've met in my life, you're absolutely the most up-frontest."

Dani smiled. "Yeah, well it comes with the territory."

"What territory's that?" David asked.

"See," Dani said, "I can be a fortune-cookie too."

The Capitol Promenade was a window shopper's paradise. Specialty shops resided in storefronts of nineteenth century décor. Dani and David strolled along a cobblestone sidewalk under Dickensian light posts that bathed the outdoor promenade in a soft yellow glow. What it may have lacked in congruity, it more than made up for in sheer quaintness. Cherry and maple trees lined both sides of the almost four-city-block plaza. Troubadours and street magicians plied their trade up and down the promenade, and women, as if right out of the original cast of *My Fair Lady*, peddled flowers to passersby.

It only took a mere forty-five minutes into the excursion before Dani had David toting two shopping bags. The subject of Mozart was brought up only briefly when David wandered into a second-hand record store and looked at a Vladimir Horowitz recording of Mozart's Grand Concerto for the fortepiano.

"He was amazing," Dani said over David's shoulder.

"Mozart or Horowitz?"

"Yes," she replied with a grin.

They were watching taffy being pulled at a candy shop when Dani asked from out of the blue, "David, you ever been to Moscow?"

David did a double take. "Moscow? Like Moscow, Russia?"

"Yeah."

"What kind of question is that?"

Dani huffed. "Can't you ever just answer a question directly?"

"Uh…yeah, of course I can."

"So?"

"Why you want to know?"

"You're impossible," Dani said, rolling her eyes. "Okay, answer this. Did you go to Juilliard?"

"Yes."

Dani threw her arms in the air. "Finally, a direct answer. Piano?"

"Yes, piano major."

"Wow, you must have been good. Not an easy program to get into."

"I was all right."

Dani laughed.

"What?" David asked.

"Oh, nothing. I just never would have taken you to be the humble type."

"Uh...okay?"

"What did you think of Red Square?"

"Dani, what are you talking about?"

"I talked to Paul. I told him about the Mozart, he's excited."

"Good," David said, trying to follow where she was going.

"He remembers Henry Shoewalter."

"He does? Did he have him?"

"No, he'd stopped teaching by the time Paul went to Juilliard, but he was still on the faculty."

"Too bad, he was a great teacher."

"He's also heard of you."

"Me? How?"

"He said you were pretty famous—big man on campus type."

David shrugged, "It's a small school."

"Oh, for cryin' out loud, David, let it go. You won the Tchaikovsky Competition in Moscow, for heaven's sakes. You know how big that is?"

"Why do I get the feeling you're going to tell me?"

Dani grunted. "Okay, let's try this. When did you move to L.A.?"

"About twelve years ago."

"Why L.A.?"

"Why not?"

Dani scowled.

"Sorry. I like the weather...the weather's real nice." There was an uncomfortable pause, then he asked, "So, where are you from?"

"Oklahoma, born and raised," Dani answered with no inflection.

"Family still there?"

"Dad and brother."

"How'd you end up in DC?"

"The museum. I got the job after I got my doctorate."

"Why music history?"

"Why not?" Dani replied.

Both were silent for a several moments.

Finally, David said, "Listen, Dani, it was a long time ago. I don't talk about it because it has nothing to do with who I am now. It's complicated."

Dani looked into David's eyes and nodded. When she spoke, her voice had a noticeable softness to it. "You know, everyone thinks you're dead. Paul told me the rumor is you were killed."

David offered a half smile and began erratically opening and closing his hand. "I was," he said, in a near whisper.

Dani started to respond, then stopped herself. Instead, she smiled and said, "Come on, time for you to buy me that dinner you promised."

FOWLER SAT HUNCHED IN A CHAIR.

"It's not your fault, Tom," Greenfield said. "You know that, don't you?"

"The hell it's not," Fowler spat back. "I should have never sent that kid after Petrovic. He was too young."

"He was a trained federal agent, Tom. What happened to him could have happened to any of us."

Fowler sat up. The bags under his sixty-two-year-old eyes showed the strain and anguish of the past few hours. He spoke quietly, but with sharpness. "I want that sadistic bastard, Bob."

"I know. I do too."

"And Woo, I want to talk to that son of a bitch. He knows more than—"

Greenfield interrupted, "That's not going to happen."

Fowler looked up. "What do you mean?"

"He's incommunicado, Tom. We can't get to him. Right after he ID'ed Petrovic, he went under. I've talked directly to the director of the CIA, and I quote, 'Woo is not available.'"

"My ass. We have a hacked-up federal agent in the morgue——"

"Tom, I even tried the secretary of state. Negative, Woo's under."

"On what? What's he working on?"

"It's classified, highest level. No one's talking."

"This is bullshit, Bob."

Greenfield leaned back in his chair and looked up at the ceiling. "What about Webber and the girl?"

Fowler let out a frustrated breath. "We have them both under surveillance, six-man teams on both. All agents have digital cameras, and each team leader is equipped with a laptop with direct interface to the mainframe's Comparative Imaging Processor. We'll know in minutes if Petrovic is around."

"What if he's in disguise?"

"I don't care if he dresses up like Ronald McDonald. We have his image now, so if he shows up, the C.I.P. will ID him."

"But you don't think he will, do you?"

Fowler fell back into the chair. "Highly unlikely. He knows we're on him. If he is following them, we'll have to take pictures of half of DC to find him."

"So what's your plan?"

"I wish I had one, Bob."

Chapter 30

Kathryn leaned back in her chair and rubbed her eyes. Her back ached and the words on the computer screen were getting blurry. She looked at the clock—it was eleven thirty. She'd been working for over ten hours.

Daddy's clout had gotten Kathryn Depriest, then Kathryn Whitebridge, admitted to Juilliard. But it was an accidental epiphany that kept her there. An average mezzo, Kathryn discovered her true calling her second year at the conservatory. As a researcher, she possessed an almost psychic ability to know where to look for information others couldn't find. It was Professor Henry Shoewalter who first recognized the talent when he begrudgingly brought the eager sophomore on as his research assistant for a paper he was commissioned to write for inclusion in a book published by Cambridge University. As it turned out, her work on Franz Liszt for the book, *A Comparative Study of Composers from the Romantic Period*, was brilliant by anyone's standards, including those established by older and far more experienced researchers. Her gift was simple common sense. While *eggheads*, as she called them, spent their time mulling through letters, examining and then reexamining famous works for insight into composers' lives, Kathryn would look at a subject's life outside of music. What were their hobbies? What were their loves? "That's where you discover the gold," she used to tell Henry. And more often than not, she was right.

Kathryn printed out the page on her computer screen. She'd gone over her notes for the last assignment Henry asked her to undertake, Mozart circa 1778, and compiled them into a single page. *It has to be here*, she thought, walking downstairs to the kitchen. She saw the light on in Anthony's study.

"I didn't hear you come in," she said, sticking her head into the room and seeing Anthony sitting at his desk.

"I came home after the concert. You looked busy, so I didn't want to interrupt. What were you doing?"

Kathryn walked into the study. "Going over the notes on Henry's project."

"Find anything?"

Kathryn sighed. "I don't know. It all seems so trivial. I can't imagine what Henry found so interesting about this period in Mozart's life. It was one of Mozart's least prolific."

"When was it?"

"1778."

"Hmm." Anthony thought for a second. "Why don't you tell me what you found? I doubt if I can come up with anything new, but if nothing else, it might help if you speak it out loud."

"Okay." Kathryn scanned her page. "Well, let's see, first of all, Wolfgang had left Salzburg the previous September and had been traveling through Europe with his mother, Anna-Maria."

"His mother was with him?" Anthony inquired.

"Leopold knew his son's lesser attributes and refused to let him go alone."

"How old was Mozart at that time?"

"Twenty-one, but Daddy still held quite a bit of dominion over him. When he resigned from the Court of Salzburg, Leopold said in essence, 'get a job.' You know how Mozart was with nobility. He hated crawling to them. It drove Leopold nuts, and he was constantly urging Wolfgang to be more polite to important people— something I can relate to. Anyway, he went to Munich, and in true fashion, pissed off an Elector there and thus failed to find employment. He had to go on to Mannheim. That's where he started out the year 1778. Mannheim."

"Okay, I'm with you. How was Mannheim to him?"

"Actually, pretty good. Wolfgang loved Mannheim."

"Of course, the Mannheim Orchestra," Anthony said.

"At the time, the greatest orchestra in the world. They changed eighteenth century music completely. So, with his mother keeping him out of debtors' prison, Wolfgang filled his life with composing and partying with friends."

"But he didn't stay."

"No, he didn't. Leopold again."

"Why?"

"Why do you think? A woman—well actually, a girl. Just after his twenty-second birthday, Mozart fell madly in love with fifteen-year-old Aloysia Weber."

"Excuse me, dear, don't you mean Constanze Weber?"

"No," Kathryn chuckled, "Aloysia. Constanze was her sister. She came along much later after Aloysia dumped Mozart. Can you believe that he fell in love with one and ended up marrying the other?"

"Oh, I can believe it," Anthony replied.

Kathryn realized what she had said the moment it came out of her mouth, but she tossed off Anthony's comment and quickly moved on.

"Anyway, Aloysia's father was only a poor music copyist with little chance at prosperity and a huge family to support. Leopold was mortified. He wrote Wolfgang a slew of angry letters and commanded him to go on to Paris."

"Which, of course, Wolfgang did."

"Of course."

"Is this when he wrote the Paris Symphony?"

"Very good, Anthony, you remember your music history. Yes, he did, and that was about all he composed. Wolfgang hated Paris. He despised the pretense of the wealthy and pitied the lot of the poor.

His heart was back in Mannheim with Aloysia, and on top of that, his mother had fallen gravely ill."

"Was that before or after the Paris Symphony?"

"During. The only reason he wrote the symphony was because he needed the money to take care of Anna-Maria. A man named Jean Le Gros commissioned the piece. He was the director of the Concert Spirituel, and from what I can gather, a real opportunistic shmuck. He knew Mozart only by reputation, but because Mozart was Austrian, as was the queen…"

"Marie-Antoinette?"

"Bingo. Well, Mozart got the job, and the world got the Paris Symphony."

"When did his mother die?"

"A few weeks later, July third. After that, Mozart left Paris and returned to Salzburg. Eventually, he got his old job back as concertmaster with the Archbishop Colloredo. The rest of the year Mozart did more arguing with his father than composing." Kathryn put down her notes. "That's it. Any thoughts?"

"Yes." Anthony got up and walked around the desk to where Kathryn was sitting and gently kissed her on the head.

"What was that for?"

"My way of saying I'm sorry again."

"For what?" Kathryn asked, totally confused.

Anthony leaned against the desk in front of her and smiled. "Back in school when you did this sort of thing for Henry, I thought it was because of David. I was wrong, Kathryn. This is a brilliant piece of work."

This was the first time Anthony had ever complimented her on anything other than how she looked—and he hadn't even done that in years. "Thank you," she replied.

"So what's next, Miss Marple?" Anthony said, returning to his desk.

Kathryn sighed. "Tomorrow I want to go back to the library and triple check these facts. Then I have to find out why Henry wanted them."

"How do you plan to do that?"

Kathryn thought for a moment. "I think...I need to go to Henry's."

"In Westchester?"

"Yes. Maybe I can learn what he was working on."

"Good luck," Anthony said.

Kathryn stood to leave. Halfway out of the room she stopped. "Anthony?"

"Yes, dear?"

"Thank you."

"For what?"

"For understanding why I need to do this."

Anthony went to his wife and they embraced. "If there's anything I can do..."

"You're already doing it," Kathryn said.

Anthony smiled and squeezed her tighter.

Chapter 31

The first words out of Paul's mouth when he picked Dani up the next morning were, "Well, is it him?" Dani confirmed that indeed it was the same David Webber he'd heard about when he was at Juilliard, and then she told him not to bring it up because David didn't like to talk about it. After Paul made a few disparaging remarks about David's sanity, he promised he wouldn't.

But the first order of business before picking up David was the museum. Dani retrieved both original manuscripts from her office safe and took them downstairs to the lab. Meanwhile, Paul took a photocopy of each piece to the department's ProTools studio located in a small room below the Ripley building. An hour later, Paul and Dani met up and went to get David.

When men are with other men, they are lions, boastful and fearless; battles are never lost, ground seldom given, and never do they give up a chance to prove whose king of the jungle. When men are with women, they are fine gems, dazzling and coveted, carved so close to perfection they appear flawless to the untrained eye. But when men are with men in the company of a woman, they are neither animal nor mineral, they're definitely vegetable, corny as a Kansas back forty, and as ridiculous as broccoli for breakfast. Dani pondered this truth as she sat in the back seat of Paul's minivan and observed the two men in front.

"Nice car," David said.

"Thanks. It's a straight six," Paul replied.

"Really?" David came back.

"Yep, she's got some power," Paul proclaimed. "What do you drive?"

"A Honda," David mumbled.

"Hot hatchback?" Paul asked.

"Accord," David replied.

"Oh, I had one of those when I was younger."

"Yeah, this is nice, especially if you have children."

Dani was sure Paul sensed her growing interest in David. Despite everything before, the previous evening had turned out to be one of the most enjoyable nights she'd had with a man in years. After eating their weight in king crab legs, they continued walking around the promenade for another two hours. To her surprise, she found David very easy to talk to. She told him about growing up in Oklahoma, her father, and her work at the institution. David even opened up, telling her about his parents, how they were killed in an automobile accident when he was nine, and how foster families in Indiana raised him until he went to live with Henry. He even talked a little about his life in Los Angeles and J.P. She asked about why he and Henry hadn't spoken for such a long time but didn't press it when David sidestepped the issue. By the end of the evening, Dani realized she wanted to know David better, much better. She had a sense David felt the same way, and that concerned her. There were still too many secrets. And until she knew what those secrets were, she had to keep her emotions in check.

The minivan rounded the hill, and Paul pulled into the parking lot alongside of the university library.

"Who are we meeting here again?" David asked.

"A friend of mine on staff here at the university."

"What's his name?"

"Wilbur," Dani said, drawing out the name.

"Wilbur?" David said with a smile.

Paul shot both Dani and David a look.

The trio entered the library, and Dani and David followed Paul to a circular staircase in the middle of the first floor rotunda leading to a glass-enclosed lounge on the second floor. Once reaching the comfortable lounge, where people talked freely behind soundproof glass, Paul went to the information desk. He returned a minute later.

"Wilbur's on his way," Paul said, taking a chair.

Less than thirty seconds later the double glass doors flung open.

"Pauly," the high-pitched voice rang out.

"Wilbur," Paul replied, getting up and reaching for the large, fleshy hand.

"You look good, Pauly."

"As do you, big guy."

At six-five and tipping the scales at three hundred seventy plus pounds, Wilbur the librarian filled every doorway he went through. Riding atop the huge African-American's size seventeen shoes were thighs the circumference of a waist. The man's belly was large but hard and only equaled in enormity by his chest. He defied his girth, however, by moving with the ease of a dancer as he followed Paul across the room.

"Let me introduce you to a couple of friends. This is David Webber, and this is Dr. Dani Parsons."

"Pleasure, ma'am," Wilbur said, gently taking Dani's hand.

"You're Wilbur Wallace," David said as he stuck out his hand.

The large man shook David's hand with a smile.

"You two know each other?" Dani asked, looking at both men.

"Well, he doesn't know me, but I know him. What was it, five years ago?"

Wilbur smiled. "Nah, eight."

"Eight years ago, has it been that long?" Paul interjected, knowing exactly what Wilbur and David were referring to.

"Sure was," Wilbur said. "Can you believe it? It seems like yesterday."

David said, "I remember watching you in Pasadena."

"Somebody want to fill me in here?" Dani asked, feeling completely left out.

"Wilbur Wallace," David explained, with a grin. "Defensive lineman for the Michigan Wolverines. Three-time All American, rated one of the nation's best nose guards and a sure bet to go in the first round of the NFL draft."

Wilbur smiled. "Oh, I don't know if I could have made it in the pros, don't think I was fast enough."

Paul broke in. "Bull. You were the quickest lineman in the NCAA before the injury."

"What injury?" Dani asked, feeling very much like a woman doing the backstroke in a pool of testosterone.

"Homecoming game against Ohio State my senior year. Full-back went one way, I went after him, my knee stayed where it was—which happened to be in the way of a two hundred and fifty pound guard. Busted it up pretty bad."

"Ooo, I'm so sorry," Dani said, wincing.

"Oh, don't be. Things turned out all right for me."

Paul interjected, "After graduating from Michigan, Wilbur went on to get his masters and doctorate here at Georgetown. Today, Wilbur's one of the foremost authorities on African-American history in the country."

The big man smiled. "I'm just very blessed to have the job."

"Georgetown is darn lucky to have you, Wilbur. The administration should send a Christmas card every year to that Ohio State guard."

Wilbur laughed.

"So, Wilbur, were you able to come up with anything for me?" Paul asked.

"Boy, I sure hope you folks didn't come out here for nothing. There are not many pre-civil war records on people of color. I was up late last night going over what the university had on Dr. Cook. It was practically nothing. The Georgetown Historical Society had a little more, but it's sketchy at best."

"Whatever you can tell us would be very helpful, Dr. Wallace," Dani said.

"Call me Wilbur, please. Well, we have to go back to a man named George Beall," Wilbur said, letting his bulk fall onto an over-stuffed couch. "George Beall was the grandson of the man who owned much of the land Georgetown is now built on. When George died sometime in the early 1800's, an inventory of his property was made. Beall owned slaves, and of course, slaves were counted as property. The Society has that inventory in its database, and I was able to learn as part of Beall's property was a boy named J. Cook and a woman listed as his mother. We also know a free man of color named Henry Cook purchased them. Henry Cook was a tobacco merchant by trade, but was very active in the Pennsylvania aboli-tionist society."

"Was he related to James and his mother?" Dani asked.

"Indeed. He was James's father."

Paul chimed in, "You mean he bought his own wife and son?"

"We don't know for sure if the woman was his wife, or even the mother of James, but in essence, yes, that's what he did—not all that uncommon. Even though some free blacks in the north did own slaves, more often than not the slaves were freed after they were purchased. In fact, records indicate Henry Cook purchased two other families, one including his daughter, who he freed listing her love as payment."

"That's so sad," Dani said.

"Yes, it is," Wilbur replied. "But it was the way it was."

"What happened to James?" David asked.

"As I said, the history is sketchy. What we do know is James became a doctor and was scheduled to immigrate to Liberia to prac-tice medicine. He changed his mind, along with many other free blacks who claimed the right to stake their family's futures here in America."

"Why would he do that after all he'd been through?"

"The same reason many other free blacks didn't leave—the Underground Railroad. James was very involved in relocating Southern blacks to the north."

"We were told that Dr. Cook was a musician," Dani said.

"Yes, and quite a good one by all accounts. He taught violin."

Paul and David looked at each other, thinking the same thing, but it was Paul who spoke it. "How did he learn the violin?"

"Well, this isn't fact, but the story is Thomas Jefferson taught him."

"WILBUR WALLACE, wow, could that guy play," David said, getting into Paul's minivan as Dani slid the rear door shut.

"I bet the Rams would have taken him," Paul said, turning on the ignition.

"You think? I would have thought the Bears."

"Really, why?" Paul asked.

"They would have liked his size. Also, with his speed you get the pass rush."

"I don't think he would have stayed a nose guard in the pros. I think they would have moved him over to offense."

David considered Paul's statement and nodded in possible agreement.

Paul looked in the rearview mirror and saw Dani smiling. "What?"

"Oh, nothing," Dani said with a smirk. "I'm just thinking what a lucky woman I am to actually witness the ancient ritual of male bonding in person."

Paul pulled out of the driveway and negotiated traffic back onto M Street. Dani gave Paul the address to Sugarberry's, and he drove directly there.

The Brink's truck Dani had called for was already parked in front of Sugarberry's when the three arrived, but the two couriers from the company were only standing beside the truck with their arms crossed. Paul came to a stop behind the truck, and Dani was the first out.

"Hey, guys, I'm Dr. Parsons from the Smithsonian. There a problem?"

The gray-haired man closest to Dani did all the talking. "Nobody's home."

Dani made a face. "She has to be, she knew you were coming. Did you ring the bell again? She's old and may not have heard you."

"I rang, knocked, and rang again. She's not here, Dr. Parsons."

Dani looked at Paul and David. "This doesn't make sense. She couldn't wait to have her collection exhibited in the museum."

"Maybe she just forgot you were coming." Paul said. "She is old."

"She wouldn't have forgotten."

"You folks looking for Trudy?" a man walking a tiny Pomeranian called out from across the street.

"Yes, sir," Dani answered. "Do you know if she's home?"

He picked up his small dog and approached. "She left."

"Left?" Dani replied.

"Yes, last night, about eleven o'clock."

Dani looked at Paul and David, and then back to the man. "Are you sure?"

"Well, of course I'm sure. I was walking Sasha here, and I saw her leave with her suitcase."

"Her suitcase?"

"Was she alone?" David asked.

"No, sir. A younger gentleman was helping her into a car. They were in a hurry too."

All eyes looked at David as he fell against Paul's van and rubbed his eyes. "Welcome to my world, people."

THE BRINK'S TRUCK LEFT, and Dani, David, and Paul sat silently in Paul's parked van for several minutes. Finally, Dani whispered what all three were thinking.

"God, please let that sweet woman be okay."

"Of course she's okay, Dan," Paul said. "Why wouldn't she be? She probably just forgot to tell you she was leaving town, that's all."

Dani looked at David, who said nothing.

Paul continued, "In fact, I bet if you check your voice mail, you'll find she left you a message."

A slight smile of hope crossed Dani's face. She took out her phone and listened to her messages. Her expression said it all.

"Okay, so she forgot to call you, big deal," Paul said. "Dani, she's fine. She'll remember she was supposed to meet you and call apologizing, you'll see."

Dani looked at David again, who was still silent. "What do you think?"

David looked at Dani and then Paul. "Yeah, Paul's right. She's probably fine."

"You don't believe that, do you?" Dani was on the verge of tears. "You think this is connected to the Mozart manuscripts, don't you?"

David struggled to offer a lie, "No..."

"Yes, you do," Dani interrupted. "And I do too."

"Dan, your imagination's running away from you," Paul said. "Now look, you two, I don't know what happened to Professor Shoewalter or to your friend J.P., David, but just because an old woman forgets about an appointment and decides to go visit a sick relative somewhere doesn't mean we have a conspiracy at work. She had her suitcase, for goodness sakes, you guys—how many kidnap victims take a suitcase?"

Dani and David looked at one another. Paul was right; they had no evidence Sugarberry had been taken against her will and no real connection between J.P. and Henry. But without saying it to each other, they both also knew Paul was wrong—Sugarberry was not on vacation.

"I need to go to New York," David said.

"Why?" Paul asked.

"I'm coming with you," Dani added.

"No," David shot back.

"Yes, I am."

There were several seconds of silence before David spoke, "Bad things are happening to people around me, Dani. I'm not going to let you be one of them. This is my problem. The best thing for you...for both of you to do, is let me out of this car and forget you ever met me."

Dani looked at Paul and then back to David. "Cut the macho

crap, Webber," Dani said with a gentle voice. "I'm coming with you, end of discussion. And you're wrong, it's not just your problem." She looked at Sugarberry's house. "Not anymore. Besides, you need me in New York."

"What are you two talking about?" Paul interjected. "Why do either of you need to go to New York?"

Dani answered, "Because we have to find out what Henry Shoewalter was working on and why David's Mozart sketch was so important. Do you know where Henry lived?"

David felt ashamed of his pathetic neediness. The brief moment of bravado was an act he suspected Dani didn't buy for a second. She was right. He did need her in New York. But not for any scholarly reasons—he just needed her. He nodded and looked out the window. "Yeah, I know where he lived."

Chapter 32

Thurman Winfield reclined on a leather couch in the opulent Harlem offices of Electric Chair Records. His spectacles were perched on the end of his nose, and a book entitled *This Business of Music* rested open upon his chest. With no forewarning from his body, his eyes suddenly popped open. He got up and walked over to a desk sitting in front of a tinted-glass window.

As if looking into a crystal ball, he stared down at the desk. He picked up a lead-weighted ashtray and moved it in front of him. Then he took off his glasses and placed them off to the left and set the book off to the right, creating a perfect triangle. He studied the geometric design he'd created.

Satisfied, he turned his attention to a bowl of wrapped chocolates sitting on the table beside the couch. He retrieved the bowl and brought it back to the desk. He counted out ten pieces of candy into the ashtray. He pulled out all the change in his pockets and divided it equally between his eyeglasses and the book. Then he sat down and studied his work.

Like a chess player, he reached for his eyeglasses and pushed ten coins to the ashtray. He then took a chocolate and placed it beside his eyeglasses. He slid five coins from beside the book next to his eyeglasses, each time taking a candy and putting it back into the ashtray, followed by pushing the ten coins from the ashtray over to the book.

He went through the drill twice more. Afterward, he sat back in his chair, unwrapped a chocolate, and popped it in his mouth. "Old Nick," he said, chewing on the candy, "you crafty little Italian. So that's what you're up to."

"BOWEN, its David. The Sugarberry woman is now missing. I don't know what the hell is going on, so Dani and I are going to Henry's house in New York. Maybe we can find out what he was working on. We're catching an afternoon shuttle and should be back tonight, but I won't be staying at the hotel anymore. This is costing a fortune, and I can't leave my cat, so I'm checking out and will be crashing at the house of a guy named Paul Rogers. He's a colleague of Dani's. I'll call if I come up with anything...no, I'll call you tonight either way. And please, Bowen, you do the same."

Petrovic finished listening to David's message and sat down on the bed. His face was expressionless as he cracked his knuckles. "It's time this comes to an end," he said, looking down at J.P.

A WHITE-PANELED furniture truck was parked at the end of an abandoned taxiway at Washington's Reagan National airport. Inside the vehicle, three men in suits sat. No one spoke. The only sound was a low hum coming from the three computer terminals and two GPS receivers lining the interior of the cargo area. Two of the men wore headsets. The third, Thomas Fowler, did not. Instead, he was hunched over a makeshift desk looking over the latest batch of images pulled from the printer.

"Sir, the assistant director is pulling up."

Fowler grunted as he stepped from the cargo area and into the cab of the truck. Greenfield opened the door and pulled himself into the cab of the mobile control center just as Fowler fell into the driver's seat.

"Can't remember the last time you actually joined me in the field, Bob."

"Probably the last time you put the bureau's collective butt in a sling." Greenfield glanced back into truck. "How's it going back there?"

Fowler shook his head. "We've been on them all day. No sign of Petrovic."

"Where are they now?"

"Getting on a shuttle for New York."

"Shoewalter's?" the assistant director stated more than asked.

"That'd be my guess. We thought we were getting a break. There was no way Petrovic was going to be able to stay incognito in an airport. We have agents all over the terminal, on the tarmac, even in the baggage area. Zilch."

"Too bad," Greenfield said.

"Yup," Fowler replied, rubbing his eyes. "So why *are* you here, Bob?"

"I'm meeting the Los Angeles district attorney's plane in a half hour. Thought I'd drop by to see if you have anything I can tell him."

"You could have just called."

"Yeah, well I wanted to be able to tell him I'm personally on top of the situation, and assure him all is being done that can be done, and what is being done is the right thing. Tell me it's the right thing, Tom."

"You think we should pick up Webber?"

"How about you, you still think it's best to just follow him?"

"I talked with New York. Fifteen agents are waiting to cover Webber and the girl the minute they get off the plane at La Guardia. And there's something else."

"What?"

"Kathryn Depriest's got a tail."

"Really, who?"

"None other than Jimmy Depriestiano."

"That is interesting. What's Old Nick up to?"

Fowler finally smiled for the first time since the massacre in the subway station. "I don't think Old Nick put the tail on her."

"Her husband?"

"I think Anthony is playing both ends against the middle."

Greenfield considered the possibilities. "What are you going to do?"

"First, see what happens with Webber in New York. I still don't think he's involved, but I'm not sure what Anthony thinks. Then I want to accelerate the operation—force Depriestiano's hand."

Greenfield nodded.

"Any word from Woo?" Fowler asked.

"Are you kidding?" Greenfield scoffed. "It's like the guy never existed."

Fowler chuckled. "Oh, he exists, Bob. That little rascal definitely exists."

THE LIMO BATTLED its way down Fifth Avenue until crossing Forty-Second Street, where it pulled over to the curb and stopped. Jimmy Depriestiano, wearing ear buds, leaned against one of the two giant stone lion statues keeping watch over the entrance of the New York City Public Library. His eyes were closed, and he was in the middle of a drum solo when the massive car honked its horn. Jimmy pulled out the earpieces, stood, and casually strutted to the vehicle's rear window, lighting a cigarette.

"Get in, you idiot," the voice yelled from inside. The car door opened, and Jimmy slid into the seat across from Anthony. "How stupid are you, anyway?"

"What the fuck you talking about?"

"I thought I told you to stay out of sight."

"I am. Kathryn's got no idea I'm scoring her."

"Has she been in there all day?"

"All fuckin' day, man. I'm bored shitless. Can I go home?"

"No, cousin. I'll tell you when you can go home, understand?"

"Yeah, yeah."

"Have you talked to your father?"

"Oh, yeah, I almost forgot. He talked to his friend at the FBI. He don't know nothin' about Webber except they's got some agents watching him. He said it's all pretty hush-hush."

Anthony grit his teeth. "Did he happen to mention where Webber was?"

"Yeah, he said he heard Webber and some other bitch was on their way up here. Whatta ya think of that?"

Anthony thought for a second and then smiled. "I think things are about to get very interesting, dear cousin. That's what I think of that."

Chapter 33

As David negotiated traffic out of LaGuardia airport and onto the Whitestone Expressway, Dani sat in the passenger seat, engrossed in a report she'd been reading ever since getting on the plane in DC. She'd hardly said anything for an hour, but David didn't mind, he needed the silence. Returning to New York, to Henry's, wasn't something he was sure he was prepared for.

Little time had been wasted after leaving Sugarberry's. While David checked out of the hotel, Paul and Dani swung by the museum's lab and picked up the report on the two pieces of music, returning the original manuscripts to her safe. There was no time to check in at the ProTools studio—Paul would have to see to that after Dani and David made their plane. Twenty minutes later they were at Paul's house dropping off David's belongings, which included Ravel. All in all, it took an hour and a half from the time David made his pronouncement that he had to go to New York to Paul asking Dani at Reagan National to call once they reached Shoewalter's.

"Well, you're right," Dani said, her eyes still on the pages. "Your manuscript is consistent with the paper stock Mozart was using in

Vienna in '91. The watermark on the left of the manuscript is a CS over a small c in reverse, and on the right there are three moons over REAL in reverse. The measurement between the staves, highest line of the first stave to the lowest line of the bottom stave, is 182.5 mm to 183 mm, and it looks like they were ruled by hand, not machine. It's from exactly the same stock Mozart used for *Così fan tutti*, *The Magic Flute*, and the requiem."

"Yeah," David replied, his hand holding the wheel tighter than usual.

Dani knew returning to New York was not something David was eager to do. Though she didn't know why, she was sure it had to do with why he and Shoewalter hadn't spoken in years. And more than likely, why a world-class concert pianist had ended up in obscurity playing in Los Angeles piano bars.

"You okay?" Dani asked.

"I'm fine," David answered, giving Dani a quick glance.

"How long has it been since you've been back here?"

"About twelve years. So what does it say about the other piece?"

"Get ready, this is going to blow your mind."

"Why?"

"A couple of reasons. The watermark on Sugarberry's piece made it very easy to date. A Pennsylvania manufacturer named Nathan Sellers created the mold. He was a famous late nineteenth century paper artisan. He was the only person in America to create his watermarks by the wire method. That, along with a chemical analysis of the ink, puts the manuscript around 1810."

David thought for a second. "If what Wilbur told us about Dr. Cook is true, then Cook would have been just a boy when it was written."

"Right, which makes perfect sense," Dani said with a smile.

"Why are you smiling?"

Dani took a deep breath. "The hand that wrote this piece—"

"Is not Cook's," David finished.

"No, that's not true, some of it is Cook's."

"Some of it?"

"The handwriting analysis shows three different hands on this music."

"Three?" David responded.

"Yes, you care to guess who one of the other writers was?"

"You mean they came up with a name?"

"In this case they did," Dani answered.

David thought for a second before letting go his own smile. "Thomas Jefferson."

"None other," Dani giggled.

David was caught up. "So Jefferson did teach Cook to play the violin?"

"It looks that way. When Cook was a boy, he must have lived at Monticello. It's common knowledge Jefferson loved music, so it's not hard to imagine him discovering one of his boy slaves having an ear, and him teaching him the violin and basic music notation. That would explain why the piece contains both their handwritings and why Cook's hand is so similar to Jefferson's. The confirmation over the last few years about Jefferson and his mistress, Sally Hemmings, makes it even more plausible. Jefferson obviously had a very different relationship with his slaves than most masters." Dani smiled and added, "It's elementary, Watson."

"Okay, hang on, Sherlock. That all makes sense, but we still have the same question. How did Jefferson know any of Mozart's work? We're still talking almost fifty-years before the first Kochel was published."

It was Dani's turn to think for a moment. "Jefferson had to have met Mozart at some point. Maybe when he was in Europe?"

"We need to find out more about Jefferson."

Dani smiled. "This is what I do. I'm in the finding-out business. When we get back to DC, we'll check Mr. Jefferson's travel schedule around the year 1790 and 91. I also want to go to the National Archives."

"Why?"

"That's where they house genealogical records. We need to find out more about Dr. Cook and his family—maybe we can put him and Jefferson together."

David nodded. "You said there were three hands. Who was the other?"

"Unknown. But it's certain it's not from the original notation."

"You mean it was added later?"

"Much later." Dani turned several pages in the report. "I'm reading: analysis of the letters C-K and F inscribed in the lower left corner of the artifact, identified as exhibit B, reveal the writing to be from a third, unknown source. Instrument used is a number two leaded pencil. Date of creation, within the last three months."

"ATTENTION, the National Museum of American History will be closing in fifteen minutes. Please begin moving toward the exits on the first and second floors. Thank you for visiting the National Museum of American History."

As the recorded voice began repeating its command, the young monsignor tossed his bottle of water into the trash can and stepped onto the down escalators leading to the gift shop and cafés.

"Excuse me, ma'am," the priest said to the young girl behind the register in the gift shop. "I know you're closing, but I was wondering if I could purchase some hats to take back to my boys at the orphanage."

"Sure, Father, they're right over there in the corner," she said, pointing to the hat tree filled with baseball caps, all displaying the Smithsonian logo.

"Yes, I know, but I really need about thirty of them, and it would be nice if they were all yellow—that's the color of our athletic shirts. I was wondering if you might have a box of them in your storage room I could purchase?"

The clerk looked around. The store was almost empty. "I don't know—"

"Oh never mind, I'm sorry, it's too much of an inconvenience. You must be exhausted and ready to get home."

"Well, can you come back tomorrow, I'm sure—"

"No," the priest answered. "I'm leaving tonight to go back to Chicago. It's okay, it was just an afterthought. I thought the boys at the home would enjoy them. God bless you and have a lovely evening."

The monsignor turned to walk away. The girl stopped him. "Father, wait."

The priest turned.

"I tell you what. Why don't you grab me one of those hats over there. I'll scan it and multiply the purchase by thirty. You go ahead and pay, then leave with me. I pass the storage room on the way out the employee exit, and I know we have plenty of those hats down there."

"Bless you, dear. As long as it won't get you into any trouble."

"Nah, I'm the assistant manager, it'll be okay. I'll just tell security you're my priest. Go on, you get the hat while I lock up the front."

As the girl walked to the front of the store, Petrovic slipped on latex gloves and put his hands in his pockets.

"DO YOU REMEMBER WHERE HE LIVED?"

"I remember," David answered, his voice low and almost monotone.

David's face was stone. He showed no emotion as he drove through the town of White Plaines. He looked straight ahead, as if refusing to acknowledge the existence of anything that wasn't five feet directly in front of the car. He came to a stop sign and for the first time looked around. "That didn't use to be there," he said, nodding at a small strip mall.

He turned right and entered a tree-lined residential area where small houses sat a respectable distance off the street, and front lawns sprawled all the way to the street in the absence of any sidewalk. He began slowing and pulled over to the curb just before reaching the end of the second block.

David sat back in his seat and let out a heavy sigh. "That's it."

It was a modest, white wood-framed two-story with a large screened in front porch. It was small and old but far from being a run-down shanty.

Neither got out of the car. Dani waited as David stared at the house.

"It's nice," Dani whispered.

"It's...smaller."

Dani smiled, suddenly understanding. "Yeah, I know. I feel that way too every time I go home."

David looked at Dani, nodded with a sad smile, and opened the car door.

At first, Dani thought David had stopped because he decided he couldn't go through with it. But then she saw what he saw. Across the front door was strung yellow tape that read WESTCHESTER COUNTY SHERIFF'S DEPARTMENT.

"I didn't even think of that," David said.

"Is there a back door?"

David nodded, and Dani followed him around the side of the house. The backyard was huge, and the grass was green and trimmed. There was no fence, but a flower garden was planted up and down each side of the back yard, and a vegetable garden bordered the rear of the property. They came to three wooden stairs that ascended to a back door—there was no yellow tape.

"Now, how do we get in?"

David walked up the stairs and looked around. Potted geraniums, desperately in need of watering, were clustered together on the wooden planked platform. David tipped each pot and looked underneath. He found the key under the fourth pot. He inserted the key and opened the door.

"YOU SURE ARE WORKING LATE," Charlie said as Paul handed him his ID.

"No rest for the wicked, Charlie."

Charlie smiled. "Where's Dr. P?"

"I put her on a plane for New York a couple of hours ago."

"Well, she didn't say nothing to me about no vacation."

"No, it's business. She'll be back tonight," Paul said, taking his

ID card. "Listen, Charlie, I have some reports I want to leave on Dani's desk, and I also want to pick up my email. The computer in my office is down, so I thought I'd just use hers. Think that'll be all right?"

"Don't see why not. You need me to let you in?"

"No, I have a key," Paul said, jangling a key chain.

"Them dang computers. That's why I refuse to get one."

Paul grinned. "You may be on to something, Charlie. I'll be down in a few minutes." As Paul got onto the elevator, Charlie saw a single sheet of paper fall from a file folder and land on the floor.

"Dr. Rogers, you lost a—" It was too late, the elevator doors had shut.

Paul stepped off the elevator and walked down the empty corridor to Dani's office. He was within ten feet of her door when he noticed it was ajar and the light was on. "Dani, you lame-brain," he muttered, pushing open the door.

Their eyes met. But the man kneeling at the safe said nothing. If he was surprised, he didn't show it. His face was relaxed, his breathing calm. Paul's attention was diverted by a high-pitched muffled cry. He turned toward the sound. The girl was sitting on the floor in the corner of the office with tape across her mouth. Tears were streaming down her cheeks. Fear swept through Paul's body, and he began backing out the door.

The stranger finally spoke, "Don't move."

Paul looked back at the man. He was a priest. And he was pointing a gun three feet from Paul's head.

"We're leaving."

Paul swallowed and answered the statement with only a nod.

Petrovic motioned for Paul to turn around and start walking. As Paul turned, he heard a loud spit. His head involuntarily spun to the noise—he wished it hadn't. The girl had fallen onto her side. She'd stopped crying. The bullet had entered her skull directly in the center of her forehead.

"Walk," the voice behind him commanded.

There was no floor—he had no feet. He was completely numb with fear. They were still several feet from the elevator when Paul heard its ping as it arrived at the floor. When the doors opened, he saw the barrel come over his shoulder.

"Charlie, no!" Paul yelled, grabbing the man's arm.

The hard concrete walls caused the spit of the weapon to reverberate through the corridor. Paul's grip on the assassin's arm was short lived, and he felt himself being shoved to the floor. As he fell, he saw Charlie, his weapon drawn and in a firing position. Paul's mind raced. *Shoot, Charlie, shoot! Why aren't you shooting?* As Paul hit the floor, he looked back for the assassin and understood why Charlie wasn't returning fire. The man wasn't standing any longer—he was lying on the floor behind Paul using him for cover.

Petrovic fired twice, one bullet hitting Charlie in the shoulder, causing the security man to spin to his right. Petrovic stood and fired again, this time hitting Charlie in the chest. As the priest started walking toward his target, Paul swung out his leg, catching Petrovic in the back of the knee and causing him to stumble. Petrovic regained his footing and turned to Paul. His eyes were steel, cold and dead. Paul had never believed in the concept of the devil before, but at that moment, he knew he was looking at the face of pure evil.

Paul stopped breathing as he watched the killer point the gun at his head. *This is it*, he thought. *This is where the mystery ends.* Paul closed his eyes and waited for the sound. He heard it, but it wasn't the lethal spit. It was a loud blast from several feet away. Paul opened his eyes and saw the priest falling backward. He looked down the corridor and saw a completely blood-soaked Charlie sitting on the floor, his back against the wall with a smoking gun in his hand. The old man's eyes were wide, and his head was frantically shaking up and down. "The gun," he moaned.

Paul looked on the floor beside him and saw it—a gun.

Paul lunged for the weapon and felt a sudden dull pain in his side. He saw the priest raising himself off the floor. Paul grabbed the gun but couldn't lift it. It was like a nightmare; no matter how hard he tried, his body wouldn't obey. Suddenly, he realized he was no longer able to move at all, the pain in his side overtaking him. He looked back for the demon. The priest was now on his feet and standing directly over him. Paul watched the killer lean closer. He felt the pressure from a hand pushing on his back. The corridor started spinning. The killer said something, but all sounds had become distorted and slow. He was drifting, and there was no connection to his own body as he watched the priest return upright and wipe the blood off the knife. Then there was darkness.

Chapter 34

Nothing had changed. The veneer curtains, the braided rugs, the flannel slipcovers, and the tarnished brass lamps were all in their place just as David remembered. The walls were still cluttered with the same strange paintings by artists no one had ever heard of—just as they were twelve years ago—probably as they were ever since Henry moved in. He stood in the small living room and silently took it all in. The old wallpaper was peeling in places, and the hardwood floors were in need of waxing, but the old place still looked pretty good.

"Is this you?" Dani asked, picking up a picture frame off a dusty old TV set in the living room.

David walked up behind and looked over her shoulder. "Yeah, that's me."

Dani started laughing. "Look at all that hair. And look how skinny you were." She set the picture down and scanned the others clustered together. "Oh my, they're all of you." Dani heard David trying to catch his breath. She turned and looked at him. She could tell he was doing his best to hold it together.

"Come here." Dani put her arms around his neck.

"You know," David said, clearing his throat, "I'm not really a crier."

"What?" Dani whispered.

"I'm not a crier. It's...just something I don't do."

"Oh, so you're the strong silent type?"

A soft chuckle was forced out. "Yeah, something like that."

"Well, should you become one, it's okay. I cry at AT&T commercials."

David gently pulled back. He was smiling. He looked in her soft hazel eyes and said nothing for a long moment. Dani was sure they were going to kiss. She felt her lips being pulled to his. Her heart was racing, and then David said, "I guess we should go check out Henry's office. It's across the hallway." Her arms fell to her sides as David pulled away and started across the room. She closed her eyes and exhaled, still teetering.

The room was a cluttered mess. It was also how David remembered it. Books everywhere on the floor, the desk, the windowsill, and stacked three high in the bookcase itself. As David stood in the doorway and surveyed the small office, memories flooded his mind. He looked at the old Steinway sitting in the corner and could still see a *little him* practicing scales as Henry graded papers. He remembered every time he was sure Henry wasn't listening, Henry would shout out of nowhere, *legato, Davey, legato!* David could still see the old man surrounded with books and music at the huge mahogany desk in front of the only window in the room. Reading and making notes and then reading some more, or on the telephone, giving an interview to some academic publication, or advising a fellow professor, or as was often the case, on the telephone encouraging some petrified student who was about to perform his final in front of Henry's jury. Henry loved his work, and only now did David realize just how much he enjoyed watching Henry love it. Yes, it was a cluttered mess. But this was the inner sanctum of a scholar. This was who Henry was. This was Henry's life. This was David's home.

"This isn't going to be easy, is it?" Dani said, looking at the chaos.

"Whenever Henry was working on something, he always kept

that project on his desk." David entered the room and went behind the desk, taking a seat in an old and cracked high-backed leather chair.

Dani followed David's lead and starting thumbing through the stacks of papers and books piled on the desk.

"Here's a text book on Gregorian chant—don't think that'll be any help. A book on Copland—a biography on Ellington, I'd like to read this." Dani continued to lift items off the desk and place them on the floor. "This looks like the first draft to a letter of recommendation for a student. I have about a half dozen here, all different students."

"Yeah, I've found a couple of those myself," David added, carefully sifting through the rubble.

"Was Henry ever married?" Dani asked, digging into a new pile.

"Yes, to his work."

"You know what I mean," Dani said, lifting a stack onto the floor.

"No, he never married. He dated a little but nothing serious that I know of. Then again, I was pretty much into myself by the time I would have understood that sort of thing. But as far as I know, there was only his work."

"Must have gotten lonely."

David didn't reply, but wondered why he had never considered that.

For the next twenty minutes the two meticulously went over everything on the desk and in each of the four drawers. Neither found anything remotely pertaining to Mozart. The desk was almost cleared off when David leaned back in his chair and looked around the room.

"What?" Dani asked.

"Hang on." David walked to the bookcase and ran his hand over all the titles. Then he walked to the other side of the room and repeated the process. He canvassed the room, scanning the titles of the books scattered around. He stopped and did a three-sixty, looking in all directions. "Okay, this is weird."

"What's weird?"

David walked to the piano, opened the lid on the bench, looked in, closed it, and sat down behind the piano.

"David, what's weird?"

"Not only are we not finding anything on Henry's desk about Mozart, I can't find anything in this office about Mozart."

Dani shrugged her shoulders. "Maybe this isn't where he was working."

"Whether he was working on a Mozart project here or not, he still would have books on Mozart. I mean, come on. Henry loved Wolfy. Besides, Henry was a music scholar. How many music scholars do you know who don't keep a vast array of material on the greatest composer who ever lived? No, this is wrong. It's almost like someone has come in here and removed anything pertaining to Mozart. I can't even find so much as a piece of sheet music."

Dani said nothing in response. David was right; it didn't make sense.

Dani was glancing over the last few remaining items on the desk when she heard the music. David was playing the piano.

She got up and walked over. A piece of music was on the music stand, but David wasn't reading it. His eyes were closed, and he swayed as he caressed the keys. The melody was beautiful and hypnotic. The line flowed through the lush yet simple chords like a bird, never *trying* to be sentimental or emotional—it just was incredibly sentimental and powerfully emotional. David came to the final retard, ending with a chord progression played softer than Dani ever thought a piano could be played.

"Oh my God," Dani whispered.

David looked up and smiled. His eyes were red.

"That was amazing—you are amazing. What was that?"

"It's a concerto I wrote for Henry my first year at Juilliard. I gave it to him for Christmas. It was sitting here on the piano. I haven't played it in years."

Dani walked around the piano and sat beside David on the bench.

He looked up from the music and saw she was staring at him. "What?"

Dani didn't immediately respond. She only smiled and looked into his eyes. "Who the heck are you, David Webber?"

They didn't hear the back door open or the intruder walk through the house. Dani saw her first. She was standing in the doorway. When David saw the startled look on Dani's face, he turned around. He almost threw up.

"Hello, David," Kathryn Depriest said.

Chapter 35

"I'm sorry. The door was open, so I just came in…I, uh, I thought you might be the police and…" Kathryn realized she was babbling, stopped mid-sentence, and smiled at Dani. "Hi, I'm Kathryn Depriest."

Dani recovered from the shock and returned the smile. "Dani Parsons," she said, extending her hand.

Kathryn shook the woman's hand and then looked at David. He wasn't smiling. His face was drawn, and his left hand was flexing. "So, David, not even a hug for an old friend?" Kathryn asked, doing her best to keep the tremble out of her voice.

David hesitated before he got up and mechanically put his arms around Kathryn. He had yet to say a word.

"I'm fine, David, thanks for asking," Kathryn said.

Dani didn't need to be hit over the head. Though she didn't know who this Kathryn Depriest was, she knew from David's face *what* she was. If ever a graceful exit was in order, it was now.

"Uh…listen," Dani said, "you two look like you have some catching up to do, so I'll just go…uh…I know, I'll go find the kitchen and make us all some coffee." Kathryn and David just stared at each other as Dani continued, "And you know what,

271

David? I forgot to call Paul and tell him we made it. I should do that too." Dani could tell no one was listening to her, so she smiled and walked out of the room without saying anything else.

Kathryn let out a nervous laugh. "Whew, this is...awkward."

David said nothing.

"You know, I always wondered what it'd be like when we saw each other again. I sure didn't expect it to be like this."

He was still silent.

"You look good, David."

David nodded. There was another prolonged pause.

"She's pretty. How long have you two been——"

"She's a friend, haven't known her long," David finally said.

"Oh."

"How's Anthony?" David asked on top of Kathryn's response.

"He's fine."

"Yeah, so I read."

Kathryn looked confused for a moment and then smiled. "Oh, you must mean the magazine article. Yeah, that was a little too much. I didn't want Anthony to do it—photographers coming into the house and following——"

"What are you doing here, Kathryn?" David interrupted.

She smiled. "Same old David Webber, get right to the point."

David didn't respond.

Kathryn's face became serious, and she looked David in the eye. "I heard about Henry...and you. I guess I'm here to try and help."

Just then Dani stuck her head into the room. "Sorry, I can't find any coffee. I hope tea will be all right. I have some water boiling."

Kathryn looked at Dani and smiled. "Tea will be fine, thanks."

David didn't take his eyes off of Kathryn. "Henry hated coffee."

"Yeah, he did, didn't he?" Kathryn added.

David walked over to the desk and sat down. His face was hard and his body rigid. "Kathryn was just informing me she was here to help. I guess my problems are over. Isn't that great?"

Dani didn't know how to respond, so she didn't. The David she had sat with at the piano was gone. The one from the café was back.

"David——" Kathryn said.

"No, really, I didn't know what to do. Now I don't have to worry."

Kathryn looked away.

Dani decided that if she was going to be dragged into the middle of something, she might as well get dragged in with both feet. "Ms. Depriest, how can you help?"

"Please, it's Kathryn. As David knows, I used to work with Henry as a researcher. When I heard Henry was killed and that David was—"

Dani jumped on Kathryn's words, "You know what he was working on?"

"Yes, well, sort of. He contacted me about a month ago. I hadn't heard from him in years." Kathryn looked at David to make sure he had heard what she had just said. "He wanted me to do some research for him."

"Did it have anything to do with Mozart?" Dani asked.

"Yes, it did."

Dani started to say something else but was interrupted by a shrill whistle from down the hall. "That's the water. I'll be right back."

After Dani left the room, Kathryn looked back at David. He was leaning back in the chair. His mouth was tight and his jaw locked.

"I guess it isn't true what they say, is it?"

"What's that?" David responded dryly.

"That time heals all wounds. You still hate me, don't you?"

David looked at the woman standing in front of him. Her hair was blonder, there were some crow's feet around her eyes, and her face was fuller, but she was still as beautiful as ever. What was he to say? What could he say, and what was the true answer? He honestly didn't know.

"How'd you find out about Henry?"

"Anthony told me. He heard from the musicians in the orchestra. Friends out west informed him about how they suspected you."

"He must have loved that."

Kathryn took a deep breath and refused to look at him as she spoke. "Listen, David, I should probably just leave now. It's obvious you have no desire to see me, much less take any help from me. But

I want you to know I'm not going to stop trying to figure out what happened to Henry because I know you didn't kill him. And I owe it to Henry to prove you didn't…that you couldn't." Kathryn swallowed hard, holding back the tears. "You know I loved that old man too. I hated what happened between the two of you because of me, but David, it wasn't his fault, it was mine, mine alone. It was so long ago, and we were both little more than kids—I was a kid, a kid that screwed up. I'm sorry, I'm sorry for you, I'm sorry for me, and most of all, I'm sorry for Henry. Because he didn't deserve what you gave him—what we gave him. This is my chance to make it up to him. And I'm going to."

"How?" Dani asked, appearing in the doorway.

"Whatever Henry was working on was important, very important. He told me so. I think *that's* what got him killed."

Dani walked behind the desk and kneeled next to David. She spoke almost in a whisper, "David, if she can help, you owe it to Henry to let her."

David looked at Dani, his jaw loosened, and he closed his eyes as he rubbed his hand through his hair and nodded.

Kathryn spoke without being prompted. "Henry asked me to do a study of Mozart focusing on the year 1778. That's all he was interested in, that year. I don't know why. Does that year mean anything to you, David?"

David got up and walked to the bookcase. *My God*, he thought, *Kathryn is here in this room right now*. The years of reliving the last time he saw her at the hospital, the anger, the pain, the regret. So much of his life had been affected by this woman, whose memory had held such power over him for so long and now, here she stood.

"David," Dani asked, "*does* that date mean anything to you?"

David nodded and tried to focus. "Yeah, maybe. It was the year Mozart's mother died. We need to talk to a man named Sullivan."

"Raymond Sullivan?" Dani asked.

David jerked around. "You know him?"

"No," Dani said as she started looking through the papers she'd tossed on the floor, "but just before you started playing the piano, I found something—where did I put—here it is." Dani held up a message book. "Dr. Raymond Sullivan. It's in here several times, with a phone number."

"Why does that name sound familiar?" Kathryn asked.

"Because back when we were in school, he published a theory Mozart had written a requiem mass for his mother that's remained missing. I was preparing to refute it when…" David stopped himself, "well, I lost interest."

Dani intervened. "David, that could be it. Henry must have learned a requiem for Mozart's mother really did exist. That must be what we have."

"You have it?" Kathryn jumped in. "You have the requiem?"

"No, but we each have a piece of music, the same piece of music from two different sources. David's is from Mozart's actual hand, mine's from…" she stopped herself, "another source."

Kathryn looked at David open-mouthed. "The sketch Henry gave you—that's what she's talking about, isn't it?"

David nodded.

"It's part of a mass for his mother. How did you—"

"I work for the Smithsonian Institution in DC. I was working on another project when I acquired the piece. David learned of me because Henry had my name and phone number in his possession when he was killed."

"Why?"

"We don't know."

"But you're sure it has something to do with the Mozart?"

"Yes," Dani acknowledged, "and if what we have is part of a requiem Mozart wrote for his mother, then this would be the most important Mozart work to turn up in decades—certainly the most personal. It'd be worth a fortune."

"It's not a requiem," a stone-faced David said.

"Why?" Dani asked.

"Because for one, the dates don't work. My sketch is from '91. Mozart's mother died in '78. Why would he write a sketch to something he composed thirteen years earlier? Second, if he did compose a mass in '78, he would have had plenty of opportunities to perform it, and there's no record he ever did. We certainly know about every other work that was performed. Hell, we even know the names of the original singers in his operas. And how about the fact that of all the letters Mozart wrote to Leopold, not a single one of them mention anything about a requiem? Don't you think that would be something a son would share with his father, especially this son and this father? No, I didn't believe it when Sullivan first posed the theory, and I don't believe it now. Mozart never wrote a requiem mass for his mother."

"Maybe Henry found the proof you say doesn't exist," Dani said.

David still shook his head defiantly.

Kathryn spoke up, "But, David, what else could it be? The thing that has baffled me about Henry's request is that 1778 was the least productive year of Mozart's life. Anna-Maria's death was the only significant thing that occurred."

"Why are we stuck on 1778 all of a sudden?" David yelled. "My sketch is from 1791. Just because Henry gave you an assignment doesn't mean shit. Jesus, Kathryn, you still think the whole fucking world revolves around you."

Kathryn didn't respond, and no one spoke.

After a moment, Dani headed for the door.

"Where you going?" David asked with a much softer tone.

"I'm going in the other room to call Paul," Dani said sharply. "Then I'm going to come back in here, and we're going to call Dr. Raymond Sullivan. You may be right, David. Maybe Mozart never wrote a mass for his mother. But Henry had Kathryn researching that specific year for some reason, and I can't believe it's just a coincidence Sullivan's name and phone number are here on Henry's desk. In the meantime," she added, her tone sounding like a mother scolding her children, "I suggest you two say whatever it is you need to say to each other. It looks like we're going to be working on this thing together, and I refuse to deal with all of this old ex-boyfriend/girlfriend crap. Now grow the hell up and clear the air. I'll be back in a minute."

Dani stormed out the door and left the room silent. David

ambled back behind the desk and fell into the chair. Neither spoke for several moments.

Kathryn sat down across from David. "How's the hand?"

David looked up. "It does what it needs to do."

Kathryn nodded.

"Does Anthony know what you're doing?"

Kathryn nodded. "Yes, he's even encouraging it."

"Admirable. He's a better man than me."

She leaned forward. David could see that her eyes were filled with pain and pleading. "Are you going to be able to handle this? Because to be honest, I don't know if I can."

David took a deep breath and closed his eyes before he spoke. "Yeah, I can handle it. Like you said, it was a long time ago, and we were just kids."

Suddenly from the other room they heard a loud crash and Dani's voice cry out. David was already on his feet and heading for the door when he met Dani stumbling back in. Her face was white, tears were pouring from her eyes, and she was hyperventilating. "P—Paul, oh God, Charlie!"

"What's wrong?" David asked, steadying Dani by the arm.

"Some—someone broke into my office. Oh God, David, Charlie's dead and Paul, he's—he's—" Dani laid her head on David's chest and sobbed.

Chapter 36

David crouched in front of Dani as Kathryn handed her a glass of water. Dani took a small sip. She was still shaking but breathing easier.

"We have to get back to DC. Paul was stabbed and is still in surgery. David, they've removed a kidney and…" she started crying again, "…they don't know if he's going to make it. David, what's going on?" She sobbed, letting her head fall on his shoulder.

"I don't know," David muttered. "I don't know."

"Charlie was shot four times. He was dead before anyone got to him—oh God, I can't believe this is happening."

Kathryn kneeled beside David. "Who did you talk to, honey?"

"DC police. I called Paul's cell, and they answered. They were looking for me."

"Do they know what happened or who it was?"

Dani shook her head as she wiped her nose with a tissue. "All they said was someone broke into my office and Paul walked in on them."

David took Dani's trembling hands. Then he turned his head. "What was that?"

"What?" Kathryn responded.

"I heard the back door—someone's here."

David jumped up and went to close the door to the office. As he put his hand on the doorknob, two men in dark suits appeared from the hallway. David fell back into the room. The men entered and surveyed the scene. One withdrew a cell phone from his inside jacket. "We've got them, sir."

"Who are you?" David demanded.

The man put the phone back in his pocket. "Mr. Webber, Ms. Parsons, Mrs. Depriest—I'm Agent Grimes, this is Agent Burns, we're with the FBI. Would you three come with us, please?"

"Why? Where are you taking us?" David asked.

"We've been instructed to escort the three of you back to DC."

"DC?" Kathryn half yelled, "I can't go to DC."

"You don't have a choice, ma'am."

THE FEDERAL AGENTS HUSTLED DANI, Kathryn, and David to Westchester County Airport where a private jet was waiting. Forty-five minutes later, they were met on the tarmac at Reagan National by a black SUV that transported them directly to Dani's office.

Dani's knees buckled when they stepped off the elevator onto the fifth floor. David grabbed her under one arm and Agent Burns took the other. Kathryn stood back and closed her eyes, unable to look at the gruesome scene.

The wall opposite the elevator was painted black-red with dried blood, and the floor below was a puddle of ooze. Men in suits dodged men in white lab coats, and photographers were taking pictures of the crime scene.

"Watch your step," Agent Grimes instructed as they walked around tiny yellow cones bearing numbers marking the placement of used shell casings. There was ten feet or so of clean flooring before they came upon another puddle of blood. This one had not yet coagulated and was still bright red—the pool was at least a quarter of an inch deep. A gurney was being rolled out of Dani's office—the body was covered.

"Oh, Charlie, no," Dani cried out.

"No, ma'am," the man following the body said, "this isn't Charlie."

"Who is it?" David asked, also in a state of shock.

"Her name is Christine Foster. She worked in the gift shop downstairs. We think the perp used her to get into a restricted area and ultimately up here."

They all watched in silence as the corpse was taken down the corridor, and then the man spoke again, this time almost to himself, "She was eighteen. He got what he wanted and killed her. He didn't have to, he just wanted to." The man pulled his attention back to the people in front of him. "Mr. Webber, Ms. Parsons, Mrs. Depriest, I'm Agent Tom Fowler with the FBI. Would you please step into the office, we need to talk."

Agent Grimes and Burns nodded to the senior agent and departed. The three entered the office, and Fowler closed the door behind them.

"Everyone, have a seat."

Dani looked around the office.

"It's okay," Fowler said, seeing Dani's apprehension, "there's nothing else in here. Most of it happened in the hallway."

Dani sat down in the chair across from her desk, and Kathryn took the one beside her. David remained standing between the two until Fowler rolled out the chair from behind the desk. "Here, son, have a seat." Fowler sat on the corner of the desk. "First, let me say, Dr. Parsons, I'm sorry about Mr. Cheevers—Charlie. I understand he was a friend. He was a good man. If it's of any comfort, he died a hero. He's the only reason Dr. Rogers is still alive."

Dani looked straight ahead, her eyes drenched with tears. "Paul?"

"He's in recovery—too soon to tell."

Dani closed her eyes and nodded.

Fowler continued, "It's time all of you know what you're involved in."

"I didn't kill Henry or J.P.," David blurted out.

Fowler didn't respond. Instead he addressed Kathryn.

"I guess the best place to start is with you, Mrs. Depriest. This might be harder on you than anyone."

"I didn't know any of these poor people," Kathryn said.

"I'm talking about your husband, Mrs. Depriest."

"Anthony? Is he—"

"Anthony is fine. He's not a part of this, but he is in a lot of trouble."

"I don't understand," Kathryn responded.

"I know you don't. And that's why *you're* here."

Fowler took a beat then began. "Several months ago the IRS and Federal Trade Commission were involved in a joint investigation of a man named Thurman Winfield. Winfield is the founder of a rap music record label called Electric Chair Records. I won't bore you with the details of what Winfield was being investigated for, but tax evasion and the bribing of an IRS auditor topped the list. They'd had Winfield under surveillance for some time and were prepared to make an arrest when Winfield was contacted by Bernie Freeman."

"Uncle Bernie?" Kathryn muttered.

"Yes."

"Who's that?" David asked, looking at Kathryn.

"The Depriestiano's family attorney," Fowler answered. "Mrs. Depriest, are you aware of...let's say the colorful reputation of your husband's family?"

Kathryn looked at David and then back at Fowler. "I'm not sure I should answer that, Mr. Fowler, without my attorney present."

Fowler raised an eyebrow. "I'll take that as a yes." He continued, "When it was brought to the bureau's attention Freeman had contacted Winfield about a quote, 'lucrative business venture,' we saw an opportunity."

"What does this have to do with what happened here?" David asked.

"To be honest, Mr. Webber, probably nothing."

"Then why the hell—"

"Just listen," Fowler ordered. "Mr. Webber, the night Henry

Shoewalter was killed, you had been arrested earlier that evening, correct?"

David's face turned pale. "How...how do you know——"

"Because we were watching."

Fowler got up and walked around the desk. "The business venture that Bernie Freeman came to Winfield with was conceived by Anthony Depriest."

"What?" Kathryn exclaimed under her breath.

"It involves Winfield turning Electric Chair Records into a record company dedicated to classical music."

"Why would Anthony want to do that?" Kathryn asked.

Fowler paused and then looked at Dani and David as he spoke. "Because he wants to release a very rare and never before heard work by Wolfgang Amadeus Mozart, and he plans to own it. Lock, stock, and barrel."

Chapter 37

It was as if someone had punched all three in the stomach at the same time. Dani audibly gasped, Kathryn just hung her head, and David lost his mind.

"That son of a bitch!" David yelled, leaping toward Kathryn. "He killed Henry. Your fucking husband killed Henry."

"Sit down, Mr. Webber," Fowler said without raising his voice. "Anthony Depriest hasn't killed anybody."

"But he——"

"Sit down," Fowler ordered.

David sat down. Kathryn couldn't look at him, and it wouldn't have mattered if she did because David fixed his stare forward.

The door opened, and Robert Greenfield entered with another man. Fowler nodded but didn't introduce them. He went on, "Now nothing about Anthony's little enterprise would necessarily be illegal, except to pull it off, Anthony needed his uncle's machine. And Old Nick being Old Nick wasn't satisfied with just owning and publishing a rare piece of music, even if it is worth a small fortune. See, Old Nick's nothing if not greedy. So, Ms. Depriest, your husband's plan got bigger and more illegal. Here's the deal. Renaissance Records, through its international distribution networks, will launder money for every criminal organization in the world. Here's how it'll work. Pick a criminal organization. Let's say the Mexican drug cartel. Let's say they need to launder some money. Let's say for the sake of easy math it's one hundred dollars. Renaissance Records will sell to the cartel, or more likely a phony cartel company, CD's. They will charge them the one hundred dollars the cartel needs laundered. Then Old Nick, through another company, probably retail, and most assuredly doing business in another country, will purchase that product from the cartel for fifty dollars. Bang, money's clean. Old Nick makes a hefty little profit that either goes into another business or an off-shore account."

Dani interrupted, "But won't he know you are watching him the minute his record company starts doing business?"

Fowler nodded. "Dr. Parsons, I can assure you, the Depriestiano name won't show on any document of ownership of Renaissance Records. Besides, the practice itself is done all the time and isn't in and of itself illegal."

"What do you mean?" David asked.

"Of course you have to remember I haven't bought a record since...well since they made records. But I've learned in the record business, music is bought and sold in this manner every day, especially on the worldwide market. And not just by small homegrown companies. The major multi-media conglomerates do it also, buy-outs, trade-outs, you name it. That's what makes it such an ingenious idea. Even when it's legit, the money trail is practically untraceable. And in this instance it's made easier because you're dealing with classical music. Unlike any other genre of music, classical music naturally crosses all borders. And don't forget, you're dealing with an intellectual property that is public domain, so there's no one outside the family to pay."

"That's brilliant," David said almost under his breath.

"Yeah, it is," Fowler agreed. "Old Nick will make millions, maybe even billions. The Mexicans, Colombians, the Russians, the Sicilians, even terrorist organizations from all over the world will want to do business with Old Nick. In essence, he'll be the clearing house for all money laundering."

"How did he know?" Kathryn muttered, to no one in particular.

"About the Mozart? From Henry Shoewalter," Fowler answered.

"But Henry didn't have any contact with——" She stopped and put her hand over her mouth. "Oh my God."

"Yeah, that's what he did," Fowler said. "How did you and Shoewalter correspond?"

Kathryn closed her eyes and nodded. "Mostly by mail."

"For a long time, Mrs. Depriest, we thought you might be involved. By the way, you're being followed. Jimmy."

Kathryn felt sick.

Dani finally spoke, "Mr. Fowler, are you sure? Anthony Depriest is one of the most respected conductors in the world, and this Thurman Winfield doesn't sound like the most reliable source."

"He's not. But *our* Thurman Winfield is."

Dani and David looked at each other.

Fowler continued, "You see, the Thurman Winfield the Depriestiano family is dealing with is not the real Thurman Winfield. He's one of our agents. We did a deal with the real Thurman Winfield and made the swap before anyone had met face to face." Fowler looked back at Kathryn. "I'm sorry, Mrs. Depriest, our facts are accurate. Your husband has been using you."

Kathryn stood and walked to the back of the room. Fowler exchanged brief glances with Greenfield and the other man. When she turned around, her chin was up, and her eyes were dry. "What do you need me to do?"

Fowler looked at Greenfield and nodded. "I was hoping that would be your reaction. We'll get to that in a minute, but right now I need to go on with my story. And that leads me to you, Mr. Webber."

"I haven't seen Anthony Depriest in years," David said.

"I know, and I know why," Fowler said, looking at Kathryn. "First, let me tell you what you want to hear. This man right here," Fowler said nodding toward Greenfield, "is the assistant director of the FBI. He wants me to inform you the FBI doesn't believe for a second you killed Henry Shoewalter or had anything to do with the disappearance of Jean Ann Peterson."

David closed his eyes and released a long breath. Dani took his hand.

"But," Fowler said emphatically, "the fact remains, David, people didn't start dying until you came onto the scene."

"Mr. Fowler," David pleaded, "I don't know why."

Fowler stood and patted David on the shoulder. "I believe you, son." He turned to the desk and picked up a folder.

"This isn't the *why*, but it is the *who*." Fowler opened the folder and handed David an eight by ten photograph. It was of a bearded man in a Yankee's cap.

"Who's this?" David asked, looking at the picture.

Fowler glanced again at Greenfield and the other man and then handed David another photograph. "The same man this is."

David looked at a photo of a young priest standing behind a cash register.

"The first photo we took, the location is the Mall just outside this building. The second one is from the surveillance cameras downstairs in the gift shop. David, that's the man that killed Henry."

David's hand began to tremble, and the photos fell to the floor.

"Mr. Fowler," Dani asked, "is this the man that—"

"Yes, he's responsible for this too. As well as a young FBI agent."

"But why, who is he?" Dani asked, her voice shaking.

Fowler picked up the folder again and withdrew another photograph.

"David, I want you to look at this photograph and tell me who you see."

David took the picture and immediately shot upright in his chair. "That's me and Bowen," he said almost as a question.

"Who?" Fowler came back.

"Me and Joshua Bowen. He's a Los Angeles police officer. He's helping me. He's the only person who believed I didn't kill Henry and J.P."

Fowler looked at the two men in the back of the room. Then

Greenfield spoke for the first time. "Why did he tell you he believed you?"

"Because he met J.P. the night I was arrested for that bar fight. They spent the night together, so he knew I couldn't have done it." Greenfield looked at the man beside him. David continued. "Bowen hasn't got anything to do with this. He's the son of the D.A. in Los Angeles."

"Who?" Fowler responded, his eyes widening.

"The D.A., Arthur Bowen, he's his kid. That's why I was released from jail. He told his dad about spending the night with J.P. and how I couldn't have done what I was being accused of, so his dad got me released. He couldn't vouch for me because it would ruin his old man's career."

Fowler looked over at the men in the corner and shook his head in disbelief. Then he looked back at David and put his hand on his shoulder again.

"Mr. Assistant Director, would you introduce our guest to Mr. Webber?"

Greenfield looked at the man beside him and then back to David. "Mr. Webber, I'd like you to meet the District Attorney of Los Angeles, Arthur Bowen."

The distinguished-looking man stepped forward. "Mr. Webber, pleasure to meet you, especially since I did you such a service. One problem, though. I don't have a son."

David's face went pale. "What?"

"Three daughters—no sons."

"But...no. Bowen told me...you got me out of jail."

"No, I didn't. I went over your file on the flight here. One of my assistants was handling your case. You were released for simple lack of evidence."

David looked at Dani and then back to Fowler, his face twisted with confusion.

"David," Fowler said, pointing to the photograph, "this man, the one you know as Mr. Bowen's son, and this man, and this man," showing David the photos of the priest and the man in the Yankee's cap, "are all the same man. His name is Viktor Petrovic, and he's a wanted international assassin."

"No, it can't be," David mumbled. "I spoke to him, he's not here, he's in L.A."

"You spoke to him recently?" Greenfield asked, looking at Fowler.

"Yesterday, and I left him a message today. He couldn't be the same guy."

Fowler sat down on the desk again and spoke over a sigh. "Where was he when you called him, David?"

"I told you, Los Angeles, he couldn't be——"

"No," Fowler interrupted, "Where did you call? His home? His office?"

"His cell phone," David answered.

Fowler nodded. "Mr. Bowen, do you have your cell phone with you?"

"Of course."

"Would you mind giving me the number?"

He gave Fowler the number.

Fowler picked up Dani's office phone and dialed. Ten seconds later a high-pitched chirping came from inside Arthur Bowen's suit jacket. Fowler looked at David and hung up the phone.

David fell back in his chair.

"David, we need that number."

David didn't respond.

"David," Fowler said again.

David reached for his wallet, pulled out a slip of paper, and handed it to Fowler.

Fowler looked at the number and walked to the door. He opened the door and handed the slip of paper to another man.

David looked at Dani and shook his head.

"We'll run the number," Fowler said, "but my guess is it's a burner. I also doubt Petrovic can be reached there anymore."

"So he's been here all along," David said.

"I would hazard to say within hours of your arrival."

"After he assassinated an LAPD detective," Arthur Bowen added.

David looked up. "Ryan?"

"Yeah," Fowler said. "Ryan was a good cop. When he couldn't ID Petrovic through LAPD or the bureau, he sent his fingerprints to INTERPOL. It only took them minutes. Unfortunately, Petrovic was paying attention. Here's the rest of it, David, at least how you were dragged into this. We were following two of Depriestiano's men, who were following Henry Shoewalter. Shoewalter surprised them and unexpectedly caught a last minute flight to Los Angeles. Why, we really don't know." Fowler looked at Kathryn. "But whatever the reason, your husband was certain Shoewalter was going to L.A. to meet David about the Mozart piece. To be honest, I'm not so sure about that, but Anthony was." He looked back to David. "So, to buy his two goons time to catch up, he arranged for you to get yourself arrested."

David opened his eyes in disbelief. "Harshbarger?"

"They were following you from the minute Ms. Peterson bailed you out. But at some point that night Depriestiano's men vanished from under our noses. Until this afternoon, we didn't know what happened to them. They and one other person turned up floating in Echo Park Lake."

David's face went white. "J.P."

"No, not J.P.—an LAPD officer. His throat was slashed, and he was stripped naked. Now we understand why," Fowler said, looking at Greenfield and Bowen. "Petrovic needed the uniform."

"Where's J.P.?" David asked, not wanting to hear the answer.

Fowler picked up the folder. "We don't know, but we think she's alive."

"What? J.P.'s alive?" David shouted.

"I said, *think* she's alive, David. We need you to confirm her identity."

Fowler handed David another photograph. "We just got this a few hours ago. Since you left L.A. so unexpectedly, we assumed Petrovic wouldn't have had time to secure a well thought-out place to hold up. We knew he was tailing you and reasoned he had to be staying in close proximity, so we confiscated the security tapes of all the surrounding hotels. This is from the Marriott on Twelfth. I need you to tell me if the woman in the wheelchair is J.P."

David looked at the photo of a tall, masculine woman pushing a wheelchair. Fowler got his answer without David saying a word.

"That's what we thought," Fowler said, taking back the photo.

David leaned back in his chair. His heart was racing. He didn't know if he should be happy or sad or relieved or petrified. His hand was resting on his knee, erratically shaking, when Dani reached over and took it in hers. "She's still alive, David, she's still alive. We can't give up hope. We'll get her back."

David squeezed her hand and forced a smile.

"Mr. Fowler," Dani asked, "what does he want?"

"The same thing we all want."

"The Mozart?"

"It would seem so. What is this thing, anyway?" Fowler asked.

Dani shook her head. "We think it might be a requiem Mozart wrote for his mother. If it exists, it would be worth a great deal of money."

"Are you any closer to locating it?" Greenfield asked.

"No," Dani answered.

"How about Shoewalter, was he?" Fowler asked.

"We don't know. David doesn't even think it *is* a mass."

"Why?'

Dani looked at David before she answered—he was still shaking. "Because the date of David's sketch doesn't work with the date of Mozart's mother's death. I have a piece by a woman named Sugar-berry—" Dani suddenly stopped. "Oh God. She must be—"

"We don't know that, Dr. Parsons," Fowler said. "The Sugar-berry woman lives in the house you, Dr. Rogers, and David were at earlier today, right?"

"Yes," Dani answered.

Fowler nodded. "Go on, you were saying the dates conflict?"

"Here, I can show you." Dani got up and went toward her safe but stopped before she'd taken a step. The door to the safe was open. It was empty. "Oh, no," Dani said, her voice cracking.

"I assume," Fowler moaned, "that's where the pieces were?"

Dani closed her eyes and shook her head.

"That's just great," Greenfield said from the back of the room.

Fowler smacked the photos against the desk.

The room was silent for several moments. Fowler walked to the door and opened it. He said something to the man outside. No one could hear what he said. He closed the door, walked close to Greenfield, and whispered in his ear.

Greenfield nodded.

Fowler returned to the desk. "All right, everyone. I don't know about you, but I'm sick and tired of being led around on a leash by Viktor Petrovic."

"What do you mean?" Arthur Bowen asked.

"I mean," Fowler answered, "that bastard has been pulling the strings long enough. I say it's time we start pulling his strings."

"How?" David asked.

Fowler started to speak and then stopped himself. He looked at Greenfield. "No, Bob, we can't do it, it's too dangerous."

Greenfield nodded without protest.

"What?" David half yelled. "Mr. Fowler, if there's something I can do, ask me. Hell, I volunteer. You need me, and I want that bastard."

It took several moments while Fowler wrestled with every conceivable option. Finally, he surrendered to the truth of David's statement. "You're right, I do need you. But I need Dr. Parsons too."

David looked at Dani and then back to Fowler. "No, not Dani, she's out of this. I'll do anything you want, but not Dani."

Dani spoke as if she hadn't heard David, "What do you need us to do?"

"Dani, no. I'm not letting you—"

"David," Dani cut him off. "He was here in my office. He killed Charlie. Paul's just barely—" she put her face in her cupped hands.

David placed his hand on her back and gently rubbed. He let out a breath. "What do you need us to do, Mr. Fowler?"

Fowler nodded. "You and Dr. Parsons are going to find that Mozart piece. You'll have the full resources of the United States government. Anything you need, you'll have. If it can be found, you two will find it. We have a safe house in Virginia. You'll work and live there until this thing is over."

Dani started to protest, but Fowler cut her off. "I'm not letting either one of you out of the FBI's sight, so don't even try to argue with me."

"I want to help—I can help," Kathryn said.

"Oh, you're going to help, Mrs. Depriest," Fowler replied. "But I need you for something else. Dr. Parsons, how are you at acting?"

Dani looked up.

"Because I need you to give the performance of a lifetime to the press."

Dani said, "Mr. Fowler, I don't think I can—"

"Dr. Parsons...Dani, all of you, listen to me. Petrovic now thinks he has everything you have. That means he thinks he doesn't need any of you anymore. And that means he doesn't need Ms. Peterson, either. If we have any hope of flushing this monster out and getting Ms. Peterson back alive, we have to make him think he's wrong—that we know something he doesn't know."

The room fell silent.

Fowler continued, "I'm not going to lie to either of you, this is very dangerous. I can't make you...hell, I shouldn't *let* you do this. I'm using you as bait to draw Petrovic out. So what do you say?"

"Of course we'll do it," Dani answered without hesitation.

"Mr. Webber? I need to hear from you too."

David looked at Dani and then turned to Fowler. His face was hard; his eyes were calm. "J.P.'s alive. I'll do anything you say."

Fowler nodded.

TWENTY-FIVE MILES WEST OF WASHINGTON, DC, a white rental sat in the empty parking lot of a rundown motel. Inside room number four Viktor Petrovic sat naked at a desk looking into the mirror. Sweat poured from his body as he held a pair of needle-nose pliers over the flame of a butane lighter.

He laid the instruments down and untied the bloody T-shirt he used as a bandage from around his shoulder. The wound had stopped bleeding and was now a sticky and matted glob. He reached into a brown paper sack and removed a bottle of alcohol. Taking a deep breath, he poured the liquid over his shoulder. His head snapped back as fire shot through his body. He made no sound.

He opened his eyes and gasped for air as the pain subsided. Without waiting, he picked up the tool, moved closer to the mirror, and inserted it into the tiny hole. His face turned red, and his eyes began to water as he pushed the pliers deeper into the wound. He heard the squish of broken and mangled cartilage, ripped muscle, and torn tendons as he twisted the instrument toward his neck. He felt nauseous, his sweat had intensified, and he was sure unconsciousness was only moments away. He bent the handle upward until he felt the tiny piece of lead pushing against his collarbone. He maneuvered the tool to an open position and squeezed tightly when he was sure he had snagged the invader. He let go a low growl as he pulled the bullet from his body.

Gasping for air, he ripped open a bandage and placed it over the bleeding wound. The nausea was getting worse. He looked back at the bed. J.P.'s eyes moved with him as he walked over to her. Her eyes showed the fear and profound hatred she felt for the man standing over her.

"Jean Ann," Petrovic panted, his genitalia swinging inches above her face, "after all we have been through, have you no pity for me?"

J.P. stared without expression. If she could have, she would have reached up and ripped his sac off with her mouth. But the drugs were too strong.

"Don't worry, it's almost over." Petrovic walked back to the desk. He picked up the slug that had been lodged in his body. He turned to J.P., held it up, and let go a sadistic laugh. "They thought this little thing would kill me."

He turned to the mirror and smiled. Then without warning, vomit spurted from his mouth. His eyes rolled back, and his head fell onto the desk.

A small leather book sat open on the desk beside Petrovic's head.

An unfolded brown piece of parchment lay under a magnifying glass atop the two pieces of music from the museum.

Dear Wolfgang, the letter began in German. Petrovic's hand covered the middle of the letter. But the words at the bottom were large and in English, *God be with you brother, Ben.*

Part III

Chapter 38

The Washington Post
   Morning edition
   MOZART LIVES!
   At the Smithsonian Institution last night, Curator of Musical Antiquities,
Dr. Danielle Parsons, announced the discovery of a previously unknown work by
Wolfgang Amadeus Mozart. In a brief statement to the press, Dr. Parsons said,
"We know the piece exists and have a good idea where it is located. We'll have it
in a matter of days."
   Dr. Parsons denied the premature nature of the announcement was to draw
attention away from the attempted burglary that occurred at the Museum of
American History earlier in the day. In that incident…

Conrad Woo watched the black Lincoln Continental pull off Pennsylvania Avenue and roll into the empty parking space below Capitol Hill. The morning sun caused the dome of the edifice to glisten and cast back the still waters of the capitol's reflecting pool. Wearing tan pants and a navy blue windbreaker, Woo leaned against a concrete wall circling the water and waited for the driver to turn off the engine. Once the car's parking lights went out, Woo approached, opened the rear passenger side door, and stepped into the vehicle without invitation.

"Have you seen this?" Douglas asked, tossing the newspaper in Woo's lap.

"Yeah, I've seen it."

"And?"

"It's a ruse."

"Are you sure?" Douglas asked.

"No, but it will have the desired effect either way. I gotta hand it to Fowler, this was a bold move. I didn't think the old guy had it in him."

"So you think Petrovic will go for it?" Douglas asked.

Woo shook his head. "He'll go for it, God help them."

Douglas sighed. "Good. We're running out of time."

ON THE OUTSKIRTS OF ALEXANDRIA, just off the George Washington Parkway, a large white-framed house sat nestled behind tall ancient oaks and weeping willow trees. To anyone who might venture up the winding gravel driveway, the two-story home would appear no different from the scores of other homes built in this historic region of Virginia. What the intruder would not see—or more precisely, could not see—were the infrared security cameras situated in the branches of the trees and the electrified barbed wire fence surrounding the perimeter of the property.

David's hand slipped along the banister as he trudged down the rear staircase leading from the upstairs bedrooms into the den located at the rear of the house. Stepping into the room, he saw Dani and Agent Fowler listening to another man explain the specific purpose for each of the computers Fowler had delivered the night before.

"Morning," David said, rubbing sleep from his eyes. "What time is it?"

"Almost seven thirty," Dani answered, looking up with a soft smile. "There's coffee in the kitchen."

David nodded. "How long have you been up?"

"Since about six—went to sleep about five minutes before that. How'd you sleep?"

David spoke over a yawn. "Okay, I guess. Ravel is getting a little sick of the constant relocating and woke me up a couple of times, but he likes this place better than any of the others." David looked around the beautiful room—hardwood floors, walls of alabaster, and twelve-foot ceilings. "What am I talking about, probably more than his own home."

Dani smiled. "Yeah, Hemingway's adjusted quickly too. He doesn't know what to do with all that backyard. Thanks for getting him, Mr. Fowler."

David added, "Yeah, thanks for getting Ravel also."

Fowler was watching the technician tie in the phone line to the computers' modems and acknowledged the appreciation with a casual salute.

"I'm gonna get a cup of coffee. Either of you need anything?"

"No, I'm fine, thanks," Dani answered.

Fowler answered with a gesture that said no.

David stopped before he exited the room and turned around. "Uh, Mr. Fowler, did Kathryn get off okay last night?"

Dani kept her head down and made sure she didn't react to David's inquiry.

Fowler looked up for the first time. "I put her on a private jet myself. I also arranged to have her picked up at LaGuardia and taken home. She made it safe and sound."

"Wonder how she's going to explain it to Mr. Depriest," Dani said.

"Don't worry about her. She'll be just fine. In the meantime, you two have other things to concentrate on."

David took a deep breath. "Yeah, we do. Let me get a cup of coffee and a quick shower, then we can start."

"First things first, though," Fowler said. "Before you two dive into this thing, I want to try something."

"What?" Dani asked.

"I want to put David under hypnosis. A man from the bureau should be here in about an hour to perform the procedure."

"What," David said with a half-laugh.

"Relax, it's nothing weird, just some relaxation."

"You've got to be kidding? I don't need to be—"

Fowler interrupted sharply. "David, I think you've got some things locked in that head of yours we need to let out. Now we're going to try this. Go get a shower, but why don't you lay off the coffee for an hour or so?"

JIMMY SAT on the balcony across from Anthony, inhaling a bagel stuffed with cream cheese, smoked salmon, and red onion.

"What time did she get in?"

"I don't know," Anthony answered. "So tell me again, where were they taken to from Shoewalter's?"

"The airport. The Feds had a Lear waiting. You talk to her yet?"

"No, she was asleep when I got in from the concert. And your contact at the FBI has nothing?"

"Nada," Jimmy replied with cream cheese on his chin. "Only thing he said was something went down at the museum where the Parsons chick works, burglary or something. That's all he knows."

Anthony dabbed his mouth with his napkin and stood. "Well, we'll just have to ask her what occurred, won't we?"

"You mean you're just gonna ask her direct like?"

"Yes," Anthony answered. "Haven't you heard? I'm the supportive husband now. Besides, it'd be suspicious if I didn't ask."

Jimmy drained his glass of orange juice and wiped his mouth on his sleeve. "Yeah, guess you're right."

"Okay, get lost. I hear Kathryn moving around upstairs."

"You're always telling me to get lost."

"Beat it, Jimmy."

"Okay, I'm goin'. Call me, *capisce*?"

"Yes, yes, I'll call you, now goodbye."

Jimmy had no sooner shut the door than Kathryn came down the stairs.

"Honey, you're up," Anthony crooned, kissing his wife on the cheek. "I was so worried about you yesterday. Where were you?"

"Oh darling," Kathryn cried as she wrapped her arms around Anthony's neck. "It was horrible, just horrible."

"What? What was horrible?"

"You were right, David has changed. He's nothing like the old David."

"You saw David?" Anthony asked.

"Yes, at Henry's house. He was there with a woman, then..."

"Then what?"

"Then the police came—I mean the FBI. They arrested all of us and took us to DC. That's where I was all day yesterday."

"Washington, DC.? You were taken in by the FBI?"

"It was horrible."

Kathryn released her hold on Anthony and sat down on the divan. Anthony joined her, taking her hand in his. "Why would they take you in?"

"Because they thought I was with David. Anthony, he did kill Henry."

Anthony was caught completely off balance. This was not what he was expecting. "Did he confess? Did he say he killed Henry?"

"He as much did. Oh, Anthony, he's filled with so much hatred. He said he was going to get back at all of us for how his life had turned out."

"By what means, dear, did he say?"

"The Mozart. You were right again. Henry did go out to L.A. to get David's help on his Mozart project. But instead of helping him, David killed him."

"Why? For what purpose?"

"Money, just money," Kathryn said, breaking into tears again. "It's a requiem mass Mozart wrote for his mother. It's worth a fortune, and I'm sure David knows where it is. But he's not saying anything. He's holding it over everybody's head. He said it was his ace up his sleeve."

Anthony heard the words but couldn't believe it. "Darling, I'm so sorry you went through this. Did David give any indication where the piece is, any at all?"

Kathryn wiped her eyes and thought for a moment. "No, he hardly said anything after the FBI arrived."

Anthony pushed further. "Maybe before they showed up. Think, dear."

"All he said was that he had it and no one else would get it. He did say something very strange."

"What?"

"It's about you. He must hate you very much." Kathryn broke down again. "I can't believe I'm responsible for all of this."

Anthony, working hard at being patient, took a deep breath and raised his wife off his shoulder. "What did he say that was so strange, darling?"

Kathryn took a deep breath. "That he and ol' Winston had a big surprise for you and Uncle Nick."

Anthony thought for a second. "Winston, who's Win...?" Anthony stopped. A chill went through his whole body. "Darling, could he have said Winfield, Mr. Winfield?"

Kathryn nodded. "Yes, that's what he said, Winfield. He and Winfield had a surprise for you and Uncle Nick."

Anthony leaned back into the sofa and said nothing

"What does that mean, Anthony? Who's Winfield?"

Anthony looked at his wife and forced a smile. "A friend of my uncle's. Don't you worry about it, sweetheart. It's over now."

Anthony took Kathryn in his arms. His eyes were closed but not without vision—the vision being of Thurman Winfield biting down on a shotgun.

Chapter 39

"How do you feel, David?" the man with the gray Van Dyke beard asked.

"Good," David answered with a soft and relaxed tone.

Doctor Richard Wright, the bureau's leading psychiatrist, turned to Fowler and nodded. All of the curtains had been pulled, and save for the tiny desk lamp sitting in the corner, the room was dark. David was stretched out on a Lazy-Boy recliner. Fowler sat close-by with an opened note pad, and Dani sat on the sofa biting a fingernail.

"David, it's Tom Fowler, can you hear me?"

"Yes," David replied.

"I want you to go back to the last time you spoke with Henry."

"Yes."

"What were you doing at the time?"

"Sleeping."

"Sleeping?"

"Yes, I was sleeping, and Henry called me—woke me up."

"What time was that, do you remember?"

"Three fifty-eight in the morning," David replied.

"Good. And you know the exact time because…"

"I looked at the clock."

"Good. Do you remember the first thing he said?"

David squinted his closed eyes, trying to remember. "He said, Davey, Davey, it's me—are you there?"

"Davey, he called you Davey?"

"Yes, that's what Henry calls me."

"Okay, what did you say?"

"I said—" David's breathing became shallow, and his head twitched. He was back in his apartment. "I said, Henry, I can't believe it's you."

"You haven't heard from him in a long time, have you, David?"

"No, it's been years."

"Why is he calling you now?"

"I don't know."

"Well, what does he say is the reason?"

"He says…he needs to borrow something from me."

"What? What does he need to borrow?"

"The gift."

"And you know what he means."

"No."

"When do you know what gift he's talking about?"

"When he says…the one by the master."

"Then you know he's talking about the Mozart music?"

"Yes."

"David, do you know why he wants to borrow the Mozart music?"

"No. He's…" David's face contorted.

"He's what, David?"

"He's…very excited, agitated—something's wrong."

"Like what?" Fowler asked, scribbling in his note pad.

"I don't know…he's just…very nervous."

"So he's more nervous than excited?"

"Yes, he's nervous."

"Does he calm down when you tell him he can have the music?"

"Yes—no, a little, but…"

"But what David?"

"He calms down until I tell him I don't have it. Then I tell him I have it in a safety deposit box at the bank, and I can't get it 'til the morning."

"Then he calms down again?"

"Yes."

"David, do you ask him why he wants it?"

"Yes."

"And what does he say?"

"He says he can't tell me about it on the phone—he will when we meet."

"And what do you say?"

David swallowed hard, and tears start rolling down his cheeks. "I say...I'm sorry...and...it's going to be great to see you again, Professor. I've thought about you a lot, and I can't wait to talk to you...I really need to talk to you..."

Dani listened from the couch with her hand over her mouth, trying to muffle her breathing. She was crying.

"And what does he say, David?"

"He says, it'll be great seeing you again also, Davey..." David begins sobbing.

Fowler pushes on. "What time are you to meet him, David?"

"Eleven."

"So you're—"

"No, I mean ten, I say eleven, but Henry says ten would be better because he has some business at eleven. Afterward we'd spend the day together."

"That's what I thought," Fowler said, writing in his notebook.

"I should go over there," David began babbling. "I should go and see him now. I know I should...I shouldn't wait." David inhales abruptly and holds his breath. "Oh God, no," David says with an intense whisper.

"What, David?"

"TV—there's a murder at Henry's hotel—I know—oh God, I know—it's Henry, I don't know how, but...I can feel it, I can—"

"There was nothing you could do, David," Fowler said.

"The police…in my house, they say I did it. It's crazy. It's—"

"Okay, David, relax."

"Why?" David screamed. "Why, why?"

"Oh, David," Dani said from across the room.

"They tell me he was killed after I talked to him—they say they know because he ordered breakfast. If I'd just gone over there—"

"Doctor?" Fowler looked over at the FBI psychiatrist who was already kneeling in front of David.

"Okay, David, deep breaths," Wright said. "Listen to my voice, deep breaths. You're feeling your body floating on water again. Just floating, it's very peaceful. Deep breaths, deep breaths."

David's breath became slow and steady, and his body relaxed.

"I think that's all we should do," the psychiatrist said to Fowler.

Fowler nodded.

"Okay, David, I'm going to count to three, and on three you're going to open your eyes. You're going to feel wonderful, like you just had a good night's sleep, and you will remember everything you said here, okay? One, two, three."

David opened his bloodshot eyes and looked around the room.

"He didn't go to L.A. to see you," Fowler said, opening the drapes. "He was there for another reason—and he was scared. He knew somebody else was after the music. We have to find out who his eleven o'clock was with."

Dani walked over to David and put her arms around him. As she released the embrace and pulled back, she saw David staring into space.

"David, are you okay?" Dani asked.

David looked at Dani and then Fowler. "Henry wasn't alone."

"How do you know that?" Fowler asked.

"Because he had breakfast."

"David, it's not your fault. You had no way of—"

"No, that's not what I'm talking about," David interrupted, his voice calm and in control. "I remember when the police came to my apartment, Ryan told me one of the ways they determined the time of the murder was because Henry had ordered breakfast—I think Ryan said it was around five thirty."

"Okay, so?"

"He said Henry had ordered strudel and coffee." David looked at Dani. "Henry hated coffee."

Chapter 40

Petrovic sat in his car and watched as Thomas Fowler pulled out of the underground parking structure of the J. Edgar Hoover building. Keeping a three-car distance, he followed the federal agent across Constitution, under the Ninth Street tunnel, and onto the 395. He followed him across the Virginia state line, into the small township of Alexandria, and to the gravel driveway of a two-story white-framed house.

Petrovic continued on two miles past the house before he deemed it safe to pull over. He picked up the newspaper in the seat beside him and read the story again. Moments later, a Virginia state trooper rolled by. He shifted the car into gear and prepared to head in the opposite direction. Suddenly, he stopped. He looked back and watched the police cruiser turn into a parking lot. The officer got out of the car and walked into the diner. Petrovic smiled, turned the car around, and headed back to the restaurant.

ON ANTHONY'S URGING, Kathryn went back to bed. Anthony,

the ever so attentive husband, prepared her a warm cup of milk with a shot of rum. Kathryn sipped the concoction and waited until she was sure Anthony had left.

She'd known about the hidden safe for years. She even knew the combination, though she never had the need, nor the least bit of interest in using it. She waited for the green light to appear and turned the handle to the safe. She saw the thick brown accordion folder sitting by itself in the safe. She retrieved the parcel and set it on Anthony's piano. Her heart pounding, she unwound the nylon twine and opened the folder. She knew what she'd find, but it didn't matter, it still was a shock, still unthinkable. First was a photocopy of the letter Henry had sent to her, the letter where Henry apologized for *his sins of the past* and asked for her assistance. Then the return letter from her saying, *any apologies should come from me*, and accepting Henry's offer. She caught her breath and squeezed the folder when she saw the stack of papers—her report. She picked up the bundle and stared. It was still paper-clipped, still in order, the postage on the envelope never cancelled. She gasped for air and started slowly pounding on the piano lid. "He never saw it." The blows getting harder each time. "Never!" She yelled as tears rolled down her face. "You son of a bitch. You never let him see it."

She saw one other object in the folder. She wiped her eyes and withdrew the envelope—it was addressed to her. She removed its contents and looked at the photocopied piece of music. On top of the piece, Henry had written, *Kathryn, this might help. Yours, Henry.*

She fell across the piano and sobbed.

EXCEPT FOR THE hum of the computers and the click of the printer, the room was quiet. Dani sat on the edge of a swivel chair, periodically rolling from one terminal to another, downloading data from various private servers at the National Archives, the Museum of American History, and Georgetown University, printing those documents, while reading other documents, while downloading yet still more documents from another computer. It was the paragon of a high-tech assembly line.

David lay sprawled on the floor, surrounded by textbooks and all of the notes Kathryn had given to Agent Fowler before returning to New York. *God, she still is good*, David thought to himself as he poured through the mounds of information she had accumulated on Henry's behalf. He was amazed at how she not only gave the facts as they were—dates and locations—but speculated on Mozart's state of mind at the time. If she ever so desired, he mused, this was a book in and of itself.

It was the afternoon, and the two had been working nonstop for over five hours. They'd hardly said a word to each other, both preoccupied with the work, so preoccupied neither heard Fowler when he came into the room.

"Henry went to L.A. to see Dr. Raymond Sullivan," Fowler proclaimed, forgoing any salutation.

"Are you sure?" David asked from the floor.

"Yeah, I'm sure."

"Was he who Henry had breakfast with?"

"I don't know, we couldn't find Sullivan."

"What?" Dani asked.

"The university said he retired a few years ago after his wife was killed."

"Is that related to this?" Dani asked.

"No. It was a carjacking in Los Angeles. The kid that did it was caught. He's serving thirty-five to life. The old guy's had a tough few years, though. He also lost his only child about the same time."

"Oh, the poor man," Dani said.

"Yeah." Fowler paused, and his eyes drifted off to the side.

"Anything wrong, Mr. Fowler?" David asked.

Fowler quickly refocused. "No…just something I need to check out. Anyway, we got an address. No Sullivan, and none of the neighbors have seen him in a week."

"A week?" David said, standing up. No one needed him to say more. Everyone was thinking the same thing.

"So how do you know that Henry—"

Fowler jumped on top of David's question, "They went through the house. It's not what they found as much as what they didn't find."

"What do you mean?" Dani asked.

"Nothing, the agents found absolutely nothing pertaining to Henry or Mozart. But while the agents were there, Sullivan's cleaning lady showed up. They questioned her and learned several interesting little tidbits."

"Like what?" David asked.

"Sullivan was very excited about a project he'd been working on. He told her he was about to be validated for all his years of work. She also said Sullivan had instructed her to take last Friday off. He said he had an important appointment that morning."

"I'll be damned," David uttered, almost to himself.

"Now, if he was working on a Mozart project, where's the research? There was nothing pertaining to Mozart, or Henry, in his house. See what I mean?"

"Yeah, Henry's house was the same way," David replied.

Fowler looked off again. "It was, huh? Hmm, I wonder?"

"Wonder what, Mr. Fowler?" Dani asked, leaning back in the chair and stretching her arms above her head.

Fowler re-engaged. "Nothing. Just something else I need to check out. You two are probably hungry. I got some sandwiches in the kitchen. Let's move in there, and you can both bring me up-to-date on what you've learned."

NICHOLAS DEPRIESTIANO SAT with his elbows on his desk and his fingers massaging his temples. Jimmy and Uncle Bernie sat on the couch, and Anthony sat directly in front of the old man with his legs crossed. After a long silence, Old Nick leaned back in his chair and spoke in a soft but firm voice, "So how did Webber learn of Winfield?"

"It's my guess, Uncle, that Webber didn't learn of him, but rather the other way around. You remember Winfield said it was a contact of his who informed him of the old man's death and Webber's arrest? I think we can safely assume that Winfield made contact with Webber."

"And you believe they've been working together ever since?"

"I do. Kathryn told me the FBI was very interested in a piece of music Webber had in his possession. It was then I remembered Shoewalter had given Webber a Mozart sketch when we graduated from Juilliard. I believe Shoewalter decided that sketch held the key to finding the missing requiem and that's why he went to Los Angeles. I think Webber killed the old man over a grudge he held against me, and that Winfield convinced him to partner-up to further his vendetta. I'm sure Winfield made taking us down sound very attractive. I think Winfield either knows where the piece is, or already has it in his possession."

"How can you be sure?" Bernie Freeman asked from the couch.

"Because of this." Anthony tossed a copy of the *Washington Post* on the desk. "I think they got Webber to roll on his new buddy."

Nicholas picked up the paper. When he finished reading, he threw it down. "If this is true, they'll be picking up Winfield."

"Yes, which is why we must move fast."

Nicholas leaned forward in his chair. His face was tight and red. "Nobody does this to me, Jimmy," Old Nick barked. "Call your friends."

"OKAY, WHAT HAVE WE GOT?" Fowler said, leaning against the counter and unwrapping cellophane from around a turkey sandwich.

Dani and David sat on stools at a breakfast bar. Dani swallowed her mouthful of chicken salad and picked up her notes. "Well, I started with trying to put Dr. Cook with Thomas Jefferson."

"How'd you do?" David asked.

Dani smiled. "I think I did it. Wilbur was right, there are not many records on slaves before the Civil War. I went through everything the National Archives had on the Cook family and George

Beall, who was supposed to have owned Dr. Cook when he was a child. I came up with the same thing Wilbur did. Actually, Wilbur had more. Then I remembered slaves were counted as property. So I started looking into the property records of Thomas Jefferson."

"You can get those?" David questioned.

"They're part of the National Archives. They house any and all important records pertaining to the federal government. Jefferson was a president, his records would be important."

"Go on," Fowler urged.

"In February of 1817, Jefferson was experiencing severe financial difficulties. So he had a garage sale at Monticello. In other words, he sold off assets—slaves. George Beall is listed as one of the purchasers at that sale."

"He bought Cook," David said.

Dani grinned. "I think he did."

"Good," Fowler said, returning Dani's grin. "That's very good work."

"I'm not done," Dani said, looking at her notes. "I decided to go ahead and try and put Mozart and Jefferson at the same place at the same time."

"And?" Fowler asked.

"I can't. Jefferson wasn't in Europe until 1785 when he was named ambassador to France. He never got near Austria, Germany, Poland, or anywhere else Mozart was from '85 to his death in '91."

"Damn," David said.

"No, that's okay. It's still information, and that will eventually lead to the truth. And that's all we're looking for, isn't it?"

David wasn't in the mood to be scholarly. "How did he get that music and learn it well enough to teach it to Cook? That's all I'm looking for."

Fowler broke in, "How about you, David? You come up with anything?"

David let out a frustrated breath. "I've been going over Kathryn's notes. She's right, the only thing interesting about that year is Mozart's mother died. But I still can't believe Henry actually thought Wolfy wrote a requiem for her. In fact, I know Henry didn't, we'd talked about it too many times."

"He could have changed his mind, David. People do change their minds."

David shook his head defiantly. "Not that much."

"Sure they do," Dani responded. "I did about you."

David's hostility was instantly squelched. He smiled in spite of himself and then broke into a slight chuckle. "Okay, you might have a point. Maybe Henry did change his mind, but I'd like to know what changed it?"

"How about your piece of music?" Fowler asked.

"No, he'd had that music for years before he gave it to me. Besides, he and I went over the piece and the prosody isn't there for a requiem."

"The what?" Fowler said, narrowing his eyes.

Dani clarified, "David means it doesn't fit into any of the sections a requiem is supposed to have."

"Right," David said. "A requiem mass is musically unique. The tension and release, the texture, the harmonic structure, the mode of a requiem is singular. It has to be, given the weight of its subject matter." David continued, "Look, a requiem is a setting of the Latin text of the 'mass for the dead' and begins with the word *requiem*, meaning 'rest.' All requiems are pretty much the same on one account—the libretto. The sections of all requiems are first the *introit*, it says…" David closed his eyes and searched his memory banks, *"requiem aeternam dona eis Domine*, that means…Eternal Rest Grant Them, O Lord. The second section is the *Kyrie*, meaning Lord Have Mercy. Then comes the *Dies irae*, the Day Of Wrath, then the Offertory, *Domine Jesu Christe*, O Lord Jesus Christ, King Of Glory. Then we get to the *Sanctus*, Holy, Holy, Holy, next, *Agnus Dei*, meaning Lamb of God, and finally the Communion, *Lux aeterna*, My Eternal Light Shine Upon Them. Also there's sometimes a *Libera me* section, meaning Deliver Me O God From Death Eternal, and an *In Paradisum*, Into Paradise May The Angels Lead You.

"Now folks, I know I've been out of the longhair academic

world of music for a while, but believe me, the sketch I have, the one Henry gave me, just doesn't fit any of those movements."

No one responded. Fowler, and even Dani, knew they were outmatched when it came to this man's knowledge of music.

"Come on, Dani," David added, "surely you can see that."

Dani smiled. This was not the boorish and crude lounge piano player she had first met. This was David Webber, the brash and confident musical phenom from Juilliard Paul had heard about. And she liked this David Webber very much. She nodded, "You're right, David. It doesn't seem to fit."

David let his head drop. "Finally."

But when he lifted his head, he saw Dani looking at him. Her soft hazel eyes were glistening. He felt a warmth go through his body and an overwhelming feeling of joy in his soul. He'd never felt anything like it. He returned her gaze. For a moment, all the evil that had fallen upon his life vanished. It was just the two of them.

"So what is it?"

David heard the words as if they were coming from another world.

"David, hey, you with me here? What is it?"

David snapped back and saw Fowler looking at both of them. "Uh, I think it's a symphony," David said, his mind still not completely in the room.

"A symphony?"

"Yeah, a symphony." David collected himself. "I need to see the music again, but that's what I think it might be, part of the adagio section of a symphony. That's usually the middle movement of three movements. After going over Kathryn's note, it's the only thing that makes sense. Mozart was into symphonies at the time, and it works musically."

Dani too had gone away. She pulled herself back and added, "We need to get Marcus Burg over here."

"Who's that?" Fowler asked.

"He runs the recording studio for the Smithsonian. We need to hear what he's come up with. He also has photocopies of both pieces."

"I'll have him over here in two hours."

"Umm, Mr. Fowler," Dani said.

"Yeah?"

"It's Marcus…I just want to warn you, he's a real sweet guy, and brilliant but…" Dani smiled, "not your typical Smithsonian employee."

Chapter 41

Exactly two hours and seven minutes later, Marcus Burg was sitting in a swivel chair staring at a computer monitor. He was hitting keys on an adjacent synthesizer when Fowler ushered Dani and David into the converted garage located off the main house. Marcus turned, peered over his round John Lennon specs, and stood with a smile. "Hey, Dan, dig the hang, babe."

"Marcus," Dani said, extending her arms to the six-foot bag of bones with stringy blonde hair. "Great to see you, honey."

"You too, babe," Marcus replied as the two hugged.

"This is my friend David Webber. He owns the sketch."

"Dude, awesome piece, man, really kicks major classical butt."

David looked at Dani as he took Marcus's outstretched hand. "Uh…yeah, thanks. What's your T-shirt say? I can't make it out."

"Hendrix, dude! You know, excuse me while I kiss the sky."

"Oh," was the only reply David could offer.

Fowler broke in, "We've set up his unit out here so both you and he can work independently and undisturbed."

"Man, this place rocks, Dan. Check it out. I could live here. It's even got a kitchen? Fridge is poppin'. I'm talkin' major score."

"Yeah, it rocks," Dani said with a chuckle as she looked at

David's bewildered face. "Marcus, did you bring the two works Paul gave you?"

"Yeah, got 'em right here," Marcus answered, handing Dani the two copies she'd copied in her office in what now seemed like a lifetime ago.

"Can I see them?" Fowler asked, taking the music from Dani.

"I heard about Pauly, bad thing, man, real bad. How is he?"

"So far so good," Dani replied.

"I'm sending out positive energy, Dan, lots of it."

"Thanks, I know he appreciates it."

"So, this is it?" Fowler asked, showing David the sketch.

David nodded. "Yeah. You read music, Agent Fowler?"

"Third chair trombone in high school marching band. I've also been told I play a respectable 'Unchained Melody' on the organ. So, Mr. Burg," Fowler continued, handing Dani the music, "do you have anything we can hear?"

"Sure, have a seat and let me entertain you."

As David, Dani, and Fowler sat down, Marcus entered commands into the computer.

"My grandson has this same thing," Fowler said.

"Not like this, G-man," Marcus replied, talking as he typed. "This ProTools system looks like any other PC, but the software's anything but. Basically, it's Abby Road all tucked into thousands upon thousands of beautiful gigabytes. And the editing capabilities are totally bitchin'. Ain't nothin' I can't do."

"Meaning, if I sing off key, you can make it so I'm on key," Fowler said.

Marcus chuckled. "That's child's play, dude. You give me fifteen minutes, and I can make you sound like freakin' Pavarotti."

"So, there's really no tape recorder involved?"

Marcus laughed. "Oh man, you're so last millennium. It's all digital, dude."

"What's the microphone for, Marcus?" Dani asked, referring to the rectangular microphone and stand sitting by the keyboard.

"I like to record ambient sound from the room. It adds nice texture to the digital recording."

"How did you choose the instrumentation?"

"I mostly worked from Mr. Webber's sketch since it had a more complete outline of what Mozart intended. The bitch is we really don't know what the piece was actually meant to be. That, of course, would help in selecting the appropriate instrumentation the old dude planned to use. The Kochel had nothing even close. The notations gave me some idea, but it's far from complete. I had to guess at the rest, so I just used the typical instrumentation of orchestras of the period. But one thing is for sure, it was meant to be performed with the piano as the main instrument."

"How do you know?" David asked.

"Because of the way he wrote the melody and counter-melody. It really had me messed up for a while. I was trying to assign each note in the melody an instrument. When I did, it left me no instrumentation available for the counter-melody and lower-register accompaniment. I was totally bummed until I realized I was dealing with a polyphonic melody, and all the other instruments were designed to support just one instrument playing the lead—an instrument that can play at least six notes at one time, like a fortepiano."

"That's unusual, even for Mozart," Dani said.

"Yeah, especially for something written in the mid 1700's."

Dani and David looked at one another. "Why do you think it was composed then?" David asked.

"Once again, because of the melody. Listen."

Marcus hit the space bar, and the cursor on the screen began to move along the music staff pictured on the monitor. The sound came from two twelve-inch speakers located on either side of the computer. David had played the melody hundreds of times but had never heard it like this. The adagio was rich and warm, and if he didn't know better, would have sworn the London Philharmonic was performing it. He also instantly knew how Marcus settled on the date.

"See what I mean?" Marcus said, swiveling around in his chair.

David nodded. "Bartolomeo Cristofori, Viennese action. How were you able to—"

"I sampled one a couple of years ago in Italy," Marcus answered.

"I told you he was good," Dani said, smiling at David.

"I don't get it," Fowler admitted.

David explained, "The piano Marcus is using is an eighteenth century fortepiano. A man named Bartolomeo Cristofori invented it in the early 1700's. There're only three of those pianos still in existence, by the way."

"Okay," Fowler said, still not understanding, "but why is he using a...whatever you called it, and how does that tell us the date?"

Marcus answered, "By the mid-1700's the instrument had become the thing but was still nothing like the piano we know today. The keyboard was shorter, about four octaves, and the soundboards were considerably thinner, so the sound of the instrument was much thinner."

Dani took up the explanation. "The only differences in pianos of that time was how the action was set. Viennese action was very light. It complemented eastern European composers like Mozart and Haydn who wrote quick arpeggios up and down the scale, whereas English action was much stiffer. It complemented more chord-oriented music. There was a guy named Clementi who was a rival of Mozart's and was a master of the English action."

Marcus broke in, "But by the late 1700's, almost all pianos, including Mozart's, had combined the two actions to allow for the more versatile music being composed by the new composers coming onto the scene, like Beethoven. But this piece, with the counter melodies in the left hand and the arpeggios in the right, was stone-cold written for an instrument with Viennese action."

David jumped in, "And since by 1790, Mozart, along with every other composer of note, was writing music that was more vertical than horizontal, we can safely assume this piece was written well before 1790."

"Right, dude," Marcus said.

"I don't know," Fowler said, "seems like a huge leap."

"Not really," David explained. "Consider if you came from another planet and saw a piece of music by...Jimmy Hendrix, let's say," David said, pointing to Marcus's T-shirt. "You'd know it was written well after the time the electric guitar and the high-watt amplifier had been invented and was in common use."

"Art always follows technology and vise versa," Dani added.

"Learn something new every day," Fowler said with a nod.

David paced to the back of the room. Everyone waited for him to say something. Finally Fowler broke the silence. "What?"

David looked up, his frustration obvious. "Same question. Why did Mozart write a sketch in 1790 to a piece he'd composed in 1778?"

"Maybe he was trying to remember it," Marcus said.

"Yeah, right," David came back sarcastically.

Dani jumped in, "No, wait. Marcus may be right."

"Come on, Dani, you know as well as I do about Mozart's ability to transcribe massive amounts of music from his head."

"Yes, for works he was creating at the time, but this is different. What if this is something he'd written years earlier, like in 1778, and he was trying to remember it? Also, remember, Mozart was not well the last year of his life."

"But why didn't he still have it?"

"Maybe he'd lost it." Dani paused and thought for a moment. "Or maybe he'd given it to someone."

"Why? And who? And don't say Jefferson, we already know he wasn't in Paris, Mannheim, or Salzburg in 1778."

Dani started to respond but stopped herself. She thought for a moment and then a smile gradually crept over her face. "Yeah, but I know who was. And I bet Henry did too."

Chapter 42

Before anyone could ask Dani to explain, she was out the door, running back to the main house, with the three men racing to keep up. For more than ten minutes, David, Fowler, and Marcus sat silently in the back of the room as Dani scanned page after page on her computer screen, mumbling as she made notes in a notebook. Finally, she pushed back from the computer and smiled.

"Well, are you going to tell us?" David asked.

"No, you're going to tell me."

"What?" David came back.

"Dr. Parsons," Fowler interjected, "time is not on our side—"

"I know," she said, "and I'm sorry, but this is necessary. It's how we historians do our work, with checks and balances. I need all of you to go through this with me and validate my thinking. Okay?"

"What do you need us to do, babe?" Marcus asked.

"I'll ask the questions, you answer."

Fowler and David nodded.

Dani took a breath. "Okay, what do we know?"

The three men looked at one another, and then David answered, "We know we have a sketch composed by Mozart to a piece nobody knew existed."

"Not exactly," Dani corrected. "We actually have two versions of the same music composed by Mozart. One, a sketch in Mozart's own hand from around 1790, and the other, a melody line in a combination of two other hands from the early 1800's. Go on."

They thought for a moment, and then Marcus spoke up, "Well, we know the composition was composed in the mid 1700's."

"Good," Dani acknowledged, "what else?"

David again, "We know one piece was transcribed by a Dr. James Cook and Thomas Jefferson, probably when Cook was a slave owned by Jefferson."

"And Jefferson was nowhere near Mozart," Fowler added.

"Right. Next?"

"So Jefferson didn't learn the piece from Mozart directly," David said.

"Correct," Dani said with a smile.

"So how'd he hear it?" Fowler asked.

Marcus answered, "From a friend who did hear it from Mozart directly."

"Good, you guys, you're doing great. Now what about Henry?"

David said, "We know Henry once owned the sketch he gave me. We know he wanted it back, and we know he had Kathryn researching Mozart in the year 1778."

Dani smiled.

David got where Dani was going. "1778. Who was in Europe in 1778?"

"Benjamin Franklin," Dani answered.

"Benjamin Franklin?" David echoed.

"Yeah, remember I said Jefferson wasn't in Europe until 1785? He went there to replace *his friend* Benjamin Franklin as Minister to France." Dani looked at the computer screen. "Here it is, in August of 1776, Franklin was sent to Paris for the purpose of persuading France to help America in its fight for independence. Jefferson replaced him in 1785. David, do you have that itinerary Kathryn made?"

David jumped up and went to the stack of papers on the floor.

"Ben Franklin," Marcus whispered. "Totally awesome."

"Here it is," David said from the floor.

"When was Mozart in Paris?" Dani asked.

David read, "Mozart left Mannheim in March and arrived in Paris at the end of the month. Anna-Marie died on July third, and Mozart left not long after."

"So we're only talking about three or so months in the spring of 1778."

Fowler asked, "For what?"

"To put Franklin and Mozart together," David answered. "Are you sure?"

Dani stood and began pacing. "Henry had Kathryn researching Mozart's life in 1778—only that one year. I think Henry went through much of the same process we have, starting with the strong proof that your sketch, David, was written around that time. But *we* have the advantage of having something Henry didn't have, another piece of music, Sugarberry's. We know it's also a part of the same Mozart piece no one's ever heard—except the person, or in this case, persons who transcribed it. Those persons happened to be a freed slave who was once owned by Thomas Jefferson, and Jefferson himself. Now how did they hear it? Obviously, Cook heard it from Jefferson when he was a boy living at Monticello. But how did Jefferson hear it? We know he didn't hear it in passing, otherwise it would be a known work, and there'd be no mystery. No, he either had to have gotten it from Mozart directly, which we know is impossible, or somebody who was in direct contact with Mozart. Fact: Franklin was in Paris at exactly the same time Mozart was in Paris, 1778—the year Henry wanted Kathryn to research. No other American of any note was anywhere near Mozart at that time. Remember, this was in the middle of the Revolutionary War. Colonists weren't doing a lot of traveling back then."

"So why isn't there a record of Franklin and Mozart meeting?" Marcus asked.

"I don't know. Maybe there is, and we just don't know it. Or, more likely, Mozart wasn't famous enough at that time to warrant anyone making a big deal out of it. But think about it. Franklin was a superstar in Paris. He was always around royalty and heads of state. Now I ask you, who did composers perform for? Answer: royalty and heads of state. It's not hard to imagine Franklin meeting Mozart at one of his performances, hearing this work, and then showing it to his friend Jefferson when he showed up in Paris to replace him. Remember, Jefferson was a musician."

"Just one problem," David said. "If he'd heard it performed, then we and the rest of the world would know about the piece."

Everyone was silent for a moment.

"What if," Dani said slowly, "Mozart's and Franklin's relationship went beyond audience and performer? What if they actually knew each other?"

No one spoke—everyone was considering the possibility.

"What's next?" Fowler said, breaking the silence.

"We need to go over line by line the itinerary Kathryn created. And we need to make one for Franklin. Marcus, how are you on the Internet?"

"Screen name's buddyhackit. Whatta you think?"

Dani smiled. "Find out what you can about Franklin. There's going to be a library of information, so just hit the highlights giving special attention to the year 1778 from say…let's give us some room, the first six months of the year. David, you continue going over Kathryn's notes. Let's see if we can put these two boys together. Agent Fowler, can I call my dad?"

Fowler thought for a second. "Sure, but you can't tell him where you are."

"That's fine."

"Why your father, Dani?" David asked.

"Something about the doodles on your sketch. They've bugged me since you first showed it to me. I've seen them somewhere."

"And your dad can help?"

Dani nodded. "Yeah, I think he can."

Fowler was about to ask if there was anything he could do when the door opened and Agent Burns stepped into the room. He whispered into Fowler's ear, and Fowler reacted, "Are you sure?"

The agent nodded.

Fowler tried to be nonchalant—he failed. "Folks, it looks like you have things handled, so I'm leaving for a little while. I might not be back until tonight, but I'll check in. If you need anything, Agent Burns here will help you."

David and Dani looked at each another. David asked, "It's Depriest, isn't it?"

Fowler considered for a moment before replying. As casually as he could, he said, "Yeah, it is. I'll call you. Keep up the good work. Remember, time is not our friend." The FBI man hurried out the door.

GRAVEL FLEW as Fowler spun out of the driveway and onto the main road. He didn't see the state police cruiser parked on the side of the road, two hundred yards in the opposite direction.

"Patrol 32, do you copy?"

The officer in the car didn't respond.

"Patrol 32, this is dispatch, what's your twenty?"

Still there was silence.

"Patrol 32, do you—"

Victor Petrovic, wearing dark sunglasses and dressed in the green khaki uniform of a Virginia state trooper, reached over and turned off the radio.

Chapter 43

His thumbs were tied behind his back with piano wire. The end of
the wire led through the index and middle finger of his right hand,
under the seat, to his legs, both of which were bound to the front
legs of a wooden chair. A tennis ball was cut in half and stuffed in
his mouth, secured with duct tape. His right cheek was bruised, and
both lenses in his glasses were shattered. Two giants in dark suits
stood on either side of the black man—one was rubbing his knuckles. Jimmy stood in front of the man, biting into an apple.

The Clifton, New Jersey, warehouse was empty except for the
chair and the single light bulb hanging over Winfield's head.

"My turn."

"No," Jimmy said to the man who was not rubbing his knuckles.

"Awe, come on, Jimmy boy, let me have some fun."

Jimmy took a bite and smiled as he chewed. "Okay, Lenny, just
one."

The man stepped in front of the chair and put his left hand on
Winfield's shoulder. He made a fist with his right hand and drew
back his elbow. Just as he was beginning to release the bomb, the
screech of a metal door opening came from the back of the build-

ing. The man halted his assault and returned to his position beside the chair as the footsteps on the concrete floor neared.

"Thurman, Thurman, Thurman," the voice crooned from the dark. "You really stepped in it this time, didn't you, ol' boy?" Anthony Depriest walked into the light, wearing a black tuxedo. "Thurman, you look terrible. Have the boys been a little rough on you?"

Depriest glanced at one of the hulks standing beside the chair and nodded quickly. The man ripped off the tape holding the tennis ball in Winfield's mouth. The half-ball fell to the floor, and Winfield immediately began hacking.

Anthony looked at Jimmy. Jimmy nodded, opened a bottle of water, and poured it over Winfield's face. Winfield desperately lapped for the liquid.

"Now then, feel better?"

Winfield dropped his head, barely able to look up at Depriest. "Why?" he asked in a raspy voice.

"Oh, I think you know why, Thurman. Did you really think you were going to pull it off? My god, man, I have to hand it to you. I thought I was the only one with an ego that inflated. I almost admire you."

"I don't know what you're talking about."

The impact from the back of Anthony's hand echoed through the cavernous building. "Where is it?" Anthony said, taking a handkerchief from his pocket and wiping his hand.

Winfield raised his head and whispered, "I don't know what you're—"

Anthony struck him again. "Where's the Mozart? Does Webber have it?"

"I don't know what you're talking about," Winfield mumbled.

Anthony nodded to the man Jimmy called Lenny.

Lenny wasted no time. He returned to his previous position in front of Winfield, drew back his elbow, and released a vicious blow. The chair toppled backward. Winfield groaned in agony, not so much from the punch itself but from the excruciating tension that the fall exerted on his thumb sockets.

Jimmy and the other man lifted Winfield back into place.

"Thurman, I'm not enjoying this, but you must understand, the requiem is mine. It's ordained, if you will. So again, and remember, I have a concert tonight so I don't have a lot of time to waste, but these men do. Where is it?"

Winfield jerked his head to keep conscious. Blood was coming from his nose and mouth. "I want to talk to the old man," he mumbled.

"No, that's not—"

"I want to talk to Old Nick. I'll tell Old Nick," Winfield shouted.

"Shut up, nigger!" Jimmy yelled, slapping him with the back of his hand.

The high voice cut through the sound of Jimmy's slap. "Enough!" Nicholas Depriestiano hobbled into the light and shoved his son out of the way. He turned to the bleeding man in the chair and stared. The old man's eyes were cold, his face expressionless. "Tell me," Old Nick said with no inflection.

Winfield waited before he spoke, "How do I know you won't kill me?"

"Young man, I'm going to kill you either way. The only thing you should be concerned with is if I do it quick and easy, or slow and painful."

Winfield looked in the old man's eyes. "You can't kill me."

"And why not?" Old Nick responded.

"My company—for distribution—I know what you're planning to do. You need me for the laundering operation to work."

Old Nick stared blankly at Winfield. If he was surprised by Winfield's knowledge, he didn't show it. After a moment, a wide grin spread across Depriestiano's face. Then he broke into a hideous high-pitched cackle. Jimmy joined his father and started laughing as well.

Anthony didn't even break a smile. "Where is it, you son of a bitch?"

Old Nick said, "Start with his fingers. If he still refuses to talk, kill him."

Anthony broke in, "No, he has to tell us."

"Nobody does to me what he has done and lives. The Mozart is secondary—reputation is everything. I'm sure you understand that, Mr. Winfield?"

"No, Uncle, we——"

"I've spoken, Tony," the old man snapped back.

Old Nick looked at Lenny and nodded. Lenny reached around the back of the chair, untied the wire, and wrestled Winfield's right hand onto the arm of the chair. The other man took something from his pocket. Winfield watched as the man flicked his wrist, releasing the steel blade from its case.

"For god sake, man, tell us where it is," Anthony pleaded with Winfield.

Winfield's head shook, and his breathing became faster as the man brought the blade to the top of his hand.

"Now," Old Nick spit, "last chance. Where is it?"

Winfield's eyes widened as he felt the sharp edge of the blade break the skin of his little finger above the knuckle.

No one saw it coming. Fowler's invasion was quick and precise. "Drop the knife!" Fowler ordered as he came into the light. The man with the knife looked up to see Fowler's 9mm aimed at his skull. He dropped the knife by reflex.

"Who the hell are——" Old Nick's thin voice screamed.

"Nicholas Depriestiano? Agent Thomas Fowler, FBI," Fowler said as a team of federal agents appeared from nowhere. "You okay, Rick?"

The man the Depriestiano's knew as Thurman Winfield nodded as agents started freeing him from the chair.

"Sorry we took so long, but we had to wait for Old Nick here to make his play. Nicholas Depriestiano, it is my pleasure to tell you that you are under arrest. You have the right to remain silent. You have the right to an attorney. If you give up this right, anything you say can and, may I add, most assuredly will be used against you in a court of law. Do you understand?"

Anthony went white as the cuffs clicked shut around his wrists. "This is a mistake. Don't you know who I am? I'm Anthony

Depriest. I have a concert tonight. Take these off of me. I'm famous. I know the mayor."

"Sir, do you understand your rights?" Fowler asked Old Nick again.

Old Nick watched as Jimmy and the two men were led away. He glared down at the African-American whose wounds were being tended to by another agent. "He with you?"

"Oh yeah," Fowler answered. "Say hello to special agent Richard Ballard."

Old Nick kept a tight face and nodded. He looked at Anthony, whose babble had turned into pleading. "I'm not supposed to be here. This is a mistake."

"Shut up!" Old Nick yelled. "You're as pitiful as your worthless father." Depriestiano turned to Fowler. "Get me out of here."

"Agent," Fowler said to the man handling Anthony, "would you escort Mr. Depriestiano out to the car? I need a moment with that one."

"Sure thing. Right this way, Mr. Depriestiano."

As Old Nick was led out, Fowler approached Anthony.

"Can you help me? This is a mistake," Anthony pleaded again.

"It's not a mistake, son," Fowler replied. "As I heard you say just a few minutes ago, you really stepped in it this time."

Anthony hung his head. "What can I do?"

Fowler shook his head. "That's between you and the federal prosecutor."

"Then what do you want?"

"I made a promise I need to keep. Ms. Depriest?"

Kathryn stepped from the darkness. Her eyes were dry, her face serene. She walked to within inches of Anthony and stared into his eyes.

"Darling," Anthony began again, "this is a big—"

The slap echoed through the building. "Anthony," Kathryn said, "I want a divorce."

"HOW BAD IS IT FOR HIM?" Kathryn asked as Fowler opened her car door.

"It depends on how much he knows about his uncle's operation. If he has information, the prosecutor will deal. If Anthony's smart, he'll talk. Lord knows, Jimmy's already singing like Sinatra. He's not saying a word, though, about Daddy. That could be Anthony's good luck. He wasn't in too deep up until tonight. All he was really guilty of was some minor racketeering and being a jerk. But tonight, he was party to assault, torture, and the attempted homicide of a federal agent—that's pretty bad stuff."

Kathryn stared out the window and nodded.

"Where can I take you?"

Kathryn desperately looked at the agent. "How about to DC with you?"

Fowler didn't answer.

"I can help. Please, I need to get out of New York."

"Ms. Depriest, I don't think it would be a good idea—"

"I've found something that David and Dani don't know."

"What?"

"A piece of music. Anthony had it in his safe. Henry sent it to me, but Anthony intercepted it, and I never saw it. Mr. Fowler, I know it's a Mozart."

Fowler looked back at Kathryn. Every inch of her beautiful face was pleading. "Do you have it with you?"

Kathryn nodded and withdrew the photocopy from her purse.

Fowler looked at the music and then closed his eyes. "I knew it. That son of a bitch," he uttered over a long sigh.

"Who? Anthony?"

"No, another son of a bitch," Fowler answered. He retrieved his cell phone from his inside jacket pocket and dialed. David answered on the third ring. "David?" Fowler said surprised. "Where's Agent Burns? Why didn't he answer?"

"He just got called from outside by one of the other agents."

"Why?"

"I don't know. They said there was a state policeman at the front gate who was looking for somebody or something...I don't really know what the story was—it's nothing, really—how's the situation up there?"

"Complete. I'm heading back to DC. How's the work going?"

"I think we're onto something. It's pretty weird, but we might have found the link between Mozart and Franklin, and maybe more."

"Like what?"

"I'll wait 'til you get here. It's too bizarre to go into."

"Did Dr. Parsons talk to her father?"

"Yeah," David replied. "That's part of it. She's with Marcus right now in the garage. She turned up some new info on Dr. Cook, and she's checking it against Marcus's info on Franklin. She's really something, instincts of a bloodhound."

"That's her job. You okay?"

"Yeah, I just finished Kathryn's notes. Like I said, I think we've got something, but we need to put it all together." There was a pause. "How is she?"

"She's fine. Listen David, Kathryn found something. It's a piece of music Anthony Depriest had in his safe that was Henry's. It's a photocopy of the Sugarberry piece."

"What?" David responded.

"Yeah."

"How did Henry get—"

Fowler interrupted, "I can't explain right now, but I think I know. David, Kathryn wants to bring it down herself for you and Dr. Parsons to go over."

There was a momentary silence on the other end of the line.

"David, are you there?"

"Yeah, that'd be fine. Mr. Fowler, are you sure it—"

"Yeah, I'm sure. Even an old third chair trombone player like me can tell it's the same. I'll see you in an hour or so."

Fowler turned off the phone and looked at Kathryn. "We don't have time to stop and get any of your clothes."

Kathryn smiled. "That's fine."

Fowler returned the smile and turned the phone back on.

"Bob, it's Tom, we got him. Old Nick is in the cage. And you're going to love the tape. Agent Ballard was brilliant and—" Green-field interrupted.

As Fowler listened to the assistant director, his smile faded. Fowler, with phone still in hand, turned on the car and spun out of the parking lot.

"Bob, get every man you can over to the house right now. And call Alexandria PD. He's there. Petrovic is there. Jesus Christ, I'm on my way."

Fowler turned off the phone and redialed the number to the house in Alexandria. One ring, two rings, three rings, four rings. Fowler let the phone ring twelve times, but there was no answer. He cursed as he threw the phone on the floor and swung the car onto the New Jersey Turnpike en route to Newark airport.

"What?" Kathryn asked, fastening her seatbelt.

"A Virginia state trooper was just found on the outskirts of Alexandria with his throat cut."

Chapter 44

It was dark by the time Fowler turned off the main road and into the driveway of the safe house. Kathryn held onto the dashboard as the FBI man gunned the car over the gravel. He was frustrated, irritated, and flat-out worried to death. Not only for the safety of David, Dani, and Marcus, but for the past hour and a half, Greenfield hadn't answered his cell phone.

Fowler slid the car to a stop in front of the house. With gun in hand, he leaped from the car, ordering Kathryn to stay put. He was halfway up the steps to the house when Bob Greenfield opened the front door.

"Bob," Fowler yelled, lowering his gun, "what the hell's going—"

"Turn off your cell phone," Greenfield interrupted, his voice low and short.

"Where's Webber and—"

"Gone," Greenfield snapped back. "They're all gone. Turn off your cell phone, that's an order." He called out to Kathryn. "Ms. Depriest, do you have your cell phone with you?"

"No," Kathryn replied, jumping from the car.

"Bob, what—" that was as far as Fowler got before Greenfield turned and stomped back into the house.

Fowler turned off his phone as instructed, and he and Kathryn followed.

The assistant director spoke as the three made their way toward the rear of the house. "The assault was nauseatingly simple. Agent Burns, shot in the head, dead at the scene. Agent Grimes, shot in the head, dead at the scene. Anderson, Williams, Gardiner, all shot once in the head at nearly point blank range—Anderson and Williams, dead at the scene. Gardiner's in a coma."

"Sweet Jesus," Fowler responded under his breath.

Greenfield continued, "All the agents were found within yards of each other midway down the drive. Petrovic apparently was lying in wait, allowing his victims to come to him, lambs to slaughter. The fact all the agents' firearms remained holstered suggests each approached without hesitation. No struggle, no breach of our so-called high-tech security system, and of course, no sign whatsoever of Webber, Parsons, or Marcus Burg."

"No," Kathryn whimpered.

"Alexandria police found her," Greenfield went on, leading Fowler and Kathryn into the makeshift office. "Thank God the patrolman who was first on the scene was ex-military with a background in demolitions. This is Agent Morris of the anti-terrorist division." Greenfield pointed to the middle-aged man wearing a headset and sitting in front of a TV monitor. "This is what we've got."

Fowler and Kathryn looked over the agent's head at the monitor sitting on the table beside the computers Dani and David had been working on.

"What are we looking at?" Fowler asked.

"The garage where Mr. Burg was working," Greenfield answered.

Fowler got closer to the screen. The image was in color but jerking erratically. It took him a moment to make it out, but once he did, he understood everything—why the outside of the house was deserted and why Greenfield wasn't answering his cell phone.

J.P. was unconscious. She sat in a chair with her head down, chin on her chest. Around her torso was strapped a vest of dyna-

mite. Attached to the dynamite with primer cord was a cell phone—
and the phone was on.

IT LOOKED different in the dark—without form, a cold mass filling
an empty void, a gigantic shadow cast upon an even larger shadow.
The lush lawn, the floral landscape, the canopy of trees, all hidden
by the night and anointed banal by the situation.   ·

Single file, Dani led the way up the cobblestone path to the
house atop Georgetown Heights, the house of Gertrude Sugarberry.
Marcus followed close behind, then David, who held a bloodied
cloth to his brow. Petrovic brought up the rear, still in the uniform of
a Virginia state trooper, a gun in his holster and one in his hand
pointed at David's back. In his other hand, he carried a cell phone.

The hostages were silent. Few words had been uttered by any of
them since David had entered the garage in Alexandria and found
the phony officer holding a gun on Dani and Marcus. He held it
together until he saw J.P. Then he erupted into insanity. Dani's
pleading scream went unheeded. David flew into a blind rage,
ignoring the assassin's weapon and lunging for the man's throat,
shouting, "Bowen, you son of a bitch!" The attack was met with a
swift blow to David's head with the butt of a pistol. After that the
rules were simple. Talking was forbidden unless it was in reply to a
direct question, punishment for disobedience was execution and
death to J.P.

Dani reached the porch and stood motionless at the front door.

"Why are you stopping?" Petrovic demanded.

"It's locked," Dani replied in a monotone, refusing to look at
the man.

Petrovic's eyes stayed fixed on the three as he walked up to the
door. Without a moment of hesitation, he withdrew a black cylinder
from his pocket and attached it to the barrel of the weapon. One
shot was all it took for the doorknob to be completely obliterated.
Petrovic shoved Dani into the dark foyer and motioned with his gun
for the others to follow.

"Which way?" Petrovic asked, standing in the doorframe.

Even in the dim light, David could see the look of defiance in Dani's eyes.

Petrovic held up the phone. "Dr. Parsons, the only way for you to save her is for you to complete your task successfully. Now where is it?"

"It doesn't matter," David said. "Regardless if we find it or not, you could care less if J.P. lives or dies, you sick bastard."

"You willing to bet Jeep's life on it?" Petrovic started dialing.

"No," Dani shouted.

Petrovic stopped and smiled.

David stared at the man he once knew as Bowen. The person he actually felt lucky to have on his side. The feeling was overwhelming. He was scared, yes, but not nearly as scared as he was filled with pure hatred, hatred like he'd never felt before—all-consuming hatred. He wanted to kill this man as much as he wanted to take his next breath.

"IT'S PRETTY BASIC, SIR," the calm voice said over the small speaker placed beside the monitor so all could hear.

"What have you got, Kosik?" Morris asked, looking at the monitor.

"Triple threat, sir. Chair moves, she moves, phone rings, result's the same. Good news is the link starts with the phone. It's a simple hot and ground connection. He must have been in a hurry."

"Kosik, can you get to it?" Morris asked.

"Affirmative, sir, give me a moment."

Everyone froze as they watched the gloved hands of the specialist insert needle-nose wire cutters into the open back of the cell phone. A moment seemed like eternity.

"That's it," the voice said over the speaker. "Baby's dead."

Fowler let out a breath, and Kathryn put her face in her hands. Greenfield immediately issued orders to the other agents in the room. "Get in there."

Fowler turned and stomped out of the room.

"Tom, where you going?"

"To the garage," Fowler mumbled over his shoulder.

"OKAY, I'm tired of these games," Petrovic shouted, pointing the gun at Marcus's head. "Last time, which way?"

Marcus closed his eyes and stiffened. "Oh man."

"No, it's this way," Dani said.

Dani walked from the foyer into the living room where Sugarberry had received her. "It's over there."

Everyone's eyes focused on the painting above the mantle.

"Behind the picture?" Petrovic asked.

"No, not the picture, the fireplace," Dani corrected.

Petrovic walked in front of Dani, held up the cell phone, and put his face within centimeters of hers—their noses actually touched. "Behind the fireplace?"

Dani didn't move from her position. "Not behind it, in it."

The assassin's eyes remained locked on Dani as he backed away. It wasn't until he finally turned to the fireplace that Dani released a held breath. They all watched as Petrovic walked over to the fireplace and ran his hand over the mantle. He looked at the painting above and then down at the hearth. "In it," he mumbled to himself. He swung his bag off his shoulder and retrieved a parchment. He opened the article, studied it briefly, and then glanced at the fireplace once again. He turned back to all in the room and over an insane chuckle whispered, "In it? Yes, I see, in it," nodding his head as a broad smile swept across his face. "I understand," his whisper turning to a shout. "It's in it."

FOWLER, Greenfield and Kathryn waited as EMS rolled Jean Ann Peterson on a gurney out of the garage. The three entered, and Fowler quickly looked around the room. He saw what he was expecting to see—nothing, not so much as a scrap of Dani's, David's, or Marcus's research. He fell into Marcus's swivel chair, leaned back, and rubbed his eyes.

"We've coordinated with the Virginia and Maryland state police," Greenfield said, looking around the room himself, "and we've set up roadblocks on the north, south, east, and west sides of the beltway."

Fowler rubbed his forehead. "Any idea what Petrovic's in?"

"We found the police cruiser in a ravine about five miles north of here. Witnesses at a local burger place up the road, where the real trooper stopped for dinner, said they saw him talking to a man in a white car. Nobody got a make or model, much less a license plate. Petrovic must have had the Peterson woman in the trunk."

Fowler nodded. "A white car. That narrows it down."

"You all right?" Greenfield asked his friend.

"Yeah," Fowler replied, his shoulders slouching. But he wasn't all right. He was far from all right. His brain physically hurt. He couldn't remember the last time he'd slept. The adrenaline rush he'd experienced in New Jersey had only left him spent. Now his mind refused to focus, and his legs were like jelly. He desperately needed sleep—a long sleep. But he knew that was impossible, even if it were possible. He needed to call his wife. He hadn't talked to her since four thirty that morning. One of his daughters was coming in tonight for a visit—would he get to see her? How could he? As long as the animal named Victor Petrovic was breathing, how could his life return to any normalcy? And there was the punishing self-doubt. *Is this my fault? Should this be it for me? Maybe I should retire. Would a younger mind have let this happen?* The questions to himself caused him to rise from the chair. He walked to the back of the room totally ignorant of Kathryn and Greenfield's stare.

When he spoke, it was a combination of rage and helplessness. "How could anyone be so bold as to walk into a federal protection facility, kill federal agents, and abduct three people?" His hand trembled as he rubbed it through his oily gray hair. "Who is this maniac? Where did he come from? Men like him aren't born—they're created."

"Is he going to kill them?" Kathryn asked, her voice shaking.

Her question was met with a moment of silence before Fowler answered. "If he wanted to kill them, he would have done it here. No, he's got what he wants. My stupid little plan worked, may God forgive me. He thinks they know where the Mozart is."

"Do they?" Greenfield interjected.

Fowler looked at the assistant director. He hadn't thought of that. "I don't know. David did say they were onto something weird after Dani talked..." Fowler stopped cold and looked at Greenfield and Kathryn. He quickly moved back across the room and picked up the phone beside Marcus's computer.

"Who are you calling?" Greenfield asked, confused.

"I hope Dani Parsons's father." Fowler pushed redial and waited. The call was answered on the first ring.

"Y'hello."

"Yes, Mr. Parsons, please."

"Speaking, who's this?"

Fowler nodded to the assistant director.

"Mr. Parsons, I'm sorry to bother you. I'm Agent Tom Fowler. I'm with the FBI. Your daughter is helping us on a case."

"Oh, sure, Mr. Fowler," the robust and happy voice replied. "Dan told me all about it. Sounds like you folks are on a big one. You're very smart to have my daughter assist you. She's a sharp one, that girl."

Fowler was sure that Dani hadn't told her father the details of the case, otherwise he wouldn't be so keen on his child being used as bait to catch a cold-blooded killer. "Yes, sir, she is. And we're very grateful for her help."

"What can I do for you, Mr. Fowler? I talked to Dani a couple of hours ago."

"Yes, sir, I know." Fowler paused briefly. "Uh...it's just...another agent needed your daughter's assistance, and she's gone now. I wasn't able to get with her before she left. You see, she was going to fill me in on your conversation but didn't get the chance. I was wondering if you'd tell me what you told her?"

Fowler held his breath, hoping the man had bought the lie.

347

"Well…I guess it'd be okay, you being with the FBI and all."

Fowler released the breath.

"From the way Dan described the symbols, I'd say they're of the craft."

"The craft?"

"Yes, sir."

"You mean…witchcraft?"

The man on the other end of the line let out a bellowing laugh. "No, not witchcraft. Good lord, what has my daughter been telling you? The craft, the Brotherhood—"

"You mean the—"

"Yes, of course, the lodge, the Freemasons. I've been a Shriner for thirty-one years—grand master of my lodge for the last eight."

"So, Dani thinks the scribbles on the music are Masonic symbols?"

"Yes. And I think she's right too, as best as I can decipher without seeing them. Dan knows Freemason trivia is one of my little hobbies, so—"

"I'm sorry to interrupt, Mr. Parsons, but *do* you know what they mean?"

"Well, now you know I'm not supposed to reveal the secret symbols of the brotherhood to strangers. I took an oath, and I'm just—"

"Sir, this is very important. Your daughter would want you to tell me."

There was a slight pause.

"Well okay, I mean, it's nothing really. Despite what you might have heard, we Masons aren't trying to overthrow democracy. We build hospitals for children, for cryin' out loud. Wheelchairs and things like that."

"Yes, sir, the Masons do fine work. But about the symbols—"

"Well, let's see, she described several symbols to me. One was a couple of triangles, one right side up and the other upside down. She said they were kind of laying over one another. That sounded to me like the compass and the square. An ancient Freemason symbol for the craft and one of the great lights of Freemasonry, it's the centerpiece of almost everything connected to the craft. It's on our signs, our letterhead, the apron—"

"The apron?"

"Yes, the apron…you know, like something that's worn around your waist. It's one of our most symbolic articles. It's supposed to represent the type of apron worn by the actual stonemasons and artisans from whom the craft originated. It's very ceremonial, you understand?"

"Uh…I believe so," Fowler replied, taking out a pen and note pad.

"She also described something resembling a sword, and she said it looked like it was pointing at something. I asked her if it could be a heart, and she said yes. Now if it is, then that's a symbol that demonstrates that justice will sooner or later overtake us, and that although our thoughts, words, and deeds may be hidden from the eyes of man, they are not hidden from the all-seeing eye. Which, by the way, she also described to me."

"And the all-seeing eye would be…?"

"God, of course."

"Anything else?"

"Yes, and this one I had to go back to my books for. She described something that sounded to me very much like a coffin."

"A coffin? You mean like a casket for the dead."

"Yes. Now that's an old one, goes all the way back to the beginning of Masonry in the eighteenth century. It always symbolizes death, but she said the coffin had the Sprig of Acacia drawn on it— now I'd never heard of that."

"The what?" Fowler asked, not catching the last word.

"The Sprig of Acacia, well she didn't call it that, but that's what it sounded like. The acacia tree is the shittah wood of the Old Testament. It has long been used to symbolize immortality, which is why it's odd that it's on a coffin."

"Uh-huh," Fowler replied, writing as fast as he could.

"Let's see, there was another symbol—sounded like the nine-layered wall."

"The wall?"

"Yes sir, the nine-layered brick wall, actually. That's an old one too. It's popped up now and again in eighteenth century Masonic writings, but no one really knows what it symbolizes. The best anyone can guess is it's the place in the old lodges where the altar sits. The Bible, the square, the compass, and the Master's apron would have rested upon it. To give it meaning is just speculation."

"Sir, would you please speculate?"

Mr. Parsons hemmed. "Well, there are some who think it's meant to represent the Ark of the Covenant."

"Like in the Ten Commandments?"

"Yes." Parsons chuckled. "Must sound pretty strange to you, huh? Yeah, it did to me at first too. You see, Mr. Fowler, much of this symbolism in Masonry is based upon the myths and legends surrounding Solomon's temple in Israel. We have stories and rites that coincide with these symbols. But it's all completely allegorical, you know, just good, moral life-lessons, nothing more. So, as for the nine-layered wall for instance, you could take it to mean the place in the lodge that houses the great symbols of faith—literally or figuratively."

"I see. Is that all?"

"Yes sir, that's all the symbols she mentioned. Was it any help to you?"

"Yes, sir, maybe. I thank you very much."

"Oh, there was one other thing, but I don't know if it's important or not."

"What?" Fowler asked quickly.

"She asked me if I'd ever heard of any black lodges before the civil war."

"Have you?"

"Oh sure, the Freemasons were very much against slavery and helped form many lodges for free blacks living in the North. As far back as the Revolutionary War, free black Masons were holding meetings and ceremonies in their very homes. In fact, many Masons, both white and black, were very involved in the Underground Railroad. That's something we Masons are very proud of. Then she asked me the easiest question of all."

"What was that?"

"If Benjamin Franklin and Mozart meant anything to a Mason?"

"And?"

"Well of course. Every good Mason knows Mozart and Franklin were two of the most famous Freemasons of all time."

Fowler nodded. This was the connection David was talking about. "Mr. Parsons, thank you. You've been a great help. Good night, sir."

"Good night, and tell Dan her daddy loves her."

Fowler's heart fell. "I will, sir. I most certainly will."

Fowler hung up the phone and turned to Kathryn and Greenfield.

"Freemasons, that's the connection. Mozart and Franklin were both Freemasons, and the sketch that David had was filled with Masonic symbols."

"Meaning what?" Kathryn begged.

"I don't know, but I'd bet those symbols tell anyone who knows how to read them where the full piece is."

"Do you think Dani and David figured it out?"

Fowler fell into Marcus's chair again. "I hope so. For their sake." Fowler rested his arm on the desk and accidentally hit the mouse of the computer. The screen saver went off, and the screen turned into a large panel that looked like the front of a cassette tape deck. He looked at the screen but didn't notice it at first. Then the numbers in the lower corner got his attention. He looked at the screen and the numbers again—it was running.

He took the mouse in his hand and moved the cursor over the stop button. He clicked the mouse and looked at the numbers. They stopped. He then moved the cursor over to the rewind button and clicked the mouse. After a couple of seconds, he clicked the stop button again. Then he moved to the play button and clicked.

"Freemasons, that's the connection. Mozart and Franklin were both freemasons, and the sketch that David had was filled with Masonic symbols."

"Meaning what?"

"I don't know, but I'd bet those symbols tell anyone who knows how to read them where the full piece is."

"Do you think Dani and David figured it out?"

"For their sake, I hope so."

Fowler, Kathryn, and Greenfield all looked at each other.

"It's been recording us the entire time," Greenfield said.

It hit all three at once. No one asked it, but Fowler answered the question anyway. "I don't know, let's find out."

Fowler moved the cursor over the rewind button again and clicked the mouse. This time he waited until the numbers rolled all the way back to zero.

"Come on, Marcus," Fowler said in an intense whisper. "Be that brilliant."

Fowler positioned the cursor over the play icon and clicked.

Chapter 45

Petrovic wasted no time. He grabbed Dani by the hair and threw her on the sofa beside David, making them sit back to back. "You two wait here," he said, taking out two sets of handcuffs and locking the two together. "Marcus and I will be right back."

"Oh, dude, don't kill me, man," Marcus pleaded.

"Relax, we're just going to the car for some tools." Petrovic looked at his captives and smiled. "Yes, I came prepared. And remember?" Petrovic sang, waving the cell phone in the air.

David began fussing with the cuffs the minute Petrovic was out of sight.

"No, David," Dani said. "There's not time, and he wouldn't think twice about killing us or J.P."

David stopped and relaxed as much he could.

"Dani, are you sure about the fireplace?"

"It has to be the nine-layered wall, representing the Ark. And look at that painting—the sun—but it's not a sun, is it? It hit me when I talked to Daddy. It's the all-seeing eye of God looking down on the scene below. It's the Underground Railroad. Those people are being taken to freedom and why they have that expression of hope. After I realized what the painting was about, I went back and

353

pulled the land records on this house. This place is a Georgetown landmark. It's been here since the late eighteenth century. Henry Cook, James's father, remember how Wilbur said he was a free black and tobacco merchant? Well, he was also a noted Pennsylvania abolitionist and a leader in the Underground Railroad. And he was Grand Master of the local black Freemason lodge. David, this house was a lodge, and that fireplace was the altar."

"But how did Franklin—"

"Marcus learned that in the last years of Franklin's life he occupied his time by writing his autobiography and articles. Guess on what subject?"

"Slavery," David answered.

"Slavery. He abhorred it. The fact that this country, the country he helped give birth to, was practicing what he viewed as a barbaric act enraged him and broke his heart at the same time. His final public act before he died was to sign a memorial to the state legislature as president of the Pennsylvania Society for the abolition of black slavery."

"And Franklin was a Freemason. He knew Henry Cook."

"Yes."

"Then that also means that—"

Dani finished the loop. "That young James didn't learn the Mozart from Jefferson but the other way around; Jefferson learned it from young James."

"My god, then that would mean—"

"—that James taught it to his former master long after Jefferson had sold him to George Beall, and Beall had in turn sold him to James's father, Henry Cook, who freed him."

David added, "So James's father, Henry Cook, learned the piece from Franklin, who got it from Mozart?"

"Yes, circle complete."

"But, Dani, if it's in this fireplace—or altar if that's what it really is, then why did Franklin give it to Cook? By the end of the late 1780's Mozart was famous. Why didn't Franklin make it public?"

"I don't know," Dani answered. "I don't have all the answers, but David, if it's not in this fireplace, I don't know where it is. And if we don't know where it is, then we're—"

"Having a nice chat?" Petrovic said reentering the room.

The bag clanked. Marcus stumbled into the room and dropped the duffel bag on the floor. The recording engineer looked like he'd just carried a boulder up the side of a hill.

Petrovic unlocked Dani's and David's cuffs. "All right, my friends, in the bag are two hammers and two chisels. I want that fireplace in bits and pieces in one hour or Peterson dies. And so do one of you."

"OH GOD, J.P.. You son of a bitch!"

"David, no!"

There was indiscernible background noise.

"No one speaks unless told to. Speak and you die."

A moment of silence.

"Do you know where it is?"

Silence—then a metallic clicking sound.

"I asked you a question. Do you know where it is?"

"Yes." Dani's voice. *"In Georgetown. At a…"*

David's voice interrupting, *"What have you done to her, you goddamn—"*

"You spoke, David. That was dumb." Another metallic click.

"Please don't kill him!" Dani's voice shouting.

Silence.

"If you don't care about yourself, then maybe you care about her."

The man laughed.

Silence.

"All I need to do is dial this number and boom. Understood?"

"It's in a house…in Gertrude Sugarberry's house." Dani's voice crying.

"Show me. Let's go."

David's voice. *"J.P., it'll be okay. I'm so sorry, I'm so—"*

Rustling footsteps, and then there was nothing.

Greenfield was already on the cell phone. "That's right, two twelve-man teams. Code red, highest tactical, repeat highest tactical. Ground zero is the house of Gertrude Sugarberry in Georgetown—address is forthcoming. Target is white male, six-two, hair color unknown. He has three hostages. Most likely dressed as a Virginia state trooper. He's heavily armed and should be considered lethal. Agent Fowler and I will be waiting."

"Waiting my ass," Fowler said, heading for the door.

Kathryn started out behind him.

"I'm sorry, Ms. Depriest, you have to stay here."

Kathryn had no time to protest. Fowler and Greenfield were out the door.

"DANI, I don't think we're going to find anything in here," David whispered while knocking a piece of mortar free from between the red brick.

"Why?"

"This is brick and mortar—it isn't two hundred years old."

"He's right, Dan," Marcus added, leaning in close. "I put myself through college doing this type of work. This mortar isn't even completely set yet. Can't be more than a couple of weeks old."

"I hear talking," Petrovic yelled from across the room. He looked at his watch and then held up the cell phone. "You have seven minutes."

The three hostages were all on their knees. They were covered in dust and surrounded by shards of red brick and rock. Dani and David were positioned at one corner. David hammered and chiseled as Dani cleaned away shattered brick. Marcus did the same at the other end. They had broken through the first layer of brick only to find a second layer.

"You mean this wall is new?" Dani whispered.

"Not all of it," Marcus answered, "just the top section. It's that quickset stuff. But the bottom is very old—a sand, mud, and gravel type of mix."

"Oh God," Dani breathed, "then that means someone's already been here."

"Yeah, I think so," Marcus replied.

"What are we going to do?"

David answered, "Take it one problem at a time. We have about five minutes to get this thing down."

Chapter 46

Sparks shot from the bottom of the car as it bounced through the intersection of Wisconsin and P Street and began ascending the hill. Greenfield glanced at his note pad. "At the top of the hill turn right, first house across the street from the cemetery."

Fowler rolled through the stop sign and coasted to a stop by the curb. They both saw the white Ford Escort parked in front of the house. Fowler opened his door.

"Tom, let's wait for backup. They should be here in minutes."

"You wait. I can't."

"Tom," Greenfield said, taking his friend's arm. "It's not the smart play."

"I'm going around the back of the house. There has to be a back door. I won't move in 'til the units arrive."

Greenfield nodded, knowing a direct order would be pointless.

Fowler jumped from the car and headed straight for the cover of the trees.

IT WAS A CRAGGED TWO-FOOT OPENING. David knocked the

surrounding bricks out with the hammer. Dani and Marcus huddled on the floor.

"Move," Petrovic ordered, pushing David away.

David dropped the hammer and stepped back. Petrovic shoved his weapon down the front of his pants, positioned himself a few feet from the wall, turned sideways, and readied his attack with three short, swift bounces. The kick was lightning quick and fierce, accompanied by an animal-like roar. Two bricks released. Then another kick, four more bricks broke loose. After five sorties, the two-foot opening expanded to the size of an oblong manhole.

Petrovic retrieved a flashlight from the duffel bag, fell to his knees, and shone it into the opening. David, Dani, and Marcus braced for the worst.

"It's empty," he spit. "It's...wait..."

Dani squeezed David's arm.

"...there's something...a door."

Petrovic removed his head and picked up the hammer. The sound of steel against steel reverberated through the house as Petrovic sat on the floor with his arm inside the wall and pounded. Finally, there was a snap. Petrovic stopped, threw down the hammer, and shone the flashlight back into the wall. He turned to the three exhausted people on the floor beside him and smiled. "You," Petrovic said to Dani, "hold the flashlight."

Dani took the flashlight as Petrovic lifted the wooden hatch.

David saw the look on Dani's face.

"What?"

"Looks like a ladder," Dani answered.

Petrovic moved out of the fireplace and removed his gun from his trousers. "Why? Where does it lead?"

"I don't know."

He pointed the pistol at Dani's head.

"I swear," Dani pleaded. "This must be a station."

"A what?"

"A station. It was a term used in the Underground Railroad. It must be to a tunnel for hiding and relocating slaves. But I didn't know about it—I swear I don't know where it leads, if anywhere."

Petrovic lowered his weapon and looked at the opening. "We're all going down, same rules——" Petrovic stopped mid-sentence and cocked his head. He moved from the fireplace to the front window and fell against the wall. He separated the curtains with the barrel of his gun. "Fools!" He ran back to the fireplace, grabbed Dani, and pulled her in front of him.

It was mindless, the insanity of it never entering David's consciousness. "No!" David yelled, hurling himself at Petrovic, hitting him waist-high.

The attack took Petrovic totally off guard, his hold on Dani broken on impact. The two men stumbled across the room, clutching one another like Sumo wrestlers until Petrovic's feet came out from under him. They crashed on top of the coffee table, its legs disintegrating from the weight. David was on top, but the advantage was short-lived. Before David knew what was happening, Petrovic had him rolled over, his hands around David's throat. David's mouth gaped wide open, begging for air as Petrovic's grip got tighter and tighter. David looked into the killer's eyes—they were completely without emotion. He heard Dani screaming and Marcus say something, but it all seemed far off in the distance. Then he heard a familiar voice.

"Federal agent!"

Then a gunshot.

Blood spurted over David's face, and Petrovic released his hold.

David gasped as air rushed to fill his lungs. He wasn't completely cognizant when he saw Petrovic's gun. Not thinking, just acting, David rolled to his side and grabbed the weapon.

Then another shot.

David's head jerked down by reflex. Her face filled his mind. *Dani.*

He got to his knees and looked toward the fireplace. Petrovic had Dani by the hair and was reaching into the bag for something. His shirt was covered in blood, but the gun from the holster was now in the killer's hand.

"Let her go!" David yelled, raising the gun.

Petrovic looked at David and began firing off rounds while

rustling through the bag. David fell to the floor, scrambling behind the four-feet high stone partition separating the living room from the dining room. He wasn't expecting to find what he found. It was Fowler, and he'd been shot. The FBI man's eyes were open, but blood was everywhere.

"Get down," Fowler ordered.

David didn't reply. Instead, he took a breath and peered over the wall, the gun shaking in his hand. What he saw horrified him. Petrovic was halfway into the fireplace. Dani was still outside but bent over and screaming in agony. Petrovic had a rope wrapped around her neck like a leash and was pulling her in behind him. David raised the gun but froze when he saw Petrovic remove the cell phone and begin dialing. For David, everything moved in slow motion. David raised the gun. Petrovic raised the cell phone. David fired but missed by a mile. Petrovic extended the phone out from his body. David heard his own heartbeat as the killer smiled and mouthed, "Boom."

"No!" David howled like a wounded animal. He never heard Fowler say, "No, David, she's—" as he cocked the pistol and bolted from behind the wall.

But it was too late. Petrovic and Dani had disappeared into the fireplace.

"Dani," David whispered. He ran to the fireplace. Marcus had taken cover behind a pile of brick. The man was shaking uncontrollably.

"You okay?" David asked, pulling a flashlight from the duffel bag.

"Yeah, he's got Dan."

"Tell them Fowler's been shot," David said, stepping into the opening.

"What are you doing?"

"I'm going to get Dani. And I'm going to kill that mutherfucker."

And he was gone.

"SHOTS FIRED! SHOTS FIRED!"

Greenfield fastened his flak vest and started up the stone path, adjusting his headset. "Copy Unit Two, cover the back. Remember we have four friendlies—one of those is ours. Unit one, fan out, watch for an ambush."

Except for Greenfield, the six men from the elite FBI Tactical Unit behind him wore all black with helmets, headsets, and goggles. All carried semi-automatic weapons.

"Leader, this is Unit Two. We're behind the house—back door is open."

"Damn it, Tom," Greenfield said under his breath, "Roger, Unit Two."

"Shot's fired! Shots fired!"

"Go, Unit Two. Go," Greenfield ordered. "Unit One, we're going in."

Greenfield hit the porch first, waving for the others to follow.

"Leader, we have a bogey, repeat we have a bogey."

"Where, Unit Two?" Greenfield said, stopping his men with a raised hand.

"Running around the side of the house. He must have come out of another entrance—I've sent three of my men after him. Should I follow?"

Greenfield paused for a millisecond. "Negative, I'll send two of mine. Get in that house." Greenfield pointed to two of the men, and they were off.

"Leader, this is Renegade," another voice reported. "Bogey has crossed street and entered cemetery."

Greenfield didn't respond. He pushed open the door and entered the dark foyer. The three-man team entered behind him. Greenfield motioned to the living room.

"Leader, we've lost bogey. Repeat, lost bogey."

Greenfield gave the signal.

The three men stormed through the alcove into the living room. One took a firing position on one knee, the other two entering in a crouch.

"He's got Dani," Marcus yelled from the floor. "David went after him."

"Where'd they go?" Greenfield demanded as the two men from Unit Two ran in from the kitchen.

Marcus pointed to the fireplace. "Down there."

A sound came from the back of the room. Greenfield raised his weapon.

"No," Marcus shouted. "It's Agent Fowler."

Greenfield rushed behind the partition. Fowler was sitting up holding his arm. "Jesus, Tom."

"I'm okay. Go get him."

Greenfield clenched his jaw.

"Leader, we've lost him. He just disappeared."

"Damn it," Greenfield exclaimed. "Roger, Renegade, hold your position."

"What happened?" Fowler asked.

"We lost him running out of the house."

Fowler shook his head. "Bob, that wasn't him. Petrovic went into the fireplace."

"Then who—"

Fowler started to stand. "Help me up. We're going into that hole."

Chapter 47

After a twelve-foot drop into total darkness, David stood in an eight by ten foot chamber. He shined the light on the walls of red clay surrounding him. Eight wooden beams, two on each wall and all differing in size, extended upward from the dirt floor to a crooked ceiling of rock. Where he stood, the clearance was a good twelve feet. On the opposite corner, however, it was less than five. The structure looked as if a good sneeze could bring it all down. Three exits were visible; the wooden ladder behind him, a chasm to his right, and one to his left. He'd already ventured down the one to the right only to run into a wall of red clay ten feet in. The one to the left had to lead him to Dani.

With the flashlight in one hand and Petrovic's gun in the other, he trotted into the tunnel. The air smelled of mud, but it wasn't stagnant. There had to be an opening somewhere at the other end. Petrovic had a head start, so David prayed the descent into the chamber had taken Petrovic as long as it had him.

Thirty seconds into the tunnel, David noticed he was having a hard time keeping his trot from becoming a run—he was descending, and quickly. The walls had changed too. The red clay had become hard and coarse like limestone. He stopped and listened.

The temperature had dropped at least fifteen degrees, and he heard the sound of running water from above. He shined the light over the walls. A steady stream of water was running from a jagged rock formation to his right. He raised the light beam and understood why. The clearance was now at least thirty, maybe forty feet—the tunnel had become a cavern. Stalactites dripped from the ceiling like gigantic tears, as stalagmites rose to meet them from balconies of rocks that shelved the cragged walls. The builders of the room below the fireplace had excavated a cave. It was beautiful, but it was also dangerous. David realized Petrovic could be hiding behind any of the formations.

With that thought, David began moving again, alternating the light from ground to wall. He'd gotten used to the path being relatively smooth, so he wasn't prepared when his foot slid out from under him, throwing him off balance and nearly putting him on his back. He held the light to the ground. It was a thin, off-white, cylindrical object that was the culprit. David put the flashlight under his arm, bent over, and picked it up. He held the object high so it would catch the light. He turned it in different positions when it finally hit him what it was. A chill surged through his body, and he dropped it to the ground. It was a bone, and it was human. Moving the light, David saw there were a few others, four or five and varying in size. But as he raised the light and shined it farther down the tunnel, he began seeing more of them. Then he saw it in an alcove off to the right, not ten feet from where he stood. If he didn't know differently, he'd have thought the image was someone's idea of a clever Halloween decoration. But this was no decoration, this was real, this was a burial ground. Complete skeletons, at least fifty of them, some huddled together, bone wrapped around bone, lined the wall, tossed aside and piled up like someone's dirty laundry. He didn't have to guess what he was looking at. These were slaves. Slaves that for one reason or another didn't make it. "Oh my God," he muttered as he walked closer. Tattered rags still hung off many of their frames, and personal items like walking sticks and women's bags littered the ground nearby. Then he spotted something else, a skeleton off to the side. His heart sunk as he got closer. It was small, much smaller than even the smallest of the others. It was on its side in the fetal position, a brown piece of cloth draped over its little ribcage and what looked like a small handmade doll of corncob and cotton still clutched in its tiny hand. The air left his body, and he fell to his knees, his eyes filling with tears.

He thought he was used to it, the perpetual cruelty man perpetrated against his fellow man on an everyday basis. He thought he was immune. He thought that after spending the better part of his adult life consorting with people who exist only after midnight, he'd witnessed about every sick example of mankind at its worst. Bitterness, selfishness, callousness, pettiness, and loneliness—he couldn't forget loneliness, the most common of them all. These were the diseases of night people. But he was immune—he'd seen it all. Or so he thought. But here, in this cave surrounded by the most heinous act of cruelty this country had ever witnessed, he was both infected and affected.

His mind flashed on a happy old security guard at the Museum of American History and his two grandchildren. And a brilliant yet humble athlete turned scholar at Georgetown University. And a woman named Sugarberry whom he'd never met, but that Dani had described so vividly as the essence of grace and dignity, he felt as though he knew her. He thought of all of them and realized that if today was a hundred and fifty years ago, any one of these skeletons could be them. He walked next to the small and fragile remains. He felt nothing but shame as he knelt and pulled the small cloth over the tiny skull. It was only a few seconds. But he'd later confess to have totally gone away, and that it was only the sound of Dani's voice that pulled him back. *"No!"*

He couldn't tell how far off it was, but it was Dani. He started running deeper into the cave, his legs beginning to burn because he was now running uphill. It was getting warmer, and he smelled fresh air—he was nearing an exit. The tunnel began to get smaller and the incline steeper. Voices could be heard up ahead, but he still couldn't make out the words. A few more steps and he saw a beam of light flash across the wall. It was Petrovic. It was only then he asked himself the questions. What would he do? Could he really pull the trigger and end another man's life? Then he thought of J.P. and Dani—and the answer was yes, he could.

David knew he had left the cave and was now in something man-made. The ceiling had progressively gotten lower until he had to finally go to his hands and knees and crawl the last ten yards. But the voices had become clearer, and he could see the opening twenty feet in front of him. He turned off his flashlight and pushed his way up the narrow shaft. He got to the opening and waited. Petrovic was talking.

David raised his head out of the portal and saw it exited into a large enclosed structure with an opening at the far end. He could only see Petrovic's and Dani's legs. He pulled himself from the hatch and found he was below a table of some kind. Making sure Petrovic was still facing away, he crawled out from under the table—but it wasn't a table, it was a tomb. He was in the cemetery across the street from the house—this was a mausoleum.

David took cover behind the large concrete block and waited before he peered around. Petrovic was standing in the shadows at the far end of the room, looking out through the rusty iron gates. He held Dani in front of him, the rope still around her neck.

"When they leave, we leave," David heard Petrovic whisper.

One shot, that's all it would take, David thought as he aimed the gun at Petrovic's back. His hand was steady, and he was certain he could do it—but not that certain. Petrovic could move at the last minute, and he'd miss him and hit Dani. He couldn't risk it. He had to get closer.

Just as he began to move from behind the mass of concrete, Petrovic spoke again, "They're gone, let's go."

Without releasing tension on the rope, Petrovic shoved open the gate and pushed Dani into the open air. David jumped from behind the tomb and ran into the shadow Petrovic and Dani vacated. He watched the killer make sure the cemetery was empty. This was the moment. He could wait no longer. He stepped from the shadow, moved a few feet closer, and turned on the flashlight.

"Let her go," David ordered, gun raised.

Petrovic didn't turn around. He didn't even flinch. He stayed motionless, tightening the tension on the rope. Dani audibly inhaled.

"I knew I should have killed you back at the house. Very good, David."

"I said, let her go. I swear to God I will kill you."

Dani gagged as Petrovic tightened the tension on the rope. "Oh, I'm sure you would. But I have your girlfriend in a very compromising position. Do you know how quickly I could crush her windpipe? I bet quicker than you can pull that trigger. Want to race?"

David pulled back the hammer. "Yes."

It wasn't the answer Petrovic was expecting, but he still didn't move. Then without warning, Petrovic let go of the rope and opened his arms wide.

Dani bolted to David's side, gasping for air, pulling the rope over her head. Petrovic turned and faced them. He'd been shot, the upper right side of the uniform was covered in blood, but still he smiled. "Now what? I'm unarmed."

David stepped back and held the gun at Petrovic's head.

"No, David, don't," Dani begged.

"He killed J.P.," David said, his arm straightening even more. "He killed Henry, and Charlie, and God knows who else. Why shouldn't I kill him?"

Dani squeezed David's arm and said, "Because you're not a killer."

David held his pose. He wanted to pull the trigger. He wanted to rid this soulless creature from the face of the Earth. Dani was right, he wasn't a killer, but this thing in front of him wasn't human. He knew he could send a slug of lead into this man's head, and no one would question the decision—no one except him. David understood whatever he did in the next few seconds was going to be a decision he'd have to live with for the rest of his life. But as it turned out, it was a decision he'd never get to make.

"Drop the gun," the unfamiliar voice ordered from the darkness.

David's head jerked toward the voice. He instantly moved Dani behind him, looking quickly at Petrovic and then back toward the voice.

"I said drop the gun," the man said, emerging from the shadows beside the mausoleum. He was all in black and held a gun leveled at David.

David's head snapped from the stranger and then back to Petrovic and then back to the stranger. He still couldn't see his face.

"Mr. Webber," the man said, "I *will* shoot you if I must."

It took another beat, but David dropped the gun, immediately wrapping his arms around Dani.

Petrovic grinned. "Well, hello, my old friend."

"Shut up," the man replied, pointing the gun at Petrovic.

Petrovic's smile abruptly disappeared.

"Mr. Webber, Dr. Parsons, time for you to leave."

David and Dani looked at each other, but neither moved.

"Back through the tunnel to the house. Leave now, please."

Dani hesitantly moved first.

"Do you understand? Leave now."

The force of the man's order caused both to run into the mausoleum. As David was helping Dani down the shaft, he looked back into the cemetery. The man was gone, as was Petrovic.

They slid on their butts down the narrow tunnel until it opened wide enough to stand. David held Dani's hand and the flashlight as they ran from the tunnel back into the cavern. It wasn't until they'd reached the other side of the cave that they heard the voices. Both stopped when they saw the lights. Greenfield was the first one they recognized. Then beside him, his shoulder wrapped in a bandage, they saw Agent Fowler. Dani looked at David, her eyes filled with tears of relief. David smiled, took her in his arms, and held her tight.

Greenfield and Fowler were within feet of the embracing the couple when they all heard it. A single gunshot from somewhere above.

Chapter 48

Dani just giggled. David on the other hand, if not flustered, was more than a little uncomfortable by Marcus's robust display of emotion upon their safe return to the house. He greeted both with an overjoyed, three-way embrace. So overjoyed and so robust, David had to physically dislodge the man's arm from around his sore neck to breathe. Afterward, Greenfield ordered two agents to drive Marcus home. They could still hear the wired sound engineer as he left the front porch. "Dudes, the guy was like eight feet tall, really. His hands were like baseball mitts. Hey, did you guys ever watch the *X-Files*? You ever investigate any UFO stuff? Man, I'm jonesin' for pizza, you guys hungry?"

The scene in the house had calmed. Greenfield stood by the demolished fireplace and conferred with agents from the tactical unit as Fowler, suffering only from a flesh wound, sat across the room talking on his cell phone. David and Dani took the opportunity to be still. They sat on the couch; neither spoke. David's arm was around Dani's shoulder, her head on his chest.

Greenfield walked over to the couch. "We've combed the cemetery and the cave. No sign of Petrovic or the other man. You didn't see his face?"

David answered with a shake of his head.

"David," Fowler interrupted, handing the phone across the broken coffee table, "someone wants to talk to you."

David took the phone, and without asking who it was, said, "Hello?"

"Oh luv, you'd do anything to get out of paying me back the seven hundred and seventy dollars you owe me, wouldn't you?"

David's eyes filled with tears. He could barely speak. "Jeep?"

"Hi," she responded is a weak, slurred voice.

"Jeep, oh, God...I'm so sorry...so sorry."

"They tell me it wasn't your fault...for once."

A smile broke over David's face as he wiped away the tears. "Yeah, that's what they tell me too, can you believe it?"

There was no response.

"Jeep?"

"I'm here, just a little tired. They gave me something, I think."

He had so much to say, so much to apologize for. But he could tell she was fading fast, so it would need to wait for now. But eventually he would say it. "It's okay, Jeep. You go to sleep. I'll see you in the morning, okay?"

"Hmm, okay."

David squeezed the phone. "I love you, kiddo."

Her voice was barely audible. "I love you too."

David handed the phone back to Fowler and nodded thank you.

"Where is she?" Dani asked, wiping away her own tears.

"Washington General," Fowler said, turning off the phone. "She's in the room next to Dr. Rogers. We don't think it's necessary, but we put a twenty-four-hour guard on both of them just to make us all feel better." He looked at David and smiled. "Doctors say she's going to be fine. Just needs some rest."

David closed his eyes and released a breath he felt like he'd been holding for years. "Thank God. I thought Petrovic...with the phone—"

Dani took David's hand. "See, I told you she was going to be all right."

He smiled. "Yeah, you did, didn't you?"

Dani kissed him on the hand.

"Well, folks," Fowler said. "I hate to be the one to get back to business, but we still have a couple of unanswered questions. Dr. Parsons, shall I assume the Mozart piece wasn't where you thought it would be?"

Dani shook her head in bewilderment, "No, it wasn't."

"Any chance it was there at one time and moved?" Greenfield asked.

"A very good chance, but why and by whom? That cave must have been a flurry of activity two hundred years ago. Cook and his lodge of Freemasons probably used it for everything, both practical and ceremonial. You saw the bones in the cave. I'm sure that spot was once a switching junction between two lines for the Underground Railroad. That's the place where one conductor would pass off the slaves, or freight as they were referred to in Railroad's terms, to another conductor to continue the journey north. It would have been a place of great importance to the free black Masons who operated this section of the line. I suspect if the Mozart manuscript was ever here, it was probably kept at that spot in the cave."

Fowler interjected, "So it's not a grave as much as a——"

"A shrine. Those bones are there so we'd never forget."

"It worked," David said.

"Yes, it did," Dani agreed, looking up at David.

Everyone was quiet.

A young agent walked into the living room and whispered something in Greenfield's ear. Greenfield nodded. "Show her in."

Kathryn Depriest ran into the living room and headed straight for David. "Oh David, thank God!" She leaned over and hugged him.

Dani didn't move from David's side.

"I was sure——" she couldn't get the words out.

"We're okay, Kathryn," David said, patting her on the back.

David's use of the collective pronoun *we* did not go unnoticed by Dani.

Kathryn looked at Dani and then at Dani's hand on David's

chest. She moved back a little and forced a smile. "I'm glad you two are okay."

"Ms. Depriest, can I get you something?" Fowler asked, sensing the situation and remembering it hadn't been the best evening for her either.

"No, thank you, I'm fine."

Fowler responded with a reassuring smile.

The leader of the tactical unit rushed into the room. "Assistant Director, Agent Fowler, there's something downstairs you should see."

"What?" Greenfield asked.

Fowler approached, and the man whispered the information in Fowler's ear. Fowler let go half a laugh and shook his head. "Well, well, don't that just pop your buttons?"

"What?" Greenfield asked.

"Ladies and gentleman," Fowler said, "I think we're about to have some of those unanswered questions answered."

They were led out of the living room, through the foyer, and into the study on the other side of the house. Dani immediately realized they were heading to the stairs off the study leading to the lanai music room on the back of the house. Fowler entered the music room first and then Greenfield. Next was Dani and then Kathryn. David was the last in.

As David entered the room, he saw everyone else standing completely still. Completely still—barely breathing.

"What's going on?" David asked.

Dani was the only one who responded and only with a look.

David walked up to Dani. She was white. He started to ask what was wrong when he heard a sound coming though the bodies in front of him. He pushed past Fowler and Greenfield and almost tripped over Kathryn, who had fallen to her knees.

"What the hell's wrong with—" First he saw her, an elderly African-American woman sitting beside a piano, smiling sheepishly at her cavalcade of visitors. For David, the following seconds moved in slow motion. He looked at the woman for a long moment, but said nothing. Then he looked at the piano beside her and then back at the woman. Finally, almost as if his mind refused to let him take it in, he looked back at the piano. He saw, but didn't see. His brain couldn't connect the image to reality.

He swallowed. Then the image became clearer. At the piano, sitting on the bench slouched over the keyboard, he saw the small man with thin gray hair. The man turned around and smiled sadly.

David audibly exhaled but uttered no words.

"Hi, Davey," the old man said.

"Hi, Henry," David replied.

Chapter 49

Henry got up from the piano and approached David, saying nothing, only looking into his eyes. The two stared at one another for several seconds; neither spoke. Finally, Henry raised a trembling hand and touched David on the cheek. At first, David showed no reaction. Then after a moment, his bottom lip began to tremble, and the first tear broke free and rolled down his face. Henry reached out his frail arms. David's eyes widened, and he let out a painful wail, burying his face in Henry's shoulder.

Henry held him tightly, stroking his head. "Oh Davey, I'm so sorry."

Kathryn was sobbing.

Dani, her eyes soaked and red, rushed to Sugarberry, fell on her knees, and took the woman's hand.

David raised his head. His face was distorted with confusion. He gazed at the ghost in front of him and ran his fingers over Henry's wrinkled brow. Finally, with a broken voice, David said, "You're...alive..."

Henry forced a smile through his own tears. "Oh, Davey, I'm just fine."

"I...I...don't understand."

"I know…"

"But…I…why…?"

"Oh, Davey, I…I didn't know, I didn't know."

"Didn't know?"

Henry looked desperately around the room.

"He didn't know about you, Mr. Webber," Scott Douglas said, entering the room unannounced. "I'm sorry, it was for his safety. I just learned of him myself."

Everyone showed shock and confusion as Douglas walked over to the old man and patted him on the back—everyone except for Agent Tom Fowler.

"Who are you?" David asked.

Fowler answered. "This, David, is the man who's going to answer our unanswered questions. Aren't you, Mr. Douglas?"

Douglas ignored the question. "I'm so happy you're all safe. I've just been informed Viktor Petrovic is no longer a threat. Congratulations, Assistant Director and Agent Fowler. Job well done."

"Informed by who? And where's Mr. Woo?" Fowler demanded.

Douglas smiled. "Just informed by those who know, Agent. I really can't say any more than that. And Mr. Woo is unavailable."

Greenfield was seething. "Okay, Douglas, let's have it. Why is Professor Henry Shoewalter sitting here in what appears to be perfect health?"

Douglas shook his head. "Well, as I understand it—and again I was just brought into the loop—Professor Shoewalter has been assisting his government."

"With the search for the Mozart?" Fowler shot back.

"Yes. And to get Petrovic," Douglas answered. "Mr. Webber, Professor Shoewalter didn't know about you being involved. He was told you were contacted in regard to canceling the meeting the two of you were to have."

David stayed fixed on Henry. He was still reeling. "But…how… you were dead…they found you? Petrovic killed you. Agent Fowler, you told me—"

"No, they didn't find *him*," Fowler interrupted. "Petrovic killed somebody, but it wasn't Henry. Was it Mr. Douglas?"

"For the love of God, who?" Dani asked, sitting at Sugarberry's feet.

"Agent Fowler, we really shouldn't be…" Douglas stopped himself, thought a moment, and smiled. "No, obviously it wasn't Professor Shoewalter. It was Professor Raymond Sullivan."

"Sullivan? Why?" Dani asked.

"Because Petrovic wanted something Sullivan had, and he had to kill him to get it. The murder was actually committed hours before Professor Shoewalter even arrived in L.A. The switch was made later that night."

"Again, why?" an exasperated Greenfield asked.

"Because, just like you and your little newspaper stunt, it was imperative Petrovic believe we knew more than we did. And, of course, when I say *we*, I mean the US government. As I said, I just became aware of this."

"Of course," Fowler said with as much sarcasm as he could muster.

Douglas continued, "You see, Petrovic knew someone else was after the Mozart, namely your husband, Ms. Depriest. By putting the man he really killed, Professor Sullivan, in Henry's room and releasing it to the press it was Professor Shoewalter, it forced Petrovic to believe Shoewalter, who he knew was still alive, must be close to finding the Mozart. We made him think the switch was made to protect the professor from Old Nick and keep Depriestiano off track. Also, if we didn't, we knew finding Petrovic would be next to impossible."

"So when Professor Shoewalter called David that night, Sullivan was already dead?" Fowler asked, already knowing the answer.

"Yes," Douglas answered without apology.

Henry's eyes filled with tears as he looked at David. "I had told Raymond over the phone about you and the sketch I had given you. I told him that he, not me, should be the one to contact you to retrieve it. I…" Henry hung down his head, "didn't want to intrude on your life."

David closed his eyes in shame.

"I'm so sorry I involved you, Davey. But after Raymond was

killed, I knew it was more important than ever to get the sketch from you. I had no choice."

David reached for Henry, and the two embraced again. Kathryn, overwhelmed with guilt, put her hands over her face and began sobbing.

Fowler looked at Greenfield. "That explains how Petrovic knew of David Webber—he'd probably been on him from the get go. And Depriestiano's goons were sitting ducks the minute they landed in L.A."

Douglas moved across the room. "Four months ago we got intel that Viktor Petrovic was stateside. He was ID'ed on the UCLA campus hanging around the music department. When Professor Raymond Sullivan was murdered, we knew by whom. What we didn't know was why."

"The Mozart," Fowler stated.

"Yes."

David chimed in, "He committed murder for a simple Mozart symphony?"

"How do you know it's a symphony?" Douglas asked.

"Because he's David Webber, that's how," Henry stated loud and proud, dabbing his eyes with a handkerchief and looking admirably at David.

David looked back at Henry. It had been twelve years—a lifetime since he'd heard that high, tiny voice and seen those perpetually laughing blue eyes.

Douglas asked again, "Mr. Webber, how do you know—"

"It just is," David shot back. "It's not a mass, it's a symphony." David looked at Henry. "Trust me."

"Actually, Mr. Webber," Douglas said, "we do trust you. It is a symphony. And if Professor Shoewalter and the late Professor Sullivan are right, it's not so simple. And it's worth quite a lot of money."

"Why?" Fowler asked.

It was Henry who answered. His expression changed, and he looked at David with boyish excitement. "Because it's not just a symphony, Davey—it's *the* symphony. The Master wrote a symphony just for us."

"What? For...for us?" David stuttered back.

"It's called 'Sinfonia 'a 11 Instrumenti Neo-Americana.' The Symphony for the New America. Mozart composed a symphony for the United States of America. That's what the sketch I gave you is. Can you imagine? All those years, Raymond Sullivan thought he was looking for a requiem, but instead, he was looking for something far more important."

"And it'd be worth that much?" Fowler interrupted.

Douglas answered, "It's on par with owning the Declaration of Independence in Jefferson's own hand—in short, it's priceless. We know that Petrovic was already accepting bids starting at two hundred million dollars."

"And of course you just learned this," Fowler said with a clinched jaw.

Douglas raised his shoulders in innocent denial. "Hours ago."

Fowler shook his head. "You said you had proof, Professor."

"A letter—actually two letters. One Marie-Antoinette sent to Jean Le Gros."

"The director of the Concert Spirituels in Paris," Kathryn interjected.

"Yes, the same," Henry confirmed with a smile to Kathryn. "Sullivan found the letter years ago when he was on fellowship from the Louvre museum. It was the catalyst that led him to believe Mozart had composed a requiem for his dead mother."

"What did the letter say?" Dani asked.

"Most of it is praising Le Gros for his service, but it closes with the Queen writing, 'If you see the talented Monsieur Mozart, please tell him I saw his latest work and believe it is a stunning and fitting tribute.' Now, since the letter was dated July ninth, 1778, and Mozart's mother died on July third, naturally Sullivan believed the reference was to a mass."

"Of course he would. I probably would've too," David said.

"I'm not so sure, Davey. Did you notice the problem with Marie-Antoinette's statement?"

David thought for a second and nodded. "Yes, she said, I *saw* his latest work, not heard. How could she have seen an unpublished piece of music?"

Henry smiled. "Yes, and it's obvious from the statement, 'if you see the talented Monsieur Mozart,' that the Queen wasn't personal friends with Wolfy. Raymond should have been tipped off from the beginning. He was just too willing to believe his own story once he created it."

"You said two letters, Professor?" Fowler asked.

"Yes." Henry reached over to the piano and retrieved an old piece of brown parchment from the lid. "This one."

Fowler leered at Douglas while everyone else focused on Henry as he unfolded the paper. "This was what finally changed Raymond's mind. Like most of us old professors, it sometimes takes getting hit over the head. This was Raymond's hammer. Until a few minutes ago, when Mr. Douglas gave it to me, I'd never seen it—only knew what Raymond had told me about it. That's why I went to Los Angeles, to inspect this letter. But poor Raymond was murdered before he could show it to me."

"What's it say, Henry?" David asked.

"I shall read it to you all. It's in German, so pardon my sloppy translation."

Henry placed bifocals on his nose and began to read. "It's addressed to Mozart himself and dated February fourth, 1790. It begins, *Dear Wolfgang, I pray this greeting finds you well and in good spirits. I hope*—no, I'm sorry—it's not I hope, it's—*I wish I could say the same. The days are long and my nights are labored. But I do not fear. I have had a good life, certainly more than a mischievous old man such as myself deserves. You must be surprised to hear from me after such a long time. It has been many years since you and I congregated in that small salle in Paris. I remember fondly that glorious evening, trading naughty jokes and hearing your music. The memory warms this old man's cold and brittle bones.*"

"He must be talking about the night of the first performance of the Paris Symphony, the opening of the Concert Spirituals," Dani offered.

Henry looked up from the page and smiled briefly at Dani.

He read on, "*I receive many letters from my friends in Europe. I have frequently asked of you, and they tell me you are very renowned, and you have become very much respected. This does not surprise me for you are the great Mozart. Which brings me to the heart of this correspondence.'"*

Henry took a deep breath and moistened his lips. "Okay, here it comes. *'The beautiful and inspired gift that you so generously and graciously bestowed upon me has as yet to be enjoyed by all, save for a few close companions. My reason for this has not been stinginess, though I do confess to a certain amount of stinginess in this regard, but moreover disgust. In candor, my brother, I do not feel my homeland deserves your masterpiece at this time. Indeed, injustice reigns. It heartens me. When we spoke those many years ago, I told you of a place where all men were free and all ideas were held level, an idea that you yourself hold so dear. I fear I proclaimed too much. For now, as I write this, all men are not free in my land, and all ideas are not level. Some men still feel the need to hold dominion over others. This saddens me and is my great regret in these, my final days. Therefore, I have made an arrangement. Your masterpiece will stay silent until that time when this new Nation can hear with the ears for which the 'Sinfonia 'a 11 Instrumenti Neo-Americana' was intended to be heard. When this is a Nation whereupon all men from every corner of the Earth, regardless of race or creed, can come and say, I am home, and be honored with the same dignity and import as those who were born on the soil. This is my prayer, and I pray you will not think ill of me for this decision. For our brothers understand. And it will be they alone who will keep your gift, my treasure, and this Nation's soul in a safe place until they deem appropriate. I have held this beautiful work close to my heart from the day I received it. And I will surely miss its absence in the life hereafter. Be well. God be with you, brother. Ben.'"*

Henry looked up and removed his glasses.

Everyone was silent, letting the words of Benjamin Franklin sink in.

"Professor," Dani asked almost reverently, "the *brothers*—Franklin's talking about the Freemasons, right?"

Henry nodded. "Yes, dear, Raymond was given the letter by an old Mason in Vienna—he'd stumbled upon it when he was looking for proof of the mass. The guess is that two hundred or so years ago a brother Mason found the letter after Mozart died and returned it to the lodge for safekeeping."

"Returned it?" Kathryn asked.

383

"Yes, that's where Franklin had sent it to begin with. Somehow, probably through a friend who was a Mason in Europe, Franklin learned Mozart had joined the brotherhood, so he must have surmised that would be the most efficient way to contact him. He was obviously right."

A light went on for Dani. "Because you knew of the Masonic connection, you had already excavated the cavern beneath the fireplace?"

"Yes, dear. Unfortunately, no Mozart."

"But, Professor Shoewalter, how——"

"Please, call me Henry. I have a feeling we're going to become quite close."

Dani glanced at David and smiled. "Okay, Henry. How did you know about the fireplace? I only figured it out after I had met Mrs. Sugarberry and had seen the picture over the mantle."

"And Henry," David added, "how did you get involved in all of this to start with?"

Henry looked at David and patted him on the cheek. "Quite by accident, Davey. Though I must admit it has been most exciting for Trudy and me."

David looked at Dani, Mrs. Sugarberry, and then back at Henry. "Trudy?"

Henry smiled. "Yes, Davey." Henry released David's hand and walked over to Gertrude Sugarberry and took her hand from Dani's. "Trudy, this is Davey. Davey, I'd like to introduce you to my wife."

Chapter 50

Gertrude Sugarberry-Shoewalter got up with an enthusiastic smile and extended her hand. "Oh my, it's little Davey Webber. Well, it is such a pleasure to finally make your acquaintance. I can't tell you how much Hanky has told me about you."

"Hanky?" David replied.

"But," Dani said, completely taken aback herself by the announcement. "Your husband, Edgar…he—"

"Edgar and I had forty-five wonderful years together. I never thought I'd ever find anyone again. Then I met Hanky."

Henry kissed Gertrude's hand. "Almost three years now. I was giving a lecture at the university. I looked out in the audience, and there she was."

David finally found words. "But your house, your office, it's still —" At that moment David looked around the room and everything was clear. The books on the shelf: *Portrait of a Genius*, Emily Anderson's *The Letters of Mozart*, the *Oxford Dictionary of Music*, all the books that weren't in his office. David looked back at Henry. "You live here now."

Henry shrugged. "Most of the time, but I still keep the house in White Plains. I'm on the board at the conservatory, and Trudy prefers it to a hotel. Though, since I've met these gentlemen," he said, looking at Douglas, "I haven't been either place much. They've had me in a nasty little apartment downtown."

"And I have missed him so much," Gertrude added, looking up at Henry. "When this nice young Asian man named Mr. Woo came by and got me a few nights ago, it was the first time I'd seen Hanky in nearly a month."

Douglas didn't look at Fowler nor Greenfield, but he was aware of their leers.

Dani broke out with a laugh. Then she noticed the piano. "Mrs. Sugarberry, I mean Mrs. Shoewalter——"

"Either's fine, dear. I've been Sugarberry so long, I don't make a fuss."

"But I do," Henry said with mock seriousness.

Dani smiled and continued, "The piano. I thought it strange you owned such an instrument and didn't play. Now I understand, it's…" Dani looked at Henry, "…your husband's."

"Oh, no, it's mine, isn't it, dear?" Gertrude said, looking up at Henry. "Hanky got it for me as a wedding present. He tried to teach me to play, but you know, can't teach an old dog new tricks." The woman put her hand to her mouth and laughed with Henry.

Dani smiled. She was looking at the picture of young love.

Fowler had to interrupt, "Professor, you were going to explain how you got involved with these…" he looked at Douglas and sighed, "gentlemen."

"Oh, yes, I was, wasn't I? Well, let's see, I guess it started last summer, just after Trudy and I were married. I started doing research on a new book. It was to be called *The Lost, Incomplete, Arranged, Doubtful, and Spurious Compositions of Mozart*. I know the title is too long, but the subject's a good one. My contention was to be that many of the compositions omitted from the Kochel, because they were considered not to be actual Mozart compositions, actually were. And even if they weren't, I would contend they were still important for the sake of the false composers feeling compelled to write like the master. It was going to be a vast undertaking. But before I got too far into the project, Trudy and I had a honeymoon to go on. And so we did, to Paris. It was beautiful, wasn't it, dear?"

"Yes, dear, it was," Gertrude replied.

"One day when we were visiting the Louvre, whom do we run into but Raymond Sullivan. Raymond and I had known each other for over fifty years, but ever since he'd gotten on his missing Mozart requiem obsession, we'd locked horns. I wanted to avoid him, but Trudy, the peacemaker, wouldn't hear of it."

Gertrude smiled again at her husband.

"So in spite of our differences, I decided it was time to bury the hatchet." Henry looked directly at David. "Davey, it was wonderful. We talked and laughed for hours about the old days when we were both at the conservatory in Vienna and the exploits of youth. Well, it was over a delightful dinner I told Raymond about my new book, and to my surprise Raymond was very enthusiastic. Raymond was never enthusiastic about anything other than his obsession, but alas, in this case, he was. He told me he had to play me something, so we retired to his small flat a few blocks away. Naturally, I thought to myself, oh lord, the missing mass again, and indeed what he played me he claimed was part of the missing mass Mozart had started for his mother, Anna-Maria. Well, of course I immediately recognized the piece as the same I had purchased years ago in Vienna and given to you."

"There's another copy of the adagio?" David blurted.

"Yes. Raymond said he'd discovered it in Paris. He had a test made of the watermark and learned it was written on the same paper stock as the Paris Symphony. Well, this only added fuel to the flame for his missing mass theory."

"Unbelievable," David said.

"Yes, but I was determined not to ruin an otherwise wonderful evening with the old feud, so I stayed mum and just went along with him. Besides, I was genuinely intrigued by the fact that Raymond had come by another copy of the adagio, but composed on a paper stock Mozart used thirteen years earlier than the one I had given to you. Then to beat all, my dear bride chimed in."

"What did she say?" Dani asked.

"She said not only had she heard the piece before, but she possessed it as well. Well, needless to say, both Raymond and I laughed. I believe you were a little perturbed by our response, weren't you, dear?"

Gertrude patted Henry on the hand again.

"Anyway, the evening concluded with Raymond promising to send me a copy of his sketch for me to make my own examination —he said I could use it for my book if I wanted. So I agreed."

"Did he?" David asked.

"No, I never got it," Henry answered. "But when we returned home, Gertrude wasted no time in showing me the piece she was referring to." Henry looked at Douglas. "The dear woman had it buried in the bottom of a cedar chest. Can you imagine?"

Gertrude chuckled.

Kathryn broke in, "Was that the piece you sent to me, Henry?"

Henry smiled. "Yes, Kathryn, it was."

"The Cook," Dani said to Gertrude with mock annoyance. "That's what he's talking about, isn't it? I *didn't* find that piece by accident, did I, Mrs. Sugarberry?"

Gertrude lowered her head and put her hand on Dani's arm. "I'm so sorry, dear—yes, you caught me. I just missed Hanky so much, I thought if I helped a little, he'd get home quicker. Henry, you must admit after I told you about Dr. Parsons from the Smithsonian, you thought it was a good idea too."

Henry shook his head disapprovingly. "Yes, Trudy, I did, but you were still very naughty for doing it."

Dani was figuring it out. "So the whole sheet music thing was just a—"

"Yes, I called your Dr. Beckman and used my sheet music collection as an excuse to get one of you experts up here. Though, I really was going to donate it at some point."

Dani just shook her head in disbelief.

"As I was saying," Henry continued, "Trudy's piece was from a different pen and transcribed for solo violin, but yes, indeed it was the same melody Raymond had played for us, and the same one from the sketch I had given to David. It was the adagio. I was baffled."

"I thought it was romantic," Gertrude interjected.

"Romantic?" David asked.

"Well, yes, dear." Gertrude smiled like a little girl. "Here we were, two people in our golden years, from vastly different backgrounds, who fell in love and married. Then we learned we each owned the same rare piece of music. It was like we were meant to be. Don't you think that's romantic?"

"Oh, yes," Dani responded, matching Sugarberry's dreamy expression.

"Anyway," Henry continued, "Trudy told me the stories about Dr. Cook." Henry focused his attention back on David. "It was unheard of. How did an early nineteenth century African-American come to learn anything composed by Mozart, especially something no one else knew existed? I called Raymond in Los Angeles and told him Trudy was right, she did indeed own the same piece of music. That was also the first time I told him about you and your sketch."

"What was his reaction?" Fowler asked.

"Surprisingly, not that surprised. But I didn't know Raymond had already made the Franklin/Mozart connection, as well as their involvement with the Freemasons. All he said was I should focus my attention on the year 1778. I realize now he was being the perfect scholar, wanting me to take the same steps he had for the sake of seeing if I came up with the same conclusions. That's when I asked Kathryn to research Mozart's life in 1778." Henry looked at David seriously. "I'm sorry, David, but she was the best research assistant I ever had, and I needed help."

David looked at Henry and smiled. "It's okay, Professor."

Kathryn's face gave nothing away to the contrary.

Henry nodded and continued, "Most of what she learned was common knowledge, but it still led me to Jean Le Gros and the Concert Spirituel. I learned all dignitaries traditionally attended its opening, and if Franklin was in Paris, and he was, he surely would have been one of them. I immediately contacted Raymond and told him I had narrowed my research to June, 1778, Corpus Christi day, opening night of the Concert Spirituel."

"The debut of the Paris Symphony," David added.

"Exactly. Don't forget, Raymond's sketch was on the very same paper stock as the Paris Symphony. It was all coming together."

"What did Dr. Sullivan say to that?" Fowler asked.

"He was elated, of course. I had corroborated his findings, though we still couldn't explain how Trudy's piece came to be, or why Mozart felt compelled to rewrite the sketch thirteen years later. So we agreed further research was warranted. Raymond suggested he continue researching his piece and that I should shift my attention to Trudy's piece and Dr. Cook. I agreed."

"Then you learned about Dr. Cook's father, just as we did, and that led you to Franklin. Full circle," Dani said.

Henry smiled. "You're very good, young lady. Yes, that's exactly what happened. I discovered Cook's father was a leading abolitionist and a Freemason even before Sullivan told me about the letter he'd found from Franklin. Afterward, it was just a matter of figuring out where a devoted brother might enshrine a precious relic. As soon as I realized this house, Cook's house, was once a lodge, all I had to do was figure out where a shrine might have been two hundred and fifty years ago. David, you know my fascination with unique art. That painting over the mantle always intrigued me. When Trudy informed me it had been hanging in the same place since this house was built—well, it wasn't a difficult assumption."

David and Dani looked at each other and nodded

"But," Henry went on, "you didn't know about the letter to Mozart from Franklin, so how did *you* know to look in the fireplace? The painting alone couldn't have told you, and I know there's no mention of it on Trudy's music."

David answered, "From the sketch, Henry. Remember all of those little doodles? Dani found that they are really Masonic symbols."

Henry's mouth opened. "Well, I'll be. I should see that music again."

"Petrovic took—"

"I have it right here, Professor," Douglas broke in.

This garnered another leer from Fowler. Douglas handed Henry the sketch.

"This is fascinating," Henry said, looking through his bifocals at the sketch. "They are symbols. And now I believe I know why Mozart began a sketch to something he'd composed so many years earlier."

David shot a confused glance to both Dani and Kathryn. "Why?"

The teacher addressed the student, "Davey, Franklin wrote that letter to Mozart just a little over two months before his own death. I think Wolfgang was just trying to remember the piece. Perhaps it was even his intention to perform it in honor of Franklin at some point in time." Henry turned to Dani. "Tell me, dear, do you know what all these symbols mean?"

"We *thought* so," Dani replied, "but if you didn't find anything—"

"What's this?" Henry interrupted, pointing to a symbol.

"It's called the all-seeing eye, and it represents God. That was the main connection I made to the painting over the mantle upstairs."

"Fascinating," Henry mumbled. "And this?"

"A sword pointing to a heart, it means justice will soon reign."

Henry smiled and nodded.

David spoke, "Henry, the letters C-K-F in the bottom corner, did you—"

"Ah, yes," Henry uttered, "that was about the only thing I could remember from this piece. It always baffled me as to its meaning. I even scribbled it lightly in pencil on Trudy's copy so I wouldn't forget about it."

David looked at Dani. "Our third hand."

"This is odd," Henry said.

"What?" Dani asked.

"This, it looks like a coffin."

"Yes, it is. We're not sure about the meaning because it contradicts itself. The coffin symbolizes death, but the leaf on it symbolizes immortality."

"Hmm, very interesting," Henry replied.

"What are you thinking, Professor?" David asked.

Henry looked across the room at Kathryn.

"Kathryn," Henry said. "You have an idea, don't you, dear?"

Kathryn got up, walked across the room, and took the sketch from Henry. Everyone was silent as the woman scanned the page.

"It's a letter," she said, almost matter-of-factly.

"A what?" David came back.

Henry looked at the page again and then up at Kathryn and nodded with a smile. "Very good, very good indeed."

Dani unsurreptitiously nudged her way between David and Kathryn and looked at the page herself. After a moment, she saw it too. "I think you're right."

It hit David last. "Of course, why didn't I see that?"

Henry patted him on the arm. "Because we weren't looking until now."

"What?" Douglas asked. "What letter?"

Fowler put his hand on Douglas's shoulder. "Relax, will ya? What do you all mean a letter? I thought the sketch was a piece of music?"

It was Kathryn who answered, "It is, and this might have started out to be a sketch to some music Mozart was trying to remember—something he'd written thirteen years earlier. But it ended up a letter—a letter in symbols."

"To who?" Douglas asked.

Dani answered, "A brother mason, probably here in America—maybe even Dr. Cook's father."

Henry took it up, "The letter from Franklin to Mozart would have taken weeks to reach Mozart. Once it did, Wolfy wasted little time since he knew Franklin was in his last days. You see, Mozart was nothing if not somewhat of an egomaniac, and the thought of one of his works being lost to the world forever, let alone to himself, would not be acceptable regardless if he sympathized with Franklin's motivations or not. So he took matters in his own hands. And why not? He was a full-fledged brother of the lodge, he could still obey Franklin's wishes—just be in control of his baby's destiny. This is Mozart telling his brothers where to hide the symphony upon Franklin's death."

All three government men looked at one another.

"So where is it?" Douglas asked.

The quartet ignored the blunt question and went back to the sketch. Kathryn turned to Dani. "Dani, can you start at the top and read exactly what you know each symbol means?"

"Sure." Dani put her finger at the top of the page. "This is the compass and the square, it's the center piece of almost everything connected to the craft."

"That's the greeting," Henry said.

"This is the sword pointing to the heart, it demonstrates justice will sooner or later overtake us, and although our thoughts, words, and deeds may be hidden from the eyes of man, they are not hidden from the all-seeing eye."

"Referring to the *injustice* of slavery Franklin spoke of in the letter," Kathryn said.

Henry added, "And though they may not live to see it, justice would prevail."

Dani continued down the page. "This is the all-seeing eye of God. And this is the coffin, death, with the sprig of the acacia, immortality. But I don't know what it all means when they're together."

"That's okay, dear, continue," Henry consoled.

"This is the nine-layer wall, it's the symbol for the Ark of the Covenant, or a place to house the great symbols of faith. Here are the letters C-K-F, which to my knowledge, have no Masonic meaning. That's all." Dani didn't notice until she stopped, but Kathryn was holding a pen and writing down what she said.

David, on the other hand, was staring into space.

"David," Dani said, "you okay?"

David took the old parchment from Dani.

"What is it, Davey?"

David spoke like he was speaking to himself, "What would Mozart have declared to be immortal even after death?"

"Christ," Kathryn answered. "He was very religious."

"True, but what else?"

There was silence.

Then Henry said, "His music."

Dani, Kathryn, and Henry all gathered and looked again at the sketch. It hit them all at once, but it was Dani who vocalized their collective reaction.

"Oh my God."

"What?" Douglas asked, the question almost coming out as a shout.

David looked at Douglas. "Does the president know about all of this?"

Douglas shot a look around the room before he answered. "Perhaps, why?"

Douglas's response caused Fowler to laugh out loud.

David smiled. "Because if you want to get your hands on this particular piece of music, you're definitely going to need to call him."

Chapter 51

STREET TEMPORARILY CLOSED—CITY OF PHIL-
ADELPHIA. The barricade erected at the intersection of Arch
Street and Fifth blocked both pedestrian and automobile access.
The same type of barrier shut off the perimeter at ten other locations from Second to Sixth between Market and Race. The official
explanation: a leak had been detected in a natural gas line running
directly under the Independence National Historical Park. So at five
forty-five a.m., the City of Brotherly Love's most historic area was
officially evacuated and sealed off. The media was assured crews
from the city's Department of Water and Power as well as a crack
team from the Army Corp of Engineers were on the case, and the
area would be reopened, safe and good-to-go by nine a.m. There
was no immediate danger. That was the official line.

Two men in orange vests and hard hats waved the large black
van through the barricade. The vehicle proceeded down Arch and
pulled in behind a city utility truck. The doors flung open and eight
weary people stepped out.

After boarding the Bell helicopter at Andrews Air Force Base,
Scott Douglas had suggested everyone should use the opportunity to
get some sleep. None did. Regardless of fatigue, the sheer weight of

what they were about to do was too heavy, the consequences too great.

"Mr. Douglas, I presume?" asked the military man with the chiseled face.

"Yes."

"General Stanley Turner, at your service."

No handshakes were exchanged.

"Thank you, General," Douglas replied. "Is the area secure?"

"Locked down tight as a drum."

"Good work. Your men didn't waste much time, did they?"

"We were dispatched from Bragg at oh four hundred," the old soldier replied. "We've been ready for you since oh six hundred."

"Were you instructed as to protocol?" Douglas asked.

"It'll look like no one was ever here," the general answered. "Follow me."

Douglas looked back to the others and motioned for them to follow. Two marines stood sentry as they entered through the wrought-iron gates. "Make yourself comfortable, it'll still be a little while," General Turner said as the group entered the cemetery of Christ Church and the final resting-place of Benjamin Franklin.

High-intensity halogen lights transformed dawn into high noon within the cemetery gates, and the thin whine of power tools assaulting stone reverberated throughout the courtyard. Each of their hearts pounded a little harder as one by one the group filed into the courtyard and passed the two concrete slabs to their left. One bearing Franklin's name, the other his wife's, Deborah.

Dani flopped to the ground midway in and leaned against the red brick wall of the old church. Henry and Gertrude made themselves comfortable on a bench in the back of the cemetery away from the noise, and Gertrude instantly nodded off on Henry's shoulder. David, who had not allowed Henry to stray more than a few feet from his side since leaving the house in Georgetown, found another bench close to the elderly couple. Kathryn sat beside him. Fowler, Greenfield, and Douglas remained with the general by the grave.

"You know, Mr. Douglas," Fowler said softly, "I was just thinking."

"About what, Agent Fowler?" Douglas answered, watching the progress of the work in front of him.

"How you're so full of shit your eyes are brown."

Greenfield shot a look toward his agent and then toward Douglas for the reaction. There was none.

"Well, I'm sorry you feel that way, Agent." Douglas replied.

Fowler smiled. "You know, two things have bugged me from the moment I met you and the mysterious Mr. Woo."

"And what would those be, Agent?"

Fowler crossed his arms and looked straight ahead as he talked. "How did the CIA just happen to have stumbled onto that particular FBI surveillance photograph of Webber and Petrovic? We must have thousands of photos going through our office. You tellin' me the CIA found by accident a photograph of a guy whom by its own admission was impossible to ID? No, I think they knew where to look. Which leads me to the other thing. How did an international assassin ever come to learn of a missing Mozart piece to start with?"

Douglas remained nonchalant.

Fowler's smile disappeared. "You should have told us, Douglas."

"Told you what, Agent?"

"That Viktor Petrovic was with the company." Fowler opened his note pad and started reading aloud. "Real name: Major Michael Peter Sullivan, son of UCLA music professor Raymond Sullivan. Listed as killed in action in Iraq."

Douglas responded with only a blink, but it was a response.

"Yeah, I know. After I learned Professor Sullivan once had a son, a little birdie told me I needed to look into it. See, I've been around a while too, Mr. Douglas. Also, I have friends in some very convenient places." Fowler read again. "Major Michael Peter Sullivan, Special Forces, trained to infiltrate and eliminate specific targets. Black Ops. Discharged for mental instability. Last known whereabouts, Montana. In short, your hit man became a white supremacist. How am I doin'?"

Douglas didn't say a thing.

"I'll make the rest up, but I bet I'm pretty close. Major Sullivan is just another isolationist whacko until an African-American boy kills his mother in a botched carjacking. He goes over the edge and decides to aim higher. With skills courtesy of Uncle Sam, he can do it. He changes his name to something nice and eastern-European like Viktor Petrovic and puts himself on the open market. Oops, the company's got a problem. A very well-trained international assassin with Made-in-America written all over him. Pretty close, aren't I?"

Douglas looked Fowler in the eye. "Interesting story."

"Isn't it, though?" Fowler replied. "Now, I only have one question for you, and I want a straight answer. Is Major Sullivan still a problem for me, or did Mr. Woo take care of him in that cemetery back in Georgetown?"

Douglas took a moment, licked his lips, and then turned back to the graves. "You have no further problems, Agent Fowler."

"The man killed his own father, for the love of God. We had a right to know."

Douglas sighed and shrugged his shoulders. "You know, Agent Fowler? You might be right. Oh well."

Fowler looked at Greenfield. "I'm getting too old for this, Bob."

Across the cemetery, Kathryn watched David watch Henry and Gertrude. "I don't remember ever seeing him this happy."

David didn't reply.

"We haven't really had a chance to talk, have we?"

"No, I guess we haven't," David answered, still looking at Henry.

"I wish—"

"Yeah, me too."

"I wish," finishing her sentence, "after all these years, we would have met again under different circumstances. I feel like there's so much to say."

David finally looked at the woman. "There's nothing to say, Kathryn."

"Isn't there?"

David answered softly with no edge at all. "No, it *was* a long time ago."

"You've never thought about us?"

David lowered his head. He started to lie and then stopped himself—he'd been lying for too many years. "Yeah, almost every day."

"Then—"

"But I've been wrong to do so."

Kathryn didn't reply.

David continued, "Kathryn, I don't hate you, but I did. I hated you. I hated Anthony. I hated Henry. But most of all, I hated myself."

"Yourself? Why would you—"

"Because I always knew it was my fault."

"I don't understand."

David took Kathryn's hand. "Kathryn, why did it happen? Why did you start up with Anthony when we were still together?"

Kathryn pulled her hand away. "Oh, David, I don't know—"

"Yes, Kathryn you do know. More importantly, so do I." David let out a long breath and looked over at Henry and Gertrude. "I was not a very nice person, was I? Certainly not what anyone would call attentive. No, it has always been about me, my career, my life, my..." David stopped and looked back at Kathryn. "If it hadn't been Anthony, it would have been someone else, eventually. I'd have made sure of it."

"What I did was childish rebellion. And I paid for it. You weren't—"

"Kathryn, I was. And I've paid for it." David looked off. "I never appreciated what I had—you, Henry, all the award and accolades. You know why? Because from the time my parents were killed, I thought the world owed me something, some sort of reimbursement. But you know what I finally understand? The world doesn't owe me a thing. It doesn't owe anybody anything. Bad things happen—that's life. I asked for the life I've lived these past twelve years. I'm to blame, not the world, and certainly not you or Henry. But I think I can forgive myself now. I don't have to be that way anymore."

Kathryn squeezed his hand. What she wanted to say, she

wouldn't. What she wanted to do, she couldn't. So she just smiled. "You're a good man, David."

Both were silent for a moment.

Kathryn looked over to Dani, who had her eyes shut. "Do you love her?"

David didn't reply immediately. "I think so."

Kathryn's forced a smile. "I like her a lot."

David looked at Kathryn, the woman who, even though not in his life, had been so much a part of his life for so long.

"I'm sorry about Anthony," David said.

"Really?"

He grinned. "Yeah, really. He and I aren't all that different."

Kathryn shook her head. "Yes, you are."

David smiled. "So what will you do?"

Kathryn sighed. "I don't know. It's been so long since it's been only me, I might like it. Maybe I'll go back to school, finish my master's. I seem to still have a knack for the research thing. Who knows? Maybe Dani can get me a job at the Smithsonian."

David chuckled. "You? Working? That'll be the day."

"Hey," Kathryn protested, slapping David's arm. "I used to work. Or have you forgotten those all-nighters at Henry's?"

David looked in Kathryn's eyes for a long moment before answering. "No, I haven't forgotten. And I never will."

Kathryn's eyes filled with tears, but the smile never faded. She leaned over and gently kissed him on the cheek. But as Kathryn pulled back, David caught Fowler out of the corner of his eye approaching quickly.

"They're bringing up the casket."

They set the decayed black box on a steel grate beside the broken earth. It was wooden and small, very small. One soldier reached over and brushed away the loose dirt atop the lid. In gold leaf all read the simple words, "Rest In Peace—Benjamin Franklin." Below were the letters, CCC.

David saw it immediately. "CCC, I'll be damned. It was there all along."

"What, Davey?" Henry asked softly.

"CCC, Christ Church Cemetery. In German it's *Christus Kirche Friedhof*—C-K-F."

Henry looked at the letters and shook his head. "Well, I'll be."

Another man, this one not in uniform, stepped up and began circling the casket with a metal detector. "General, we only have two latches on this side. I suggest we use the plasma to burn through the seal. It'll be cleaner."

"Carry on," the general ordered.

The plasma torch was handed to the man. A soft hum emitted from the instrument as the man squeezed the trigger. It took less than a minute. The man looked up to his superior and nodded.

General Turner turned to Douglas.

"Do it," Douglas ordered.

The three women huddled together, Gertrude in the middle of the two younger ones. Henry and David approached the open coffin. Henry looked in and then looked back at David. David tried to take a deep breath but couldn't. Then, his hand shaking, David reached into the coffin and withdrew a folded cloth. He gently unfolded the cloth and found it was an apron, rectangular with strings on each side. The Masonic symbol of the compass and the square was embroidered in red above a pocket. The pocket was not empty. David pulled out a tightly rolled parchment. Henry held the top of the parchment as David unrolled it. Both men stared at the paper.

"Well?" Douglas asked.

David looked at Henry. Henry looked at David. They both smiled.

Douglas raised his phone. "Mr. President, we have it."

PRETTY DESCRIBED the young and effeminate blond male who stepped off the elevator on the top floor of the Grand Hyatt Hong Kong. He walked to the end of the hall and pushed the buzzer. A North Korean soldier opened the door.

"Enter," the soldier ordered.

He walked in.

"Raise your arms."

He did as he was instructed.

The soldier ran his hands down the young man's body and over each leg.

"Shoes—off."

The sneakers came off.

After inspecting each shoe, the soldier walked to the door and turned down the light. "Undress, the general will be in momentarily."

Alone, the boy/man took off his jeans and shirt and stood naked in the middle of the suite. After a moment, the bedroom door opened. A husky Asian man, roughly sixty-five years old, stood in the doorframe wearing only a black robe. He gazed at the figure in front of him and smiled.

"Come here," he ordered.

The boy approached.

General Kim Chul ran his hands down the muscular ivory body. "Nice," he whispered, dropping his robe and falling to his knees.

The young man wasted no time. With one hand on the general's head, he reached around his back and withdrew a syringe from between his buttocks. He jabbed the needle into the back of the North Korean's neck. The general only had time to look up in horror before falling to the floor.

General Kim Chul was dead.

Victor Petrovic picked up the man's lifeless body and dropped it on the bed. He dressed, sat down in a chair, and waited. After a suitable amount of time, he got up and opened the door to the hallway. As he suspected, the soldier was standing guard.

"General Hotcakes told me to tell you he didn't want to be disturbed. Personally, I think he's very disturbed, if you know what I mean," Petrovic cooed, heading toward the elevator, rubbing his crotch.

The soldier didn't conceal his disgust. But he did not enter the suite.

Petrovic got off the elevator on the third floor and went directly to Room 300.

"Done?" Conrad Woo asked from a chair as Petrovic walked in.

"Of course," Petrovic answered, pulling off the blond wig. "There's one less chink in the world tonight. Doesn't that just warm you all over?"

Woo didn't respond.

"So tell me, Conrad, why did I just kill that old man?"

Woo remained expressionless. "Do you care?"

Petrovic thought for a second and then shrugged. "No."

Woo nodded.

"However," Petrovic added, taking off his jeans and putting on a pair of black trousers, "I do care a great deal about something else."

Woo, never taking his eyes off the assassin, picked up a cell phone and dialed. The call was answered immediately. "Complete the transaction." Woo ended the call and tossed the phone to Petrovic.

Petrovic punched in another number. This call too was answered quickly. "Account two-three-zebra-seven-alpha. I'll wait."

Both men were silent.

"Could you repeat that figure, please? Yes, that's correct. Thank you."

Petrovic closed the phone and tossed it back to Woo with a smile.

"Satisfied?" Woo asked.

"You know," Petrovic said, putting on a white button-down, "we wouldn't have had to go through all of that ridiculousness back home if you guys had just met my price when I asked for it. I mean really, Connie, what do I care about a stupid old piece of music?"

Woo got up and spoke as he headed for the door. "Tell me, what's it like to kill your own father?"

Petrovic looked in the mirror as he wrapped a silk tie around his neck. "Hmm, interesting. But not real different than killing an old communist queen."

Woo looked at the man for a long moment and then opened the

door. "Michael, stay off of US soil. Otherwise, I just might have to kill you myself."

Petrovic smiled as he straightened his tie. "In your dreams, Connie, in your dreams. Besides, you guys would miss me."

Woo turned and left, letting the door slam behind him.

"By the way," the now proper looking businessman yelled with a German accent, "the names Viktor. Viktor Petrovic. Don't forget it."

Epilogue

Washington, DC—July 4th

Pandemonium. Hundreds of men, women, and children pushed, pulled, and bartered their way for a better vantage point along the red-carpet entrance to the Kennedy Center. One by one, limousines delivered celebrities from every sphere of show business, politicians from every party, and religious leaders from every faith. Lights and camera crews were everywhere. NBC, ABC, CBS, FOX, MSNBC, and CNN were all carrying the extravaganza live. Both ShowTime and Pay-Per-View made a run at buying the exclusive rights to air the concert but were denied. The weeks leading up to the night had been a constant barrage of anything having to do with Mozart and Franklin; interviews with leading musicologists, an endless montage of biographies, and countless round table discussions on the political and historical significance of the lost symphony.

The scene backstage, though much more subdued, was still electric. Henry wore a smart black tuxedo with a continental style lapel. His wife, Gertrude, was quietly elegant in a light-violet tea dress with matching satin shoes. Both stood calmly and listened to Dani, who hadn't stopped talking since they arrived. "I know he'll do fine. Great, I predict. Oh, I hope he does okay. Henry, will he do okay? I mean, did he used to get stage fright? He said he didn't, but it's been so long. He says he knows the piece, but I haven't heard him play it yet. He wouldn't let me. He's been practicing at the university six hours a day for the past two weeks. I know he'll do okay. Oh God, I think I'm hyperventilating."

Henry tried his best not to laugh but couldn't stop himself. "Dear," Henry said, taking the insane girl's hand, "Davey will perform wonderfully."

Dani wore a strapless, cream-colored gown that just touched the floor. Accessories were sparse—a simple silver cross around her neck and a single silver bracelet around her wrist. Her lips were softly colored, cheeks delicately blushed, and her chestnut hair was pulled back, allowing her hazel eyes to sparkle and her smile to catapult across a room. She took a calming breath. "Where's Kathryn? I need to tell her I spoke to Wilbur Wallace, and he's interested in bringing her on board as a researcher."

"She's taken her seat," Henry answered. "She's here with some male model, Phillip something-or-other. I swear he couldn't be more than eighteen."

Dani looked around. "What's taking him so long?"

The question was no sooner asked than David emerged from his dressing room wearing white tie and tails.

"Oh, Mr. Webber," Dani breathed. "You look amazing."

David smiled. "Thank you, Dr. Parsons."

David pulled her near and passionately pressed his lips to hers.

"Oh, get a room, luv."

David pulled back and looked over Dani's shoulder. J.P. and Paul Rogers were approaching, holding hands.

"Good lord, J.P., what's this?" David asked with pretend annoyance at the sight of her and Paul together.

Paul extended his hand. "What can I say, old boy, she's great medicine."

"Oh, she's a pill all right," David replied, kissing J.P. on the cheek.

Dani gently wrapped her arms around Paul. "How are you feeling?"

"Okay. Doctors say I'll be a hundred percent in a month."

Dani smiled.

"Listen, David, we need to talk." J.P. pulled David aside. "I've been talking to the producer of this concert tonight. He told me he would be interested in taking this show on the road. Chicago, Atlanta, San Francisco, he's even talking the Bowl. I told him we'd sit down with him tomorrow to discuss terms. Also, get this, *The Tonight Show* called. I told them—"

"Whoa, whoa, whoa, Jeep," David said, holding up his hands. "Hey, I'm glad you're feeling better, but...honey, I can't think about all that right now."

"For heaven sakes, luv, why not?"

David chuckled. "Well, for one, I have to play the biggest concert of my life in about five minutes. And two, I haven't decided what I want to do after this."

"Are you kidding? You'll play. What could be more important than that?"

David looked over at the picture a few feet away. Henry, Gertrude, Paul, and Dani were holding hands as Gertrude offered a prayer. He smiled. "That."

J.P. looked at the four people and then looked back at David. She nodded and smiled too. "You know, luv," she said, her voice getting much softer, "I think I'm getting tired of L.A. Maybe it's time for a change of scenery."

"Like DC, maybe?"

J.P. raised an eyebrow and blew David a kiss as she walked away with Paul.

"Places, ladies and gentlemen," the stage manager announced.

The orchestra began filing onto the stage and taking their seats. Dani walked over to David and kissed him on the lips. "Nervous?"

"No. Petrified."

"I don't know if this will help, but I just wanted to tell you something," she said, straightening his tie.

"What?"

She stopped and looked into his eyes. "I love you."

"I love you too," David whispered back.

The stage manager interrupted with a tap on David's back. "Mr. Webber, excuse me, sir, but I need you stage right with me."

Dani gave David another kiss, smiled, and backed up. "Don't screw up."

As the orchestra began to tune, David stood alone in the wings, rolling the fingers on his left hand. He looked at his hand. There had been no miracles—there was still discomfort between his ring and little finger, but it was manageable.

"Davey?"

David turned around. "Henry, you should be in your seat. The concert is about to—"

"I know. I'm going right now. I just wanted to say...I'm proud of you."

David's eyes filled, and his throat got tight. He could only nod in reply.

"You play well now, okay?"

David shook his head and smiled. "Okay, professor."

Henry turned and began to walk away when David called out, "Henry."

The old man turned around.

"This is a long way from Mr. Ramsey's in South Bend, isn't it?"

Henry's eyes glistened, and he smiled, "Yes, Davey, a very long way." He turned to leave again.

"Dad."

The old man stopped and turned.

"I love you."

Professor Henry Shoewalter raised his chin. It took two tries before he could get the words to come out. "I love you too, son. Now go play well."

The audience rose and applauded enthusiastically as President Hartley and the first lady entered the presidential box and took their seats. The house lights went down, and the curtain rose on a huge American flag hanging behind the orchestra, bringing the audience to their feet once more.

"Ladies and gentlemen," the low voice announced, "the conductor of the National Symphony, Maestro Hugo Corrine."

The audience offered a generous ovation as a bald, stocky man entered from stage left, bowed, and took his place at the podium.

"Ladies and gentlemen, featured soloist, David Henry Webber."

Again the audience applauded ebulliently as David entered from stage right. He bowed with his head, shook the maestro's hand, and took his seat at the nine-foot Steinway.

A hush fell over the audience as Corrine raised his arms. Then with a swift downward thrust, the Kennedy Center erupted, and history was made.

If sound could be a color, it would have been bright red. If an emotion, it would have been pure joy. If weather, this surely would have been a hurricane. The audience quickly became hypnotized as they were taken on a journey into genius. Those present would later say their very breathing changed as they listened. Others would confess that what they heard was so new and unknown they actually became frightened, while still others would swear, on that summer evening in Washington, DC, God had been revealed in the tension and release of a masterpiece.

About the Author

Phil Swann's career has spanned over 30 years as an award-winning performer, songwriter, and author. As well as having songs recorded by hundreds of recording artists, Swann is the composer of nine musicals including Play It Cool, The People Vs Friar Laurence, and Musical Fools.

As an author, his work includes The Song of Eleusis, The Mozart Conspiracy (published in Italy as Il Codice Amadeus), Cold War Copa, Mekong Delta Blues, and Tinsel Town Tango.

Phil lives in LA where he teaches the craft of writing at UCLA and the Los Angeles College of Music.

For more information about this author, click here.

For additional books by this author, click here.

Printed in Great Britain
by Amazon

66466391R00241